The Galactic Mage Series

Book 1: The Galactic Mage
Book 2: Rift in the Races
Book 3: Hostiles
Book 4: Alien Arrivals
Book 5: (in progress)

Prequels

Ilbei Spadebreaker and the Harpy's Wild
Ilbei Spadebreaker and the Zombie Apple Collapse
(in progress)

John Daulton
www.DaultonBooks.com

ALIEN ARRIVALS

Book Four: The Galactic Mage Series

John Daulton

This is a work of fiction. All characters and events portrayed in this book are fictitious. Any resemblance to real people or events is purely coincidental.

ALIEN ARRIVALS
Book 4: The Galactic Mage Series

The phrase "The Galactic Mage" is the trademark of John Daulton.

DEDICATION

In memory of Michael G. Burke.

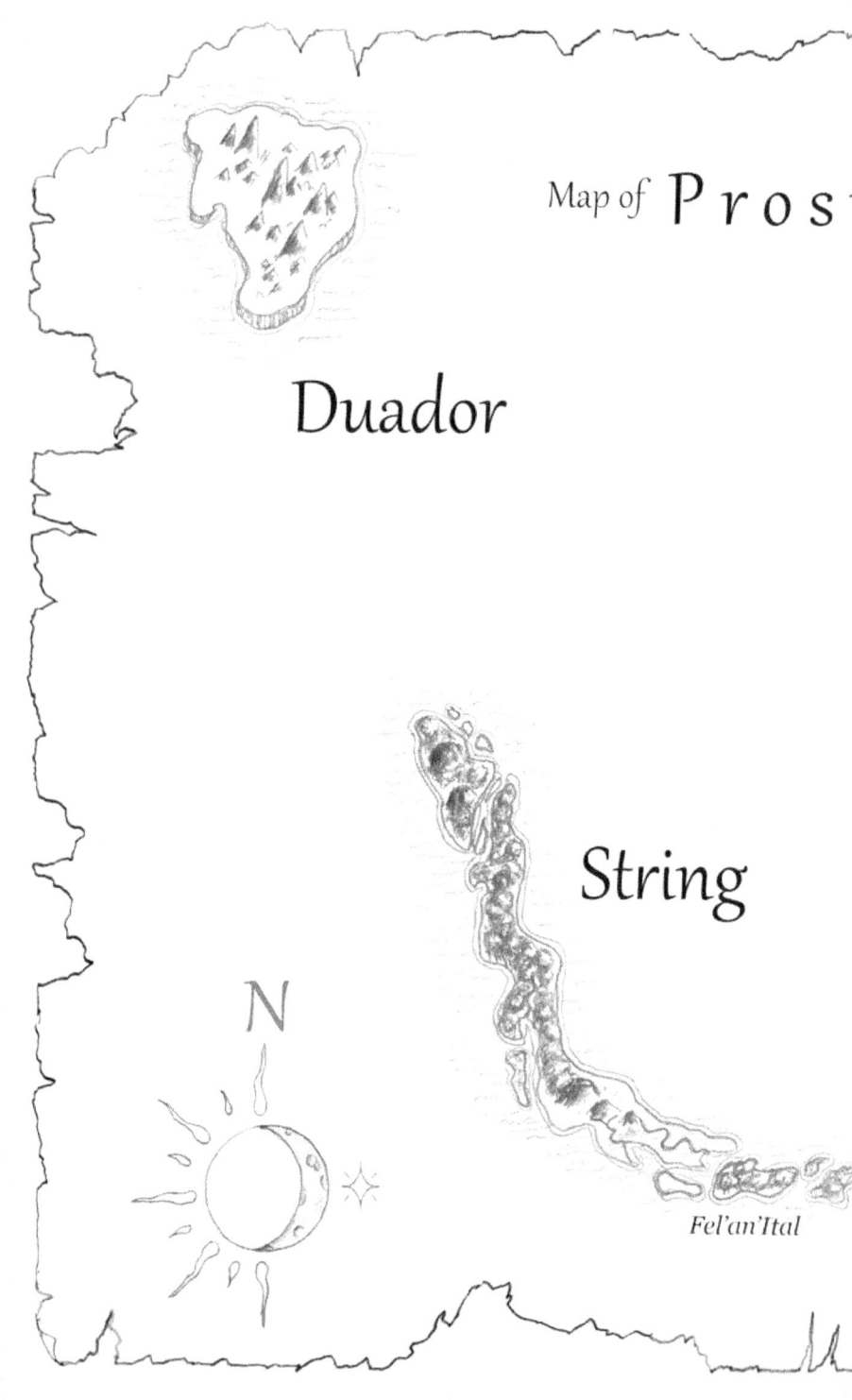

Map of P r o s

Duador

String

N

Fel'an'Ital

Chapter 1

Pernie woke in darkness, her cheek damp where it lay upon something soft. She knew she was awake because her eyes were open. She blinked a few times, but there was nothing to see. The smell of damp stone surrounded her, mixed with a hint of sea air, as it had been when she'd gone to sleep.

Voices murmured from around a bend. They belonged to the elves and that old woman with them. The three of them sat a few paces beyond the small chamber where Pernie was. Guarding her, she knew. The elves were the ones who had taken her. She'd tried to fight them off, to escape and run free. She even bit the Queen's elf, Shadesbreath, on the hand, a good bite that drew green blood. Elves were salty and tasted like the sea.

She sat up and looked in the direction of the sound. Somewhere in the darkness, a passage led from this small chamber into the outer one, but no light defined its opening. She didn't want to go out there and talk to them anyway. That's what they wanted. She wasn't going to give them anything they wanted. Ever. But she was hungry. So perhaps she would have to in the end.

Petulant lips pouted, unseen in the blackness, as she

debated what to do, the stubborn side at war with the hungry side, a battle between mind and body. Inevitably, body won.

Shadesbreath, in his black leather armor, dagger hilts protruding everywhere, sat upon a stool of carved coral near a boulder, watching as Pernie's head poked out of the dark passage. He watched her as she emerged, already looking her way as if waiting for her all along. He glanced across the boulder, which served as table for all assembled there, to where Seawind sat. The two elves nodded. Seawind even managed something like a smile as the corners of his mouth grew a hair's width wider into his pale green cheeks.

"So, little one, you have decided to come into the light," said the third figure seated there, a human woman of indeterminate years, many of them. She was wrapped in leather armor as brown as bark and which matched the color of her eyes so perfectly it had to be by design. "My elven friends suggested you wouldn't be doing so for another half day."

Pernie frowned at the woman, but didn't say anything. She scanned the tabletop of the boulder in search of food. There was nothing there.

"I'm hungry," she said, stepping out into full view. "You'd better not let me starve, or Master Altin will come and burn you to ash."

The old woman laughed, a long and throaty thing, her head tipped back and a few loose strands of gray hair dangling like vines around her neck. "Oh, I should think he would at that," the woman agreed. "But don't you worry about going hungry, young miss. We haven't brought you all this way to starve you to death." She turned in her seat, an orange-and-brown bit of coral work to match those upon which the elves sat, and took up a small leather sack lying near her feet. She tossed it to Pernie, who caught it naturally. "There, child, is enough to keep you for a week."

Pernie frowned at them all again, the three strange

figures sitting there watching her, then pulled at the mouth of the sack and peered inside. It smelled of fish. She opened it further and found within a tightly packed block of fish strips, salted and dry. She looked up at the three of them. "I have to eat this for a week?"

"You'll get used to it," the woman said. "The elves, for all their finery with wine and long lives, have not the patience for quality cuisine. I've had to make do on my own. After the first fifty years or so, you get over the old cravings. Food becomes fuel and little more. You will enjoy the fruits of the island, though. Those more than make up for what you've grown used to in the past."

Pernie's thoughts flickered back to the heaping tables put forth by Kettle, the old kitchen matron back home and the only mother Pernie had ever known. The stout old woman would have a fit if she knew what the elves intended to serve as Pernie's permanent repast.

"Well, I don't want to get used to it." Her gaze flicked toward Shadesbreath. Her eyes narrowed. She looked to see where she'd bitten him on the hand, but there was no sign of the injury anymore. "I want to go home."

"You have already been told that is not going to happen, *dra'hana'akai*," said Seawind as Shadesbreath quietly studied her. "It is best if you settle in."

"I don't want to settle in. I want to go home. When Master Altin finds out where you've taken me, you'll see. This whole cave will be filled with fire, and Sir's dragon will gobble you up alive and chew your bones to dust. Just wait and see."

"Sir Altin has already been informed, and the War Queen of Kurr has already acknowledged our right to take you. You are here because you are The Bodyguard, Protector of the High Seat, chosen by Tidalwrath himself."

"I'm not a bodyguard. I'm only a girl. Even I know that. Kettle always said the elves are supposed to be smart, but that doesn't seem very smart to me."

The old woman laughed. The elves seemed incapable of it.

"You are correct, child," the woman said. "You are not a bodyguard, at least not entirely. One day, though. Perhaps one day soon, if my friend Shadesbreath has the right of it about you."

"I don't want to be a bodyguard. I want to go home."

"That is not possible."

Pernie pulled out a strip of salt fish and nibbled on it. It wasn't as bad as she'd thought it would be. They watched her eat.

The old woman rose and went out for a time, then came back with a silver goblet filled to the brim with water. "Here, child, drink."

"Stop calling me *child*. My name is Pernie." She would have refused the water as a show of defiance, but the salt fish required that she drink, leaving the name issue as the only convenient one for the display.

"I am Djoveeve."

Pernie thought the name sounded weird, like there was something stuck in the woman's mouth. She might have laughed at it another time.

"If you'll let me," the woman said, leaning down and putting her hands on her knees, "I'll show you how to use your magic."

"I don't need you to show me how. Master Grimswoller is my teacher back at magic school. And once I'm done with my lessons, Master Altin said I could be his apprentice."

"Well, Master Altin is going to have to find another apprentice because Tidalwrath has plans for you."

Pernie scowled up at Djoveeve then, her eyes narrow, feral. If she were a cat, she would have hissed. The old woman watched her silently, the two of them watching back and forth. They might have stayed that way for hours had not Pernie been distracted by the pink edges of the woman's eyelids, bright pink, so bright they seemed lit from within. They reminded Pernie of raw meat. A few eyelashes still grew from them, the last and hardiest weeds clinging to ground in which nothing else could grow. Time had killed the rest. Pernie had always thought of Kettle as old, but this woman redefined aging. Pernie had never seen a woman that looked as old as Tytamon, the ancient magician who had presided over Calico Castle for most of Pernie's life, a man rumored to have been approaching an eight hundredth birthday had he lived another pair of years.

Djoveeve noticed Pernie's distraction as it began to glaze her eyes. She watched as Pernie's thoughts turned inward. She smiled patiently and looked up to her elven companions. "She is still very young."

"No younger than you were when you arrived," said Seawind. "And she is far more accomplished than you were at that age, far more and in many ways. Yours was better magic, surely, but you had nothing on her with a knife."

Djoveeve nodded at that. There was no question about Pernie on that account. She'd heard the stories of the young girl's ferocity during an orc invasion on Calico Castle. The child possessed every instinct of a killer, and she had the courage of all the greatest predators. She would make a powerful *Sava'an'Lansom* for the High Seat.

Pernie heard them talking about her. She knew grown-ups well enough to recognize when they were trying to talk over her head. She made a face, mostly to herself, and pulled another stick of fish out of the pouch.

Djoveeve considered her for a bit longer, then returned to the table that was a boulder. She drew in a long breath, looking up at the ceiling not far above. Pernie followed her gaze, tilting her head as she regarded the flecks of pyrite sparkling in the dark brown stone like stars of pale gold. "Is that gold?" she asked, pointing with a half-eaten bit of fish.

"No, child. But it does look that way."

5

"I said stop calling me *child*. I'm nine years old. I'll be ten at the end of summer."

"But you are a child. That's what being nine is."

"I've fought orcs, you know. I've even killed some before. Just like grown-ups do."

"Yes. That is why you are here."

"Orcs?"

"In a manner of speaking."

"I hate orcs."

"Everyone does."

That made her think. Somehow she expected more arguments from them. "Elves aren't afraid of orcs," Pernie pointed out, looking to the elves sitting silently nearby. "So why should they hate them?"

"Are you afraid of them?"

Pernie had to think about that. She didn't want to be afraid of them, but they were very scary. They had huge long teeth, and their lower jaws stuck forward in terrible ways. Their skin was green, greener than the pale shades of the elves, green like the leaves of oak trees and the needles of pines. Some were lighter hues, like pond scum. She'd seen one that might have been the color of earwax once, had it not had just that touch of green. Pernie thought they were green in a way that seemed an insult to forests, grass, and even weeds. They were mean and they ate people when they could. They'd almost eaten her once. And it was true that she had killed a few in the raid on Calico Castle, but she'd been terrified. She didn't want to admit that she was afraid. Not to this old woman with the pink-rimmed eyes and the two pale green elves sitting there.

"No," she said. "I'm not afraid."

"Hmmm," hummed Djoveeve. "We shall see about that." She turned to Seawind, who had already gotten up. He left the chamber, his movements fluid and graceful. He wore a suit of scale mail armor that appeared to be made of leaves,

6

silent leaves that rippled as if stirred by the wind as he walked away.

He left through a passage whose entrance was at such an angle that Pernie hadn't known it was there. She watched him vanish through it as if he'd simply walked into the stone. She went over to it, peered around it as if looking around a dressing screen. Seawind was just rounding a bend in a narrow tunnel leading away.

She turned back to Djoveeve with her lips twitching from side to side. "Where are we?"

"You are on *Fel'an'Ital*. It is one of many islands in the elven lands of String. In the common tongue of your homeland, Kurr, *Fel'an'Ital* means 'Island of Hunters.'"

"What kind of hunters? I'm a hunter. I hunt all the time." She reached down to her waist, feeling for the homemade sling that was usually wound around her as a belt. "You took my sling," she accused. "Give it back."

"We took your necklace as well."

Pernie reached up to her throat and felt for the small pickaxe amulet that had hung there by a leather thong. "That's mine too!" she snapped. "You give it back. That was a present from Master Spadebreaker. It has magic in it, and Master Altin says I can keep it. You give it to me right now."

"You can have it back when you are able to use it properly."

"I can use it just fine." She tried to intimidate Djoveeve with crossed arms and an icy glare, but the old woman's face was as immutable as the stone all around.

Seawind came back into the room, leading a prisoner in chains. Pernie let out a cry and scrambled back so suddenly she struck the wall, her eyes wide with fright. The prisoner was an orc.

"So you *are* afraid," said Djoveeve, though there was no condemnation in her voice. "I thought as much."

Pernie stood stiffly, as if pinned to the wall.

7

"You'll have your magic weapon back when you can face this creature without the fear that fills you now. Not sooner."

Pernie barely heard the words. She could only gape at the orc. The fact that it was battered and worn looking made no difference to her. It was an orc. The most horrible of all creatures. Manlike. Men who ate men. She shuddered, a whole-bodied tremor from head to toe.

The orc looked up at her, saw her through glassy eyes. She was sure she saw hatred there. Or at least that's what she convinced herself was there. In truth the orc made no movements, no aggressive acts. No expression came upon its broad green face at all. Another observer might have reckoned the orc looked tired, worn out. Pernie, however, did not, and she remained where she was, teetering on the brink of flight. To where, she had no idea.

"Take the pet away," Djoveeve said. "You've seen what you needed to see." Seawind and the other elf, Shadesbreath, who served as the Royal Assassin to the Queen of Kurr, exchanged glances once more before Seawind led the orc out of the room again.

Pernie was a few moments before she calmed herself.

"You must learn to face your fear," the old woman said, rising and coming once more to stand before Pernie. "The Sava'an'Lansom cannot be afraid of an orc, not even an orc with magic. I will teach you not to fear them. When you are ready, you will face that one and defeat it on your own."

Pernie's eyes went wide with fright again. She tried to summon up her courage, tried to remind herself how it felt to jam her tiny knife into the firm green flesh, but all she knew was fear. She'd been afraid the whole time she fought the orcs last time. It was as if the person who'd been in those fights hadn't been her, the frightened her who lived behind her eyes and who had looked out and watched as someone else operated her hands and feet that day. It was someone else who had stabbed and stabbed and stabbed. When it was

8

done, when the screaming and bleeding was over, the inside Pernie had come back out, bringing the fear with her.

Djoveeve seemed to see all of that. It was as if the old woman looked right in through Pernie's blue-eyed windows and saw it too, even felt it. Her expression softened, and she got down on her knees. She leaned back, resting on her heels, and smiled. "You won't fear them when you are through. I promise. That is the gift of the Sava'an'Lansom. You will see. You will hunt without fear. Fight without fear. You will decide the fate of humans, elves, and orcs. This I promise."

The two elves stood and said it too. "This I promise," each of them repeated in turn.

What remained of fright was washed away by the oddity of what she'd just seen. They both looked so severe.

Pernie's lips twitched from side to side again as she contemplated all of it. She looked back to Djoveeve, who remained seated on her heels. "So what does *seven land some* mean?"

"*Sah-vah ahn lan-sohm*," Djoveeve replied, pronouncing the elven words phonetically. "It means 'Assassin of the Vale.'"

Pernie looked suddenly to the Royal Assassin standing there beside Seawind. Shadesbreath, the bodyguard of the Queen of Kurr. That was the only assassin she'd ever seen. The only one she'd ever heard about.

"You mean ...," she began, sorting it out and unable to help a certain flicker of giddiness, eagerness shaping itself from the possibilities. "You mean, I get to be like him?"

Djoveeve nodded. "If you are up to it. Which we will have to see."

Pernie frowned down at her at that. "I can do anything I want to if I want," she said. "Kettle told me so a thousand thousand times."

"As I said, we shall see."

Pernie was sure she saw Shadesbreath smile before he turned away.

Chapter 2

Pernie stood amongst twenty elves beneath a jungle canopy that spread high above her and seemed as if it must never end. A warm, sweet-smelling humidity hung heavily in the air, filled with the calls and cries of birds and creatures for which Pernie had no mental imagery. Of the elves, Seawind was the only one among them that she recognized. They were all male, not a single female in the lot, not even Djoveeve, who Pernie hadn't seen in at least a day. With her absence came the absence of anything resembling a kind look or sympathetic eye. There were only stern stares and a smattering of derisive smirks.

"So, young Sava," Seawind began, striding toward her as he spoke. "Today is your first hunt. Today we will see what you are made of."

Pernie looked to the slender black-shafted spear he carried, then glanced around at the rest of the group as well. Each elf held a spear just like the one Seawind had.

"Where's mine?" she asked, reaching out for his somewhat hopefully.

He pulled it out of reach, shaking his head as he spoke. "You've got no need for one of these just yet, Sava. It will be enough if you can keep up with the rest of the hunt."

Pernie glowered at him and looked back at the gathered elves again. One of them, a bit leaner of frame and smoother of skin than the rest, leaned forward and regarded her dubiously. "Look at her, she's hardly even a runt," he said. "Skinny as a reed. She has no chance of running with us, and we all see it. She may be a human, but I see no point in getting her killed. Her people will complain and use it to begin the wars again."

"She will be fine. And I believe the humans have had enough war for now, friend Sandew. Their lands are still damp with the blood of the dead, as is the ink, still wet upon their treaties."

"Well, I won't die to save her. She is your responsibility, Seawind, not ours."

Seawind inclined his head slightly, a gentle nod in acknowledgment.

"Let's be off," said an elf standing beside Sandew.

In the time it took Pernie to turn her gaze from him toward Seawind, the rest of them were gone. Only the subsiding movements of a few broad leaves and low branches marked where they had disappeared into the jungle. She couldn't hear them running at all.

"Good luck," Seawind said. "Keep up as best you can. Now run!" He ran off after the rest, gone so fast she had no time to call out that he might wait and tell her where to go. He moved like a deer, darting away in an instant, and in moments he and his green-leaf armor were gone after the others. Vanished into the mass of greenery.

Pernie stared after him, trying to make sense of what she saw: the crisscrossing tree trunks, the dangling vines, the upthrust fronds and brambles and shovel-shaped leaves of so many unfamiliar plant varieties. She'd spent her entire childhood roaming freely in a forest that was just as large as this, she was sure, but despite all that time and experience, nothing in Great Forest had prepared her for this. The whole jungle seemed a great bramble of entangled everything.

But still, the elves had run right off through its density, and they were all bigger than she. If they could, she could. And so, off she went, running right after them.

She sprinted through the section of jungle Seawind had vanished into, slapping aside the leaves and leaping through the dense patches of dewy ferns. She fought off the tangling vines as she ducked and darted under and around great limbs and tree trunks completely hidden beneath blankets of ivy. She leapt over puddles that splashed warm water when she landed short on the far sides. She wove her way around large clumps of thorny bushes, and had to slow and scoot sideways through a thick patch of odd bulbous things that sprouted long, narrow leaves shaped like sword blades and which were just as sharp. By the time she came out the other side, she was crisscrossed with red lines of blood on her face, neck, legs, and arms.

But still she ran. She ran as fast as she could. She startled creatures large and small as she ran. Brightly colored birds squawked and flapped noisily out from hiding places near her head, and a small group of brown-and-orange-striped foxes went scooting for cover as she plunged through a clearing suddenly. At the far end of it, a dozen huge black birds, crows with reptilian heads, flew up like slicks of tar as she ran at them, the lot of them rising together from the half-eaten and rotting carcass of something very large and, by its stench, long dead.

These startled her and put a fresh burst of speed into her wild, careening pursuit of the hunting elves. She continued to crash into the jungle depths after them, her breathing growing louder as she leapt and scrambled through vegetation that was completely alien to her, not only unlike any she'd ever seen but unlike any she'd ever imagined. Some of them made noise. Others grabbed for her or bit at her or threw up strange clouds of spores, which she knew well enough to avoid. She saw plants fighting with one another. She saw plants fighting with animals. She even saw one plant eating some sort of wild pig, the stout body of the animal half-swallowed as if by a python, wrapped up in a roll of wide yellow leaves like a cigar. She paused long enough to watch the pig until it stopped thrashing. She shuddered and ran on.

She had to fight her way through a thorny thicket, and when she burst through it, she tumbled down a steep embankment and landed with a splash in a stream. When she rolled to a stop, she sat up, one eye twitching and the corner of her mouth curling into a snarl, intent on being in a mood. But no sooner had she blinked the water from her eyes than she found herself nose to horn with a giant rhino, which stared back at her with its tiny little eyes and huffed a hot, wet breath at her, coating her with slime. This made her forget about moodiness. She squealed and scrambled back, the sweet smell of chewed grass in her nostrils and a greenish film slicking her face.

Sidling up the creek, she slowly worked her way farther and farther upstream until she found a place where the trees grew too close together for the rhino to pursue—or at least she hoped they did. With heart pounding, she inched a little closer to the trees, then, finding a burst of courage, she took her eyes off the rhino and charged once more into the verdant maze of the jungle all around.

As she ran, she listened for sounds of the rhino's pursuit as much as she listened for any sound of the hunting elves. Preoccupied as she was, it was only by purest reflex that she was able to duck beneath the spear-thrust of the giant mantis that tried to stab her through.

She saw the blur of movement, yellow like maple leaves in the fall, a blur against the green and yellow of flowering vines. She sensed the movement more than she really saw it in the way one sees normal things, and with that gift of reflex with which natural athletes are blessed, she managed to tumble aside and roll under one of the arcing roots of an enormous rosewood tree.

The mantis jabbed at her again. She slipped back under another protective arc, the whole of the root like a great wooden serpent rising in and out of the soil in waves. Her assailant stabbed once more. Splinters of wet wood flew. Pernie dove back the other way.

This time, the mantis' spiked limb thrust itself a hand's width deep into the hardwood flesh of the tree root, allowing Pernie to roll to her feet. She spun round and got her first good glimpse of her attacker: an insect twice as tall as she was, working to yank itself free, having struck so violently its spiked forelimb was stuck in the root. It jerked at its caught extremity, scrambling with the five that remained free for purchase to brace itself. Its spindly legs articulated like fingers made of sticks, and its angled feet thumped on the mossy jungle floor. It turned its head toward her, facing her, its huge eyes staring down at her, emotionless and watching. They gleamed wetly in the filtered morning light, each eye shaped like an inverted tear bubbling out of its triangular head. Its mandibles opened slowly, just once, then closed, giving the impression of its having licked its lips. It looked back to its work, yanking at the trapped spear tip of its forelimb.

Pernie knew better than to wait and see how long that extrication took, and without another thought, she was off and running yet again. She sprinted for all her skinny little legs were worth, her little heart pounding in her chest as she stretched every stride to its fullest. Perhaps at this pace she would catch the elves soon.

She burst out of a thick stand of trees and ran up a short incline, coming upon a wide patch of ferns. They were big ones, bright green and nearly as tall as her waist, with delicate leaves all intertwined, transparent together like a vast silk screen. The gentle rise and fall of them all had the effect of a green mist clinging to the ground.

She searched for sign of the elves, but found none. She risked a glance back over her shoulder to see if the mantis was closing in, but the jungle was so dense and so dripping with vines and ivy that she couldn't see more than a few paces into it, the rest an impenetrable mass of unchecked growth.

Still, she heard something back there, something slapping leaves and snapping limbs. So she ran on. It didn't matter whether it was the rhino or the insect.

She ran through the ferns and found as she did that they threw up clouds of strange yellow dust. It got in her eyes and blurred them some, but it didn't sting. It tasted sweet, like citrus in honeyed tea. She kept on as best she could, but she startled something living beneath the ferns, something big, which ran heavily across her feet, a cascading passage of many, many pointy feet. She caught a glimpse of something greenish gray and then traced its path by the rustling of the ferns, headed off in a direction to her left. Whatever it was, it moved with astonishing speed. She was glad that whatever it was, it was running from her rather than after her. She was certain she could not have gotten away.

She shuddered, but pressed on in her chase, running once more through the ferns, stirring up the powdery fluff. Twice more, something brushed against her legs, and twice more, she saw it—or them—run off and disappear beneath the cloud of ferns. The fourth time it happened, she tripped over it and fell, crashing into the ferns and landing face first in the powder beneath the misty fronds.

She found herself in another world of sorts, a jungle canopy in miniature, one that existed beneath the larger one. The ground was covered by a layer of the yellow dust, soft like crushed chalk. She looked around in the filtered light and saw that there were creatures everywhere, long, flat creatures that seemed to hug the ground with what had to be at least a hundred long, slender legs. They reminded her of the centipedes back home, only these were much larger than those by far. A pair of them skittered closer to her as she lay there, and she dared not move.

They watched her through eyes that waved atop antenna-like appendages that sprouted from their heads. As they drew near, she could see that their bodies were segmented, and from the dull sheen of their gray-and-mottled-pink backs, she thought they might be covered with some kind of shell. They emitted a twittering sound from mouths that were tiny compared to the rest of their bodies, almost absurdly so, barely as big as an apple seed, yet meant to feed a creature nearly as long as Pernie was tall and more than three hand spans wide.

Pernie noted it and counted herself fortunate, for it seemed unlikely that such creatures would eat meat, at least not meat as large as Pernie. However, she wasn't completely comfortable yet, given the way they were looking at her. Others were coming too, the chorus of their vocalizations coming in response to the first two.

Pernie looked out across the micro-jungle she'd fallen into and realized that she was being surrounded by the strange creatures, or at least nearly so, and she had to throw off the natural curiosity that had left her there staring as she was.

She climbed to her feet and found that she was somewhat dizzy. She blinked to clear her eyes.

One of the creatures touched her leg.

With a shriek, she sprinted for the trees again, but found that she was having trouble seeing where she ran. Twice she ran straight into giant tree trunks, and a third time she tripped over a fallen limb and went sprawling into a patch of mud. The hundred-legged creatures were everywhere.

She staggered down a steep embankment, trying to grasp limbs, vines, or trunks for balance as she stumbled along. Every time she touched one, there were the soft touches of those many legs upon her heels, the chattering twitter in her ears.

Glancing around, she spotted a rock nearby, small enough to lift, but big enough to use against one of these strange ... bugs?

She went to it and bent to pick it up, and as she did, one of the creatures rushed at her and ran right up her back. It was heavier than she thought, and its weight bore her to the ground.

She blinked, trying to see through her blurry eyes as the ground came up at her. She could feel all its legs moving upon her skin like so many staccato heartbeats as the creature skittered around. It stayed on top of her as she rolled, scrambling in place like the woodsmen did back home when they rode the logs down the river toward Leekant. No matter how she rolled to get out from under it, it stayed right on top of her.

She stopped rolling and, with a thrust of her arms, pushed it off, at least twenty of its pointy legs all waggling to hold onto her hands and wrists.

She had to fight to break it loose, screaming and jerking and kicking at it until she was finally free. She ran back and picked up her rock. The creature was already there waiting for her. She smashed its head in with the rock.

Two more were behind her, one once again crawling up her back. The second one began climbing up the front of her legs, but she bashed it off with the rock as well, denting in two segments of its shell.

She tried to shake off the one on her back, but it was too well placed, its gripping legs too efficient at holding on.

She scanned around her everywhere, looking for something else she could use.

She saw there was another stream a few hundred spans away. She wondered if the creatures knew how to swim. They were awfully heavy—but then, so were horses, and Pernie knew they swam just fine. But perhaps the creatures couldn't hold their breath. Pernie could, and she could hold it for a good long time. She'd been practicing all her life.

She threw down her rock and ran through the haze of her increasingly cloudy vision. She ran toward the gurgle of the water flowing over stone. The creature came around to her front, entangling her arms and covering her face. The second one, apparently not dead despite the bashed-in body plates, caught right back up to her with ease and entangled itself in her feet. Once again she sprawled face first to the ground. The creature covering her face adroitly scrambled around her, logger-like, and managed to be on her back by the time she hit. She screamed as the second one also clambered aboard, and she soon realized the weight of them both was too great for her to stand.

The first one slid around her ribs as she got to her hands and knees and once again put itself right in her face. She saw the small mouth open right before her eye, only a vague black spot in the thickening goo that was her sight. Something was coming out of it, something short and sharp, but hollow at the tip.

She screamed again and found a spasm of strength and rage. She teleported herself into the creek, some twenty paces away. She didn't do it on purpose. She couldn't even say how she'd done it, but it happened just like it had those times before, back at Calico Castle—like when she'd somehow teleported onto that orc's back as it was attacking Altin; like when she'd teleported out of harm's way in the fight upon the knoll as the orcs laid siege to their home; and like she'd done when she suddenly found herself teleported inside of Tytamon's tower, all alone with the orcs just down the stairs from her. It was her magic manifesting, nascent power, uncontrolled.

But, uncontrolled as it might be, it worked. She was out of their grips, but not out of danger, for the two creatures were there immediately, right at the edge of the stream. They'd run the distance almost as fast as she'd teleported, but perhaps this time it wasn't fast enough. They darted back and forth along the water's edge, but they didn't come in.

Soon it was clear that they couldn't swim, or at least that they weren't so inclined.

Pernie grinned, relieved, even jubilant with the sudden victory, the magic victory. Master Altin would be proud when he found out.

But the creatures weren't going away either. Worse, one of them ran upstream, streaking off at a speed nearly impossible to see, and then, a few moments later, it came back again on the other bank, cutting off her escape. On land, she was surrounded.

She weighed her options. Obviously she didn't want to go upstream, for there was something up there that had allowed one of the bugs to cross. That meant she could either stay where she was and wait for them to go away, or head downstream and hope for better luck.

She stared off in the direction of the current, trying to see what might lie ahead, but the creek vanished—like everything else had today—into the green knots of the jungle. It occurred to her she was never going to find the elves.

Downstream seemed the only option that didn't involve waiting helplessly, and who knew what the hundred-legged bugs were going to do. They were obviously communicating with one another, so there was no telling how many more were on their way. Which meant it was time to get moving.

She lifted her feet and began to swim with the gentle current, her efforts and the flow moving her along at a pretty good clip. The creatures ran right alongside her.

She hoped maybe they would run off when they got into the thicker part of the jungle, but they did not. They kept up with perfect ease, each of them running up and over obstacles. At one point, the one on Pernie's right had to run off into the distance to get round the curve of stone that slowly rose up and became at first a sheer cliff and then a slick overhang for a time. But it came back when Pernie swam farther along. It ran right down the rock face once the overhang became simply vertical again, like a spider on a wall, and when the wall of stone diminished and became low, moss-covered bank again, it scrambled along as if nothing inconvenient had happened to it at all.

The creatures stayed with her for the better part of what she gauged to be an hour, until finally the little stream meandered its way into a large pool, gently tumbling down a short slide of rocks, over which Pernie slid before being dumped into the pool. She saw that three other streams all joined here, and it was with some hope that she looked back to see if her many-legged assailants were finally going to be thwarted by this watery impasse.

Sure enough, both of them were atop the slope of stone, neither willing to get their feet wet apparently, and both staring down at her, waving their eyes on those long, sinuous eyestalks, and emitting their strange twittering. She wondered what they were saying to one another as they looked down. She hoped they would remember not to mess with her again.

Suddenly, as if startled, they both spun and ran away, the movement so fast their turning and departure made them look like vanishing puffs of smoke. Pernie laughed. Finally. She also realized as they ran off that she could see again, and had been able to since she'd teleported into the creek. That was a fortunate accident, she thought. It must have been the powder in her eyes, she realized. What else could it be?

A nasal, keening sort of sound spun her around to look behind her. Four giant creatures, a little bit like dragons but standing on just two legs, stared across the pool at her. The smallest of them could not be less than three spans high, and the largest one was pushing five. They seemed to balance upon their tree-trunk legs, sort of stooped and tilting forward, with long tails that thrust out rigidly behind them and moved slowly side to side. Like the insects that had just been chasing her, these too had eyes that moved on long stalks, though not so long proportionately as the bugs' had been, and all eight of those eyes watched her as she trod water considering her new predicament. She moved herself farther away, daring a glance down to see how deep the pool was. It was clear enough to see the bottom, no more than four spans deep. The big one could wade right in and get her if it wanted to.

She slowly swam away from them, backing toward the opposite edge of the pool. Another nasal whine sounded from behind her. She turned to see another one of the monsters standing there. It stalked back and forth along the edge of the water, gnashing its teeth hungrily. From the side, she could see that it had stubby little wings on its back, like the wings of a bird that's just been hatched, wings that didn't seem to have grown with the rest of the creature.

This one roared at her as it made its way back and forth along the edge of the pool. It continued to do so for quite a while. Roaring and pacing. She couldn't get out downstream now either.

Pernie looked back and forth from the four to the one. Hardly any difference when it came down to it. Four or one, she couldn't get past any of them.

She looked back up the way she'd come, from atop the waterfall. She didn't think they could get up that. Maybe she could teleport again.

She closed her eyes and tried to remember what she'd done all those other times. What she'd done to get out from under those wide, flat bugs with all their gripping legs. What she'd done to get to Master Altin when the orc attacked.

She thought and thought and thought. But nothing came. Still she trod water in the center of the pond. She cursed Master Grimswoller for not teaching her how to use her teleportation magic. He'd been too busy teaching stupid healing instead. Healing flowers. Who cared about stupid flowers? Teleportation was real magic. It was magic like Master Altin had. He was the greatest teleporter in all the world, a Z-ranked teleporter, the highest of the high. Nobody had that much power. And she was going to be his apprentice one day.

Maybe after she finished learning how to be the Sava'an'Lansom. That wouldn't be so bad, learning that. They could teach her that first. Then she could go back and finish off that Earth woman, Orli Pewter. Pernie might have missed with the blaster when she tried to shoot Orli last time, but next time there wouldn't be an elf to save her. Then Pernie could marry Master Altin as soon as she was old enough. She figured that would be pretty soon anyway.

The loud gnashing teeth of the strange dragons turned her toward the bank with the four monsters on it. There were figures moving all over them. It took her a moment to realize it, but it appeared that the monsters had suddenly broken out with a terrible case of elves. The four beasts, in that span of time Pernie had spent in thought, had contracted the outbreak and were now crawling with elves, who filled the beasts' leathery hides full of spear holes.

Pernie watched in awe as a score of elves dispatched the monsters so quickly it was as if the great creatures were but likenesses of themselves, illusions easily dismissed with the prod of a spear point. They hardly had time to snap their jaws or swing their mighty tails around before they were all dead.

And in the next set of breaths, four of the elves, just four, ran around the pool, leapt the stream, and set themselves on the lone creature on the other side. It was dead in just over twelve seconds.

Pernie smiled as she watched. They were wonderful killers. She'd never seen anything like it except in those few moments she'd watched the Queen's assassin, Shadesbreath, do his work fighting to free her in the stairway beneath Tytamon's rooms. There was a grace to their brutality that moved her like music, a song in harmony with her very soul. Not that she understood such things in such terms, of course, but she felt them, deeply. She was affected by what she saw as others are affected by great art or profound philosophy.

By the time the elves were pulling her out of the water, she was laughing, just this side of hysterically.

Chapter 3

Sir Altin Meade stood beside his fiancée, Orli Pewter, staring openmouthed at the Queen. Her Majesty, Queen Karroll of Kurr, sovereign of all humanity on planet Prosperion, glared back down at the two of them from her throne, her expression implacable, cold as the marble columns rising to the ceiling high above. "Absolutely not," Her Majesty said as she summed up her decision. "The fact that Director Bahri or anyone else in the Northern Trade Alliance or, frankly, anyone on Earth at all is willing to consider this idea is appalling. The Hostiles killed hundreds of thousands of people on *their* world too. I cannot fathom what the man is thinking. Perhaps he isn't. He is a kind soul. I gathered that about him immediately. Kindness is a fine thing, but when it is not convenient or prudent to practice it, I do not."

Orli swept a strand of platinum-blonde hair out of her eyes with her hand. The movement of her head, shaking incredulously as it had been for the last several minutes, kept putting the strand there. "But Your Majesty," she said. "How can you say no after all that Blue Fire has done for us, for everyone? If it weren't for her, both our worlds, Earth and Prosperion, would be destroyed. We remain alive because of her, and yet she is lying out there in space right now, all alone, in pain. Suffering. Surely you can't intend to just leave her there like that."

"I know very little of pain that can be suffered by these living planets of yours, Miss Pewter. The only one of my experience, your Blue Fire, has, in the end, done far more damage than good to humanity. You credit her with our salvation, but to be frank, were it not for her actions to begin with, all those people back on Earth would still be alive—not to mention the entire lost population of that other planet, what was it called, Andalia? I believe your sympathies are misplaced, if not entirely, certainly to a ponderous degree—though I'll grant they do speak to your kind heart in their way, much as Director Bahri's do."

Orli began to speak again, but Her Majesty cut her off.

"Miss Pewter, that will be all. I've made my decision, and you begin to press the limits of your privilege, even as the ...," the pause was long as the Queen's eyes narrowed, her face taking on a cunning, almost predatory, aspect for the span of a single heartbeat, before returning to its normal stoic state, "... as the fiancée of the Galactic Mage." Were it possible to fling dung at a word with the inflection of one's voice, it could be said such was done at the reference to their continued state of betrothal.

Altin noted the tone, and by his posture, and the long breath of air that slowly escaped his lips, the Queen knew full well his displeasure, as did all the courtiers along the edges of the great chamber. Such was the nature of that sigh that many of the silk-bedecked lords and lace-beplumed ladies all stopped in their own private conversations to watch should Her Majesty's wrathful scepter be made to fly. The War Queen, as she was known throughout the land, was not one to be sighed at like some child beneath the impatient eye of a beleaguered parent, and such was the nature of Altin's long and audible breath. They all paused, some slinking behind the protection of a colonnade, others behind the armored figure of a nearby officer of the army or the Palace Guard, watching and awaiting her certain ire.

"By the gods, Sir Altin," erupted the Queen as if on cue. "Don't you dare blow that insolent wind at me. I say, I will have you in chains if you make another such. Your title does not give you privilege to breathe your discontent at me."

Altin made a prudent inclination of his head. "I'm sorry, Your Majesty. My frustration got the better of me."

"I should say it did. You are fortunate that I adore you so, or I might have had to sic my elf on you." She glanced back over her shoulder to a space of wall behind her golden throne, which to all present appeared simply that, a space of wall, the veined amber hues of polished marble beneath the royal coat of arms. Despite the vacancy, all in attendance also knew who stood there—or at least who likely stood there—for that was the place where Shadesbreath waited in attendance to the Queen as her Royal Assassin. It was impossible to say if he was present or not, as always, but the mystery was, as Her Majesty often put it, "part of his charm."

"Thank you," Altin said, swallowing his irritation. She normally didn't put him through this sort of thing, which proved that she was still angry about the wedding that he and Orli had "tried to deprive her of." For what else could the derisive sneer have been?

And that might be of some use to him. If Her Majesty was still in a mood about his and Orli's having evaded her attempts to throw them a huge gala wedding—which she still held as a possibility now that he and Orli had been forced to put off their wedding aboard the spaceship, what with Pernie's abduction barely a week ago—perhaps he could turn the misfortune into something of an advantage after all. "I am grateful for Your Majesty's lenience" was all he said.

"As you should be," said the Queen. "Now do be a good

boy and go help your teleporter guildmates. I want my space-post network under way. I'm in a fit of anticipation awaiting the absolute colonization of outer space. My diviners do nothing day in and day out but look for possibilities. I can hardly contain my enthusiasm. I feel as if I am twenty again."

"Indeed, Your Majesty," Altin said. "The work has begun, and the Transportation Guild Service offices are abuzz with activity as we speak." Orli shifted uncomfortably next to him, her own agitation palpable. "However, My Queen, if I might be indulged a moment further on both regards, I would like to point out that there are issues of security involved with setting up TGS offices all across the galaxy. As you know, space travel is dangerous. It seems to me that the best way to ensure the safety of our people out there—particularly those manning the small TGS offices you intend to set up for our Earth friends—is to make as many allies, as many good, strong allies, as we possibly can. Which certainly means that we should make them out of all the known species that occupy our ...." He turned to Orli, his brow furrowing as he struggled for the word. "What do you call our part of space?"

"Sector," she supplied.

"Yes, our *sector*." He turned back to the Queen seated upon the dais above them on her golden throne. Were it not for the crimson velvet cushions, she, in her golden plate mail armor, might blend right in with her chair. Perhaps that was by design. "My point, Your Majesty, is to say that I believe, as your Galactic Mage, that the most prudent course to ensuring the fastest and most thorough expansion of Her Majesty's influence and power throughout the stars would be to secure such relationships as are possible, whenever possible. Given that Blue Fire is one of only four planets we know about that supports any kind of life, it seems beyond essential that we do what we can to secure to our bosom as quickly as possible that rather significant twenty-five percent of them that Blue Fire represents, especially as hers is one that is still home to an intelligent species."

Her Majesty scowled down at him, her eyes narrowed to slits, and for a time, the movement in the galleries, which had just begun to relax and murmur again, once more tightened up behind the columns and armored folk. But then, just as the storm had begun upon the royal brow, it vanished, replaced by mirth. "By the gods, Sir Altin, you've been in Crown City too long. You're starting to sound like one of us. I think I liked the barefooted country boy better. At least I could see him coming when he thought to manipulate me."

"It appears your vision is still fine, My Queen."

She laughed again. "Oh, dear, but you really are turning into a syrupy denizen of politics, aren't you? You're going to be as bad as Vorvington soon." This, of course, reddened the face of the pudgy Earl of Vorvington, who stood in the gallery not far from the throne, as he regularly did.

Altin smiled, his head tipping sideways and his eyebrows rising to acknowledge the truth of it.

"Fine, Sir Altin. I will indulge your idea to a point, though I will not give my approval for it. Besides, I've already spoken to Director Bahri about this issue. He has given his qualified permission on the condition that you not attempt to move the other Hostile's heart or whatever it is you have planned until all the dead Hostile orbs, their husks as it were, are removed from the Earth's solar system. Is that not correct, Miss Pewter?"

"Yes, Your Majesty," Orli said. "That was his condition. That, and that the NTA has emplacements built there before we try. He wants us to be ready to destroy the heart chamber again if things don't go according to plan."

"I believe you are forgetting his final condition," she said, a saccharine smile upon her lips.

"Yes, Your Majesty. There was one more. He also insisted that we do nothing without your consent."

"That is correct. And, my dear, your plan needs a lot more … massaging, before I will consider it." She shot a glance at Altin that suggested his suspicions about her motives might be right. "I will, however, grant you permission to attempt to convince me again when you have put a little more work into the idea, something besides the great bleeding of that kind heart of yours, Miss Pewter. I think you ought to do a good deal more looking into what it is you plan to do. You say you want to bring Yellow Fire back to life, but do you even know if the host world, the Hostile you called Red Fire, is truly dead? You say that Yellow Fire has merely been dormant for a million years, that Blue Fire's mate was just sleeping after some sunny accident rather than truly dead. And if we suppose it to be so, then what's to say that Red Fire hasn't simply been dormant these last five months since you say you blew him up? What evidence do you have that your explosives worked? Or, for that matter, that any of what you plan to do next will work as well?"

Altin started to answer for Orli, his mouth opening reflexively, but he shut it without speaking. He had no way to confirm that the Hostile world known as Red Fire, the world responsible for over a million human deaths, was truly dead. The orbs attacking planet Earth had all stopped moving, their angry red colors turned to ashen gray. That had seemed like evidence enough, but perhaps it was merely circumstantial at best.

"Yes," said the Queen, seeing the same expression on both faces before her. "You don't know a great deal. And while my gratitude to Blue Fire is as vast as the galaxy itself, I think the two of you ought to go gather the facts before you press me for my permission on such a poorly planned and poorly researched epic undertaking. Make sure it's dead, Sir Altin. With absolute certainty. As the Galactic Mage, that is most assuredly your jurisdiction. And find out if the yellow one is actually still alive. I hardly think it befits my position to endorse an idea that is barely half-baked, wouldn't you agree?" Again came the cunning look, flitting as it did like a flung dart meant for Altin alone, the faintest narrowing of the royal eyes. She smiled, barely perceptibly, and the light coming through the stained glass windows high above glinted beneath those lowered eyelids.

Orli started to say something, but stopped. Altin was glad of that. Clearly she realized they'd just gotten Her Majesty to move from absolute "no" to something approaching a maybe.

"You are, as always, quite right, My Queen," he said. "Thank you, Your Majesty."

"Oh, stop it," the War Queen said. "You and I both know those words taste like bile upon your tongue. If I truly wanted another Vorvington, I'd simply get myself one. Miss Pewter, what is it your people call that duplication process I've been reading about? Was it *cloaking?* That can't be right?"

"Cloning, Your Majesty," said Orli with the first vestiges of a smile.

"Ah, yes, that was it. Cloning. I believe I would rather have the NTA scientists whip me up a whole batch of fat Vorvingtons than see you turned to another fawning courtier, Sir Altin. Gods know I've more than enough backstabbing and arse kissing as it is."

Altin grinned, but he kept the tilt of his head forward, slightly submissive all the same. "Of course, My Queen."

She laughed again. A great merry laugh that filled up the gilded hall to its gold-encrusted rafters. The bonds of tension that bound the courtiers burst at once, and they all laughed with her, some nervously, some simply out of joy that they'd not been struck by the flung scepter of royal outrage today. To be included in a mild insult was, by comparison, a great relief.

The Queen, when her fit of humor had passed, looked back at the two of them standing there and smiled. Her gaze passed from one to the next, then back again. Finally, it settled on Sir Altin. The smile faded to absolute seriousness. "You play the game well, Sir Altin. And if you're smart about it, everybody wins. *Every*body." The smile returned as she waved them away with the royal scepter. "Now be off with you. Both of you. I'll hear not another word of this until you have something I can consider, something that won't make me look the fool in the eyes of posterity."

"We will, Your Majesty. And thank you." He bowed. Orli curtsied, and the two of them backed properly away. Altin kept his grin in check until they were well beyond the Palace gates. They hadn't quite gotten what they'd come for, certainly not what Orli had had in mind, but they'd gotten more than he'd actually expected that they would. Which was a start. Maybe there was hope for Blue Fire after all.

Chapter 4

The elves dashed off into the woods again, gone just as fast as fast could be. Little Pernie stood watching the last waggle of a young rubber tree as the motion of Seawind's passing settled back to stillness again. This was her third day doing this, and she was convinced now that he did that purely for her benefit. She'd seen him move enough over these last few days to know he didn't have to touch that tree if he didn't want to. Yesterday hadn't gone any better than the first day in terms of catching them, but she was determined to do it somehow. She thought perhaps it was those little things, those signs of dancing rubber trees, that she was supposed to look for to keep up. So, with a determined sigh, she set off at a run again.

She ran past the rubber tree and through the dense underbrush for a time. She came across an animal trail and stopped, looking about for some sign, something else to track them by. There was nothing.

She listened for silence in some direction, any direction, hoping for a cessation of the cacophonous screeching and squawking and howling and whistling along some sliver of the jungle somewhere. Maybe the creatures of the jungle could help her find which way the elves had gone.

They did not.

She ran on. She ran down the animal trail for so long she finally had to stop and catch her breath. She did so, and began running yet again. She came to a stream again, perhaps the same one she'd first encountered the other day, perhaps a new one. She had no way to know. She stopped and got herself a drink. She looked around. The sweat sticking her silky elven tunic to her body annoyed her. She looked all around yet again, but still there were no signs of them. She thought about running on again, even did so for a dozen steps or so, but soon realized that seemed pointless too. She might be going the wrong way as easily as the right.

Still panting, she stopped and looked up into the canopy high above. Maybe she could spot them from up there. Casting her gaze around, squinting through the green ubiquity, she found a thick kapok tree covered with climbing vines. She went to it and set to climbing it herself.

A practiced climber, she made quick progress, and soon found herself a hundred spans above the jungle floor. She took a thick vine in her hand to secure herself, and peered around to see what she could see. It looked nearly the same from up here as it did from below. Green. There were, here and there, small clearings that she could look across, but no movement at all. She supposed the creatures of the jungle didn't survive for very long making it so easy for predators as that. Especially the elves.

She thought it might be funny to make them come up here and find her instead of her running after them again. So she climbed another twenty spans up and found a comfortable place in the boughs where she could rest and watch.

She lay up there for some time, silently gloating over her own cleverness, when a wave of noise came at her from far off to the right.

She rolled onto her stomach and peered through the leaves, the line of her sight just below the lowest level of the canopy, like looking along the bottom of a great green cloud. Something was coming. Lots of somethings. Great dark things with legs like spiders, only directed upwards rather than down, reaching into the cloud. They came in a flurry of falling leaves and shrieking racket, at least forty of them all roughly in a row, a pack of them, or a herd, or whatever such things comprised.

Her first thought was to climb down before they got to her, but a glance below reminded her just how high up she was. She'd be several minutes exposed trying to shimmy down all that.

She considered climbing higher into the canopy, but the sight of those creatures frightened her. What if there were others hidden in the sea of leaves? Her fingers spidered down her side to where her little knife had always been, the little knife she'd had for many years—the one the elves had taken along with her sling and the miner's pick she'd gotten from Master Spadebreaker when he died. All she had left to her was to hide.

She crushed herself into the leafy vines around the tree trunk as best she could, wriggling under them like she might a thick blanket on a cold winter's night. She thought the noise she made was awful as she did it. The piercing shrieks of the creatures swinging toward her grew louder and louder with each passing heartbeat.

Soon the racket was nearly deafening as they approached. They came all together like the first winds of a terrible hurricane. She peered out from her hideaway and watched them as they went by, the leading edge of the storm passing on both sides.

They were great hairy things, and what she'd mistaken for spider's legs were arms. Lots of arms. At least six that she could count on each creature, thrusting out from oblong bodies that from one end sprouted long tails of pale, smooth flesh like rats and from the other, hairy-faced heads with faces that were frighteningly like those of men. They reminded her of the apes that the carnival men from Murdoc Bay brought when they came to Leekant during the Harvest Festival holiday, but only in the vaguest sort of way.

The whole group of them swung past her hiding place at marvelous velocity, their many arms reaching up into the leaves to clutch branches with absolutely surety. Occasionally, one or another of them would suddenly seem as if it were falling. It would start to plunge toward the ground, and for the first few instances of it, Pernie had watched in expectation of a mighty splat. But none of the creatures fell. They gripped vines in one or two of their hands, and they held them confidently as they fell, the vines falling with them, limply at first, but soon enough they went taut. In that instant the creatures would swing forward in long and graceful sweeps, sometimes so close to the ground that the bulging curves of their undersides—or perhaps what served as their backs, though Pernie could not be sure—would brush the tips of the low brambles before they were once again slung upwards toward the canopy. In these moments, these great swinging arcs, the creatures on the vines would get out way ahead of their companions, shrieking and raising a racket that made Pernie cringe. But then, as the rapturous noise had barely just begun, another of the many-handed apes would suddenly be plummeting toward the ground. Soon after, that one was way out in front, screeching its supremacy back to the rest. Pernie was sure it was a game.

The whole of their passing came and went in less than a minute. They swept in, swept past, and swept out of sight again, the storm gone and only the diminishing racket of their cries marking that they'd ever been by at all.

Pernie shook a little with fright at first, but she recovered most excitedly. She'd never seen such things before. Great Forest was home to nothing so wondrous as that, at least not that she'd ever seen. And as she thought about what she saw, she realized too that they might have just shown her the way. She couldn't run with the elves very well, but perhaps she could keep up with them like that. By swinging from the trees.

She pressed her lips together firmly, determined, as she stared up into the shadows of the canopy. It was so thick above her that she couldn't see the sky, not even a patch of it. She knew there would be creatures in there for sure. She'd been listening to them for days. If she only had her knife!

But she didn't have it. And she did want to learn how to not be afraid of an orc.

She supposed learning that might start with not being afraid of whatever lived up in those trees. It surely couldn't be any worse than those bugs with all their legs and waggling eyes, much less that pack of two-legged dragons with the stubby wings and giant, gnashing teeth. And besides, swinging from those vines looked like fun.

She climbed a little farther up into the canopy and found a long limb extending far out from the trunk. It made something of a tier in the canopy, and she found she could run right down it for over sixty spans. Other limbs from other trees crisscrossed it as she went along. She hopped over some and ducked under others, never losing any speed.

Soon the limb became too thin, barely as wide as her hand across, and it wouldn't be much farther before it began to bow beneath her weight. It grew increasingly springy the farther down it she ran, and there were more and more forks in it, each of them sprouting tufts of leaves that tangled up with the tufts from other trees. Still, she could get good lift from it, so, spotting another branch that looked promising, she took the last few running steps and then bounced, riding the flex of the branch down and letting the rebound launch her into the air. She flew to the next branch and landed easily, just as nimble as a chipmunk–not so unlike her play back home in Great Forest used to be.

She trotted along the new limb, looking around for one of the thick vines she'd seen the six-armed apes swing from. Soon enough she spotted one and made her way to it, straight as an arrow shot.

She paused near the end of the limb, at the farthest portion that would still support her weight, and realized there were still at least three spans' distance between her and the vine. She looked up into the leaves where the vine disappeared. She looked down to the jungle far, far below. She hoped the vine was secure up there somewhere, then backed up, all the way back to the trunk, then sprinted forward again, once more bouncing on the limb and then hurling herself toward the vine.

She was in free fall for what felt like forever. She heard the vine tearing through the canopy above her as she fell, snapping smaller branches and stripping away leaves with a particular hiss before they began to flutter down after her. Beneath her, the bristly mass of a low-growing clump of spiny palm trees seemed to rise up at her like a cluster of spears. She gripped the vine tightly and gritted her teeth. If the spider-apes could do it, she could.

Free fall ended so abruptly that, despite her firm grip, she still slid half the length of her body down the vine. The thin stems of the young leaves that grew from the vine, and the coarse fibers of its outer bark, gave way as she slid. But she clutched it with all her might, clamping down with hands and feet. The bark gave way to firmer, moister stuff beneath, and with some small amount of friction burn, she was able to break her fall.

She stopped just short of the leafy spears beneath her, and her feet grazed more than a few as she swung across the jungle floor with only three spans to spare. But three spans above it she was, and that was plenty. She swooped over it all in a rush of air, the wind blowing back her hair and peals of purest joy blowing out across her lips.

The arc of her swing carried her right back up into the canopy again, just as it had the spider-apes, and she was still squealing rapturously as the massive python caught her by the wrist.

At first she had no idea it had happened; it was all part of her thought to reach out to grab the nearest branch. But soon the green-and-yellow tendril of the serpent was winding down her arm like a corkscrew. She tried to yank herself free, but it was obvious that she had nowhere near the strength. In a matter of moments the snake had yanked her loose from her vine and hauled her up into its coils, where it began to squeeze.

Chapter 5

Orli peered out at the planet far below, her hands resting on the stone windowsill of Calico Castle's tall central tower—now far from its usual place upon Prosperion—as she leaned forward to take in the spectacle. The planet, called simply R3, was a massive, rocky world some twelve times larger than Earth. It was in the system named for its sun, Fruitfall, which was the designation Orli had given it when she'd first seen it—and a name that had been officially pulled into the networks back on Earth, making it permanent, to Orli's private delight.

In orbit around R3 were three moons, two that were approaching the size of Earth's own moon, and one that was nearly as big as Earth itself. This was the moon that she and Altin were calling Yellow Fire—for now—for this was the moon that they believed once held, and hopefully still held, the heart of Blue Fire's mate. And it was to confirm that fact that they were there.

Altin was just finishing pulling on his bulky spacesuit as Orli, already suited up, wistfully gazed out upon the grayish, planet-sized moon. It was the first time she'd allowed herself to consider that she might be wrong. What if he wasn't down there? What if Yellow Fire really was dead? What if they found the chamber deep beneath the dead moon and there was as little life within as there was without? What if?

"Well, are you ready?" Altin asked, turning her around.

"I am," she replied. "Do you really think there's a chance for them?"

Altin's left cheek pushed up under his eye, where uncertainty tugged the corner of his mouth up a bit. "Mine is not the scientific world," he said diplomatically. "Though in time, I might get to it. Until then, I leave such conjecture to you and yours. I am simply here because I love you. And, of course, because I do hope to help Blue Fire find happiness. So, in that, I am very hopeful that the, well, the flower bulb of his life force, as you once referred to it, is still viable at the least."

She smiled. Hope was good. Hope was what brought them here. "Well, let's go to it, then."

"Do you have your Higgs prism ready, so we don't have any surprises like last time?" He rubbed his back absently as he recollected how the heavy gravity of the world called Red Fire had caught them both off guard the first time he had teleported them there. It had only been a scant six months since they'd first been there, and the memories of the pain were still fresh.

She smiled, patting a black box clipped to her suit's utility belt. "Already set. This time we aren't in such a hurry as before. I had time to calculate the moon's gravity yesterday while you were still looking for the planet with your scrying spell." She moved away from the window, stepping over and around a clutter of ancient artifacts and piles of stacked books. She and Altin were in the study of the deceased mage, Tytamon, Altin's mentor of many years. He'd been murdered just before the great battle with the orcs and demons had broken out, and Altin had not been able to find the will to tidy the chamber up and make the place his own. So it was mostly as the great sorcerer had left it, which made navigating through the jumble of old furniture and magical antiquities treacherous—who knew what priceless item she might break, or worse, what awful curse or magic trap she might unleash?

Carefully, she picked her way to a sturdy table of gray and ancient wood upon which sat a small box of hard plastic, nestled amongst the heaped leather-bound books and baskets filled with a variety of nameless magical ingredients and oddities. The very presence of that box amongst all the ancient things made it stand out as entirely alien.

She opened it and pulled out a black device with a few dials and a small display screen, just like the one clipped to her belt. "I got you your own this time," she said as she approached. She turned the dials on it to a setting Altin recognized as the symbol for the numeral "one" in the writing style of Earth. "When we get down there and you drop the magic dome, tap this button right here." She pointed to a large and conspicuous button near the bottom of the unit, before clipping the Higgs prism onto his suit's utility belt and attaching the short length of its nylon tether.

"Roger that," Altin said, making a face at her as he parroted the words the Earth people used when speaking to one another on their coms.

She smiled up at him, her pretty face tan beneath the glass dome of her helmet, her time on Prosperion giving her color she'd never had while stuck on a spaceship. Her blue eyes sparkled green and red and amber in alternating turns as they reflected the lights blinking on the control panel of his spacesuit. Seeing her made him smile.

"Let me double-check the landing," he said. "One moment." He turned and went into the small chamber built into the tower's western wall—not that there was any real sort of "west" now that the tower was out in space, floating as it was in orbit above R3 and its largest moon. Inside the chamber, normally used as a "clean room" or teleportation chamber, Altin had set a large wooden basin, which was filled nearly three-quarters full with water. This was the method of magical scrying, and into that water Altin had cast a form of seeing magic through which he could now watch the surface of Yellow Fire. He locked the spell in place on a particular patch of the moon, not far from the base of a rather abruptly upthrust mountain range.

He took the time to study the area, noting the conspicuous lack of greenery and the total absence of any sign of life. Or even weather, for that matter. The whole of what he saw made it appear as if the moon was nothing but a great ball of ash.

Nonetheless, there were no apparent dangers lurking near, and so he concluded that it was safe enough to teleport the tower down to the surface, where he and Orli could begin the search for Yellow Fire, or at least, for his hopefully alive-but-dormant heart.

Casting the teleportation spell was a matter of moments. The size of the tower and all its stone, much less all its floors of books and furnishings and its two living occupants, were nothing to him. Altin was a Z-class teleporter, teleportation the strongest school of magic he possessed, the strongest of his seven schools, seven of the eight possible. Such access to the varied magicks of Prosperion was rare, and it was a rare mage indeed who could toss towers about the galaxy so easily as Sir Altin Meade. But he could, and it was through that rare gift that they found themselves there above Yellow Fire and, in the moment after Altin's glance into the scrying basin, that they found themselves upon the surface of the large gray moon.

"Well, here we are," he announced as he came out of the teleportation chamber and rejoined Orli amongst the jumble of books and dusty magical things. "Let me know when you are ready for me to drop the Polar Piton's shield."

"Well, don't drop it yet," she said, looking startled. "You don't even have your helmet on. And let me check to make sure the teleport didn't do anything funky to our suits. You people and your damn magic are always messing with our technology."

He feigned indignation. "*You people*, eh? And here I thought you meant it when you swore all that fealty to Her Majesty on the Crown City walls the day the demons came. Some subject of the kingdom you turned out to be."

She laughed. "Of course I meant it, but that doesn't change the fact that your magic tends to scramble computer brains sometimes."

He nodded, his face serious again. Many a near mishap—and more than a few that weren't so lucky as to be just that—had occurred when the channeling of magic disrupted the circuitry of the Earth machines. The people of both worlds were still working on trying to figure out why that was, why it only happened sometimes, and how distance and specific schools of magic came into play. There was so much to learn, but there was also hope that some insights would be found soon, as there were teams from both worlds working on that very thing. So much could be gained by both worlds if they found a way of unraveling that mystery. But until then, the mix could be dangerous.

"Put your helmet on," she ordered with a twinkle in her eyes. She took it off the table where it sat near a low-burning candle. She lifted it up and set it, gently and lovingly, into place. He reached up and fumbled with the latches for a time, which put an exasperated expression upon her face. "God! You're like a big infant with these things."

"Hey!" he protested. "Look at these gloves. How can I be expected to perform delicate operations when each of my fingers is as big as a pig's foot?"

"I'll give you a pig's foot," she said, smiling again. With a few deft movements, she had his helmet locked into place.

She made sure the suit's dorsal unit was secure, then checked the control panel on his chest and the other on his sleeve. "All good," she said. "Let's go. And don't forget to take it down slow. Let the air out of here easy first, or we'll be picking up Tytamon's stuff from halfway across the solar system." She pointed to the heaps of things around them to make her point.

Altin nodded, then closed his eyes. He let his mind slip into the mana, the place of magic, which for Altin was a constant pink mistiness, like a cloud had settled upon all the universe and no wind stirred. Most magicians saw mana differently: as currents, rising tides, waves, and undulating whorls of chaos. But Altin had a ring—he had the stone within the ring, really, hidden underneath—given to him by Blue Fire. It was a piece of herself and a piece of the Father's Gift, a part of that which had given her life. The ring smoothed out the tempest for Altin, gave him mana that was nearly as instant as his thoughts. He no longer had to speak the words that shaped ideas and formed the constructs of spells as other humans did.

And so, with that quickness afforded by the ring, he plunged into the mana and, with it, into the magic dome he had cast around the tower, the dome known as a Polar Piton's shield. He reached out with his thoughts and found the thread of magic that wove the dome together, holding in the air they breathed, maintaining the steady temperature, and even sustaining the very gravity that held them both comfortably to the floor. He found the thread, tugged at it gently, and, heeding Orli's warning, unraveled the invisible protective shell slowly so as not to send all the air beneath the dome blasting through the windows in a rush. He let it leak out through small openings until it was all gone. The air he could manage; the gravity he could not.

He braced himself as he opened his eyes, awaiting the crushing mash of gravity that had smote him when he'd dropped the shield on the planet Red Fire, a great weight that felt as if ten thousand smashing bricks had fallen upon him. But it did not come. Intellectually he'd known it wouldn't. Orli told him this moon was much smaller than Red Fire was. Smaller than planet Prosperion even, if not by much. But still, the mind and memory do their work, and it was a matter of several moments before the tension left him and his taut muscles could relax.

"I confess to having been nervous there," he said by way of letting her know that it was done. For without saying so, there was no other evidence that the dome was down.

Orli turned and looked out the window. "It looks kind of like our moon on Earth."

Altin, having never been there, couldn't say much to that. "Well, let's be on with it, shall we?"

Orli picked up a large tool kit and slung the strap over her shoulder. "Yes," she said, "let's go."

Not long after, the two of them emerged from the tower's stairwell and stepped out onto the dusty surface of the moon. Orli looked around, tapping the optical controls on her sleeve to get a telescopic view of the horizon all around. She scanned a long, slow arc. Only the mountainous area ahead broke the monotony of the vast gray plain. "Nothing," she said. "Looks pretty dead."

"Well, hopefully it's not all dead," he said. "Let's go see if he's still alive down there somewhere."

Chapter 6

Pernie stood amongst the hunters again, just as she had yesterday and the day before and the day before. Twenty-four days in a row, to be exact, all exactly the same. The hunt would gather here outside the cave that had become her home on *Fel'an'Ital*; they would wait for Seawind, who was always last to arrive; and when he did arrive, they would all run off and leave her to run pointlessly into the trees.

Her admiration for their killing craft had begun to wane by the seventh day of trying to run with the hunt, which had been yet another day of the elves having to save her from predators. And such had been the case on every occasion since but for one, and that had hardly been any better. By the fourteenth day she'd been stung twenty-three times by nine different types of insects, three of which were considerably taller than she was, and twice she'd actually been pulled into a giant termite lair—the same one both times. The big snake that had snatched her off the vine on her third day had nearly crushed her in its coils—actually it had crushed her for the most part, but as usual, Seawind's magic made the injuries go away—and since then it had been nothing but birds, reptiles, insects, and various types

49

of cats, canines, rodents, and, more often than not, mystery beasts, one after the next. The only day she hadn't been nearly or partially eaten was the day she'd plunged straight off a cliff with a sheer drop of some four hundred spans to a rocky beach below. She'd only been spared death on that occasion because Seawind had arrived as she went over. He was kind enough to throw his spear through her leg, abruptly ending her fall, and then haul her up by the length of slender rope he'd somehow managed to get tied to the end of the shaft. Yesterday, she'd actually been in the mouth of a twelve-span crocodile, which had begun to spin her round and round in a death roll at the edge of a riverbank when the elves finally showed up, and so today, she had decided that she was going to tell them she was done. Every day before, Seawind or Djoveeve had come into her little chamber in the cave, woken her up, and somehow convinced her to try running with the hunt again. Every time, they somehow managed it, though she could not be sure why, and every day it was the same thing: her getting mangled by some jungle beast. Over and over again. But she wasn't going to do it now. Not this time. This time she'd had enough. One croc too many, by her way of seeing things. One croc, one cliff, one centipede-thing too much.

She sat upon a log with her jaw set and her skinny arms crossed upon her chest, waiting. The youngest elf, for that is what she decided Sandew was, watched her with a look that made her even more determined to go home. He'd taken a spray of acid in the face a few days ago from a giant bird that had plucked her up and carried her off to its nest, some kind of green-and-white eagle with a parrot's beak and eyes as big as Pernie's head. For a time after, there was some fear he might lose his sight, even with Seawind appearing almost the moment it occurred and working healing magic on the spot.

"Why don't you go home, little human?" Sandew said as

he watched her staring at him. "You'll never run with us. Your species is slow and weak. I said it when you got here, and I'll say it again. What is the value of coming here to die?"

"Djoveeve ran with the hunt, Sandew," said another elf. "She is human." Pernie did not know the elf's name. She knew none of them by name beyond Seawind and Sandew, even though the elves in this group were the only elves she'd seen since coming here. Just these. They rarely spoke when she was around.

"That was before my time," said Sandew. "And in the two hundred and ninety years since, what other human has? Djoveeve was an accident. The gods forgot themselves when they made her."

"There has been no need for another," said Seawind, appearing atop the brown mounded projection of the cave mouth and having come from somewhere far beyond.

"Well, this one isn't it. I've heard the stories. Djoveeve ran with the hunt on the second day."

"That is true, she did. I was there. And before her, Belletelemew ran with us on the ninth. I fail to see your point."

"We approach the full passing of the moon, Seawind. Perhaps his time with the humans has made Shadesbreath's judgment weak. Perhaps he has misread the signs."

"He has not. If you choose not to run with the hunt to make her, that is up to you. But the rest of us will run until it is done."

"I'm not going to run," Pernie said. Her voice sounded small, snuffed nearly to nothing by the noise of so many creatures all around, the elves and the animals, the forest swallowing up her words. She felt it and repeated herself, though the elves, keen of hearing as they were, had heard it fine. "I said, I'm not going to run."

"You must run. It is the only way," Seawind said.

"I want to go home. I'm not doing it anymore."

"But you are getting better." Seawind even managed to sound as if he believed it, but she knew better. Grown-ups always said things like that, even when they weren't true.

"I am not," she said. "I'll never run with your stupid hunt. It will always be the same. Next time the croc really will eat me. Or you'll miss my leg and spear me through the head when I fall. The snake will get me, or the spider-apes. I hate it. And I hate you. I want to go home."

"I'm afraid you can't go home until you have mastered the spear."

That made her look up at him. She hadn't heard that before. "What do you mean, *mastered the spear?*"

"When you've mastered the spear, you will be eligible to take your first test. Pass it, and you will be free to go."

"I can throw one as well as you," she said, defiant and reasonably convinced she could. She'd been throwing her own homemade spears nearly all her life, ever since the first day she'd discovered the value of a good, straight stick. She reached for his. "Let me try."

"You cannot have one until you can run with the hunt. You already know how it must be."

"Well I won't."

"That is up to you." He turned to the rest. "Are you ready?" All nodded but Sandew, who sent both Seawind and Pernie a nasty look. "Very well. Off with you, then," Seawind said. And, as always, they seemed to simply melt into the trees. Only Seawind stayed behind.

"I won't go," she said, resetting the cross of her arms and huffing loudly to make sure that he would hear. "I won't."

"Patience, little Sava. You must keep trying. It will come to you."

"No, it won't. I'm slow and stupid, just like Sandew says. You said yourself the others before me could do it faster than I could."

"The others before you had different gifts."

"What gifts?"

"I cannot tell you now. You must do this on your own." He squatted down before her, and looked her straight in the eye. His huge almond-shaped eyes seemed kind to her then, possibly for the first time. "But you can do it, little Sava. You didn't come here by accident. It is the will of Tidalwrath. It is simply a matter of time."

Her mouth wriggled like a worm on a warm rock, but she didn't know quite what to say. He spared her having to, however, for he jumped up, touched her cheek gently, and ran away, off into the trees after the rest of them. Again.

She watched him go. Arrows hardly shot away so fast. She would never run like that. Not in a thousand million years. So what did they think it was that she could do? And why wouldn't he tell her how Djoveeve and that other woman before her had done it? There was obviously some kind of secret.

It must be magic, she thought. But she couldn't use magic yet. At least not predictably. Not even when she was mad. She hadn't been able to get out of the crocodile's teeth. Or the beak of that giant bird. She'd surely been about to hit the ground that day she went off the cliff. So what, then?

She sat right there on her log and thought and thought and thought. She felt like there must be some kind of riddle. But, for the life of her, she knew not what. After a time, she gave up trying to think about it and let herself cry for a while.

She missed home. She missed Kettle. She missed eating real food instead of stupid fish strips and fruit. She wished Master Altin were here to save her like he always was for stupid Orli Pewter. What had Orli ever done for him? Nothing, that's what. She kept trying to get him killed. That's what she did. But Pernie would never get him killed. She would protect him with her life.

But first she had to get out of here. But how? She wondered at it some more, and found herself wondering what Master Altin would do if he were here instead. She wondered, and then she knew. She knew exactly what he would do. He'd already done it.

With a grim smile, she got up and headed into the trees. Walking this time.

Chapter 7

Unlike even the rocky red storm that the surface of Red Fire's world had been, the moon that had once been the living Yellow Fire was now as quiet as a tomb. As Altin and Orli trekked across the ash-dusted plain, nothing moved. Not the least trace of life. Nothing to make sound, no rustle, rattle, or rumbling. There wasn't even anything to add visual noise, no color but gray. There were no flowers or trees. No weeds. No lichens clinging to the dead gray rocks. There wasn't even the least amino acid curled unseen in some hidden pond somewhere, in some puddle beneath some craggy rock. There was just nothing. It was so still and vacant even the winds had died. The very air had been terminated, burned away by the blast of the blue sun, Fruitfall; one great flare and all things were destroyed, right down to the atmosphere.

And yet, despite the bleak vacuum of lifelessness, Orli had hope as she and Altin made their way into the jagged teeth of upthrust peaks before them. Somewhere among them would be a cave, an entry that would lead them down into the place where Yellow Fire lived—or had lived, so many millennia ago. So many millions of years perhaps. No one knew, not on Earth or Prosperion. There was no way to know. And Blue Fire couldn't tell them. Blue Fire didn't measure time like they did. For her there was only the time before Yellow Fire's love, the time during, and the time after it was gone. But it didn't matter how long. As long as they had hope, there was still a chance.

In size, this world was much smaller than Red Fire, much smaller than Blue Fire too, but that hardly counted as an advantage when it came to the work Altin and Orli had at hand. In speaking to Altin as Blue Fire often did, blasting his mind with esoteric images and emotion mainly, though increasingly with some nascent grasp of words, Blue Fire had imparted a sense of direction to him, a mental map of where it was that they needed to go to find Yellow Fire. To call what she gave him a memory would perhaps be overstating the case, but he had what might be better called an instinct for finding Yellow Fire now; at least that's how he explained it to Orli. It was a feeling that would trigger when the time was right, a sense that left was better than right at some intersection of passages, or that down was preferable to up. Intangible as it was, unsettling and hard to trust, the type of memory he had received had worked before, not so many months ago. It had worked when he had led them through the caves, caverns, and fissures into the depths of the vast world Red Fire, hunting the heart of that murderous world down. It worked then, so it would work now.

What lessened her worry all the more was that, unlike their trip to kill Red Fire, for this trip, they had the advantage of Altin's magic. Without the crushing assault of Red Fire's thoughts intent on blasting Altin's brain apart, they could do without the anti-magic enchantments that had kept them safe. This was a great luxury, and so with that advantage, and the fact that Orli had brought two Higgs prisms rather than one, they hoped to make quick and safe work of the search.

She let him lead the way, and just as before, Altin's instinctive memory led them directly to a pass leading into the craggy mountains, and after an hour or so, they reached the entrance to a cavern.

"Well, here it is," he announced unnecessarily. "According to my cloudy borrowed memories, somewhere in there is where Yellow Fire's heart should be." She smiled, a short, determined thing, and strode in. He followed, then quickly took the lead.

They wound about through low caves until they came upon a great fissure. "We'll have to go down that," he said, a boyish grin upon his face.

It was a wide crack, perhaps a hundred feet across, split open long ago when the moon was still a living world, the rent made by some ancient shifting of the surface that had broken this place apart. It was pitch black inside. Orli peered down into the darkness and shuddered. Altin saw it.

"What's the matter?" he asked.

"Nothing," she replied. "I just had a flash of us falling down that damn pit back on Red Fire. I thought I was going to lose you when you drifted out of range of the Higgs prism that day."

"That was an anxious few moments, wasn't it?" His grin was even more boyish than before. "But we came out all right." He was clearly having fun.

"Yes, thank God." She looked at him through the helmet glass, then glanced down at his Higgs prism. "You're sure you are going to be comfortable using that?"

"It's only one button," he said. "I confess to being a slow learner, but I am confident that even I can handle that much Earth technology." He waggled one thickly gloved finger at her, then made a show of repeatedly poking an invisible button right in front of her. "You see? I'm really quite good at it."

She laughed, a bit of color blushing her cheeks. "All right.

Just ignore me. I think I'm just really anxious about finding him alive."

Unlike Orli, Altin seemed perfectly at ease. If anything, he was nearly as giddy as a child. This was precisely what he'd hoped to do his entire life, discover and explore things out amongst the stars. He could not have been happier if he tried, and she knew it. As much as he cared about Blue Fire, he wasn't as attached to the idea of bringing Yellow Fire back to life as Orli was. She wasn't even sure he really believed it was possible. He said he did, but she thought he might just be doing all of this because she'd asked. But she supposed that was okay. He was here, and he was a happy companion.

"Here," he said upon approaching the edge of the abyss, "this will show us how far." He pulled a rock out of a sack that he was carrying and cast an enchantment spell upon it. The spell lit the stone with a soft white glow. Then he tossed it down into the hole. They watched it fall for a time, the luminous enchantment washing the side of the fissure in pale light, revealing the lines and narrow ledges along the walls for a while until it faded away, shrinking to tininess and then blinking out of sight in the distance.

She looked into Altin's visor and saw that his eyes were closed. She knew that he was riding it down with a magical seeing spell. She smiled, to match his own. He was so carefree in all of this, so delighted to be here, so content to be with her.

If she weren't so afraid it wouldn't work, that Yellow Fire could not be saved, and that Blue Fire would be alone in the universe for all of time—and worse, that all of Altin's warnings, all the Queen's worries, all the Director's worries might come true, the Hostiles reawakened, the whole war resumed, another million people killed—if she weren't afraid of that, she might be enjoying it as much as he was too. But at least there was hope. And she was here with him. They knew they were doing the right thing, or at least she did. She knew it in her heart, but what if ....

Finally, after a long wait staring back and forth between him and the pit, which seemed to her bottomless, his eyes snapped open as if knocked wide by the rising energy of his broad grin.

"Got it!" he announced. "I'd bet it's twelve measures deep at least. Pretty spectacular crevice for a world much smaller than Red Fire was." He pronounced all this, named the distance as if it were an amusement park ride, something to be enjoyed with candy and rapturous screams as they plummeted into its depths. And before she could comment on it, they were at the bottom of it. "See."

"You're a nut," she said, but had to laugh. She'd gotten used to him teleporting her around like that. It was disorienting, but exhilarating just the same. "But you do make this much easier than falling with a Higgs prism." She checked his suit, then her own, to make sure there were no magical mishaps. Her air mixture setting had changed, and Altin's suit clock had to be reset. "Well, somewhat easier."

He shrugged and offered only a crooked smirk as she worked on their suits. It was only a matter of minutes, and then the two of them went on, traveling just as they had before on Red Fire, blindly following passages, led by the unfolding memories Blue Fire had given him of these places that he had never been. They walked on and on for hours.

Even though she understood, at least mostly, how the memories worked, Orli asked at least five different times if Altin was sure they were going the right way. When they came into a low, round chamber in which curled strange wisps of dry gray material, dangling in sheets from the cave walls and ceiling, he nodded. He reached up and touched a bit of the stuff hanging all around them. Whatever it was, it crumbled like old, dry tree bark. Altin nodded a second time.

"Yes, this is definitely it," he said as he picked up a sheet of the stuff. "All of this was bright at one time, I'd wager. It was all glowing and alive, like the green, glowing parts of Blue Fire and Red Fire that you've already seen." He grimaced as he added, "This is the dead flesh of Yellow Fire."

"I feel like a grave robber," she said. She cringed and sort of hunched her head down into her shoulders some. "Maybe this was a bad idea."

"It wasn't," he replied, sobriety replacing his merriness for the time. "You were right. Blue Fire gave up what little she had of happiness for us. We owe her this much. And Her Majesty won't sign off on it until we've determined it's all possible."

"But, what if I'm wrong? Maybe this is crazy."

"If you are wrong, then so be it. Her Majesty already thinks you are crazy, and I couldn't care less if you are as batty as a cave. I love you all the more for trying. You will be the conscience of my next several centuries. And rightly so. These creatures we've ironically dubbed Hostiles live for millions of years. Why should one such world suffer across eons for the brief happiness of Earth and Prosperion, populated with such temporary creatures as the likes of humanity?"

"Why do you say it's brief? We may die, but our race lives on. There is no need for us to be temporary at all. I agree with what I think you are saying in principle, but I don't think it's fair to write us off as a race."

"Look at how close we came to wiping ourselves out. All of us. Hells, the humanity on three worlds is already down to two, and we damned near did finish off the lot of us barely six months ago. We stopped it *that* time, but what's going to prevent us from doing it properly the next? I should say the odds are pretty high that we will get to the threshold again. The history of Prosperion certainly gives enough evidence for that, just as I am sure your world's history does as well. Why else would your people have a fortress city on the scale of that monstrous Fort Minot? Why would your people have such incredible weaponry? What were your people shooting at before you discovered life on other worlds, surely not nothing?" He didn't wait for her answer. "My people are all the same. And now we're in the process of merging your technology with our magic. You have to admit, that does seem the recipe for finally pulling off whatever will see an end to us all. Don't you think?" Despite all of it, he grinned at her. "Don't misunderstand me, my love. I am entirely for enjoying it while it lasts."

The breath of Orli's resignation was loud in the confines of her helmet. She didn't want to argue with him. She thought it was too pessimistic a view, though she could admit he was right in a way. But she wasn't ready to give up on humanity's chances any more than she was on Yellow Fire's. No matter what the future held, Blue Fire deserved better than she had gotten since the war came to an end. The only fear Orli really held to was the one in which Altin's warnings, and those of Her Majesty and Director Bahri, might come true. She didn't want her kindness to bring about more misery and death. That was the real risk here. Fortunately, Altin's levity would not allow her to dwell on her concerns, and soon they were making their way again.

For another two hours they moved farther into the moon. In places, the dead skin of Yellow Fire's corporeal flesh lay so thick in the spaces they passed through that they had to push through it blindly, the mess of it higher than their heads. It crumbled like the burnt remnants of wood, more easily in places where it turned to powdery ash and less so in others, where making progress was akin to wading through gray popcorn, chest deep and seemingly endless. By the time they'd pushed their way through the clogged arteries of the moon and into a cavern where they could move freely and see beyond their helmet glass, they were both breathing heavily. But emerge they did, and they soon found themselves in a giant subterranean space that opened up all around them in such magnitude that its distance devoured all forms of light.

"I think we found it," Altin said, looking about. The beam of his helmet's light glinted off great formations of crystals clumped everywhere around them on the walls and floor nearby. Some of the crystals were as thick as Orli's wrists, and the formations of them several feet long, all jagged and sharp.

"Looks like it," she agreed. There could be little doubt. This was just like the inner chambers of the two other Hostile worlds she'd been inside. "But how do we find the heart chamber without the help of it being a different color and glowing obviously for us? Everything is dead and gray in here."

And it was true; there was no color in the chamber at all. The crystals were as gray as the ashen surface far above. Shining light into the crystals revealed nothing unusual. They were lifeless.

Altin bent down and let his helmet light shine into a clump of crystals nearby. He peered into it for a time, and shook his head. "It's not eating the light," he said. "Like the Liquefying Stones do."

She nodded. She understood well enough. He'd been hoping for the light-eating effect the yellow magic-enhancing stones had. The crystal he called Liquefying Stone. He'd used one small piece of it when he'd first begun his journeys into space. Orli had seen the effect too. Light had this odd way of sort of vanishing into it. These crystals just reflected the light back, the gray merely becoming a little bit lighter.

Altin said that Liquefying Stone ate light. It pulled it in with an inexplicable anti-luminous gravity, an effect that was nearly nauseating to watch for very long. Altin's mentor,

Tytamon, had first found the stones on Prosperion. He'd kept three of them. Later, Altin discovered there were millions upon millions of them lining the caverns that served as Blue Fire's womb, and there were more on the walls of the tiny chamber where her heart was. The whole of Blue Fire's inner self was studded with the yellow stones, all of which ate light and all of which could soften mana in the hands of human sorcerers. But here, on this world, that effect was gone. It was obvious they were the same sort of crystal, but these were dead. It was as obvious as the difference between a living human heart and a dead one. Whatever worked within those crystals had been snuffed out with everything else. And that didn't bode well for Orli's plan.

"Hmmm," he muttered. "Maybe this isn't it after all." Orli thought he sounded like he was trying to sell that to himself.

"Why not?"

"It's not taking in the light. Liquefying Stone eats light."

"I noticed. And I think that is how the Hostile worlds find each other. Like they can sniff each other off the rays of the host sun. Or at least, it's how males find females," Orli said. "It has something to do with how Red Fire found the Liquefying Stone that High Priestess Maul had when she went with Conduit Huzzledorf to find Earth. I got that much from Blue Fire in my dream the day Red Fire attacked her like he did."

"Well, nobody is going to find these," he said, pointing down at the formations, and then pointing around in a wider arc. "It's not doing it."

Orli suppressed an urge to swear. She chewed on her bottom lip for a moment while she considered it. "Well, why should it?" she said after beaming her light around the chamber a second time. "If you think about it, it's to be expected. Yellow Fire is dead or dormant right now."

"Yes, but there's a big difference. If these stones are dead because everything's dead up there too, well, then that seems to portend disappointment." He pointed through the unseen ceiling, the ceiling they both assumed must be above somewhere. "But it should still work if the heart is alive, shouldn't it?"

Orli shrugged. "Ask Blue Fire. I only got what I got from her in a dream, remember? But if my bulb hypothesis is correct, perhaps it's all working as it should. Think about it: daffodils don't bloom while they are dormant. So, perhaps Hostiles don't either, in their way."

His brow wrinkled and he hummed low, almost too low for the helmet microphone to pick up. "I suppose." He didn't look convinced.

"Just ask her," Orli said again.

"I kind of hate asking her anything," he said. "It's so brutally sad to talk to her these days. I have a hard time recovering afterward. A conversation with her is like finding out everyone you've ever known and loved is dead. Again. And for the first time. It is like the rediscovery of the most awful tragedy. Every single time." It was his turn to shudder. "I'd rather not quite understand if I don't need to."

"Well, if you don't, how will we know we're in the right place?"

"We are. I think. We just have to find the heart chamber, like we set out to do."

"Well, then we're back to our original problem. Where is it?"

"It should be over there somewhere," he said, tilting his head to the left. "Let's go."

She knew he was guessing, but she followed anyway. She understood that Altin's way of communicating with the distant world of Blue Fire was deeper than her contact with the creature in dreams. Altin shared Blue Fire's mind when he talked to her. Felt her feelings. Great, planet-sized feelings that were overwhelming and strong. He felt those emotions as if they were his own, and amplified. She didn't blame him for wanting to avoid such an experience if possible.

They made their way along the floor of the cavern. In places the going was easy enough, and the hard soles of spacesuit boots prevented injury or discomfort caused by the points of the crystals they trod upon. But in other places, the crystal formations were very large, and squeezing through short forests of them that grew inexplicably large became arduous and risky to the integrity of the spacesuits. Twice they had to teleport to the other side of formations of that kind—also risky to the suits, though less so, perhaps. Fortunately, neither instance caused any problems with the spacesuit controls and only cost them the time it took for Altin to cast a seeing spell to find the other side.

Progress was slow, but at length they chanced upon something glowing dimly in the distance, a pale purplish radiance coming up from the floor.

"Look," Orli shouted, seeing it first. "Look, there!" She laughed aloud. "I just knew it. There. He's still alive. He's still alive!" She started running toward it before Altin had even spotted it.

"Wait," he called after her, but she was already well on her way.

They ran up to the edge of what seemed a small crater, small enough that Orli could have jumped across, but deep enough that climbing down into it would make it awkward getting back out. Peering into it, they saw the source of the purple glow, a round patch of crystals barely an arm's length across.

They stood side by side, staring down at it for a time, Orli barely daring to hope that it might really still be alive. "Do you think it's possible this is really going to work?" she said.

His head rotated in the fishbowl of his helmet to look at

her. "It was your idea. Of course it will work." He flashed his beautiful smile at her and then started climbing down inside.

"Altin," she began, reaching out to touch his arm.

"What?"

She looked into his eyes, so steady, so perfectly committed to this plan, so wholly given to the passionate entreaty she had made that brought him here despite his own misgivings at the start. She drew in a long breath and smiled. "Nothing. I love you."

He smiled again, his teeth tinged with a touch of blue by the reflected lights of his helmet controls. "I love you too. Now let's see about getting Blue Fire someone to love as well." With that, he climbed down into the hole.

Chapter 8

Calico Castle's tall central spire settled into its proper place with a great rush of air. Its sudden arrival out of the teleport spell blew dust up from between the cracks of the uneven flagstones in the central courtyard and blew the skirts and apron strings of the kitchen keeper, Kettle, all about. She squinted and looked up to the window high above, then back to the Earth man standing next to her. She pointed at the tower, her stout arm raised, as she said, "There ya be. That's the master what finally come home. Ya can keep yer questions ta him, 'cause I hanna got time fer em, and weren't likely ta have a proper answer anyway."

As if he'd heard it, Altin stuck his head out through the window, and from the perspective of poor Kettle down below, he might easily have been some form of alien monster looking down at her. She knew quite well that Altin had taken Miss Pewter to some distant world, and for a moment upon seeing that helmeted head, she was right sure they'd both been killed and this bulbous-headed freak had returned to eat the rest of them.

The engineer standing beside her, however, was entirely familiar with the spacesuit design, and he waved an eager hello. "Sir Altin," he called up. "We need your input on a few things before we can continue down here."

Altin's gloved hands came up, and they could see him pawing at the helmet for a time until a pair of smaller hands, a woman's and without gloves, came into view and deftly unlatched Altin's glassy lid. He lifted the helmet off and, looking slightly exasperated, called out, "I'll be right down."

"Well, and there ya have it," said Kettle, sounding put out by the entire affair. Without another word she set straight off for the kitchens and her culinary demesne.

A few minutes later found Altin and Orli emerging from the large central doors of Calico Castle's main hall, both out of their spacesuits and in more comfortable Prosperion attire. Altin's gray-and-brown robes fluttered in the breeze of his long strides as he eagerly approached the engineer, several steps ahead of Orli, who was hopping after him as best she could while still pulling on the second of her tall black riding boots. He reached out and shook the man's hand enthusiastically. "Master Sambua, I'm glad you are back. Orli and I were just talking about our great need for you."

The engineer's eyebrows frowned, but his brown eyes were bright and his smile wide. "I'm happy to know I might be of some use to you both," he said. "And, as I said, I do need some input from you now." He turned back and directed both of their gazes to the work being done on Calico Castle's eastern tower.

Shorter and less robust than the one that had just arrived, the eastern tower was the one that had been Altin's for much of his youth. It would still be the one he used were it not for its destruction in a terrible and nearly fatal teleporting accident several months ago. However, the rebuilding was well under way, and Altin would have use for it again.

Except just then, the rebuilding had come to a stop. Both Altin and Orli noticed that none of the workmen were doing anything. The longer they looked, the more obvious it became, especially to Altin, who had delighted in watching the bright violet lights of the welders as they joined the steel beams together with their amazing electric rods. He still fancied that the technology to melt metal so easily had to be magical, despite Orli's having assured him it was quite commonplace on her world, even an ancient bit of technology by her reckoning.

But none of that was going on; the bright stars of the welders sending down the rainfall of orange sparks were completely missing, as were the calls of the men to one another, and the droning of the machines that hoisted the girders and metal plates into place. All the work had stopped, and most of the workmen were nowhere to be seen.

Still, Altin had to smile, as he did every time he looked at it. His tower, being rebuilt by men from another world. A gift from another people. It was a strange set of coincidences that dated back through time, the rebuilding of Calico Castle's four corners, the towers all rebuilt or repaired at one point or another in time by people with the need to express their gratitude—at least, those towers that could be rebuilt had been, those that had not been enchanted beyond repair. But unlike the masonry of kings or even elves, Altin's tower was being rebuilt by, well, by aliens. And in a style so marvelously different than anything ever seen on Kurr before. On Prosperion. He could hardly wait to see it done.

But, for now, nothing was being done. The Earth men sat on their toolboxes, staring at the three of them standing there, Altin, Orli, and the engineer.

"So what is it that I can do for you, Master Sambua?" Altin asked.

"Well, Sir Altin, it seems the boys went into town yesterday and, after a few drinks, found themselves in a conversation with some of the locals, who told them about a curse. It appears the locals believe that anyone who builds a tower here will die by some terrible magic."

Altin wrinkled up his face at the absurdity of such a claim. He glanced to Orli, who only shrugged in response. "That's absurd," Altin said. "Why would they say such a thing?"

"Well, Sir Altin, and I mean no disrespect, but, well, some of the boys came back—you know, on the suggestion of the people in town—and tried to approach that heap of rubble over there." He pointed with the movement of his head to the remnants of Calico Castle's northern tower, which, as described, was indeed nothing more than just a heap of rubble. "You see, Sir Altin"—and it could be easily observed that this conversation was very uncomfortable for the engineer—"the guys here, well, they've done a lot of work with broken buildings over the years, and while I admit that the stone masonry around here is not the sort of thing we see much of anymore on Earth, well … it's just that there's something about that heap of rubble that makes it impossible to approach." His gaze darted downward for a moment, as if he were almost too embarrassed to say what came out next. "And, being perfectly honest, sir, I recognize that this may all be psychosomatic and all, but being that your people do have magic, after all, well, I tried to show the boys how to have a little backbone, so to speak, and, again being perfectly honest, I couldn't walk up to it either. Like, there's some kind of dark force preventing me."

Altin tipped his head back and laughed, and for a moment Orli looked as if she were going to scold him for being mean, but then he stopped and clapped the man on the shoulder and looked him square in the eye. "It *is* cursed," he said. "And there is a 'curse' of sorts here. But it has nothing to do with the men who built it. Or any of your men, for that matter. It's the magicians who live in them who die, not the masons and carpenters. Nor, of course, the welders as they come along."

The engineer looked relieved but still not entirely convinced. He glanced back over his shoulder at his men, who were all still watching, several of them nodding that he should go on. He turned back to Altin. "Well, they were fairly adamant about that last part," he said. "Those men back at the bar. It was the workers that get cursed, they said. Burst into flames, or turn to zombies and werewolves and such."

Altin smiled. "I suspect, Master Sambua, that they were having some fun with you and your crew. And, just as likely, more than a few of them believe some of it too. The first thing Tytamon told me when I came here as a boy was that Calico Castle got its name because Sixes always kill themselves. I was quite frightened at the time, being only eleven years old, and being told by everyone I was a Six. But I survived—although perhaps because it turned out I am a Seven. Nonetheless, wizard or not, some people have been afraid to come to Calico Castle over the centuries because of it.

"Tytamon has mentored young mages with six schools of magic over many of those centuries, and, well, Sixes have a habit of destroying not just towers but themselves. Just enough magic to be terribly dangerous, and not quite enough to hold it together. That is why the towers have all been rebuilt so many times and, well, so differently over the years. That is the only 'curse.' It's certainly not anything to do with the castle itself. And it has never ceased to amaze me how so many people were afraid of Tytamon. He was probably the kindest man who ever lived upon Prosperion."

The thought brought him pause, and with a sigh, he looked up at the tall central tower from which he and Orli had just emerged. He still thought of that structure as belonging to the great old mage. He thought he probably always would. The feeling passed, and he turned back to the engineer. "That's the truth of it, and you have it on my

71

honor."

The engineer's brow furrowed as he took it in. He knew exactly as much about magic as he'd been able to read in the fleet documents provided to him by his company prior to coming here from Earth. Still, vague as all that was, he looked as if he supposed it might make sense. He glanced back to the eastern tower where the work had stopped. "And that one," he said. "That was yours that got destroyed."

Altin blanched at that, but nodded. "Yes, that one was mine."

"So not only the Sixes destroy them, then?"

Altin laughed. "Well, you do have me there. But no, that was an accident of a different sort, although I suppose not so much different as I keep telling myself. But here I am, still alive. So, no, no curse. Just a poor bit of planning, or perhaps just bad luck."

"Ah," said the engineer. His tone suggested it was all clear now, but his expression suggested otherwise.

"Needless to say, Master Sambua, there are no curses for workmen here. Nothing magical set upon the stones. Your people are perfectly safe in that regard."

The engineer nodded then, genuinely looking relieved. "The men will be glad to hear it. Thank you, sir. I know we must look silly to you asking that."

"Not at all. I understand completely. You should hear the things I am asking Orli almost constantly about your world. If anyone looks silly, it's likely me most of the time."

"It's true," Orli said, leaning forward and touching the engineer on the shoulder conspiratorially. "But I don't dare say anything for fear that he'll turn me into a toad."

Altin pretended to be angry and threatened her with that very thing, adding after it, "And it won't be my fault if you end up dinner for some passing heron either, so you ought to watch out."

They all laughed, and it was with the expression of one

who has had a huge burden removed that the Earth man returned them to Altin's own point of inquiry. "What was it that you and Miss Pewter wanted to ask?"

"Ah yes, I nearly forgot. It appears we're going to need some considerable amount of Earth machinery, and we were wondering how well things are coming along, as we may be in need of my tower sooner than we thought."

"Yes," said Orli. "We're going to need the basement garage you guys built for us to hold some equipment, stuff we'll need for something we are working on. There's just no room in this one." She pointed with her thumb, jerking it over her shoulder at the tower that had been Tytamon's.

"Well, that's got a basement too, as I understand," said the engineer. "What do you need that will need more room than that?"

"For one thing, that basement is crammed with magic stuff," she said. "But mainly, it's just not built to be a suitable cargo hold, and we can't pressurize it in the absence of Altin's magic shield. What you guys built down there is what we need." She directed her eyes toward the ground beneath the gleaming steel structure being built.

"Well, I'm happy that you're happy with what we've got under way, Miss Pewter, but as I said before, it will be at least five more months before she's done. And Miss Kettle in there"—he looked toward the kitchens as he spoke—"has made it perfectly clear that we are not to tell Sir Altin that it's done until we've placed the last stone in the outer wall around it. She said this place needs to be sealed up tight against orcs before he takes that tower into space, or, well, basically she's threatened to brain us all with a frying pan. I saw the look in her eyes, and I'm half-convinced she could do it too."

"She can," both Orli and Altin said at once. They looked back and forth between each other, surprised, then laughed. They looked back at him, nodding in unison, as Orli added,

"Definitely."

"So there you have it," Master Sambua said. "Five or so months for our part, and we haven't even seen the Prosperion masons yet for that outer wall. We sent one of those little messenger lizards they have twice in the last week, but the master mason says they've got to prioritize rebuilding Crown City first. He says they'll get to us when they can."

"Well, that's going to be a long time," Altin said. "Crown City was nearly half-destroyed. It will be years."

The engineer nodded that he understood. "We're looking for someone on Earth, but there aren't many stonework contractors anymore."

"I suppose we could just use someone's barn," Altin said. "I don't suppose there is much difference in the end."

"Altin, it's going to have to serve as a base for our machines. It needs a power source. It needs a proper pressure hatch and vehicle access. We need a ship, not a barn."

"Well, what about Roberto?" Altin said. "Didn't Her Majesty just buy him a ship?"

"She bought him a ship?" Orli looked surprised.

"That's what I'm asking you."

"I haven't talked to him in a month. What ship?"

"Do you recall when I went to Crown City two weeks ago? It was just after Kettle threw that rather large fit, insisting that I hadn't tried hard enough to get Pernie back."

Orli nodded, clearly remembering it well.

"Well, as I was being brought into Her Majesty's private audience chamber, I heard her talking to the Lord Chamberlain about getting the gold together for 'dear Roberto's spaceship.' I didn't get most of it, but it seems the Queen and your friend have something in the works."

Curiosity flitted across Orli's face, then she nodded. "Let's find out. Take me to Little Earth, and we'll see if we can't get him up on the entanglement array."

They bade the engineer farewell—and good luck with

convincing his crew to get back to work now that the fear of curses could be allayed—and in a matter of moments, they appeared in the knee-high grass of the meadow outside of the walled fortification known as Little Earth. Within the walls was a small village built by the Queen's people to serve the people of Earth as a Prosperion base. It was a forty-acre stretch of land upon which fleet transports and other craft could land, coming and going as they pleased. The whole compound was only two measures from Crown City, near enough to be convenient for travel in between, but remote enough that the wayward effects of magic would not very often disrupt the machinery.

They strode purposefully through the grass to the gates where two Marines stood sentry outside. Wide smiles cracked the men's somber façades as the famous couple approached.

"Lady Pewter and Sir Altin," they said nearly in unison. Both of them, young enough to have barely sprouted beards, looked starstruck at seeing who had come.

"Well, I'm not technically a lady yet," Orli said. "I have to be granted that title or be married to a lord." She jerked her head in the direction of Altin standing near, and added, "And he keeps finding ways to slip out of my clutches."

"Hey," Altin said defensively. "You know that isn't true."

She relented. "I know. We do have rotten luck, though."

Altin didn't want to get her going on that point, or the whole afternoon might go up in flames, so he quickly redirected the conversation, sufficing himself to finding the right time to reset the ceremony as soon as possible. With Pernie being snatched away by the elves, it was difficult to find the right, well, mood at Calico Castle. Kettle was such a constant source of warmth and love in his life that he just couldn't bring himself to do it yet, not when she was still to be found crying in the kitchens most nights. And the Queen had been adamant about there being nothing he could do in regard to getting Pernie back. The whole affair was the makings of many centuries, the product of treaties, and, worse, the blathering prophecies of both men and elves. Interference on his part would be seen as either an act of war or blasphemy, and for many, both. He was as helpless as Kettle was. And all he could do was sigh with her, and tell her that Pernie would be okay. That she'd be famous someday, and important to all the realm. Which, of course, Kettle could not care a lick about.

They passed through the gates and entered the main compound, making their way up a modest dirt lane that was not unlike many to be found in quaint old villages all across Kurr. Orli still smiled when she saw the thatched roofs, and to Orli's ears the creaking wood of the steps was the sound of happiness.

Inside the command building they were greeted by her father's secretary, a lean, older man with the look of a longtime military bureaucrat. He looked up, nodded politely, and indicated they should go into the office beyond.

Her father, newly made general, rose and greeted them both with a smile so wide and welcoming few sunrises boded as much warmth. "Baby girl!" he said, coming around the large wooden desk and clapping her in an iron hug. "I missed you this week."

"We were busy finding Yellow Fire," she said, looking a little embarrassed given that she hadn't told him what they were up to. She hadn't wanted him to worry.

If eyes could growl, his would have, but he let it pass, moving from her to clap Altin into another bear-trap hug. The dull thuds of his strong hand clapping Altin on the back sounded like drumbeats before he finally pushed him away. "You better be careful with my girl out there, young man." The words were gruff, but there was love in his eyes. He and Altin had one thing in common: both would die for her. It was a bond that had been forged over the course of seeing how close they could get to proving that, time and again, and the two of them could not have been closer or held one another in higher esteem had they been of the same blood.

Altin grinned at Orli, who was radiant upon seeing them together and so fond of one another. They were all smiling as they took seats, the general behind his desk and the young lovers in chairs before it. After a few lingering pleasantries, Orli got to the crux of their visit. "I need to get in touch with Roberto," she said at last. "Altin thinks the Queen might have bought him a spaceship. Have you heard anything like that?"

The general laughed, his silver-haired head tipping back as he did. "Oh, she did all right," he said. "And not just any ship. I have, let me see ...." He tapped up something they couldn't see on his computer screen, before he resumed, "I have two hundred and thirty-six messages from various cartels and trade union folks within the NTA all whining to me about it."

Both Orli and Altin looked surprised, though Orli more so, since she knew what that implied better than the Prosperion did. "Why?" she asked. "What has he done? He can't possibly have had that ship long enough to piss that many people off. He only got his discharge papers a month ago."

The general laughed again, his smile wide and his eyes glinting with affection for Roberto. "You're correct. I have no doubt that your friend will piss them all off in his own good time, but for now they're mainly in a fuss about his exclusive deal with Her Majesty."

"And that is?" Orli prompted when her father paused.

"She's given him an exclusive deal on the entire Goblin Tea trade with Earth."

"She what?" That came from both Altin and Orli at once.

"You heard me right. Her Majesty gave your boy Roberto absolute and total exclusivity on all trade of Goblin Tea from Prosperion to Earth. All of it. Period. They get it from him, or they don't get it at all."

Altin took a moment to think on it, then began to laugh. "Huzzah for him! That's outstanding."

Orli, however, did not laugh. "You can't be serious?" she said. "Roberto? My God. Do you have any idea how obnoxious he will become?" She knew full well the qualities of Goblin Tea. There were no varieties of coffee on Earth as potent as Goblin Tea. Not even the synthetics or the genetically modified stuff. While Goblin Tea itself wasn't magical, there was some magic in the growing of it. Or at least that's what people said.

Both men were laughing heartily as they considered what she said, and they even more wholeheartedly agreed. "He will be impossible," Altin said between chortles. "I couldn't be happier for him."

"And well deserved," the general added. "It couldn't have happened to a better man."

Orli looked exasperated by the very idea of that much money and influence being handed to Roberto so quickly—sweet, loving, and courageous man that he was, her dearest friend in all the world, entirely aside. It was obvious by her frown that she still felt he was entirely too debauched to be given that kind of wealth. "Well, I hope it doesn't ruin him," she said. "I can only imagine how much he will abuse the power once he has it." She tried to be stern about that, but the two men she loved so much both seemed so happy for Roberto that the infectious nature of their happiness finally pulled her in. All the same, as she sat grinning with them, she added, "He will be impossible now, you know?"

"Indeed," said Altin, and at least on that they all agreed.

When they were done speculating on the nature of depravity possible in a man with uncountable wealth, a new spaceship, and powerful friends on two worlds, they finally got to the point of calling *the* man himself. It took the general some time to find Roberto, but soon enough his cheerful face lit up the large monitor on the wall behind the desk, and, as always, his brown cheeks rounded with effervescent natural humor.

"You're damn right she bought me a ship," he said to their question on that regard. "Brand new. Only the fifth one of its kind too. I got to jump the line on the waiting list. You have to see it. It's epic. Fast and tough. They say Hostile shafts will bounce off this thing even without the shields. In fact, the plant manager told me I can park this thing at the bottom of the ocean, can sit down there for a year, and it won't so much as creak. Not that I'm dumb enough to try. I'm going to get the codes tomorrow, and then that baby will be mine. I'm thinking of naming her the *Sweaty Boobs* because she's all shiny curves in polished titanium. Makes me drool just looking at her."

"Don't you dare," Orli said. "If you call it that, I'll never speak to you again."

"If I had half an NTA credit for every time you've threatened me with that, I could have paid for this ship without the Queen's gold," he said. "Plus my life would be so much quieter."

"Well, just don't think you're actually going to name that ship the ... the *Sweaty Boobs*. I swear, Roberto. I'll be so mad. Nobody will respect you. Just don't."

He grinned back a big, wide show of teeth as raw mischief ran amok behind those glittering brown eyes.

"Well, whatever you name it," Altin said, "we need to know if you might spare your ship for a time to help us bring back Blue Fire's husband. I know Orli has mentioned it to you before, but we've got a, well, a quasi-working arrangement with Her Majesty to investigate whether it's possible. We've found Yellow Fire, and we've also discovered that his heart seems to still be alive. Orli thinks the transplantation is going to require some fairly complicated machinery that only your people can provide."

Roberto's face got serious for a moment as he thought about it. One round cheek rose as he crinkled up his nose. "Why can't you just, you know, teleport it into place?" He made his signature wriggling-fingers gesture as he said it, his standard simplification of all magic, as if some form of digital spasm was all it took.

Altin only laughed. "I wish it were so easy."

"It's not," Orli jumped in. "We need a geological team. A good one. And we're going to need room for them and their equipment once they figure out what to do. I have some ideas, but I'm not going to speculate. We're only going to get one chance at this, and I'm not risking Yellow Fire's life and Blue Fire's happiness on a guess. And that's why we need your ship."

"When do you need me?" There wasn't the least hesitation in his voice.

"How long until you have your crew?"

"I've already got them," he said. He grin was a narrow-eyed thing, which caused Orli to shake her head, unwilling to ask about something she saw glimmering there.

"Well, since you are already there, can you see about finding us a science team?"

"I'm not exactly on tongue-kissing terms with the NTA," Roberto said. "They gave me my bonus and my honorable discharge—which is better than I can say for Captain Asad—but they aren't too happy about that little incident with me trying to break you out of the Fort Minot detention facilities that day."

"So don't get a military team. Go private. Check out some universities. That's where most of the good ones will be anyway."

"All right. I'll see what I can do. How soon do you need them?"

"As soon as possible. Every day we wait is another day of

agony for Blue Fire."

"Gotcha. I'll tell you what; I'll meet you guys outside of Murdoc Bay in seven days. My first mate is finishing up her contract on the freighter I pilfered her from." He grinned again, mischief openly galloping across his face. "Then I'll see you there."

"Murdoc Bay? Why Murdoc Bay?"

"I did mention I've got a business to run for the Queen, didn't I?"

Orli looked suddenly very uncomfortable. Her last experience in Murdoc Bay had nearly led to her last experience ... ever. She glanced nervously to Altin and then her father, then seemed to swallow the apprehension back, realizing Altin would be with her. "I don't even want to know. But seven days is fine. We'll see you then."

"All right. See you then. See ya, Altin. Ta-ta, General." He laughed at that. "God, I love saying *ta-ta* to a general. I'm so damned glad to be fleet-free." He winked at the general, who smiled and nodded back, then the monitor went black.

"Well, there's your ship," said the general, turning back to face the two of them. "It looks like your mission is getting under way."

"Yes. I'm glad of that," Orli said, though some of the energy in her voice was gone.

They looked to Altin for confirmation of the propitious nature of Roberto and his ship, but his expression was rather grim. He knew what had happened to Orli last time she was in Murdoc Bay too. He'd seen the look on her face when Roberto mentioned it. The course of events in recent months had caused him to postpone dealing with those responsible, but he had certainly not forgotten. It seemed perhaps the time had finally come for meting out the rest of his revenge.

Chapter 9

Pernie made her way carefully through the jungle, tracing the path she'd taken on her first day running—or trying to run—with the hunt. She walked this time, however, and she gathered a few strands of young lianas and carefully braided the vines into two lengths of cord, each of which were just a bit shorter than the length of her arm. She worked as she walked, her fingers practiced at it, having learned to plait both from Kettle, on her own hair, and from Gimmel, Calico Castle's groundskeeper, to braid her pony's mane.

There wasn't quite a path to follow the way she went, but the direction she took was directed by those places where light shone through the underbrush, stripes and spots of illuminated space beyond and between the drooping limbs and vines and roots and stems that snarled and twisted and fought to block her way. She'd come this way thrice since that first day, though at different points, she'd darted off in one direction or another, and never quite entirely retraced her tracks. Still, her long practice with wandering in Great Forest back home did not leave her entirely unprepared to find her way through this wilderness, and with a little patience, she stayed fairly straight on course.

Soon enough, she spotted the twisting roots of the giant rosewood, rising up out of the forest floor and diving back again, looking like half-exposed links in some great wooden chain. She recognized the embankment near it right away and stopped. She looked up at the crest, scanning the foliage all around. Narrow beams of sunlight made their way through the canopy and dappled the leaves and the snaking patterns of bark and vine, all of which twisted together in a chaotic sort of symmetry, peaceful and seemingly unoccupied. But Pernie knew better. Somewhere in there was an enormous yellow mantis, hiding and waiting for her to come near. She squinted and saw the wet sap that had run from the gouges the creature's spiked forelimb had caused, a red-orange ooze of tar, tacky on the top like the surface of creamed soup that's begun to cool.

She knew the mantis wouldn't move, that it was more patient than she was, so she looked about and found a large flowering lily with broad, flat leaves. She went to it and bent one of the leaves between her fingertips. It was as thick and supple as it had appeared to be, a sturdy jungle variety. She folded the leaf, bent it back and forth, even tried to poke her finger through. It tore, but not without a good deal of force.

She glanced around for signs of movement nearby. Nothing. She tore off a quarter of the leaf, a span of it a little wider than the palm of her hand and twice as long. She folded it over once, then hunted around for a stick or pointy rock. She found one right away, and soon had poked holes in two places through her leaf at the longer ends. She threaded her homemade cords through the holes, one at each end, and secured them with simple square knots. When she was done, she held up what she had made: a sling, not much different than the one she'd used so many times at home. The one the elves had taken from her the moment she'd arrived.

She spent a few more moments looking for suitably sized rocks, gathering a dozen of them into a pile. With a last check on the security of the knots, she gave her new weapon a try.

Dust, splinters, and bits of bark flew out from the tree where the rock struck, barely a hand's width above the oozing flow of sap. A second, right after, blasted away more wood and nicked the top of the sap, cutting a wedge across the rubbery flow. The third stone knocked the little bulb of goo right off the tree, stone and sap both rolling off into the dirt.

Smiling and feeling like herself for the first time since arriving on this island, Pernie loaded another stone into her sling. This shot, like the last, was perfectly on target, and with it, she concluded she had the feel of her new weapon.

She loaded another stone, and then gathered up the rest, tucking them into her waistband, her boot tops, and anywhere else she could find, given that the elves seemed opposed to stitching pockets in their hunting clothes.

Tipping her head back, she looked up into the tree, looking for signs of something yellow, something that would give away the location of the mantis hiding up there somewhere. She found it straightaway. Three spans up, in a cluster of leaves. The play of dappled sunlight made it blend in perfectly.

Pernie saw it watching her, saw the angled lines of its massive piercing spikes, the edges of each serrated like crocodile teeth, another thing she was all too familiar with these days.

She spun her sling in ever-faster loops; round and round and round it went, the air whistling as the weight of the stone passed. With a hiss, the stone flew away, followed by a dull *thunk*. There came a rustling, then the snapping of twigs, and down came the mantis in a rain of leaves.

It hit the ground with a heavy thud, and for a time, its

legs still moved, opening and closing the angles at its knees. It looked as if it were trying to run in slow motion through the air and back up into the tree. But the eyes didn't move. Not this time. There was a hole punched through one of them, and green fluid seeped out into the dirt. And not long after, even that stopped.

Pernie thought about taking one of its spiked forelimbs for a weapon, but she had no knife to cut one off, so she had to satisfy herself with the sling. But her recent success suggested perhaps it would be enough for what she needed to do next. It was time to go back to the fern meadow and face the giant centipede-like things.

Once more she made her way carefully through the trees, again braiding a length of cord, though much longer than before and this time stripped from the fibrous insides of bark pulled from a variety of long, ropy vines. She pressed on for quite some time, hopping several streams and recalling which way she had to go with her practiced woodsman's sense. It was the work of an hour's walk to find it, but finally, as the sunlight piercing the canopy came through in nearly vertical lines, Pernie climbed a narrow rise and found herself once again looking across the thigh-high fluff of what seemed a fog of ferns.

She got down on her hands and knees and peered underneath the level of the fern leaves, as if looking for something beneath a low table. The light, filtered once more through the screen of ferns, was dim enough that Pernie couldn't see beneath it very well.

She crawled right up to the edge of the fern meadow and peered deeper inside. Nothing moved. There was only the yellow powder everywhere, a soft, dusty bed of it that covered the entire expanse beneath the delicate fern leaves. She saw no sign of the many-legged monsters anywhere.

There were, in a few places, high spots in the powder, long lumps barely discernible at first, but, as she watched, distinctly dunelike in how they appeared. Modest dunes, to be sure, but they were conspicuous once she noticed them. She counted four of them within range of her sling.

Willing to take a chance at being wrong, and completely unwilling to go into the dust and risk her vision once again, she stood and crept away from the ferns. A quick scan of the surrounding jungle suggested she was still alone. She set herself to the task of setting up her trap.

She began by making a noose at one end of the sturdy cord she had made, this one nearly as thick around as her thumb. The other end she tied firmly around a nearby tree. She stretched the line of her handmade rope out toward the ferns as near as it would go and then spread the noose out on the ground near her feet. Satisfied, she hunted around for a nice big bashing rock, something big enough to mangle the many-legged monster if her plan should go awry. Once she had one of suitable size, not much bigger than a pinecone from back home and with a reasonably sharp point as well, she knelt down next to her spread noose and extracted three of her remaining sling stones.

She loaded her little weapon and squinted into the dim space beneath the ferns again. Locating one of the long lumps in the powder, she set her sling spinning furiously. The stone shot out and struck the lump with a puffy *thump.*

Just as she had supposed, up from the dusty yellow stuff came one of the long, squat creatures, its head end up and its eyestalks moving all around.

Pernie remained motionless as she watched it looking for the source of its recent injury. She couldn't tell how much, if at all, she'd damaged it, but clearly it was alarmed.

It didn't seem to see her standing there, but in a matter of moments, one of the other lumps in the powder shook itself and rose up from the dust as well. This one was bigger than the first, the flat gray length of its gently arcing shell a full four hand's widths wide. The two of them chattered at one another, the little round Os of their mouths like dark spots in the dusk-light of their under-fern world.

Pernie feared they would wake up others, so she quickly sent another sling stone on its way. This one struck the first creature right below its eye, breaking the appendage halfway off. The creature flopped over on its back with the force of the impact, and all its legs began to tie invisible knots in the cloud of dust stirred up by its violence.

The larger one let out a low, frightening hiss, and with it, up popped two more creatures from powdery dunes nearby. All three directed their waving eyes to right where Pernie was.

They chattered at one another for a moment more, and Pernie sent another stone at the smallest of the three just before they charged.

Her stone struck true, catching the creature like the last, right at the base of an eyestalk, and like the one before, this one hissed and flipped onto its back, though only for a moment before it rolled up tightly into a ball, a perfect sphere of itself, its grayish shell all wrapped around it to protect its soft parts from yet another attack.

The other two came on strong, and their astonishing speed cleared the distance between them and their assailant almost instantly. Pernie barely had time to grab up the noose lying there and hold it out before they were upon her, the larger one running straight up her thighs, belly, and chest in less time than it takes to sneeze. Its pointy feet all brushed and touched her, at least those that were upon her–half its length was still standing upon the ground, its body bent in an L shape, giving it enormous leverage. The power it had from that leverage drove her over onto her back. She fought and pushed at it, trying desperately not to let go of her rope as she fought. She punched with both hands at the soft underside it exposed to her, an endless trunk of shifting limbs, all those jointed legs moving at once all around her, tapping and prodding her body and her face.

The second creature, as eager as the first, also put itself into the mix, and between the three of them, insects and human, they were quite a tangled mess.

Between Pernie's punching and the added use of her knees, combining as well with the activities of the second creature, which were sometimes at odds with its companion, she was able to shift enough that she could lift her arms above her head, raising with them a few of the creature's legs as it reached for her face. Her assailant opened its little mouth and thrust out its hollow mouth spike. It made a flat slap with its head, aiming for her right eye.

She jerked her head out of the way and pulled her noose down over its head, yanking violently. The eyestalks were sinuous and slid right through and up again, but some of its legs snapped on one side as she mashed the noose down in a way that bent them against their joints.

She got the noose perhaps a third of the way down the creature's length, like pulling a stocking over a frenzied, fighting foot. The combination of having several of its legs entangled and the pain of three or four broken limbs set it to hissing and thrashing. In its agony, it fell away from her and rolled up in a ball. The release of its groping feet and the push and pull of its weight sent her tumbling sideways, which in turn knocked the smaller insect off of her as well.

She scrambled to her feet and ran for the bashing rock where it lay upon the ground.

Unfortunately, the smaller insect was far quicker than she, and by the time she was but a step away from her rock, the bug was on her back again. It climbed up her body so fast she staggered and pitched forward, nearly colliding headlong into the tree to which her noose was bound. As it was, she struck it with her shoulder and was spun painfully around.

She landed hard on her back, with the insect, in that

instant that she spun, clambering around her body to stand upon her chest. Once again there came a hollow, pointed mouth tube swatting for her eye.

She turned her face in time, and the little spike went through her cheek instead. It stuck all the way through and into her tongue as well, and for a moment she felt the force of the creature trying to suck it out. But the suction released an instant later, replaced by the taste of blood.

She mashed her fists at the creature and tried to roll away. It scrambled around her as she rolled, its feet astonishingly nimble, and it was on her back again when she stopped and got to her hands and knees.

She fought her way to her feet and then ran backward, slamming the creature up against the tree, pinning it against the bark. The strength of its legs was frightening. It pushed her away from the tree and quickly scrambled back around to her chest. She tried to stagger back to where her bashing rock was, but the creature was too long and its lower half was tangling her legs up all the way past her knees.

On instinct, she threw herself face forward into the dirt, intent on landing her weight upon it again. The creature, sensing it, scrambled around to her back before she struck. She got a face full of moss and dirt instead. She actually managed a smile as she reached forward and grabbed her rock, though. It was right there.

She faked rolling to her right and rolled left instead. The creature, though fast, was confused by the shift just long enough that she managed to get back onto her hands and knees. Once again she staggered to her feet.

Again the creature was at her chest. She dodged the slap of its mouth spike with her head as she struck the first blow with her pointed rock. She nearly dodged another slap, and took a long cut in her cheek, the same side with the hole in it, and this just under her eye. She dealt two more strikes with the sharp rock, one of which crackled on impact, like the crunch of dried twigs, and suddenly the bug was rolling away from her, it, like the other two, curled up into a ball.

Pernie ran to it as it rolled up against an exposed root and beat the sphere of it in with the rock. She pounded and pounded on it with the pointed end of her stone hammer, smashing through the creature's armor casing as if it were the shell of some great pumpkin-sized egg. The bug was a heap of pale green-and-yellow goo by the time she was done whaling on it, with bits of ruined shell jutting from the mushy mound like wedges of broken dinnerware. She smiled down at its corpse and thought about picking through the wreckage to see what sorts of things might be in there. But she had more important things to do.

She saw that the big bug was still curled up around the noose, so she risked a glimpse under the ferns to see if there were others lurking menacingly down there. There were not. The first one she'd hit with a stone appeared to have run off, and the second one, the one that had rolled itself up, was now lying half-opened on its side, the balled-up defensive mechanism slightly agape, like the mouth of a dead man lying there.

She nodded. Good. This had gone better than planned.

She turned back to where the big one lay, still motionless on the ground like a large gray globe, its segmented armor gleaming dully in the wan morning light. She didn't know what to say to it, but she was about to try.

Chapter 10

Pernie sat and watched the armored ball of her captive for a long time. For the first hour or so, she kept glancing nervously back toward the fern meadow, expecting more of the insects to come scuttling out and attack, but that didn't seem to be the case. So, after a while, she worried less and started to wonder more.

She'd already figured out by her first day in the jungle that these creatures somehow communicated with one another. That much had been apparent by the way they chattered back and forth and by the way the two that had chased her had clearly been working in concert. The question was not *if* they communicated but how. Was it all vocal?

Master Altin's dragon spoke to him all the time. Dragons, at least the one she knew semi-personally, communicated telepathically. She'd even heard that the little homing lizards that Prosperions sent flitting about with notes strapped to their backs had some kind of telepathic link to one another, even with other homing lizards that they had never met. So she knew it was possible for animals to do such things. What she didn't know was if that sort of contact, contact that could cross over between species, was possible with bugs.

For a half hour she'd been trying just such a thing, and it was proving less than productive. At the wizard's school in Leekant, Master Grimswoller had taught her how to use her magic telepathy. It was very simple really, once one understood how it worked. And it was with the practiced method that grumpy Master Grimswoller had taught her that she continued to reach out to the balled-up bug lying there, trying to connect to its bug mind.

She let her thoughts seep gently out across the intervening space, projected toward the insect in as friendly a manner as possible. "Hey," she thought at it for perhaps the fortieth time, shaping her thoughts in the gentle way she would have shaped the words were she speaking to a skittish pony, goat, or calf. "Why won't you talk to me?"

Still nothing. She knew that trained telepaths could block out others' thoughts. Master Altin did it constantly. But depending on what type of block they had in place, she'd noticed that sometimes she could tell that there was a block. Meaning, she knew there was someone there. Not always, as Master Grimswoller had explained, but sometimes. But she wasn't getting that with this silent bug.

She sat down on a rock near the tree and leaned back, making herself comfortable. She could stay at this all day if she had to. All week. All year. No stupid bug was going to outsmart her.

She wondered if its shell protected its mind somehow. Who knew what a weird bug like that could do? She wondered how long it was going to stay rolled up in a ball. It reminded her of the little pill bugs back home, the ones Kettle called roly-polies when Pernie was a very little girl. Thinking of those little bugs made this one seem less sinister somehow. She wondered if maybe they were related in a way. She thought it might be nice if they were family, like cousins who had gotten separated by the sea. Like she was separated from all her family. Or at least the only family she had ever known. She missed Kettle something fierce, and she was certainly sick of fish strips now. She was sure that she would never eat them again when she grew up. In fact, the best part of becoming a deadly assassin would be to beat the next person who tried to make her eat fish into a bloody pulp. She would mash them and throw all their stupid fish outside for the wild cats to eat.

Stupid fish.

She realized she had nearly fallen asleep when her head jerked up with a jolt. She blinked a few times and found herself face to face with the insect she had caught. It had crawled right up to her and raised itself up to stare at her.

She squealed and slid sideways off the rock she'd been sitting on, but she rolled quickly to her feet and darted out beyond the reach of the length of rope that tied the insect to the tree. But she need not have, for the creature once again rolled up into a ball.

Pernie frowned at it and wriggled her little lips in curiosity. She walked right up to it and prodded it with her toe. "You can come out, you know," she said. "I'm not going to hurt you so long as you don't try to bite." She tilted her head, the long drapery of her blonde hair, rather dirty and unkempt these days, swaying with the motion and partly covering her face. "Or try to climb me like a tree," she added, in case it thought to catch her on a technicality.

The creature did not respond, and it simply lay there looking like one of the big balls of pitch the siege engineers had stacked up beside the catapults the army had placed along Calico Castle's walls.

She tried once more to push her thoughts outward to it, prodding gently, seeking its mind. This time she found it. She found it so suddenly that it startled her, causing her to lose the connection as quickly as she'd discovered she had one.

She giggled and clapped and jumped up and down. She'd

known it would have a mind. She'd just known it would!

She tried again, feeling as she did that she now understood how Master Altin must have felt when he was first taming his dragon, Taot. Master Altin hadn't been much older than she was now at all. This was certainly just like that, and she was very excited. Imagine how impressed he was going to be when he found out.

Of course, she still had to tame it properly.

She sent her mind in search of the creature's again, her thoughts tapping softly across the space like one of the creature's strong but supple limbs. She patted upon the surface of its mind like a kitten batting at a string. "Hey," she thought at it. "Let me in. I've got work for you."

She got back what could be simply translated as a "no." Just that. Somehow she'd hoped for some kind of emotion and interesting intelligence. But it just said, "No." Or at least, its thought made it perfectly clear. Just, no.

"Well," she thought at it again, "I don't care if you say no to me. I need a ride." She walked right up to it and gave it a gentle kick. "Now get out of that little ball before you make me mad." She put her hands on her hips, and her face wore the very stern frown that she'd seen Kettle use so many times before. "Get up," she said aloud. "You've rolled about enough."

This, of course, did nothing to unwind the creature from itself, so Pernie gave it yet another kick. Harder this time. "You listen here, Mr. Bug; you'll do as I say or it's going to go poorly for you, do you hear?" Now she sounded just like Kettle too. She sent that thought telepathically across the intervening space, and she made the mental threat of yet another kick to go along with it.

The bug sent back another "no."

Pernie kicked it yet again. This time hard enough that it rolled down the gentle slope, bounced up into the air some when it hit a root, and then came to the end of the rope, which jerked it to a stop. "Now, unroll, you big mean bug, or I'll have at you with my pointy rock. You can see how that went for your friend." She sent that thought telepathically as well, and then glared down at the bug for quite some time, waiting for its reply.

"No," it sent back. No anger. No fear. No sense of stubbornness. Just, no.

Pernie thought about kicking it again, but that last one had rather hurt her foot. The shell on those things was pretty hard, and this one was bigger than the one she'd bashed in with her rock.

She thought back to what she knew of Altin's taming of Taot. She remembered him telling her the story once, out beside the well when she was very small. He said he'd had to scare the dragon into being nice to him. But how? How does a little girl scare a giant bug into being nice? Especially a bug that only knows how to say "no" to everything? She thought that if she should ever get this grouchy bug tamed, she might have to name it Kettle, since "no" was Kettle's favorite word too.

She watched the bug lying there at the end of the rope, the taut bit of Pernie's cord the only thing that kept it from rolling down the slope and into the little stream. And then it hit her. The water! Neither of the bugs that had chased her that first day had wanted to get their feet wet. Maybe that would be enough.

She sent that thought to the bug telepathically. "I'll drag you right down to the water and sit on you until you be nice," she told it.

"No," came its reply.

"All right, that's it, then," she said aloud. "I've had enough of you."

She went to the tree and untied her rope. She nervously unwound the last bit of knot and waited, half-expecting the creature to unroll itself and run.

It did not.

She wound the rope around her wrist securely so that the bug could not escape, then marched right back to the balled-up bug. "Last chance," she sent to it. "Straighten up or it's a bath for you."

"No."

Without another word or thought for the bug, she strode right down the slope to the creek, only needing to give the bug the least bit of a tug to set it rolling right along. It came down beside her, then bumped and bounced past her, winding the rope around itself as it went. As it rolled farther away, picking up speed, Pernie leaned back against the rope to stop it, but that only spun it around, allowing the rope to unwind as the bug continued on. Pernie ran after, though she didn't have to for more than a few steps.

No sooner did the bug hit the muddy edges of the creek than it popped right out of its spherical form and braced itself, spreading flat, legs out wide and stopping short of the water.

Startled by the nearly instantaneous transformation, Pernie's quick reflexes were the only thing that saved her from tripping over it and plunging into the stream. Instead, she seized the opportunity and hopped onto the creature's back, turning herself sideways to its length and sliding to the middle of its trunk, where she stood balancing herself with slightly bent knees. The soft soles of her elven boots flexed gently over the arc of the creature's back, and for nearly a full second she was perfectly perched up there.

Then, of course, the creature bolted back up the slope, tossing her off with its lightning-quick speed as if someone had just jerked a rug out from under her. She landed in a pile in the soft mud, and had enough time to look up before the insect hit the end of the rope again.

Had she not been dumped several inches deep into the mud, it might have dragged her off, at least for a bit, but the suction of the mud and Pernie's determination not to let it get away were enough to flip the creature over onto its back as it reached the length of its tether so suddenly.

Its legs all went to spasms as it twisted and thrashed trying to right itself, at least all those legs that were not broken and hanging limply or jutting out askew. It did manage to get itself over, and it turned back at her, its eyestalks waggling furiously. For a moment she thought it was going to charge her, so she crawled back into the water and got to her knees. Her arm was extended to its fullest length to accommodate the length of rope she'd had to play out, and she leaned back against it and tried to haul the creature closer to the stream.

The creature flattened itself against the forest floor, spreading all its legs out until its body looked as if it were bread dough ready for the rolling pin. Pernie realized that if she pulled on the rope too hard now, it might slide down the bug's length, break more legs, and then slip right off.

It seemed that they were at something of an impasse.

Which was fine. She didn't need it to get wet anyway. She needed it to be afraid of getting wet.

She sent it another telepathic nudge. "I'm going to stand on you again," she told it. "Do not move so quickly this time."

She did not get a "no" from it, and instead, she felt its pain. Its legs hurt, the broken ones that she'd snapped trying to get the rope over its head, and the one that had broken when it hit the end of the rope just now. It seemed its limbs were very strong for grabbing and running, but not so much so when bent the opposite way.

She hadn't thought about that part, or of the pain that would have caused.

"I'm sorry," she thought immediately, sending sympathy along the way. "But it is your own fault for fighting me." She approached the bug then, hauling in the rope, hand over hand as she drew near, keeping it taut and causing the bug to remain spread out in its attempts to prevent itself being dragged into the water that it so clearly feared.

She got right up to it, only a handsbreadth from what she thought of as its face. Its eyestalks tilted back to watch her, curving like a pair of snakes about to strike.

"I'm not going to hurt you," she said. "So long as you do what I say. Let me see if I can't fix your legs." She knelt down, keeping tension on the rope all the while, and with her free hand, she reached forward and touched the creature on its shell, an angular bit of armor shaped like a slice of pie between its eyes.

She closed her eyes and began to sing the song of the wilted daffodil. It was a healing song that she'd learned from Master Grimswoller back at school. A simple song, meant for healing flowers and nothing more. But she'd made it work on Altin one day when it really mattered, and she thought she could do it again now.

She reached out into the mana that seethed and roared silently all around. She still thought of it as a scary place where great pink waves and purple swells rose and fell with terrible violence. It was everywhere, and there was a ferocity to it that both frightened her and filled her with awe. She knew that someday she would tame it all and be just like Master Altin.

She knew better than to take up a lot of it, though. Master Grimswoller had taught her that much, most of all. So she plucked up a tiny little bit of it, like pinching spilled salt from a tabletop, and she dragged out a sticky strand of mana, which she pushed into the place where her hand touched the insect on its head.

She sang the song of healing then, carefully and slowly, wishing as she sang the words she'd learned that the bug might be healthy again, believing that it would be best if its broken legs were whole. She imagined them growing straight and strong again as if they were but stems of daffodils slowly rising from the ground. She even felt bad about it too, for having broken them, and her spell was infused with the simple sympathy of a child, pure and uncomplicated, and the plainspoken thoughts of merely wanting pain to go away.

After a time, she felt that it was done, for the words of the spell were gone. Sung out to completion.

She opened her eyes, her returning awareness almost dreading to see the bug looming over her again, as it had not long ago when she had nearly nodded off.

It wasn't. But it was standing normally again, no longer mashing itself down against the ground.

Pernie stood up and looked at it. It looked back at her with its bent gray eyestalks. "Are you still hurt?" she asked it telepathically.

It made no reply.

"I'm going to stand on you again," she informed it with thoughts and words alike. Then she stepped onto its back just as she had before.

"No," it conveyed telepathically as she did so, the sense of negativity. But she didn't care.

She stood on it, drawing back on the rope, hoping it might help her balance if the bug took off again. Which it did, and the rope didn't, and, while she did do a fair job of bracing for the speed of the bug's acceleration, it simply moved too fast for her to stay aboard. She tumbled off sideways when it made its first sharp turn, which it did right away. Still, she managed to ride it for nearly the length of five full spans.

What she needed was some way to balance herself from side to side. She scanned the area all around, and finally she spotted a fallen branch lying half in and half out of the creek. She made to go get it, but the bug flattened itself out again, making an anchor of its weight.

Pernie grew irritated at this belligerence. She set herself at a sideways angle, braced her feet, and gave the bug a yank with all her strength. It flipped over onto its back, its legs once more scrabbling in the air. It flopped and twisted and got back upright, again scuttling to face her flat and straight on, perhaps even understanding that she might yank off the rope.

She wondered if it was smart enough for that.

She tried to run around to get a sideways angle again, but it rotated with her all the while, keeping its body lengthwise to her, its head down and pointed at her like a dart. She feinted right, then jumped left and gave the rope a yank. She wasn't remotely fast enough to trick it, but she was strong enough to once again break one of its legs. Which prompted it to roll right back up into a ball.

"Stupid bug," she said. "That's what you get."

She half dragged, half rolled the bug over to where the branch lay up against the bank. She pulled it out of the water and studied it. It was a little longer than she was tall, and rather crooked for all that length, but it was thick enough for what she needed it to do.

She snapped off all the forking branches coming off of its main length, having to stand on it with her foot and yank mightily before some of them would break. But after a few minutes' work, she had a very crude sort of pole with which she could try riding her captured bug again.

She turned back to where it lay near the water, gazed down at its body rolled tightly up in its shell, and shook her head. "For such a big mean bug, you're kind of a scaredy-mouse, aren't you?"

She sent it a telepathic command to unroll itself, but all she got back was "no." She was rapidly becoming convinced that that really was all the creature could say. She did, however, get the vague sense of pain again.

Impatiently, she once more cast the healing spell, again

squatting down and this time laying her hand on the curving surface of the protective shell along the insect's back. In a matter of minutes, it was done, and once again all the creature's legs were whole.

She stood and stared down at it with a frustrated sigh. "Now listen up, you: I've squashed a lot of bugs before, and I've got no problems doing it again. You're going to straighten out right this moment, or that's all it's going to be. You hear? I'll break every one of your legs if you don't start listening to me." She sent that thought with all its conviction and imagery at the bug, her hands on her hips again. She was tired, it was hot, her face and tongue hurt, and the day was growing late now. The stupid elves would come find her any minute and take her back to the stupid cave.

To her astonishment, the creature unrolled itself. She smiled. "Good bug," she said. "Now take me for a ride." She took up her crooked stick and hopped upon the bug's back again. It was somewhat awkward trying to manage the rope and the stick together, but she got herself situated as best she could. "Go on," she said, sending the command telepathically.

The bug took off again, its acceleration so astonishing that despite having her stick to brace with, the slightest angular motion dumped Pernie right off again.

"Stupid bug," Pernie muttered as she once more clambered to her feet.

She saw that the bug was standing nearby. This time, at least, it wasn't flattened out and ready for another tug-of-war. That made her smile.

"Good bug," she said. "Maybe you aren't all the way stupid after all. Now let's go again before the elves come and try to take you away."

Chapter 11

A high, hot sun heated the streets of Murdoc Bay as if the city were one great kiln. The general ... frugality ... that ruled in the city of greed often precluded the wasting of wealth on indulgences for the weak—indulgences that included such devices as awnings or trees planted simply for the purpose of throwing shade. The starkest example of this tendency could be seen along the landward edge of the wide avenue known as the Decline, up which Altin and Orli now strode.

The Decline was a back-and-forth boulevard that traversed the length of the great black cliffs beneath which most of the port city was built. It slowly wound its way down, taking nearly three measures to cross three hundred vertical spans, and ultimately brought the downward-destined traveler into the heart of Murdoc Bay, a city that was home to no small number of brigands, pirates, and thieves.

All along the rock-face side of the snaking boulevard were businesses—though such a designation could only be loosely applied for most, as more than half were surely fronts for one nefarious enterprise or another. These establishments, be they legitimate or not, were built one beside the next, their bare storefronts looking out over the edge of the sloping avenue and their back rooms carved deep into the rock. And most noticeable to Orli as they climbed was the fact that barely one in five of them offered the simplest accommodation of a shady overhang. As she and Altin made their way up beneath a blazing sun, she found it hard to imagine how so many businesses could lack even the most basic of commercial courtesies, that being something as simple as shade and an invitingly opened door.

Yet despite the heat and the inhospitableness of the street, it was up this ramped row of business that Altin and Orli went, the sweat running freely from them both. They were headed to the top of the cliff, intent on meeting with Roberto on its plateau. The top of the Decline marked the end of the city, and beyond it, there was naught but open wilderness, treeless and stark. Orli welcomed it. Rough, heat-blasted lands were at least honest, unlike Murdoc Bay. The sooner they were out of this place, the better, as far as she was concerned.

Orli's hand rested conspicuously on her blaster, her fingers already curled around its grip and her lean muscles visible beneath her sun-browned skin, taut and ready to draw. Her eyes, hidden behind dark sunglasses, swept nervously back and forth. Altin kept her close, with his arm around her, his hand in the small of her back. He knew how anxious being there made her, and his green eyes scanned the faces and shadowy spaces between buildings, darting from one to the next, and up to the high places of the shallow rooftops where there were structures ambitious enough to encroach sufficiently into the avenue to make such things necessary.

Mainly she saw awe and admiration in the countenances of the people there, and no small amount of fear—fear of Altin, the Queen's Galactic Mage. She wasn't sure if it was because he was the Galactic Mage or because he was the Queen's, but either way, she counted their journey fortunate in that his face had become so recognizable as to provide some measure of defense. Although, even with that working for them, she wasn't fool enough to think his association with the crown, his title, or even his reputation as the most powerful living magician on Kurr would keep them safe in a city like this. His mentor, Tytamon, had been more powerful than he, and even Tytamon, an Eight, a wizard of nearly eight hundred years' experience no less, had been struck down by a lowly fiend. And that had happened in Leekant, a much gentler city by far. A knife in the back was all it had taken to kill the greatest magician the kingdom had ever known, and Orli had been helpless to do anything about it. She held no delusions about Altin's reputation being sufficient reason for either of them to drop their guard here in Murdoc Bay. Especially on the Decline.

So they walked together up out of the city, Altin nodding politely to those who would wave enthusiastically at the two of them and their celebrity, but mainly watching for anything provocative with the words to a fireball spell partway muttered upon his lips. He hardly needed words these days, not with his ring, but Orli knew that he muttered them out of habit anyway, holding the conflagration he would unleash to defend her only a half heartbeat away.

No fools dared tempt him, however, and neither fireball nor laser beam was let fly before they crested the cliff and found themselves looking out upon the dry lands that sprawled away from the city for measure upon measure, a vast expanse of prickly yellow weeds, squat, stunted trees, and enough loose, rocky soil to make a horse want to rub its hooves for thinking on it very long.

"Is it always this hot down here in the spring?" Orli asked as she wiped away a rivulet of perspiration that threatened to run into her eye. "This is brutal. It's as if this rotten city can't offer anything nice at all, not even its springtime weather." Having been briefly imprisoned in Murdoc Bay as part of Lord Thadius Thoroughgood's plot to capture her and then "rescue" and seduce her for himself, Orli's singular earlier experience with the city had not been a good one. This scalding heat did little to improve her attitude toward the community.

"No," said Altin, he too wiping at the moisture that poured down his brow, "this town is pretty much the dung spout of society, if the truth be told. But money seems to love it here, and the marchioness controls a great deal of wealth by having this place as the commerce capital of South Mark."

"Well, they deserve each other, that old hag and this crappy town. I can't believe Roberto would want to have anything to do with this shithole. It gives me the creeps."

"If he's going to be in the Goblin Tea business, he's going to have to do it from here." He pointed off toward the east, where barely visible on the horizon could be seen a faint green line. "That way is Gallenwood and the Feshtie River. The sea air and desert heat make a perfect humidity for growing Goblin Tea, while the river provides fresh water, and the forest gives home to the durma bees and coffee moths that pollinate when summer comes."

"Well, I do like Goblin Tea," she said. She was smiling, but Altin knew it was only partly out of her fondness for the mildly, deliciously intoxicating stimulant. "Maybe the city does have at least *one* redeeming quality."

Altin nodded, agreeing, though she knew he was not much of a fan of the bitter black beverage that most everyone else adored. He complained that the effects of the stuff took forever to wear off, which she thought was both just like him and ironic all the same.

"So where is Roberto and his new spaceship?" Altin asked as they moved out farther into the open and the heat.

They were both scanning the area from side to side. There wasn't the least bit of a dune or hillock to obscure the view, so there was no place to hide a ship, even if someone wanted to. "He said 'right outside the city,' which means here at the top of the Decline. He should be here."

Orli pulled a thin black tablet out of a flat leather pouch hanging from her belt and tapped up their present coordinates using the data stream from an orbiting starship, the *Aspect,* the same ship she used to serve aboard.

"He'll be coming in over there," she said, pointing. "About three hundred yards past that pile of rocks." From the way it looked, she suspected someone had been hastily buried there.

They made their way in the direction she'd indicated, and as they approached, there appeared before them a long, slender craft, gleaming like liquid silver in the glare of the high and blinding sun.

They both had to look away, the glare was so bright, and looking back required that they shield their eyes, though Orli only for a moment, as her sunglasses soon dimmed down enough that she could see.

"By the gods," Altin exclaimed. "It's awfully bright. And I had no idea your people could cast invisibility."

Orli laughed. "It's not. It's the surface of the ship reimaging the environment." Her lenses were finally dark enough to look directly at it. "But leave it to Roberto to get that entire surface chromed. I've never seen that before. Could that possibly be any more ostentatious?"

"Hey, I heard that," came Roberto's familiar voice from a loudspeaker mounted somewhere on the ship. "And it's not chrome. It's titanium- and silver-treated palladium glass." A moment after, a ramp lowered from a place at the belly of the ship, discernible by the dark rectangular outline that began to form and then grow until there was a tangible opening.

Two tall and strongly built women carrying large shoulder-mounted laser cannons came down the ramp first, the barrels of the guns nearly four feet long and ringed with spiral cooling tubes that were caked with frost and sent vapor into the air to be devoured by the heat. The two women took places at the base of the ramp, one on each side, each of them leaning back against the straps slung over their bared shoulders and thrusting their pelvises forward where the gun braces pressed firmly to their shapely hips. Orli could not help but notice that both women were strikingly beautiful, and dressed to express it. Each of them wore formfitting black pants and a corseted vest of satiny purple material that was far more provocative than one might expect for a pair of rather burly guards. Their bosoms bulged as conspicuously as their shoulders and biceps did.

A moment later, Roberto descended with a third woman at his side and two more only a few steps behind. All three of these women were strikingly beautiful as well, the two behind attired exactly as were the ramp guards. The fact that they too wore the corseted purple made it seem as if these might actually be their uniforms, though Orli could hardly believe it. For one thing, the woman at Roberto's side was not wearing purple, nor a bustier. Roberto, however, was wearing the same color, if not the same outfit, which drew a snicker from Orli that she only barely managed to contain. She could not help but gape at him.

The swarthy Spaniard wore a long coat of bright purple silk, which perfectly matched the bustiers of the four women behind him, excepting that Roberto's coat had an additional treatment of gleaming gold macramé at hem and cuffs, and it was decorated with carved buttons of mammoth ivory, though none of them had been put to use this hot day. Upon his head perched a large three-cornered hat—custom made, Orli was sure—black as night and festooned with a feather two feet long and just as purple as the shimmering jacket was.

While his lower half was covered with his customary black pants and blaster belt, his trouser legs were stuffed down into boots that, like jacket and feather, were as purple as anything could possibly be. Even the soles of those gaudy knee-highs were gilded at the edges with gold leaf, tacked in place and made to match the macramé and the buckle of the hatband.

Orli let go a long and most unladylike sort of snort, and she barely held herself at the furthest reaches of self-restraint as he approached.

Roberto ignored her facial contortions and nasally rasps, and he bowed with a long flourish of his three-cornered hat as he came to stand before them both. Altin bowed formally back and opened his mouth, about to give the proper Prosperion greeting when one is addressing the captain of a ship, but Orli's guffaws simply exploded into a full fit of laughter at the sweep of the hat. "You're going to get your feather in the dirt," she managed to gasp, but that was all before hilarity had her bent over completely at the waist and nearly wheezing for breath.

Immune to her ridicule, Roberto's eyes shot wide with feigned horror instead, and he snatched his hat back up and spun it around, bending the feather this way and that, and, to his further dismay, discovered that he had in fact gotten a few bits of grit lodged in there. He immediately set to picking them out with genuine irritation apparent on his face.

Orli laughed for nearly a full minute more, and it was all Altin could do to stand straight and try to be polite.

"Go ahead and laugh," Roberto said, "but do you know how much this damn thing cost me? They had to do it nine times to get the color right."

Now Altin was laughing too.

Roberto looked back and forth between them, then to the

beautiful woman standing at his right, the only one from the ship not wearing purple to match the rest. The other two women had stopped on approach and now stood a respectful pair of steps behind them, their faces stoic, though not without traces of humor twitching the corners of their mouths and glimmering in their eyes. The woman beside Roberto made a better show of keeping her expression neutral, though Orli thought she might be biting her tongue more than a little bit.

Eventually, Orli stopped laughing, and with a shake of her head and an expression that clearly declared what she thought of his ensemble, she clapped him in a long and hearty hug. He grinned a great big cheesy grin at Altin over her shoulder as he hugged his best friend in all the universe, and Altin smiled back, glad to know that Roberto was not only safe but beyond thriving by the providence of the Queen.

Finally the hug came to an end, and Orli pushed herself away. She squinted at Roberto with a devilish gleam in her eyes and asked, "So who are you supposed to be, George Washington the Pimp?"

"As if he ever looked this good."

Orli just shook her head, then turned to the woman beside Roberto. The woman stood nearly a foot taller than he did, making her three inches taller even than Altin, and she carried herself with stern dignity. Her shoulders and arms, bare for the sleeveless vest she wore, were long and sinewy, her muscles toned and her skin dark brown like the Goblin Tea coffee they'd come here to trade for. Her stance, like her physique, suggested that her body was equally suited to fight or flight, and the intelligence apparent in her eyes suggested she would know which was the better course in any circumstance. She studied Altin, then Orli, and she seemed to catch Orli studying her back. They exchanged polite smiles. Orli thought she might be the most beautiful woman she'd ever met. Possibly the most dangerous too. She wore on her hips a pair of holsters, each equipped with an old-fashioned nine-millimeter pistol, and the belt around her narrow waist was packed with replacement clips. The grips of both weapons were well worn, and Orli suspected that Roberto had chosen wisely when he put this woman on his crew, her striking beauty entirely aside.

Orli reached out a hand in greeting. "Hi, I'm Orli. Please tell me you are only working with him temporarily. If you haven't signed any contracts yet, there's still time to get away. I can have Altin here teleport you anywhere you like. Save yourself while you can."

"Hey," Roberto butted in before the woman could reply. "Don't be undermining my authority. They have to respect me and stuff." He turned and winked at the woman standing beside him, who smiled again, though mainly with her eyes.

She and Orli exchanged a knowing glance as the woman took Orli's proffered hand. "I'm Deeqa Daar," she said in a rich Somali accent. "First mate of the *Glistening Lady*. It's nice to meet you."

Orli started to speak, but then stopped, realizing what the woman had said. "Oh no," she said, turning back to Roberto. "The *Glistening Lady*? You named it the *Glistening Lady*?"

"Hey, you're the one who said you'd be a constant, nagging pain in the ass if I went with the *Sweaty Boobs*, so this was the compromise. I actually like it better. It has class."

Orli shook her head, clearly exasperated. She turned back to Deeqa Daar standing there. "Well, it's very nice to meet you," she said. "I wish you the best of luck serving under your captain there."

"I've dealt with his kind before," Deeqa said. "I'm sure there will be far more original and problematic obstacles with this work than the captain's ... eccentricity."

"Hey, I can hear you talking, you know," Roberto said. "And for what it's worth, you were in pretty desperate need of some eccentricity in your life given what I heard about that freighter you were on. I could hear you yawning from halfway across the galaxy."

Deeqa grinned at that, showing a row of pretty white teeth beneath her luminous almond-shaped eyes. "Well, you got me there, Captain."

Roberto laughed as if he'd just won a major victory. "Damn straight I did." He looked back to Altin and Orli and became suddenly serious. "She's the best damn pilot working commercial space," he said. "Might even be better than me, assuming that's even possible."

Deeqa's eyes narrowed, unrelenting mischief in them. "Oh, it's possible."

"Well, this man here needs no pilot," said Roberto, pointing at Altin and intent on finishing introductions properly. "He is strictly point to point. Deeqa, I present Sir Altin Meade, or as all the Crown City people call him, the Galactic Mage. He's kind of a big shot, but when I first met him, he was just a barefoot magician randomly poking around in space."

Altin grinned and pulled up his robes enough to expose his toes. "Not much has changed," he said. He let the folds fall back in place and reached out to shake Deeqa by the hand. "I am still at exploration too. Which is why we need your help."

"Well, the *Glistening Lady* is at your service, then," she said. "As am I. Captain Levi said we'd be assisting you, though he was a bit short on the details."

"Unfortunately, that is because we were short on them as well, which is why we need you folks and that science team. Speaking of which, *Captain* Roberto, have you had any luck in finding anyone?"

"Yes," said Roberto. "I've got a geology professor from

the NTA Branch University in New Mesa. Marks Bryant is his name. He's a geologist, anthropologist, and some other stuff, lots of letters at the end of his name. His response to my message read as if he's pretty excited, and he says he can gather up as big a team as I can pay for. Which was something I wanted to talk to you about. Who's sporting the bill on this one? I mean, I'm not stingy or anything, I just need to know."

"I am," said Altin. "It's the least I can do for Blue Fire after all her help."

"All right," Roberto said, looking relieved. "Good. I was going to hit up Her Majesty if I needed to, but I spent nearly all my start-up cash on this ship. Worse, the last time I talked with that little guy down there who's brokering most of the Goblin Tea, I got the feeling I'm going to be spending all that I have left to get my first load. Seems these people around here aren't too happy with the Queen these days, and they are taking it out on me."

Altin nodded. "No, they're not fond of Her Majesty down here. They never were, although it's worse now, I'm sure. Tensions between Crown City and South Mark have been high since the war. But none of that will matter for you, I should think. You'll find they warm right up to you once they see the color of your coin."

The gleam of bright metal was also the subject of interest for more than a few onlookers who were beginning to arrive at the top of the Decline with the appearance of Roberto's ship. Already a small crowd of people had gathered and were coming cautiously near, a handful of rather grubby folks, all eager to see a spaceship from another world. By the sounds coming up from below, many more people were on the way.

It would be a full hour before Roberto could be made to stop showing off his ship, leading little groups around the outside of it, remarking on its speed, strength, agility, and all sorts of technical things that no one on Prosperion could possibly appreciate. By the time he was done bragging, he was nearly late for his appointment with his Goblin Tea supplier down at the waterfront.

It was only reluctantly that he got Altin and Orli to agree to accompany him to the warehouse to meet, as he described it, "the littlest man you've ever seen."

Chapter 12

The six of them, five Earthborn and one native Prosperion, made their way through Murdoc Bay, backtracking at first in the direction Altin and Orli had come, but eventually working their way toward the waterfront. They walked together down the winding grade of the Decline, Altin, Orli, and Roberto three abreast, followed by Deeqa Daar and the two women Roberto described as being two of his four personal bodyguards. As they descended, Roberto commented on how spectacular the view of the bay was, and when they'd passed through town and arrived at the harbor, he couldn't get over how incredible it was to see all the sailing ships moored there, a forest of masts jutting up for what he guessed had to be at least a three-mile arc along the shore.

"It's like going back in history," he said as they turned onto Front Street, which ran along the docks. "Look at those things. Those are epic fifteenth-century caravels right there, look, three of them side by side, and look there, that's practically a replica frigate right out of seventeenth-century France."

"I didn't know you knew about that stuff," Orli said with a grin. "And here, all this time I thought you couldn't read.

I'm impressed."

"I love this stuff," he said. "I am seriously considering retiring here when I'm done. This is my third trip to Murdoc Bay, and I have to tell you, I've never been anyplace as cool as this. This might seriously be the best city in the universe."

"Yeah, and they have a thriving slave trade here, Roberto. It's just wonderful. Maybe you and that asshole, Black Sander, you know, the one who *kidnapped* me, can be neighbors and play golf together on weekends." The unexpected bitterness in Orli's voice drooped Roberto's mouth as much as it did her mood. The excitement of his new ship and his new business had made him forget what had happened to Orli here.

"I'm sorry," he said. "It's not that I forgot. And I got the whole lecture about this place from Her Majesty. But she says that's only a tiny underworld element, and they're working to root it out. I swear, if I ever find out who helped Lord Thadius snatch you, I'll burn a hole straight through their face. That's a promise." He patted the blaster hanging from his hip as he said it.

"Well," said Altin, "this is the place to do it if you do find them. They aren't much for investigating murder down here, despite what Her Majesty likely had to say. Sometimes I think that if people in Crown City knew the half of what went on down here, they'd fill the streets in front of the Palace in protest."

"Why don't they, then?" Roberto asked. "You guys got newspapers and stuff."

"I suspect most people don't really want to know, so they take pains to avoid learning too much. Active indignation takes time and energy. Most of the folks in Crown City are too comfortable to get up for something like that. Or, at least, they were before the war. Now they are too busy rebuilding. And Murdoc Bay is very far away."

"Well, I can like the city without getting involved with

the assholes," Roberto said. "It's that whole baby-and-the-bathwater thing."

Altin frowned at that, having no idea what it might mean, but he had no time to ask, for Roberto had led them down the waterfront along a row of tall warehouses built one nearly right against the next. He led them out of the street and onto the sidewalk, right up to a door, high above which was a sign that read "Gevender Enterprises." "This is it," he said, looking back.

Orli squeezed Altin's hand as she tilted her head back and read the sign. She let out a low gasp, then whispered, nearly a hiss, in his ear, "Gevender's. That's the same name as the thrift shop where Tytamon was killed in Leekant." Her hand trembled in his.

Altin's eyes narrowed as he studied the sign. His first instinct was to conjure a fireball.

"Hey, what's going on?" Roberto asked, seeing the dark mood that had suddenly come upon his friends.

"The name, up there," Altin said, jerking his head upward as he spoke. "It is the same as where Tytamon died in Leekant. Perhaps the same company."

"Or maybe a weird coincidence," Roberto said. "I've been in here twice before. There's just a receptionist and a back office where the little guy is. Master Tenderthrift, they call him. He's actually a pretty mellow dude."

Altin's teeth remained clenched for a moment more, but he relaxed a little bit. A fireball would have set the whole place on fire anyway. Besides, Gevender was a fairly common surname in the kingdom, that was true. And Her Majesty had sent the Royal Assassin to investigate. Surely the connections would have been made. All the same, he shaped an ice lance spell in his mind, just in case. In the span of two heartbeats, he could have one on its way, with no collateral damage from flames.

Roberto glanced at his two bodyguards, hoping to

perhaps take the tension down a notch. "Hey, Sami, Fatima, you two stay out here and keep your eyes open while we go in."

"What are we looking for?" asked Fatima, the dark-eyed beauty standing to Deeqa's left.

"Anyone who seems too interested that we went in here. Grab some pictures if they do."

"Roger that, Captain." Both women swung their laser rifles around on their slings and let them dangle against their chests, ready for instant use. Fatima reached up and tapped a round black com button clipped to her corset, activating the video feed. "Everything we see will be sent back to the ship."

"Good," he said. "Now everyone just take a laxative and loosen up before we go inside. These kinda people don't like dealing with people who look nervous." He looked to Orli last. "Which means you need to chill out, woman. Nothing is going to happen to you with all of us here. You've got the freaking Galactic Mage with you, for one thing. And Deeqa there can take out half a room before the other half realizes the thunder is coming from her guns."

Orli offered a flat grin and shook off her nerves. She knew he was right. But she left her hand on her blaster just the same.

They entered into a small front office where a gray-haired woman sat behind a long table. She worked with a frayed quill pen, adding figures to a parchment scroll that was so long it had run off the table and rolled across the room, stopping only because it had hit the wall. She did not move to acknowledge them until she had finished entering an entire row of numbers into a column she was working on.

At length, she looked up at them with a stern expression, her eyes moving upward in her head more than any motion of her head. Her lips were razor thin, cutting a straight line across a face absent of mirth. They only knew she had lips at all because hers were made visible by the narrow line of pale lipstick, and they puckered with irritation just before she spoke. "He's waiting for you in the back, Captain Levi. You and the dark one. Not the rest."

"They'll be coming with me," Roberto said. "Part of the deal."

"I'm afraid not, Captain. You'll do well to learn the customs of our world if you expect to thrive in its trade."

"Oh, just send them back, Terrice," said a voice that came through the door. It was so low and booming it shook dust from the ceiling. "They *are* from another planet, after all."

"Not all of them," she replied as she eyed Altin with one arched eyebrow.

"Just send them back," boomed the voice again. He wasn't yelling, his voice was just that low and loud.

"Very well," she said, making no attempt to conceal her irritation. She stood, thin as a stick, and reached into the neckline of her blouse, extracting a key from the near concavity of a bony bosom. With a quick snap of her wrist, she jerked the key on its gold chain and caught it in her fingertips, taking it to the heavy hardwood door behind her, which she opened with a click.

Roberto went through first, followed by Altin and then Orli. Deeqa pulled aside a curtain and glanced through a front window into the street before going in after them.

The door opened onto a much larger office, in the center of which sat a tiny little man who perched on an overstuffed chair of such magnitude that the sight of him upon its cushion gave him the aspect of a very small frog seated on a very large lily pad.

Immediately upon seeing him, Orli gasped, drew her laser, and shot.

"What the ...!" exclaimed Roberto as he dove to the side, having nearly walked into the shot.

The little man let go a yelp as well, and gaped at the hole the shot had burned through the leather of his chair. Had his face not already been ghostly pale by nature, he might have turned whiter still.

Orli cursed and fired a second shot, but the little man was already on the move, his speed surprising everyone in the room.

Deeqa's long stride brought her in position to intercept in a matter of seconds, and she snatched him up by the back of his satin waistcoat and hoisted him on high, with a pistol pressed firmly to his head.

"What is the meaning of this?" he boomed in a voice so loud it was like cannon fire. This time he was yelling, and the unbelievable volume of that voice stunned them all for a moment, likely saving his life, for Altin's ice lance hung hissing in the air right above his hand. Another half instant and Master Tenderthrift would have been skewered through.

"Whoa, whoa, whoa," Roberto said as he scrambled up off the floor. "Goddamn it. Everybody just freaking *whoa*." He came back to Orli with his hands out before him like a man trying to calm a wild animal. "Easy there, Tex," he soothed, reaching out and gently pushing the barrel of Orli's blaster toward the floor. "Orli. Dude. Put the gun away."

"That's him," she snarled. She raised the gun again, aiming more carefully this time.

With the tips of two fingers, Roberto carefully pushed the barrel down again. "Orli, you're going to kill someone with that. You need to mellow out before the cops come and we're all screwed. Relax. We've got this. It's just business."

"No. That's him. I told you. I tried to tell you. We haven't even been at this *business* for fifteen seconds and that's him."

"That's who?"

"That's the little shit who would have auctioned me off. He's part of it, part of the abduction too. I heard his voice when I was in the box on the slave ship." She aimed her gun again, prepared to shoot the tiny man right out of Deeqa's hand.

Roberto stepped closer to her, and with a firm hand on her wrist, he raised her arm up until the gun was pointed toward ceiling and not at anybody's head. "You said that guy was dead."

She blinked at that, as if finally coming back into possession of her mind. "No, I didn't."

"Yes, you did," Roberto said.

Altin nodded. He had heard the story too, the recounting of how Orli had been in a cage on a wide stage during a slave auction. She had specifically mentioned there being a little man with a deep voice who had served as the auctioneer. But Orli had also said, every time she told the tale, that she had watched him die. "I do recall you mentioning him," he said, speaking in low, calming tones, "but you did specifically say that you'd seen that little man blown to bits."

Orli nodded. "It's true. I did see it. He was hit by lightning. But it was lightning cast by Thadius' lackey, Annison. You said yourself Annison isn't a conjurer. Remember? So it was all for show. Or most of it."

Altin did remember that, and he knew that Orli was at least half-convinced the whole fight at the slave auction was an illusion meant to throw her off the truth. Altin had no way of knowing whether it had or hadn't been, however, as he hadn't had time to investigate. Not with everything that had happened since.

"Well, I'm not dead," shouted the man, dangling in Deeqa's hand like a little, four-limbed bag of anger. He thrashed for a moment, nearly twisting free as his waistcoat ripped, but Deeqa caught him by an ankle and lifted him up again. "Let me go, by the gods. I've never run a slave auction in all my life." His spectacles, which had fallen off, swung pendulously from a cord around his neck, somehow giving a piteous credibility to his complaint.

"You're a liar," Orli spat.

"I have contracts with the marchioness," Deeqa's gnomish bundle argued back.

Roberto started to nod to that, his teeth tightly held together, but he didn't know enough to get into the specifics. He also knew that his lucrative Goblin Tea enterprise was burning down with every lick of the flames flickering around the hole Orli had shot through the little man's massive chair. "Listen, Orli, this can't be your guy. How crazy would he have to be to get involved with slavery? He's got connections in high places. Good ones. Too good to lose. Her Majesty sent me down here to meet with him, you know? So let's hold off on conviction and execution at least until we can get a fair and proper trial."

Orli let go a derisive half laugh. "In my experience, there isn't much fair or proper about trials these days."

"That wasn't here," Roberto protested, desperately trying to save the fortune he'd already made considerable plans for. He knew she was referring to the hoax of a trial she'd gotten from the NTA right after the outbreak of the war. "And the responsible parties for that one have been punished. Asad's flying first mate on a freighter barely half the size of the one Deeqa was on. How's that for justice? No pension, no nothing. Dude will be working a junk hauler for the rest of his life."

Orli glared at him, her eyes narrowing, obviously aware that he was trying to distract her. "Do you actually expect me to believe there is another one? Another little asshole with a mouth like a cannon?"

"Orli, I just want you to not do something stupid that you can't take back."

She glared at him some more. She looked to Altin, who nodded that he agreed with Roberto. However, the fact that the ice lance still glowed brightly above his hand also made it apparent that he would do whatever she needed him to. She looked back at Roberto, one eye narrowing even more. "Fine," she said. "But I know it was his voice on that ship." She took her finger off the trigger of her gun.

"That's a good girl," Roberto said, feeling the tension in her arm release. "Now put that thing away, and let's all play nice."

"And put me down," the little man demanded of Deeqa. "I'm not some child's toy to be manhandled."

Deeqa brought him back to the chair. She wiped out the low-burning flames with a pass of her hand and then plopped him back down where he had been when they came in. She didn't holster the pistol, though.

"Good, good," said Roberto, followed by a nervous laugh. "Now, hopefully, everyone can be reasonable and not do or say anything rash. There's still a lot of money to be made, so, you know ... bygones be bygones, as they used to say."

"Don't worry about your money, Captain," said the little man with surprising calm as he wiped ash off the shoulders of his green waistcoat. "It's going to be at least a year before we can get a magician safely on their world, probably more like two. So for at least that long, you'll have the business whether your friends try to shoot me or not. I confess, in my eagerness to be about this business, to making a huge error in showing you as much courtesy as I did today. You may be certain I shall never do it again. You or the dark one. No others. Not even the Galactic Mage."

"Like you could stop him from coming if he wanted to," Orli sneered.

"Hey, can it. Please," Roberto said, the first bit a command, the last nearly pleading.

"Fine," she said. "But I think I'll wait outside."

"Yeah, good idea. Go keep Sami and Fatima company."

Altin moved to accompany her, but Deeqa saw the look on Roberto's face, and she stepped to the door instead. "Stay,

Sir Altin," she said. "I'll go with her. He asked you to come here with us specifically for what you know about the TGS."

Altin nodded. This visit was something of a trade, a service on his part in exchange for Roberto's having agreed to help with the science team. Altin was about to get farmed for information that only he had access to as an extremely high-ranking member of the Teleporters Guild.

He looked to Orli, who nodded that she was fine, then she and Deeqa went back through the office and out onto the street. When he heard the outer office door close, Roberto went straight to work.

"So, you said you'd drop the price if I could get you some information about when the visas are going to start happening."

The little man, Master Tenderthrift, nodded and laced his fingers together patiently, as mellow as if he'd not nearly had his head blown clean off of his neck a few moments before. It was as if that was not the first time someone had directed a weapon at the man. "Go on," he said.

"Well, visas are coming slower than you hoped, because the Northern Trade Alliance is an even bigger bureaucratic nightmare than the Transportation Guild Service is. Director Bahri is all for letting Prosperions come to Earth, and so is the Queen—at least that's what they all say—but both agree that there have to be policies in place first. And if you want the God's honest truth, most of those people at the NTA are scared crapless by the thought of having sorcerers suddenly coming to town. When we first got here, everyone back home was all for it, but that's because these guys"—he paused and tapped Altin on the arm as an example of what he was talking about—"were just stories being sent back in data packet videos. But now that it's actually going to happen, suddenly the idea of having a bunch of little Merlins running around has everyone privately freaking out. You should have seen the guy at the NTA Reserve Bank get all fidgety when I told him what I wanted to do. He couldn't care less about what he would have made off me on the ship loan. All he cared about was guys like Altin here jumping into his vaults and stealing everything. They're all doing it. The military guys think the Prosperions are going to steal secrets. The big corporate players do too—and those guys are all about taking risks and making money. The fact that they aren't falling all over themselves to help connect the two planets says a lot. The simple truth is that everyone on Earth with money is working nonstop to gum up the gears. Nobody wants you guys there."

Trader Tenderthrift, as he was most commonly known, let go a long, low hum, a rumbling thing that would have better fit in a dragon's chest than in one as diminutive as his own. He straightened the spectacles on his nose and looked to Altin for his opinion in that regard. "Is that how you hear it, Sir Altin? Do your fiancée's people fear you so soon after the romantic promises of Her Majesty's great speech at the Fire Fountain that day, all that rot about trust and reciprocity?"

"I could not say if they do or don't fear us," Altin said. "But I do know that the TGS council is furious with the NTA about being denied permission to look for a place to set up offices on Earth. So I would say that might align with Captain Levi's news."

"So where are the offices, then? I hear that you, Captain Levi, have already managed to get a spaceship here to Prosperion. A new one, just purchased from a shipwright on Earth, as I understand. Clearly some mechanisms for trade with us have been put in place by your people."

Roberto raised an eyebrow at that. "You heard that already? We came straight here."

The little man pointed to a cage on the lamp table across the room. There were four small lizards lying contentedly and still, basking in the warmth beneath the lamp's steady flame. Homing lizards. Roberto should have known his contact would have people in the streets. And that had been a pretty large crowd gawking at his ship.

"Well, we do have three NTA-TGS co-ops going up. But none on Earth. They're putting one up for ships on Amphitrite, but *only* ships is what I heard. No setup for moving people, just the big black platforms that the TGS wizards will turn into those giant boxes they started teleporting ships with."

"And how far is this *Amfit-tight* from Earth?"

"Amphitrite. It's a moon around Neptune. About as far away from Earth as you can get without leaving the solar system or setting up shop on an ice cube."

"Could a single seer get a seeing spell pushed that far, from that moon to Earth?" This was directed once more to Altin.

"I've not seen this base, Master Tenderthrift. But if it's an outer world, then no, not really, not without a conduit and a proper concert of magicians to help. I could do it, but there aren't any others who could that I am familiar with. Well, perhaps Guildmaster Alfonde of the Seers Guild could, but I suspect he and I are about it."

Tenderthrift rubbed his little chin as he thought about it, but there was little else he could do. Or else there was little else he wanted to talk about. He looked up at them and, as if seeing them for the first time, said, "Well then, I suppose it's for the best that I've got my friend Captain Levi here to help." His mood was so altered then, so bright, that Altin couldn't help but frown, though Roberto didn't seem to care. Trader Tenderthrift was all courtesy and respect after, and it was barely a half hour later that Roberto had a map and a signed release entitling him, to quote directly: "to fill his holds to the top at the price of twenty gold crowns per bag-weight," which was, to Roberto's considerable dismay, a full five gold pieces higher than it had been the last time he and the Murdoc Bay trader had talked.

The little man, smiling as he explained the price increase, said simply, "Ah, yes. Well, the good captain might consider asking his pretty little hotheaded friend to make up the difference." There wasn't much Roberto could say to that.

Chapter 13

Shadows deepened on the forest floor as the lines of light coming through the canopy grew frail. Pernie was anxious, expecting the elves to find her at any moment now. She knew that they would arrive and discover her trying to stand on the back of her many-legged bug, which she had named Knot due to the tangle of legs it became each time it rolled into a ball—which it did a lot, as in, every single time she had to discipline it. She knew they would find her and her bug, and then they would take it away. Or worse, they would thrust one of their spears right through it, and her whole day's work would be lost. So she had to hurry.

Her little body was bruised all over, and blood ran from cuts and scratches everywhere. But Pernie wasn't the only one showing signs of wear. The bug suffered for its part, and Pernie had been less and less willing to heal its injuries as time went on. Now, there was a stretch of broken limbs down a length of its body, on both sides of its trunk, mangled angles where several legs jutted out in tangled clumps of uselessness, snapped, bent, or broken either by the rope or by Pernie's simply mashing them with her crooked stick. She found that the creature reacted best to pain, and she did think it was slowly beginning to recognize the advantages of moving away from the pressure Pernie put upon its body, whether with her heels or the stick. Between the yank of her rope, the stomp of her feet, and the mash of her stick—all accompanied by thoughts she put into its mind—she was gaining some measure of control.

She found that simple thoughts worked best, and the sooner she'd stopped trying to communicate with it in the way she'd often heard Altin talk about speaking telepathically to his dragon, the sooner she'd started making progress with her bug. Simple thoughts, like pressure points in the mind, worked best. The creature seemed to think in the most basic of ways. It was either afraid or it was not. It was either hungry or not. And by *not*, it was a matter of total absence. It did not plan to be hungry later, nor did it look to Pernie expecting to be afraid. It simply became afraid. Or hungry. Or in pain. But this also made guiding it easier too. For she found she could put simple suggestions into its head by working its opposite. If she wanted it to go left, she would project pain on the right. Just the thought of pain, remembered pain, pain she'd sensed from it.

This discovery had led her to learn how to guide it fairly well, and she'd spent the bulk of the afternoon breaking its various legs on either side, and locating how that wound felt to it by listening to its mind, which at its most active seemed a sort of background noise. But, like memorizing the keys on a harpsichord perhaps, she'd kicked and smashed her way up and down its length and had a pretty sound repertoire of its particular agonies.

And now, at the point of having just worked most of that out, she was ready to give it another go. Her last attempt to ride it had gotten her nearly forty spans across a broad, flat moss bed, but when the bug ran up and over the great bulk of a rotting fallen tree, Pernie had tumbled right off and nearly lost her grip on the rope.

But now, she had retied her rope to her wrist, and she had a plan for how to stay on the creature even while moving vertically. With a quick glance at the dying light, she climbed onto its back again. "Go," she said, and in saying so, sent it guiding thoughts, as she'd begun to do almost reflexively by then, a little tap of pain in its rearmost extremities, and off it went.

It took off as it always did, like a greyhound at a race, but she was well used to it, and she spread her feet wide along its length and braced with her back leg. Leaning into the direction of its speed, she stayed right with it this time, and they were off like an elf-thrown spear.

With subtle thoughts of discomfort and gentle tugs on the rope, she guided the creature around obstacles and under low-hanging limbs. They rushed around the outside edge of the fern meadow where the creature lived, covering the distance in a matter of seconds. Pernie thrilled at the speed of the creature as the wind blew back her hair and whistled in her ears.

She dared a long, sweeping turn back around to her left, through which she had to lean back into the momentum of the turn, but she'd gotten better and better at that as she'd practiced throughout the afternoon. She only had to tap the crooked stick on the ground once as she came near to overbalancing midway through that time.

It was time to test her climbing theory, so she guided the lengthy creature back toward the great lumpy mass of the old rotting tree. As it approached, at seemingly meteoric speed, she crept closer and closer to the insect's head, so far up that her left foot was placed between its eyestalks as it ran.

Careful not to stand on them or pinch them beneath her boot, she waited until just before the bug got to the log, then slid her foot over the curving bit of shell that covered its face, the hard wedge she'd noticed earlier when she'd cast the first healing spell.

She shifted all her weight to that front foot as the bug went vertical and climbed straight up the mossy wall of the rotting tree. She balanced there upon its plated face, and then, as it crested the top of the tree, she stepped back onto its back and scooted to the tail end. She repeated the process going down the far side of the tree by standing on its armored rump, if it could be argued that it had such a thing.

The descent was a bit trickier, and Pernie nearly slipped off, but the bug was back on level ground so quickly that Pernie simply hopped forward just before she fell and came to land on its back again even as it began to move away. It wasn't perfect, but it had worked, and with practice, she'd surely get it down.

She ran the bug around for quite some time after that, and by the time she had it climbing up and down the trees, twilight was settling toward evening.

She didn't know the jungle at nighttime at all, and there was still no sign of the elves, so she decided to go back to the cave on her own. She knew the way well enough by now.

She turned the bug toward the cave that was her home for now, and off they went at great speed through the trees. Twice she tried to guide it through spaces that were too thick with limbs and vines, and both times she was knocked right off the creature's back. She had a great welt over one eye after the second strike, where she hit a low branch so hard little spots swam in her vision for a time. But she got right back on the moment they went away.

She was just approaching the root-covered rise where the mantis' body lay when she caught up with the hunt. She hadn't even heard them, they moved so silently, but suddenly there they were, all twenty of them, running naturally together as easily as they pleased. It would have been impossible to say who was more surprised by the encounter,

Pernie or the elves. For Pernie, she found herself among them so unexpectedly it seemed as if they'd jumped out at her from shadows and the trees. But for them, it was as if they'd just seen some new type of monster appear. Sandew actually had his spear up and was in the motion of the throw when another of the elves caught him by the wrist just in time.

Seawind began to laugh.

It was the first time Pernie had ever seen an elf laugh. All of the others began to laugh as well. All but Sandew, who was still staring at Pernie standing there on her bug.

He saw the admiration in his companions' eyes, but shook his head, saying, "No." He walked right up to Seawind and said it twice more. "No, no. This does not count. Djoveeve and Belletelemew ran with the hunt themselves. This is not the same."

"Of course it is the same. Djoveeve ran as a jaguar on her second day. Belletelemew as a hummingbird in nine. But the young Sava does not have the power to transmute. She had to find another way."

"Then she is the lesser of them by far. This is the work of *twenty-four* days, and it's not even her own weak human magic helping her. How can this be the lifewatch of the High Seat?"

"What you condemn her for, I applaud." He turned briefly and smiled at Pernie, genuine and warm. He turned back to Sandew. "Don't you see? This human runs with elves using no magic at all. She will be the greatest of the three."

Sandew shook his head again, looking at Pernie with what she thought was approaching sympathy, before looking back to Seawind. "She will be dead. And it will be on your count for eternity." He turned back to her. "My people do you a great injustice, human," he said, and then he ran off into the trees.

Some of the others seemed to lose a degree of mirth after

that exchange, perhaps agreeing with the departed elf now that the novelty of Pernie's unusual arrival had worn off. But Seawind was not among them. He came forward and placed a hand on her shoulder. "You've done it, Sava. You've run with the hunt. Something only two other humans have ever done. You're in a very small minority amongst your kind. And now you have earned the right to begin training with the spear." He held forth his own weapon, offering it to her that she might feel its weight.

She snatched it out of his hand and hurled it straight through the air, pinning a moth that had been fluttering past to a tree some fifteen paces away. "I already know how to use your stupid spears," she said. "You said you'd teach me to kill that orc, and then I could go home. I'm ready to kill him now."

He turned back behind him and, with a flicking motion of his fingers, gestured for two of his companions to hand him their spears. He gave one to Pernie and kept the other for himself, nodding only slightly in the direction of the one she now held.

She frowned at it, then back at him, and then, with speed she didn't have time to see, he swept her feet out from under her with a snapping movement of the bottom of his spear. He struck her ankles so hard and so quickly that she flipped a quarter turn and landed hard on her ribs atop her bug, who, being startled and injured both, took off at a run. She rolled off it the moment it bolted, and it dragged her half under a bush by the rope around her wrist before she could gather her wits enough to send it pain messages to make it stop.

She lay there in the leaves and twigs beneath the bush, panting heavily. She would make him pay for that.

Chapter 14

A lean, straight figure of a man watched from beneath a broad-brimmed black hat as the Earth people and the Queen's pet mage returned to the silvery spaceship resting atop the cliffs above Murdoc Bay. The watcher's coal-black eyes squinted above a hawkish nose despite being shrouded in shadow beneath the hat. Unlike the rest of the crowd, murmuring and ogling the vessel, he was silent. His interest in a ship that could travel to the stars was not rooted in awe or curiosity. No, not this man. His interest was, as always, appraisal. The appraisal of value, certainly, but mostly he appraised it for difficulty.

He'd already watched several of the young lads from town approach the two burly women standing guard at the base of the ramp. While a few of the boys were simple, uncouth drunkards, one of them had been a well-built deckhand with pockets heavy with coin. His ship, the *Hestra's Sea Hound*, had come in yesterday from a successful Pompost run. With his share jingling in his pocket, the salty youth had sashayed up to the women and made his suit with abundant confidence, for which he was politely but instantly declined. When the youth stepped closer to make a second, more insistent appeal, the nearer guard, a shapely brunette with shoulders and arms easily as cut and toned as the young sailor's were, turned the muzzle of her weapon toward him and, with a polite smile, said something to him in the alien language of planet Earth. The words were nonsense to Prosperion ears, but no one witnessing needed translation magic to understand what she had said.

The watcher beneath that wide, dark hat nodded as he observed. Pretty though these Earth creatures were, they were not the sporting type. He supposed there would be more collectors interested in an alien girl, but for now he had no orders for one. And, truth be told, the last one had been more trouble than she was worth. Three times he'd been less than a half step in front of the Royal Assassin's blade for that job, and now that the heat was off, or at least handed off to the Queen's simpletons, he figured he'd had enough of Earth women. At least until there was an offer that made the challenge worth the risk.

He lowered his head and quietly mumbled a seeing spell, doing his best to keep the gestures at a minimum. When it was cast, he pushed his magical vision toward the glistening ship, hoping for a peek inside. It was just out of his range. He cursed the gods that gave him a lowly D-class rank in Sight. Imagine what greater wealth he could have acquired over all these years with just another thirty spans.

Unwilling to move out of the crowd, he let the spell go. He saw after that the man in the purple coat had returned, the man who he presumed was the captain of the ship. He'd returned, and in his entourage still was Sir Altin Meade, the Galactic Mage, another of the War Queen's most dangerous minions. The complexity of the challenge presented by that ship was rendered all the more difficult with the young Seven in attendance. And all the more appealing. What profit could be made from the alien items on that ship, the watcher thought. If he could only see inside! What rare objects were in there that would be a first for anyone on

Prosperion, the first and finest that only he could find? Things that not even the Queen herself could have, things the alien people might not even want her to know about. Oh, the thrill of it. Just thinking of it. There hadn't been anything that piqued him so thoroughly as that spaceship since he was but a boy. Not since carving the wagging pink tongues of endless prohibitions from his parents' mouths had he felt such a rush inside. That had been a long time ago. But now the thrill was back. Now he could pilfer an entire alien world.

But he had to act fast, for it would only be a matter of time. Soon enough, the War Queen and her counterparts on Earth would open trade routes. They'd negotiate contracts. Start guilds. Objects from Earth would become commonplace in only a matter of years, perhaps a decade on the optimistic side. Then it would be too late. The greatest opportunities would be gone, the windows closed, shuttered, and barred. It would be all cronyism and inside deals afterwards. Everyone else would fight over scraps.

It occurred to him even as he thought it that the same could be said for trade going the other way. In fact, the more he considered it, the more it seemed likely that was the reason for the appearance of this ship, why it was here in Murdoc Bay. It was here to start trading Prosperion goods on Earth. The fact that it was here and not Crown City, where the deals were being done, said a lot about Her Majesty. For he knew full well it was she and not the Marchioness of South Mark behind the appearance of that ship. Had it been the marchioness, he would have known.

Which meant he was already behind the game. And worse, he had no requests. Not even that dusty old shrew in Galbrun Hall had summoned him for anything. There was no doubt the marchioness at least had wind of this sort of thing happening. But nothing from her. Nothing. He nearly spat for the indignity of it all. And it wouldn't do to go

JOHN DAULTON

calling on her to solicit an arrangement of some kind. He might as well start hawking candies and sweetmeats in the market square.

But, that was fine. He'd find his own way. He always had. And the gods do shine their favor on the ready and the prepared. And it was then that, as if by divine design, a gentle telepathic nudge pressed upon his mind. He recognized it immediately.

"Black Sander," came the demanding telepathic voice of the Earl of Vorvington. "Lady South Mark wishes to see you immediately. We have business to attend."

Black Sander's mouth cut a thin line across his angular face, like a cut made by the tip of a rapier. And out from it, like a pale drop of blood, slid his tongue, licking his lips hungrily. This was going to be fun.

Chapter 15

Pernie stood on Knot's faceplate, halfway up the ancient crater wall and looking down at Djoveeve, who was easy to see as she made her way slowly through the chest-high reeds. The wrinkled old assassin pushed apart the green blades with outward sweeps of her arms, and from where Pernie was three spans above, it seemed as if the old woman were swimming through high grass.

Pernie cast a quick glance over her shoulder, making sure she hadn't gotten too high up. If she got too close to the crater's edge, she'd stick up and be visible against the sky. The old wizard-assassin would spot her then, for Pernie's powers of illusion were not very strong. "You're only a C," Djoveeve had said nearly a month ago when she'd revealed what Pernie's third school of magic was. Even Master Grimswoller hadn't been able to tell what her third power was. But now she knew, and she'd been practicing with it since. Djoveeve said she'd never be very good with it, but it was good enough for a crude sort of invisibility.

She crouched low, gripping her blunted spear, an elven shaft with a sap-filled silk bag where the spearhead should be. She was supposed to "kill" the old assassin if she could. Another ten steps and Djoveeve would get the blunted spear right in the face.

Djoveeve stopped moving for a time, listening. She turned her head from side to side, her eyes narrowing as her vision dulled to give favor to her ears. She waited patiently for a time. "Good, child," she said after a while. "You are as quiet as a mouse."

Pernie smiled. She knew she was. Knot was too. All his little feet made no more noise than leaves settling to the forest floor. She sent him a thought for motionlessness, just enough menace to freeze him but not enough to roll him into a ball. She'd done that only a few days ago, when Seawind had finally allowed her to try fighting from atop the insect's back. She'd been high up a cave wall and been a bit too aggressive in sending it a painful thought, frightening poor Knot into spherical form. She'd fallen almost six full spans. Knot had bounced and taken no injury, but for her, well, that was the first time she'd ever seen her own shinbone so closely before, burst right through the skin and all. If it hadn't hurt so much, she would have enjoyed looking at it more.

But now she knew, and she made sure Knot was behaving properly, still as stone as he clung to the craggy rock face like a fly upon the wall.

Pernie hefted the spear, pitching the back end of it at a steep angle so as not to bump against the rock. She wished Djoveeve would hurry up and move.

Like a strike of lightning, Djoveeve's own blunted spear came hurtling up at her, so quickly all Pernie could do was jump. If she'd taken the time to urge Knot to move, she would have been struck full on.

She dropped straight down, knowing she'd land loudly when she hit the shallow water, but as she fell, her arm suddenly wrenched upward when she hit the end of Knot's rope. For an instant, she thought he might be strong enough to hold on, but he was not. His little feet, unprepared for the shock, lost their grip, and down he came on top of her, the two of them landing, first Pernie, then the bug, with a tremendous splash.

Before Pernie could clear her eyes, Djoveeve was nearly upon her, a wooden knife in her hand. Just before the old assassin could make the token slice across Pernie's throat, Knot was dragging Pernie back up the crater wall, the pulse of his fear throbbing in his insect brain.

Pernie swung beneath him like a clock pendulum, bouncing off the rock face and getting scratched up everywhere. He'd nearly dragged her all the way over the lip of the crater by the time she got him to stop. She tilted her head back, looking up to see where she was, then reached up with her free hand, prepared to climb up the rope. Two hard objects thudded against her chest, one after the next in rapid fire. She looked down again and saw that both of Djoveeve's wooden knives had left black charcoal marks on her, one right below the next. She would have been a pincushion if those knives were real.

"You've got to get that creature under control," the ancient bodyguard intoned, though needlessly. "It's going to get you killed."

Pernie hung motionlessly for a moment, her shoulder hurting from the initial jolt and all her scratches beginning to burn. She sighed, frustrated, and simply dangled there like some droopy little anchor dropped halfway into an empty sea.

"And I saw the butt of your spear above the ridgeline," Djoveeve was saying when Pernie finally began paying attention to her again. "How many times do I have to tell you that your illusions are weak? You can't hide like an elf any more than you can run like one. You've got to think. You must use your powers *and* your brain."

Pernie didn't want to hear another lecture today. And she didn't want to hear what she couldn't do. She didn't want to hear how she was weak and how she was going to die. Again. That's all anyone ever told her here. "You're going to die," they all said. Always with some big stupid "if" to go along. Well, if there were that many *ifs* going to kill her, then she expected she ought to be dead by now.

She hung there for a little longer, watching Djoveeve talk. The words made flat and round shapes of the old assassin's mouth as it moved, but the sounds all faded away. The woman was merely part of the scenery. A dull part, in brown leather, lost against the bright colors of the elven island with all its creatures and sounds and nothingness. Pernie didn't want to listen anymore.

And she was tired of eating fish.

The pain in her shoulder throbbed and broke her reverie. She might have been drifting off to sleep. She prompted Knot to pull her out of the crater slowly so as not to cause further injury. She climbed onto his back once they were up, and she set him off at a run. She was done with lessons for today. And this time, unlike last time, she was going to go someplace they couldn't find.

The biggest advantage in studying with Djoveeve out of the cave was that the old woman couldn't keep up with her anymore. Not for speed. Djoveeve's jaguar form wasn't fast enough, and her skills in transmutation prevented her from taking the shape of birds—Pernie didn't know why, but she'd figured out the weakness all the same. Which meant that Pernie could outrun her. The problem—the thing that Pernie had learned the last two times she'd tried to run away—was what the old mage-assassin couldn't manage in speed, she more than made up for in tracking ability. The woman was harder to get away from than a bloodhound or a scavenger drake.

But this time Pernie had a better plan. Riding Knot through the jungle was a tough way to run. The leaves and branches and brambles got in her way. It was impossible not to leave a trail of broken vegetation when she rode through the trees, much less her scent.

But the last time she'd gone out, she discovered something new, if belatedly: Knot left no footprints in the sand. She thought that maybe, because of it, he might not leave any scent behind as well.

So this time, as she streaked off, away from Djoveeve's lectures, she headed straight for the ocean as fast as Knot could go. Soon enough, she made it to the coast. She'd gone north last time she was here, so this time she decided to try the south. She saw that there was a high set of cliffs a few measures down. It appeared as if the beach might end there, but she knew Knot could climb them if there wasn't enough beach to go around.

Soon she discovered that there were enough rocks along the base of them to make it at least partway around, but Knot didn't like the cool mist of the water so near his feet. Rather than fight with him, she directed him a few spans up the wall and urged him to carry on. She'd gotten good at riding him along vertical faces, hooking her heels over the edge of his segmented shell, just above where his legs emerged, and leaning back carefully, just enough for balance, but not so far as to brush her back against the cliff. At the speeds Knot ran, and with altitude, that would mean death.

She well knew that what she was doing would get her yelled at if Kettle saw, but she'd been so long away from the flour-doused old kitchen matron that she'd nearly forgotten what being scolded was all about. Seawind didn't scold. He was quick with a cuff or a blow, but he never scolded her like a child. And Djoveeve only lectured. Endlessly. None of them yelled at her, either. Pernie never thought she'd miss such a thing, being hollered at, but she did. Well, not exactly the yelling part, but the rest of it. She missed the look in Kettle's face. The look after the yelling was done, when

Kettle's eyes sometimes filled with frightened tears.

Nobody cried for her here.

She tried not to cry too. But her shoulder hurt and she missed Kettle and she was tired of eating fish. She'd done everything they said, and she never complained hardly at all. But she was tired, and it wasn't fun anymore.

She wanted to go home.

As she looked out over the ocean in the direction where she thought Kurr might lie, she thought of all of them sitting at the table having tea. Kettle was serving up a plate of roast meat and steaming carrots; the carrots would be bright orange and dripping with butter and beat-sugar sauce. She could smell the wine and hear Kettle yelling at Master Altin for trying to give her some. "Ya can't give a wee lass wine!" she would say. And Altin had tried to give Pernie wine before. He said wine was good for her. Master Tytamon had said it was too before he died.

But then Orli had come along and broken the world. And her people had killed everyone, or at least gotten them all killed. And now she was trying to take Master Altin away and ruin everything while Pernie was stuck here with the stupid, boring elves.

They said they'd let her go home when she could pass their stupid test, when she'd mastered the spear and wasn't afraid of that nasty old orc, but now she knew they never would. Djoveeve would just go on talking forever, and they'd never let her go. She was already really good with the elven spear. Only last night she'd struck Djoveeve hard upon the knee when they were practicing in the cave. Really hard. It almost knocked her down. Next time she *would* knock her down.

But there wouldn't be a next time. She was going to get out of here somehow.

The cliff face fell away before her as Knot whisked them along toward the end of its length. It appeared that the flat rock face was giving way, the cliffs opening onto a little cove. The cliff rose up again on the other side, some fifty spans away.

She had no idea how long she'd been lost in thought; riding Knot had become second nature to her, but he was very fast, and she was sure she'd never been here before.

She directed Knot around the corner carefully and slowly; rounding a bend as sharp as that was a complicated affair. Doing so required that Pernie turn to face the rock, and that Knot bend himself around the corner and stop while she scooted around him from one face to the next. But soon they were around it, and she saw that she'd come upon a horseshoe-shaped cove. It was at least two hundred spans deep and nearly as wide at its widest point toward the back. And it had a bright pink beach!

Pernie sent Knot a threatening thought and had him descend at a gradual angle until they could get to the narrow strip of sand. It was obvious that this place was like no other beach she'd seen before, and she'd seen plenty since coming to String. For starters, the sand was as pink as a poodle's tongue, and it was so soft it reminded her of goose down like the kind Kettle made pillows with, luxurious and inviting. She stepped off Knot and hopped around in it for a time, enjoying the warmth and softness of it on her feet. She flung handfuls of it into the air and saw that it sparkled like a million tiny jewels.

She paused, realizing that she'd been giggling loudly, and turned quickly round, looking back the way she had come. Djoveeve was nowhere to be found. Though that was hardly cause for comfort given the nature of what the ancient woman had been doing these last three hundred years.

She tipped her head back and scanned the edge of the cliff all around, rather like Djoveeve had been doing while searching for her back at the crater they'd been practicing in. There was no sign of movement up there, though there might have been a hundred elves hiding in the trees for all Pernie could tell.

She brought her gaze back to the cove itself and saw that the crescent-shaped beach fronted an odd stand of trees, hundreds and hundreds of them, all roughly the same. They were palm trees, not unlike those that she'd seen all over the island here, but these, all of them, grew in pairs, two trunks wound around together, and seeming to share a single tuft of fronds at the top, a great mass of them all jumbled together like the green head of some spiked mace.

She went immediately to investigate, bidding Knot to curl up in a ball with just the right dose of fear, a mental blast of pain, his own, remembered and echoed back at him. It worked, of course, and confident that he was properly subdued, she left him rolled up there to go see about the trees.

Upon closer inspection, she discovered that the palm trunks had a texture like hard wax, each of them soft at the surface, but firm enough when pressed. She tried to cut into one of them with her fingernail, but she could not, and for a time, it amused her to think that they might be made out of enchanted snot.

She strolled from one to the next, noting that some had round growths like coconuts on them and some did not. But beyond this difference, they were all the same variety, and were it not for the random and haphazard dispersing of the trees, she might have thought they'd been planted here all at once.

The cove was much deeper than it looked from high above, and Pernie spent nearly an hour wandering around in its depths before she grew bored of its constancy. Unlike the rest of the jungle on the island, this place was completely without variety. After a time, she decided there was nothing novel about the trees at all.

So she returned to the beach and Knot still lying there in a ball.

She bade him unroll himself and checked his thoughts to see if he was hungry. He was, which was not a surprise. She didn't mind feeding him just now, as it gave her something to do.

With a great deal of grunting and yanking, she pulled the silk bag filled with sap off her spear shaft, making it little more than a slender quarterstaff. Still, it would suffice, and she took it right out into the waves. Surely there would be some shallow-water fish to find.

She spent some time wading deeper and deeper out, and by the time she was nearly to the mouth of the cove, which she recognized by the change in water color as the seabed dropped off steeply over a shelf, she heard the familiar bark of Djoveeve calling her name. "Do not move another step," the old woman called, just emerging from her jaguar form. "Come back inland now."

"No," shouted Pernie. "Don't tell me what to do." Just for that, she made her way directly toward the edge of the sea shelf rather than looking around for fish. Besides, she'd probably find the fish she was looking for out there.

Had it not been for the fact that her spear shaft stuck out a pace in front of her, Pernie would have walked right into the magic barrier that evaporated the smooth black wood instead. The back half of her weapon dipped into the water behind her, having lost the counterbalance of the front, and it was the reflex following that feeling that stopped her, even before her brain had time to make sense of what her eyes had seen.

She stared at the scant half-hand's width of black wood that remained jutting out from where she gripped the weapon in her fist. There was a faint and unfamiliar smell, and the end where it had been dissolved was cut cleanly and polished as smoothly as if a craftsman had decided to make it that way.

She flipped what remained of it around and, taking a half step back, poked it forward again.

Once again the foremost portion of it simply disappeared. When she pulled it back, again there was only the strange smell, and the shaft was again cut clean and smooth.

With a shrug, Pernie turned back toward the beach, still scanning the water for some signs of fish for Knot. By the time she got back to where her bug sat, Djoveeve was sitting next to the rolled-up creature, clearly preparing for another boring lecture she was going to give. And Pernie had nothing for Knot.

Djoveeve patted the sand beside her, and Pernie plopped next to her and proceeded to ignore whatever the old woman had to say because it was, as expected, just another boring lecture, this time about "carnation trees" or something like that, and lots of stuff about why Pernie wasn't allowed to come here ever again—just like everything else she was never supposed to do anywhere all the time. Rather than pay attention, she looked out beyond the strange barrier and watched the water spouting from a passing pod of whales. They were free, she thought. They could go wherever they wanted to, and nobody told them what to do. She wished she were a whale. If she was, she'd go home.

Which is when she realized what she should do. Suddenly, with renewed energy, she figured out how she could get home. She glanced over at Knot, still balled up next to her, and smiled. She patted the hard surface of his rounded shell. If she could tame a bug, surely she could tame a whale. And if not a whale, then some other creature of the sea. And unlike Knot, she was not afraid of getting wet at all.

Chapter 16

A great black box appeared fifty thousand miles beyond the planet R3 in the solar system known as Fruitfall. There were none to observe the appearance of the large black object, but had there been, they would have seen what looked like an enormous brick born from the very womb of space, and shortly after it arrived, they would have observed that object begin to dissolve. For it did dissolve, beginning at its top and one leading edge and then the rest, slowly melting away. The rate of this apparent melting increased, as if black paint were being washed away from an invisible box in which there had been placed a long, slender spaceship, which gleamed silvery in the light of the distant sun. Soon the black box was reduced to a black platform, a long, flat expanse of magically enchanted tiles as dark as space itself. The spaceship resting upon it was the *Glistening Lady.*

Inside the ship, Captain Roberto Levi was seated in the pilot's chair, with his feet up on the small console that served him as he watched through the main ship's monitor, enjoying the show as the black substance of the TGS teleportation platform "unboxed" itself. When the walls of the dark teleportation bay were finally melted away, he saw that his ship had arrived above the looming giant rock R3, and not so far away from their destination, the moon Orli said was Yellow Fire's host world before the tragic solar accident. He let go a merry laugh as the last of the black walls seemed to ooze into the platform. "You see that, Deeqa?" he said. "That there is the future of everything. You got to love those magical bastards. I'm telling you. A whole new era has begun."

"It is efficient, Captain," Deeqa replied. "I'll let Doctor Bryant know we are here. And get word to Orli and Sir Altin as well."

Roberto nodded, and while Deeqa was at that, he ordered the slender blonde at the helm to take them to the coordinates Orli had given them. The helmswoman called up the location on the monitor, then engaged the engines and set them on their way. Roberto watched with a broad grin as they approached, still giddy about how easily they had jumped so far across space. From a moon around Neptune in the system of Sol to a moon around R3 in the system of Fruitfall, thirty-four light-years in seconds. And with the TGS platforms that the Prosperions were going to be building across the galaxy for just this sort of thing, the Earth ships would no longer have to suffer the snuffing out of reactor cores. They were "in the box," as the TGS teleporters liked to say, and that somehow changed the rules. It was the same way the fighter ships and transports had worked after being teleported to Naotatica in the hangar bays of the starships, a big part of what ultimately helped end the war. Roberto didn't understand why, but he didn't care why. All he knew was that it worked. Soon there would be TGS depots everywhere, and the problems with distance in space would be gone forever. A new age truly was upon humanity.

In less than a half hour, the *Glistening Lady* was settling on the surface of Yellow Fire's moon, barely five hundred yards from the craggy stone teeth that marked the mountain pass, a pass that would lead to the caverns, which in turn would take the science team down to Yellow Fire's dormant heart.

Roberto was about to give the order for Deeqa and a few others of his crew to suit up and prepare to accompany the science team, when a loud rush of air ruffled everyone's hair. They all turned as one to see Altin and Orli standing at the back of the bridge.

"Permission to come aboard, Captain?" Orli quipped as she strode confidently up and embraced her longtime friend. She leaned away then and frowned. "Hey, where's your hat?"

He laughed, then turned and looked around. It was on the floor near the command chair, blown off the back by the wind of Altin's teleport spell. He turned a glare of mock anger on Altin. "Hey, you kink my feather, I'm going to have words with you, pal."

"My sincerest apologies," Altin said, though the grin upon his face suggested a distinct lack of sincerity.

Roberto went through a round of introductions then, beginning with the blonde helmswoman Tracy Applegate, a bush pilot from the free districts in northern Canada, and then his weapons officer, Liu Chun, who he bragged was the daughter of the late General Chun who was a hero of the Hostile war. The man had intentionally crashed his fighter into a Hostile orb just prior to its striking an elementary school being used as an emergency shelter during the worst of the attack. The video capturing his heroism had become iconic, the embodiment of the fight that had raged on Earth, and his name was known and revered by all. So much so that Orli gasped when she heard who Liu Chun's father was, and tears burned her eyes as she shook the lovely woman's hand. "I read your father's biography," she said. "He was an incredible man. There are few whose bravery comes so reflexively. And he sounded so calm on the audio. I am honored to know you, and very sorry for your great loss."

Liu nodded and smiled. "Thank you. He was a remarkable person. I miss him."

"Well, you do his legacy of giving to others justice in helping with Yellow Fire," Altin said.

She nodded again. "Yes, I think so too. It's why I left my commission behind and signed up with him." She jerked her head toward Roberto.

Orli turned to Roberto with the question in her eyes. "I thought you just scooped up all the hot chicks you could find. You mean you actually had a volunteer?"

Roberto shrugged and smiled. "I did. She saw the call for the science team on the NTA boards and applied. I saw her credentials and couldn't say no. Just my luck she's easy on the eyes too."

Orli glanced back from Roberto to Liu, who, like the rest of Roberto's crew, other than Deeqa Daar, of course, wore the low-cut, corseted uniforms Roberto had had designed. The young woman did look remarkable in the formfitting attire. Liu followed Orli's gaze down to her chest and back up. Liu shrugged, her expression that of one who has had to make some compromises. "I know. What can you say? Our captain seems like a good man, and a really shrewd combat leader from what I read. Besides, the mission matters more than the attire."

Tracy leaned back from her seat at the helm and added, "And he pays three times better than anyone else out there. I can live with the uniform for that."

They laughed, all but Altin anyway, for he was already thinking about the project under way. "So where is this science team you promised me?" he asked. "I'd like to meet them and get the gryphons in the air. Every moment we waste is another moment of private agony for Blue Fire."

"You can be such a buzz kill, dude," said Roberto as the smile died on his face. "But you're in luck; there they go." He pointed to the monitor, where just then a small gravity sled was being tugged out onto the powdered gray surface of the desolate moon by a pair of figures in bulky spacesuits whose off-white coloring practically glowed in the bright light of Fruitfall high above. "That's Doctor Bryant, I'm sure. He's been ready for this since we left Earth, probably been back there suited up since liftoff."

"Good," said Altin. "That's what I was hoping for. Someone who could really care about this project with us."

"Oh, he cares. And he's smart as hell, so don't let him scare you or piss you off. Either of you."

Both Altin and Orli frowned, and for a moment, a rare one, Roberto actually looked a little embarrassed. It was strange to see that this time it was Deeqa wearing the devilish grin.

"Well," Roberto explained, "he's just ... well—all I'm saying is if he starts hitting on Orli or something, don't blast him with a fireball. That's all. He's harmless, I swear."

"Why would he hit her? And I certainly will not tolerate it, I promise you."

"No, not hitting like *hitting* hitting. I mean, if he starts checking her out. Flirting or whatever. You know, coming on to her."

Orli laughed, but Altin looked very serious. She clutched his arm, and after a glance into her sweet blue eyes, he smiled. "Very well. No blasting. I realize that the customs of nonmilitary people from Earth may take some acclimating to for those of us from Prosperion, just as patience the other way will surely also be required. I will do my part."

Several hours later they were all deep beneath the surface of Yellow Fire's moon, nine of them, standing around the hole in the bottom of the huge chamber filled with the dull gray crystals sprouting from essentially everywhere.

"That's him," Orli said proudly as they looked down into it, the faint purplish pulse just visible below.

Doctor Marks Bryant—"Call me Professor," the geologist had said—moved up to the edge and peered down inside. He took a reading with a large blockish device that emitted a narrow green line of light. He read the data on its screen, then turned to Altin. "This is the stone you call Liquefying Stone, correct?" His gloved hand was pointing to any number of the dull gray crystals in the hole.

"It is," came Altin's reply. "Or at least it sort of is. It's not the same as the few we had on Prosperion, nor is it like those in Blue Fire's cave. At least not anymore. Hers, and the ones that I got from Tytamon, all have what you might call an anti-glow, an odd luminescence that didn't glow so much as absorb light in an observable way. It's hard to explain. But they were yellow, and there is something about that which seems in operation when you look into them. It is the same with those that adorn the walls on Blue Fire, even more so, really, for they are quite bright and do emit light, glowing wondrously at all times. These here, obviously, do not glow, nor are they yellow at all. If they are eating light at all, I can't tell it by looking. However, in terms of arrangement, they do seem to be of the same variety."

The geologist nodded, his shiny bald head reflecting the white spots of several of the others' helmet lights as he bent back down. He put his gloved hand behind a formation of crystals near the edge of the hole and narrowed his helmet's light beam. He waved his hand back and forth, evidently looking to see if any light came through, but they were too dull and gray.

He pulled his hand back and slid a small hammer from his belt. He backed away from the edge of the hole and went to a cluster of stones near Orli. He flashed her a wink before tapping on the tip of a rather long projection of crystals with the hammer. Nothing happened. He tapped on it a bit harder. Still nothing. He struck it several more times, increasingly harder with each until he stopped. "Well, it's tough," he said.

He went back to the hole and simply peered into it for a time. He straightened and turned to one of his team. "Rope," he said, holding out his hand again, this time toward the members of his team. Two baby-faced young men, obviously twins, came forward and took positions on either side of him. One handed Professor Bryant a metal clip attached to a rope, which the geologist snapped to the left side of his belt. The second youth did not wait for him to look up and instead simply clipped the length of rope he carried to the geologist's other side. Professor Bryant was all business. "All right, let's see what we've got down there that's still alive. Stacy, run the tables while I'm down there, please."

Another very young-looking member of the science team raised a tablet computer, much like the one Orli often used, though a good deal larger and sturdier of build. "Got it, Professor," she said.

The twins beside the professor moved to either side of the hole as the geologist sat awkwardly down in the bulky suit and began making his way down the fifteen feet to where the glowing pulse of the heart stones was.

"More slack on your side, Rabin, damn it," he called up to one of the brothers as he descended. He started to say something that might have been further chastisement, but he cut himself off and let out a long, low "whoa!" instead. It was more an audible and awestruck breath than a spoken word, but the effect was obvious. "You getting this, Stace?" he asked.

"I am," said his lab assistant, Doctor Stacy Walters. She was brand new to her PhD, and she wore an expression of absolute delight for having a part in the work, her eagerness visible upon her features, if barely so given that the colorful motions from her tablet were reflecting from her helmet glass and obscuring the evidence of her joy. "I've never seen anything like this. Look at the color signatures. Wow. And

I think I'm detecting that light-eating thing in it, too, lost wave patterns. That is weird. There may be some traces of the effect still in the gray ones around it too, now that I know what I'm looking at. But that's not the strangest thing. Have you seen the density readings on this glowing stuff? This is insane. Where's it getting all that mass?"

Doctor Bryant read the data her computer was sending back and shook his head. "No clue. But if it's that massive, we're going to need a lot bigger power plant to lift it out than we brought. Don't want to be in here when that thing topples into the hole."

"I'm not even sure why it isn't falling straight through the rest of this," she said. "Those other crystals should crumble under that." There followed some technical conversation back and forth.

Altin, like the others, heard everything being said, but he could make no sense of most of it. He glanced to Orli, who was too busy listening to look back. When he looked to Roberto, the captain of the *Glistening Lady* had little to add beyond "Must be heavy, I guess." And so they had to stand patiently and wait, letting the geologists do their work.

A little more than an hour later, and several failed attempts at levity from Roberto later, the twins hauled the professor up out of the hole. Without even looking any of them in the eye, he went straight to Stacy's computer and turned it round in her hands so that he could operate it himself. He spent another twenty minutes muttering to himself and finally looked up with a white-toothed grin.

"I believe I can get it out. We're going to need one of the big power plants and some digging equipment, big digging equipment, and, well, then there's the hard part. We have to cut it with a water saw."

"A what?" both Orli and Altin asked.

"A water saw," he repeated. "It's a stonecutter that works with a high-powered, very fine jet of water to cut through stone. We can't use lasers because, well, whatever the heart stone is doing to light could draw the beam and kill him. And if we try a conventional saw, we risk killing him. If this really is his brain—or his soul, as Miss Pewter's portion of the file you people sent me suggests it might be—then there's no telling what damaging any of this might do anyway. A water saw is the best bet."

"So why is that the hard part? Are they super expensive or something?" Roberto cringed inside his helmet and looked like he was preparing for an electric shock or a slap in the face.

"Yes, actually, it's going to cost a fortune to put one in here. We're going to have to have one made because the one I need is going to be a lot bigger than anything we might find lying around somewhere back on Earth. And it has to be capable of extreme delicacy too, like laser-scalpel delicacy, because the scariest part of this is going to have to be done by hand. There won't be any templates for this."

"Why not?" Orli asked.

"Because all these crystals are eating all my light. For the same reason we can't cut with a laser—even if that seemed like a good idea and didn't run the risk of overloading him or melting him or something worse, since we don't know anything about this life form—I can't get readings off of it at all. I can see what's coming out of it fine as you please. I can even see the gray ones too, at least until I get close to the heart itself. But look." He pulled out the device that emitted the green beam of light and brought it to where Altin and Orli stood. He directed it downward, centered a patch where the gray crystals met the purple heart stone in the view finder, and switched on the green beam. A line appeared on the little square screen moving straight across, and along the left edge symbols appeared. But nothing else was happening. "You see?"

"I'm not quite sure what I'm looking at," Altin confessed.

"It is not doing anything."

"Exactly," said the professor. "Which is entirely my point." He paused, looking to Orli, then got a strange expression on his face, as if he'd just noticed her for the first time. He flashed a winning smile at her and winked before turning away and returning to Stacy and the computer that she held. "There's no reading. And there's a haze where the gray crystals butt up against it, some kind of overlap, making a murky boundary. So if we can't see where he ends and the gray crystal begins, then we can't trace it to set a template. Without a template, the computer can't guide the scalpel jet. Which means it has to be done by hand. As in, it's going to have to be one of us."

Orli gasped. "But what if we hurt him somehow? You just said we might kill him by accident."

"Exactly."

Altin seemed far less perturbed than the rest. "But it does sound to me like you think success is possible. That is a good thing. Can you do it?"

"I can get it all set up with absolute certainty. But I'd be terrified to be the one to make the fatal mistake. We'll need someone else. Someone with a steady hand. Maybe a high-end sculptor, someone used to working with stone."

Stacy shook her head, looking at data on her tablet. "Nobody is used to working with *this* stone."

"Doctor Singh!" Orli exclaimed. "He's used to doing surgery. And after all, isn't that essentially what you are talking about? You called it a scalpel, after all."

The professor nodded inside his helmet dome. "As long as he's willing to live with the guilt of killing an entire world, I'm happy to turn it over to him."

Orli looked pleased, but when she turned to Altin, he did not. Her delicate blonde brows drooped.

"What is it?" she asked.

"I don't think he'll do it."

"Why wouldn't he?"

"Because he hates me," Altin replied. "He hates me, and he blames Blue Fire for all those deaths. I'm not sure he's the right man to ask."

"Well, he doesn't hate me," she said. "So let's just go tell him what we are trying to do. Maybe he'll be happy about the whole thing."

Altin's expression suggested he thought the odds long, but he let it pass. "Speaking of being happy about the whole thing," he said instead, "I suppose I should tell Blue Fire that it does seem to be possible. The last time I communicated with her, she seemed beyond the capacity for hope. This might lift her spirits considerably."

"Yes," Orli said, clapping, though the sound could not be heard. "She will be excited to hear such optimistic news. We should tell her. If you don't want to—I know she depresses you—I'll tell her in my dreams."

Chapter 17

Altin had decided it would be best to give Blue Fire the good news in person—or at least, he hoped she would see it that way—so he teleported to her world straightaway. The moment he arrived on the ledge in her great cavernous body, her womb really, she found him there and knew in that instant what was in his heart and mind.

She felt his dread for being there.

"Orli Love hate speak with Blue Fire," she said, using the rumbling of the stone all around him to make words for him to hear. She'd gotten better at speaking with sounds over the last several months, the time since she'd learned to think of humanity as a race rather than a disease. Still, she struggled with language. It was one thing to have access to all the words in Altin's memory, all those in Orli's too; it was another thing altogether to assemble those random sequences of sound, those symbols made of noise, into her own feelings and ideas. And her words were so vast they were hard to hear, for her voice was the temblor of her body, of the very stone all around.

As soon as the quaking had passed, passed beneath his feet and then beneath his knees after he had been knocked down, he pulled a pair of tiny hummingbird feathers out of a small pouch tucked away in his robes. He'd brought them just for this, for the new spell he'd taught himself to prevent these sorts of rumbling, bouncing injuries. He cast the spell quickly, the feathers vanishing, consumed and converted for their part of shaping the magic, and right after, Altin gently floated up off the ground.

Blue Fire interpreted his lifting away from the ledge, from her body, poorly.

Orli Love hate touch Blue Fire. She sent this thought straight into his mind, reverting in her humiliation to telepathy. She filled him with the ever-present sadness that filled her, grown worse in the days after the war. The great tide of her sorrow washed into his mind and soul like a wave. She added to its familiar brutality a sense of rejection as well, of repulsion. His repulsion toward her. She thought that she disgusted him.

"Oh, stop," he said aloud, trying to encourage her to use her new human words. "I am not repulsed by you at all. I find you beautiful, and I care very deeply for your happiness. But look at my poor, soft human knees." He lifted up his robes so she could see the small red puncture wounds where he'd fallen amongst the crystals, which always happened when she spoke as movingly as she did. "We humans are delicate creatures, and you are very strong. But I will touch you if you like." With barely the flick of a thought, he let the levitation spell go and settled back to the ground. "There, you see? It's not serious injury. I can have it healed the moment I get home."

His hands and knees tingled. He checked his palms and then his kneecaps and saw that the wounds were gone.

Blue Fire no hurt Orli Love. Blue Fire die.

"Oh, please, stop," he said, growing annoyed. "You're so dramatic sometimes. They are silly little wounds. I'm sorry I even brought it up. I've come to give you wonderful news."

Suddenly, he was suspended just above the floor again,

as if he'd recast the spell. The cavern rumbled all around him. "Orli Love no anger for Blue Fire."

Altin rolled his eyes. This was why, without really thinking about it, he had begun to avoid seeing her sometimes. Emotionally, she was a wreck. She had become this dried-up tuft of the great, powerful being he'd once known. But he knew it didn't have to last, even if she could not believe there was any help for her.

"Orli and I," he began, but then cut himself off. She did not know them by their names. She knew them by who loved them instead. That was the measure of one's worth. Such was the way of her kind. And so to her, Altin was *Orli Love* and, of course, Orli was *Altin Love.* He began again. "Altin Love and I have found a great doctor of her people. He is very knowledgeable about planetary things." He paused and sent images of the crystals in her womb and in her heart chamber to her telepathically. He followed those images with others of the crystals inside of Yellow Fire as well. "We believe we've found him."

Upon seeing the images in Altin's mind, upon linking those images with the words he spoke and the thoughts behind them that he hadn't spoken yet, she recognized *him,* Yellow Fire. She knew in that instant that the purplish pulse she saw in Altin's memory was her long-dead lover, her husband, gone forever, as she had so agonizingly and endlessly believed. She knew it, and then the whole cavern filled with a great quaking roar to match the torrential wail of her telepathic grief.

Altin had to summon all his magical strength to block the press of her misery against his mind, and for a time, he hung there in the air defending his sanity in a way that wasn't so much different than he had when he was fighting off the great hatred of Red Fire. He opened his mind to the mana all around him and pulled it in, using it to enforce the blockade around his thoughts. Had he not had the ring, and in it the stone Blue Fire had given him, he could not have staved off the onslaught at all. He would likely be lying there weeping and gasping for air for as long as it took her to stop. Or he would have been dead.

But he had the ring, and so he rode the storm out, becoming more exasperated all the time. But in time, it was done. When she was calm again, he apologized for showing her the thought. But still he pressed on with his point because he was sure it mattered. He and Orli both hoped that understanding what was happening might bring her cheer, lift her out of all this abject misery.

"The reason I showed you that," Altin went on, "is because this great man from Altin Love's world is going to try to bring Yellow Fire back, just like we said we would. I promised you and Orli—you and Altin Love—that we would try, and now it seems that it truly is possible. It's only a matter of a little more time. A few months while they build a machine to get him out. And then the two of you might finally be able to be together again."

There was a long quiet after that. No quakes, no images stampeding through his mind, put there by the violence of the cosmic-sized emotions that ran through her large and ever-sentimental heart.

And then one came. One small emotion, very small, hardly visible were such things to have physicality. She offered it up to him meekly, the barest mote upon an upturned hand, raised up for him to see, tentative, terrified, but for the first time, something new. It was hope.

He saw it there in his mind, felt it, the quavering fragility. She showed it to him, then gave it a gossamer sort of mass with which she shaped a ring around the image of Yellow Fire's glowing purple heart. She held that in her mind and in his, as if cupped in tremulous, loving hands. Together, they stared at it for a time.

It was the first time she'd seen Yellow Fire since his

death all those thousands and thousands, even millions, of years before. He'd been gone so long, silent and dead so long, that she was afraid to look at him now. Altin saw the image change a little, as if they were now seeing it through a haze of smoke. But still, all around the heart stone flickered that delicate ring of hope.

Altin smiled, upon his face and inwardly with his heart and mind. At last. At least one moment of happiness for her. Now if it would truly work as they said it would, if Doctor Singh and the professor truly could cut it out without hurting it, then perhaps her happiness could become as permanent as her misery had been. Then there would be justice.

He couldn't even help those last thoughts. They just came. All of them in his memories, to be read all at once.

Once again the entire chamber rumbled and rocked. Bits of dark stone fell down from temporary fissures that opened in the ceiling above. "Yellow Fire *live*. Altin Love new human make water. Yellow Fire die?" She sent along with the thunderous boom of her words the reflected image of Doctor Marks Bryant back at him. She'd pulled that right out of his memories along with all the rest. "Not make Yellow Fire die."

There came after that a series of ideas, and by the end of it, Altin realized that Blue Fire had already turned hope into a somewhat perverted form of quasi-misery. In seeing that there was a chance that Yellow Fire might be killed, it seemed she'd rather live knowing that he was marginally alive, lying as he was in a perpetual state of dormancy, than return to the knowledge that he was actually dead. She'd found hope, and now she was going to cling to it forever, even if it was hope in an emaciated state.

Altin groaned aloud, and he felt her withdraw some from his thoughts after reading them. *Orli Love hate Blue Fire. Blue Fire alone.* These came straight into his mind again, and he had to fight to not let even more exasperation through.

"By the gods, creature! Orli Love does not hate you. I will never hate you. And you have to let us try. For all we know, he's in there hoping we'll hurry up so he can come back to you. Love is a hopeful thing, my friend. Love requires faith."

"Yellow Fire no die. Blue Fire love." She rumbled the words through her colossal stone body.

"But you don't have him now. He isn't really yours. Not yet. It's just as Altin Love was once lost to me too. Do you remember? Remember the poison that took her love away?"

Blue Fire projected back an image of Thadius Thoroughgood. It was the human face of poison to her. The symbol of it. The cavern rumbled violently, but shaped no words.

"Yes," Altin went on. "Exactly. I hated losing the love of Altin Love. Thadius' poison stole her love away, even while she lived. And that's what the flare of that sun did too. The star called Fruitfall flared, and its fire took your Yellow Fire's love away. But he too still lives. And maybe we can bring him back. Like I got Altin Love back. You must at least let us try."

His mind filled with unspoken fear, terror that showed him the gray, smoky image of the pulsing heart of Yellow Fire, and slowly the gray smoke grew thick and the purple light went out, replaced by the face of Marks Bryant with water running down his face. Then he saw Orli weeping, and then himself as the image of Orli went away, obscured like the heart of Yellow Fire by graying smoke.

Altin sighed. "Yes, it's true," he replied. "We might end up killing him. It is possible. You saw that in my head. But how long do you want to remain alone?" He paused, frustrated. Floating above the ground with a spell that wasn't his added to his sense of helplessness. "This is what I know, the one thing I can tell you for certain: as long as there was any possibility that I might get my Orli, my Altin Love, back, I never gave up on her. I never would have. I never will. No matter what happens. In the end, she is all that matters to me. But, in the end, it is up to you to decide what you want to do about Yellow Fire now. I won't let them touch him if you say not to. The choice is yours."

Again there was a long and cavernous silence. He waited so long that he wondered if she had forgotten he was there. But finally she spoke again.

"Water cut. Heart stone kill." It came with the image once again of Professor Bryant sitting there, tears pouring down his face.

"Yes. The water saw might kill his heart."

"Water cut kill Blue Fire heart?" It was clearly an inquiry.

"No. Of course not. Why would it?"

"No." The cavern shook for the barest moment with the violence of her frustration with human words. She presented him with the image of Professor Bryant working in her own heart chamber, the narrow place with the glowing yellow walls and the patch of green that she had called the Father's Gift. He saw the geologist there, and then he saw the gray smoke fill it and snuff out Blue Fire's heart stone. "Water come Blue Fire. Kill Blue Fire heart."

With a jolt he realized what she was asking him. And he adamantly refused. "Absolutely not," he said. "We will not come kill you."

She rumbled all around him again, still frustrated apparently. "Yellow Fire die. Blue Fire die," she said. She showed him the purple heart fading out, then the green heart that was her own following in kind. "Yellow Fire live. Blue Fire live. Orli Love promise keep."

Altin frowned, but he understood it well enough. His first thought was to refuse again, but then he considered all that she had been through. He considered all that he had been through as well, and in doing so, he realized that what she was asking would be the only kind thing left to do. Her misery had already lasted so long. So, so long. So, with another long, sad sigh, he agreed.

"Fine," he said. "You have my word. If it doesn't work, if Yellow Fire dies, then I promise I will make them come here and cut out your heart too. If there can be no peace together in this lifetime, then the two of you can find peace in eternity."

She filled him with a swell of gratitude that was so enormous it made him cry. He was still crying when he suddenly found himself back on Prosperion, in the teleportation chamber in Calico Castle's central spire.

Apparently Blue Fire wanted to be alone.

Chapter 18

The Incredible Spectacularo stood upon a stage that groaned beneath his weight, so much so that the boards creaked at even the least movement with his hands. The stage lights were too bright, and he hated how these damn electrical things blasted their glare at him. He'd long ago stopped squinting into them trying to see out into the crowd—if one presumed to call it such. Oh, for the first two months or so, the room had filled up fairly well, but then the numbers had died away. But, as usual, there were a few patrons here tonight, a smattering of sweaty faces staring up at him, waiting for his next trick, the pittance he gleaned off their working-class salaries enough to keep hunger away ... and the authorities.

"For my next trick," he said, doing his best to force some stagecraft energy, "I'll need a volunteer." He scanned the mangy group, looking for a rising hand. Of course none came. These people were only barely alive.

He walked up to the front of the stage, raising a hand to shield his eyes, and peered into the gloom. Children were the best, if he could find them at the right age. They at least, unlike their slack-jawed parents, could find some level of excitability.

JOHN DAULTON

There were no children in the crowd.

"Come on now, people," he said again, propping up a smile on his face. "Are you not curious about the dark arts of soul stealing, and the secrets of moving time?"

This perked a few of them up, but a woman in the front row, whose needle-thin body was a dark green mess of old tattoos, yawned and shook her head, whispering to a friend who looked just like her in the seat beside. They both laughed dry laughs that scratched along the backs of their throats like wooden benches being dragged across a flagstone floor.

"Well, how about you, then?" The Incredible Spectacularo pointed to a young man perhaps not too far beyond his teens. He had the same glassy-eyed look that the rest of the dregs in this part of the city had. It was the drugs they took. Things most of them made themselves in their rat-infested apartments, apartments that were little more than old shipping containers, whole neighborhoods of them, stacked like the boxes of some giant lady's shoes. "Come on, then," he said encouragingly. "Surely you're brave enough to travel just a bit of time. Come along, then. It's all good fun. You don't look like the type who is too easily afraid."

Two young men seated on either side of the youth laughed at him. One punched him in the arm while the other called him a pussy, and between the two, they got him to get up and approach the stage.

"Ah, there we go, my good friend," said The Incredible Spectacularo through a smile as greasy and uncared for as was the hair upon the young volunteer's head. "So what is your name, my friend? And, please tell us what you do." It was difficult to keep the smile going in the bright lights. He had to force his lips to shape it, gritting his teeth and driving his cheeks up with conscious and ongoing effort. All of it made the outer corners of his eyes ache.

"Reggie," said the youth. "And I'm a 'lectrician's assistant. Lookin' for work."

172

"Ahh," cooed The Incredible Spectacularo, "what a noble trade." Of course he was looking for work. They all were. The magician had no idea what the career so described was, his command of the language still not spectacular, but he had no interest in finding out anyway. He only knew that in these first five seconds with Reggie the volunteer, he was already developing an incredible hatred for the lad.

"And so, my dear Reggie," he went on anyway, "have you ever traveled through time before?"

"Like, *duh*, dude. What do you think?"

Well, there it was. Finally a laugh from the crowd. For Reggie, of course.

The Incredible Spectacularo summoned all his will and pushed the smile even closer to his ears. He let go several notes of a laugh, "Hah, hah," adding, "What a great wit you are, Reggie." The smile died entirely for a moment as he whirled around for effect, grabbing the edge of his tatty black silk cloak by its even tattier red silk lining and giving it a flourish as he spun. "But now, friend Reggie, it is time for your first trip. Come up here, please."

As Reggie climbed the three stairs leading up to the stage, The Incredible Spectacularo went to a small plastic table near the back curtain, carefully avoiding the cracked board it straddled—Slick Danny was going to get that fixed soon, or so he'd said. He picked up a large round clock lying on the table, a flat one of the sort these people often hung on their walls. With a cursory sideways glance to another clock offstage to see what time it was, he spun back around with yet another elaborate flourish, so violently, so sped by the growing hatred of having to endure this indignity, he nearly lost his fuzzy black top hat.

He reached for it, catching it with both hands, including the one holding the clock, and both hat and clock twisted awkwardly and nearly fell. The audience laughed again. He fought back the derision that would have made a hate mask of his face. Or perhaps "a hate window" would be more accurate.

He got the hat and clock in order again, then handed the clock to his volunteer with a saccharine smile. "Good, brave Reggie, I have here a clock for you. Please show it to the audience so they can all see what time it is."

Reggie halfheartedly lifted up the clock, holding it in both hands, arms out and moving ever so slightly side to side.

"So, my friends in the audience, as you may recall, our dear volunteer was seated right over there." He pointed to Reggie's empty seat. "Raise your hands, friends of Reggie, please."

Reggie's two friends raised their hands and let out a series of uncultured *whoops*.

"Please take note, everyone, of where Reggie was," said The Incredible Spectacularo. He gave the audience time to do so. "And now, without further delay, observe as I take us all back in time, back to only a few minutes ago. Keep your eyes on our friend Reggie here, and try not to blink."

Offstage, Slick Danny flipped the switch that played a drumroll, the sound crackling ominously from the speakers mounted on either side of the stage lights.

The Incredible Spectacularo closed his eyes and began to chant a litany of words. "Oh great spirits of the underworld," he intoned, "oh to the servants of devils long gone and those yet risen. Reach out and open the portals of all time to us that we may send Reggie through."

He risked a peek out through barely open eyelids and saw that, at least for a moment, the dullards out there were all watching at least semi-anxiously.

"Friend Reggie," The Incredible Spectacularo asked, "are you ready to travel back in time to the moments before you came up onstage?"

Reggie laughed. "Yeah, dude. Whatever. Just hurry up; I

have to piss."

More laughter from the crowd.

"Are you sure you are ready for this, the greatest if briefest adventure in your life?"

"Bring it."

"Watch the seats behind you, my friends," he told the audience, "for what you are about to see will astound you and change you forever."

The magician then began the chant for real. He spoke the words easily, having spoken them hundreds, perhaps thousands of times before. He wove first a careful illusion upon the clock in Reggie's hands, all but casting it complete, and then he made the teleport, wrapping the ready and willing Reggie in an envelope of mana and sending him right back to his seat. In the instant after he sent the youth on his way, he finished the illusion on the clock, making it appear to read three minutes earlier. "There!" he proclaimed, pointing to the back of the theater where Reggie had just appeared. As an added bit of finesse, he quickly cast a second illusion, this one on Reggie himself, adding for all who had just turned to observe—all but Reggie and his two friends—the illusion of the one fellow punching Reggie in the arm just as he had done before Reggie got up.

The audience gasped all at once, the lot of them caught entirely off guard. Even the two bedraggled women with the melting tattoos could not yawn that away.

Reggie sat wide-eyed in his chair, and it was a matter of several long seconds before his friend, the same who had struck him earlier, took the clock out of his hands. He saw the time had gone backward indeed. He held it up for the rest of the room to see. "It's true; it's true!" he declared. "He really has gone back. We all have."

For a time there was general amazement in the room, but then the skinny tattooed woman turned back around and sent a frown up at the magician on the stage.

"If he gone back in time, then how come my phone still say he ain't?"

Others immediately set to checking their own devices of chronology and, as usual, the magician on the stage watched as the trick ran its inevitable course: the gap-toothed gears in the brains of the inebriated eventually turning out the consensus of disbelief. Skepticism spread through the onlookers one by one, and despite what they had seen, the doubt was soon palpable for them all.

"Alas, there are tricks to time travel," The Incredible Spectacularo said as he always did at this point. "No road runs evenly through time or eternity."

"Bullshit," called one particularly burly drunk seated near the back. "Faker. It's all bullshit." He threw a half-full bottle of beer at The Incredible Spectacularo, which the magician was just able to avoid.

"Now, now," said the magician, his hands out before him, trying to avoid another missile aimed his way. "Let's not be barbarians."

Two more bottles flew his way, and not long after, Slick Danny came running onstage and threatened to throw everybody out. Half the scant crowd seemed more than happy to have it so, but the other half, the belligerent half, began shouting that they had paid for "real magic."

In the moments while Slick Danny argued with them, and for certain assured them that there would be no refunds, the caped magician behind him silently uttered another spell. Soon after, the right side of the theater burst into flames, great orange tongues of fire licking up toward the ceiling, the roar of timbers popping loudly in perfect evidence.

The crowd all screamed in unison, and soon there was a stampede for the doors. The upside of there being so few patrons was that they all managed to get out unscathed. All but poor Reggie, who still sat staring at his hands where the clock had been.

"That was stupid," Slick Danny said, turning angrily on his stage performer. "And mean. What the hell is wrong with you?"

"They were growing rabid, as you saw."

"That's it, man. This is your last chance. You blow out another audience like that, I'm turning you in. I'll go state's evidence or something. Or I'll call that guy from that lab that was asking about you. I don't give a shit what you say you'll do. You were supposed to make me money, man. You're just killing me now."

"Threaten me again," the magician said, all the frustration, fatigue, and fear of six months in hiding surfacing in an instant. "Do it and see how it plays out this time."

Slick Danny looked like he was going to say something else, but he pulled it back. He took a visible breath, and then looked at the flames burning against the wall. He placed his hands on his hips impatiently. With a motion of the magician's hand, the illusionary flames were gone and the theater was just as it had always been, run down and filthy, but otherwise none the worse for wear. Slick Danny breathed heavily again, then nodded in the direction of Reggie still sitting there. "Now go tell him your bullshit story before he walks out of here a believer."

The magician's sigh was nearly the measure of Slick Danny's own. This really was no life for a Prosperion. No life at all.

Chapter 19

A quick check of the upper floors of Calico Castle's tall central tower revealed that Orli was nowhere to be found, so Altin made his way down into the courtyard to check the gardens. She wasn't there either, so he went to speak to Master Sambua, who was overseeing a crew of masons.

"Greetings," Altin called to the stocky fellow. The dull shine of the stainless steel plates on the east tower, his tower, made him squint as he approached. He was pleased to see that at least in some places they were getting the outer walls up. "I see you've made great headway these last four weeks. It truly is a wonder to behold. And the tower looks very sturdy with all that iron framework there."

"Oh, it'll be sturdy," the engineer said. "And we've still got a few tricks up our sleeves."

"What are all those gray lines snaking all about?" Altin asked, taking a step nearer and noticing more and more of them the longer he looked.

"That's conduit. We're running power in it for you," he said. "Electricity. We'll set you up an old-fashioned diesel generator in the basement, something your people can even make fuel for if you need to here on Prosperion once we show you how. It's pretty primitive technology, but it's reliable and won't let you down after a teleport like a fusion genny might—at least from what I've heard. With that, some batteries, and some solar panels, you'll be powered well enough for what you'll need. If nothing else, well, Orli will have enough juice to do her hair." He laughed, a great conspiratorial thing, but Altin missed the joke. "We're putting in hookups for the grid," he said, pressing on. "That way, when you come to Earth or hit some of the off-world bases, you'll be set no matter where you go. This here tower will be the only thing like itself anywhere in the galaxy. Magic castle when you want it, technological outpost when you need. Honestly, I'm a little jealous."

Altin laughed and watched with wonder as workmen were pulling the long ropes of gray tubing through the lattice of rough iron the men had put in place. "Yes, I expect that it is rather unique. I am very pleased. So do you think it will be another two months?"

"Well, that depends on whether you allow Mistress Kettle's new request."

Altin's brows drooped, and he cast a backward glance at the entry to the kitchens behind him. "New request?"

"Yes. She says the steel plates are too shiny and the glare in the afternoons is 'frightful,' to use her word. She says those two plates we put on there yesterday were throwing a sunbeam into the garden and burning through Orli's melon patch."

Altin looked back to the gardens from which he'd just come, then to the tower, which again made him squint. "It looks as if Kettle has a point."

"Yeah, she does. She says it's going to heat up the whole courtyard like that."

"So what was her suggestion?"

"She says she wants us to face the whole thing with stone to match the rest."

Altin laughed. That was hardly in the spirit of Calico Castle. "Perhaps if you just painted it black."

Master Sambua grinned. "That's what I said. But she says it will still be too hot in the summertime. And she says she's got enough in the kitchen that she doesn't want to come out here and look at a giant metal pot."

Altin hummed, then suggested, "Well, perhaps a ring wall, just halfway round to butt up against the battlements. That will get you two stories of stone. It doesn't have to be too thick, if you don't think the basement structure will hold properly after a teleport."

"Oh, the basement will hold. You could put a lot more than a tower-sized pile of stone on it and it will hold. I think that's a fine idea. It's going to look pretty strange sitting anywhere else but here, but I'll get some plans drawn up and we can go over them."

"Right. Thank you." He turned to go find Kettle, but stopped and asked, having nearly forgotten why he'd approached the man, "Have you seen Orli recently?"

"Not in the last hour or so."

He thanked him and went into the kitchens, where, as usual, Kettle was hard at work. These days, with Pernie gone, and Tytamon gone, and with a much larger group of mouths to feed given the growth of the keep's staff in recent times, the stout woman made a point of keeping herself heaped with things to do.

"Kettle," Altin called to her, "there you are. Have you seen Orli?"

"She's gone off ta see her father at the Earth fort near Crown," Kettle said, straightening herself from her work stirring a giant cauldron filled with stew. "Left near half an hour ago."

"Who took her, Gimmel?"

"She went herself."

"On horseback? She'll be days getting there that way."

Kettle's florid cheeks rounded and rose as she smiled. "Ya don't give her much credit askin' that," she said. "The girl learns quicker than that."

Altin wrinkled up his face. "Then how?"

"She done gone up and sent a homing lizard to the TGS from that clean room up in the tower. She gone straight to Crown, and meant to make the rest a' the way afoot."

Altin's dread instinct kicked him in the chest. A reflex. He panicked sometimes from merely thinking that Orli would go off alone. But she did go off alone, and frequently, at least when she could. She was much like little Pernie in that way. Turn your back on her for a moment and she'd be gone, out along the creek or wandering into Great Forest nearby, happily following whatever path curiosity tempted her to.

But Crown City was another thing. Most of the city was perfectly delightful, but there were darker neighborhoods too, and with the devastation of the war, there were still plenty of desperate people around, people who had fallen through the cracks of Her Majesty's bureaucratic aid programs, or who disdained it on principle. Orli had been taken from him once by such people and in such a neighborhood, though in Leekant, and he'd almost lost her for good.

Kettle saw what he was thinking, and it was her turn to furrow up her brow. "Now don't ya go and start frettin' her every last breath," she scolded. "I can see it in yer face. She's a fine strong lass and can fend fer herself as well as anyone. You'll smother her goin' on at her like all that worryin' in yer eyes."

"Says the woman who frets for Pernie every moment of every day."

"Well, that's a wee tiny child," Kettle said, putting her hands on her stout hips. "And there's a whole heap a' difference tween the two."

Altin laughed. No, there wasn't. He'd seen little Pernie in a fight. That child was as helpless as a prairie wolf. And like as not, after two months with the elves, being trained in the art of butchering humans, no doubt, he expected she was even less helpless now than when she left. But he didn't want to argue, so he nodded instead. "As you say."

He left the kitchen and stepped out into the hall, where he cast a quick seeing spell into the TGS office in Crown City. Of course Orli wouldn't be there.

He thought about pushing his vision through the streets and out into the fields beyond the city walls, but thought better of it. If she went on her own, she likely wanted to be on her own, so he decided the easiest thing to do was simply meet her there.

With another quick seeing spell to make sure he was clear, he teleported himself just outside the gates of Little Earth. He greeted the two guards with familiarity, went inside, and headed straight for General Pewter's office, intent on finding out if Roberto and his crew had gotten the *Glistening Lady* restarted yet back near Earth. It had been a few hours since he'd teleported them there. He was anxious to know how long it was going to take Professor Bryant to find the right machinery.

The general's pinch-faced secretary greeted him as familiarly as had the gate guards, and he was admitted right in to see the general. Orli was already sitting there.

"What?" Altin exclaimed. "How did you get here so fast?"

"I ran," she said. "I felt up for a run today. It's been a long time since I really got out at all. A little three-mile jaunt was nice, but honestly I wish they'd built this thing a little farther out. I did like running through the city, though. The rebuilding is coming along well, at least in the mile-long stretch I saw. The Temple of Anvilwrath looks like it's nearly finished now. That's amazing, such a huge building and in such a short period of time."

"The Church is never short on money. Fear and desperation make the salvation business extremely profitable, especially when you never have to deliver the goods."

"You're such a cynic. Those people helped save everyone's lives."

"As did many others, and it wasn't with the people's money."

"I've got work to do if you two are going to debate the morality of monetized theology," said the general, but he was smiling at his daughter, contented to have her there.

Altin shrugged. The fact that many of the people of Crown still struggled to rebuild their neighborhoods while the temples and city buildings went up with speed bothered him more than a spell song with a missing note, but he let it go. "Well, I'm glad I found you here," he said instead, moving to sit next to her. "I wanted to tell you what Blue Fire said."

"I was afraid of what she was going to say. That's why I needed to go for a run."

He nodded, knowing well what she meant. "Well, the good news is that she has agreed to have us do it. You might even say she holds the smallest bit of optimism that it might work. Very small, but I saw it, if briefly."

Orli perked up at that, but she saw the way Altin's expression flattened after. "But what?"

He hadn't said "but," but it was in his eyes. "Well," he began, and then started fidgeting with his sleeve. Everyone in the room was waiting impatiently, so eventually, after twitching the material back and forth a few times between his forefinger and his thumb, he finished it. "She said she'll let us do it so long as I promise that"—he paused again and swallowed—"if something happens, and Yellow Fire really does die, I will do the same to her. Cut out her heart in the same way, so that she will finally die too. She wants to be with him in death if it doesn't work out in life."

"Makes sense," the general said to that. But Orli leapt out of her chair and spun on Altin, glaring at him as if he'd already done the deed.

"You will promise no such thing! So you can go right back there and tell her that. That's not going to happen. You wouldn't dare."

"I already did. It was the only way she'd let us try."

"Altin Meade!" Orli gasped. She looked to her father for support, but there was none coming. Her mouth dropped open, but she was stunned to silence.

The general looked uncomfortable, but he was not one to lie. "She's been living in eternity without him; at least that's the way I hear you both talk about her. I have to tell you, having lost a wife myself, I can see wanting to die." His expression was one of absolute sobriety. "If it hadn't been for you, Orli girl, I would have happily lain down and died after your mother passed. Nothing ever hurt me like that did." He stared at nothing for a moment, then blinked back to them. He looked to his daughter, and the corner of his mouth twitched. "I will say, when I thought I'd lost you to the NTA death machine, it was looking like misery was going to raise the bar."

Orli's lips rolled in and her eyes narrowed, her posture like the hammer on a gun that's just been cocked, but she stopped, looking into his eyes, seeing the pain reflecting in his memory, remembering her own—not for her near fiasco, but for her mother. Orli had been old enough to know well what her mother's death had done to her father.

Slowly at first, but then all the rest at once, tension left her. She turned back to Altin with only one eye narrowed this time. "Fine," she said. "But you didn't promise you'd do it right away, did you? Like, you didn't specify a time?"

He smiled, a wan thing, then laughed a little. "No," he admitted. "I did not." He might have pressed on, explaining that the essence of his intent had been clear to both Blue Fire and himself, the implied understanding clear enough via the exchange of their thoughts, but why bother. Orli was technically correct, and that was enough to get him through the difficulty of the moment now. "But let's hope it doesn't come to that. Which is, actually, why I am here. I was hoping to see if Roberto has his ship powered up after the teleport shut everything down, and if so, to find out whether the professor perhaps has a line on our equipment yet."

Orli turned to her father and, looking as if some marginally foul odor had just blown into the room, made a face as she asked him to bring up the *Glistening Lady* on his com.

The general laughed at the way she sneered the name; so did Altin, and soon Roberto's face was up on the wall monitor. His first words were directed straight at Altin. "Listen, man, I know it's all magic awesome with you and the teleporting thing, but you really need to do something about turning out all the lights. Granted, my ship is a lot smaller than the *Aspect* was, but five hours floating helpless is still a royal pain in the ass."

"Patience, Captain," Altin said. "The TGS can only build so many platforms at a time. The secret of the engasta syrup, from which the platform tiles are made, is a well-guarded one, and the process for making it expensive and time consuming. There are only so many people who can do it at all. But, in time, there will be TGS depots everywhere."

"Yes, *Captain*," Orli added to that, pronouncing his title in a way that made it sound mildly insulting, "so until then, be thankful you are friends with people who can toss you about the galaxy as you please. Everyone else is still sitting on their hands, and ninety-nine percent of them still will be for years."

Roberto laughed. "True," he said. "But it just wouldn't be me if I didn't bitch."

She laughed. "Also true."

"So how about that water saw Doctor Bryant spoke of?" Altin asked.

"Oh, yeah, no worries. He was on that the second the power came back up. I guess the parts he needs to make one aren't that rare as long as you got the cash. He's working out the details with the vendors now. It's going to set you back big time, dude, like, we're talking bank."

Altin frowned a little, and absently fingered the amulet he wore, which was enchanted with the translation spell called Greater Common Tongues. Even with that powerful magic in place, sometimes things Earth people said only barely made sense. "I think I got the gist of that," he replied.

Orli clarified for him in his own language, she being the first person from planet Earth to have learned the common tongue spoken by most in the kingdom. "The bottom line is it's going to be expensive."

"Whatever it takes," Altin said. "Gold is not a problem."

"It may take more than you think," Roberto said. "We're talking about a really big machine and people to run it. Plus a crew to dig it all out down there and set it in place."

Altin laughed. "My friend, you forget who you are speaking to. My mentor, Tytamon, was two years shy of his eight hundredth birthday when he died. And in all those years, and all those adventures, and with all those favors and remarkable deeds he performed for lords and ladies along the way, the man amassed wealth you can't even imagine in that time. And more than amassing it, he hardly ever spent so much as a copper piece. Why, Kettle herself spends more money in a year than that man ever did."

"Good," Roberto said. "Because you're going to need it."

Altin shrugged, and smiled at Orli. "I think Tytamon would be happy to have some or even all of his fortune spent on such a noble cause."

Orli beamed and leaned into him, hugging his arm. "I

think he would too." She stared vacantly at the edge of her father's desk for a time, then added, "I miss him," with a sigh.

Altin tipped his cheek down and rested it upon her soft blonde hair, his sigh a mournful echo of hers. "As do I."

Chapter 20

The net was strung between two cliffs, stretched over a wide split that cut a five-hundred-span wedge into the island. Beneath the net, far beneath, tormented waves rushed in and out of the angularity, churning and seething. They crashed against giant rocks that had lain there since the island broke long ago, and the foaming water reached up like hands, snatching at the two figures that danced and darted back and forth across the net. But Pernie's feet were in no danger of getting wet, not from the sea-green fingers anyway. Nor were Seawind's as the two of them lunged and leapt around the wide mesh of ropes, as sure-footed as two two-legged spiders locked in mortal combat.

And it was mortal combat for Seawind, for Pernie's spear thrust forth with the speed of a toad's tongue, the sharp point aimed for the small concavity of his throat. He turned it aside easily enough, of course; the barest movement and the shaft of his own spear clacked against hers as he knocked the thrust away. With a deft movement of the bottom of his spear, he blocked the cut of her knife too, a speedy, hooking slice with which she meant to cut the tendon at the back of his knee.

She reached too far for the cut and exposed the side of

her neck, which he struck with the edge of his flattened hand, just hard enough to dim her vision for a moment and send her falling into the ropes. She tangled up in them for a moment, then fell through a wide gap, but she caught herself with her spear, flattening it horizontally just in time.

Seawind stared down at her dangling there above the churning sea far below. "You gave me your head," he said.

"I know what I did," she spat back. She threw her dagger at him as she said it, and he just leaned away as it flicked past his face. In the time it took him to do it, she'd swung back up through another opening in the net and landed neatly, straddling the gap. She held her spear at the ready again.

"You've only just earned the right to have that blade, and already you throw it away," he said.

Pernie circled him and feinted a thrust for his face. She feinted another for his groin before muttering the two-word command Djoveeve had taught her, the words for a short teleport, which brought her right behind him in the barest breath of time. She plunged the point of her spear straight for where she had learned his kidneys would be if he were human.

Seawind spun in that instant, and again came the *clack* of his spear shaft against hers. The wooden sound echoed back and forth between the cliff faces, audible even against the thunder of the surf below.

"You would kill me if you could, wouldn't you, little Sava?"

Pernie thrust for his face and then cast the teleport again. She feinted for his back, and cast the teleport yet again, this time appearing to his left and trying to sweep his legs with the butt of her spear, intent on sending him crashing into the rocky, roiling waves.

It didn't work. He hopped over the sweep so easily, so quickly and lightly, that it didn't even flex the ropes.

Seawind smiled as she came at him in a flurry of blows, her small feet dancing along the ropes and over the gaps with surety. Her thrusts and cuts, long sweeps of the spear butt toward his ankles and knees, all came in a frenzy of accuracy, and for a pair of steps, even he only just managed to dance away. The smile grew.

"Do you hate me so much, little Sava," he asked as he sidestepped another thrust, "that you would have me dead? There is more that I can teach you still." He jumped over the low, flat arc of her spear tip, which was once again seeking to knock him down. He landed catlike on the ropes as she teleported herself behind him again and thrust for his elven guts.

He spun and blocked it yet again, and danced away, and repeated his question twice more before she finally saw reason to reply.

"You said I could go home if I mastered the spear."

"But you haven't."

She made two quick stabs for his belly and teleported behind him, then back again, where she tried to split his head open with a jab toward his open mouth as he began to speak. That thrust he had to teleport away from.

"I have," she insisted, dashing along the ropes at him so quickly she was like a little monkey on a branch. She stabbed at his feet, rolling out from under a sweep of his own spear tip, and blocked two more he sent right after. He blocked her backhanded swing with his forearm, a cut that would have slashed him open along the ribs. The *clack* of her spear against his arm was nearly as wooden as if he'd blocked with his weapon. He teleported behind her and kicked her feet out from under her again, once more sending her tumbling through the ropes.

She didn't get her spear flattened out in time, and she fell right through, headed for the rocks, her spear held uselessly in her hand.

She vanished ten spans into the fall, then reappeared, right behind him, a little off balance, but with a jab of her spear meant for the back of his knee. He jammed his spear butt down into the heavy rope, violently, the angle just right to deflect her stabbing attempt and the strength of it enough to send a shock wave up the rope, which dislodged her once again.

She hooked a knee over the rope, and caught herself with her left arm. His first thrust toward her she was able to tap aside with her own weapon, but the second one scored, a blunt thrust with the butt end that caught her right between the eyes.

When she woke up she was resting against the rock face where the edge of the net was anchored to the southern cliff. Seawind squatted beside her in the way the elves did, seemingly averse to sitting most of the time.

"You're growing very strong, little Sava," Seawind said as he looked out across the ocean. "Barely a half year and already you are very dangerous."

Pernie, remembering what had transpired, chose to pout rather than respond. She was never going to beat him. He was too fast. And his magic came without words. All the elves did it that way; that's what Djoveeve had said. Two words was the best she'd ever do. Her "animal magic," Djoveeve called it. The thing that made her special because she clung to it so hard. That's what Djoveeve said. But it wasn't special.

Pernie knew it wasn't, because she knew that she was weak. Djoveeve had already told her how much power she had, her rank in her three magic schools. The old woman told her that her strongest power was growth magic, the stupid Healing sphere. She didn't want to be a healer. But that was her best one. And she was only G class in that. *G* class. That was nothing. She could only be a nurse, or some bumpkin village healer. As if she would ever want to.

Her teleporting magic was even worse, a whole grade weaker. She'd never be like Master Altin was. Never jump into the stars. The more she practiced with her magic, the more she knew her magic was stupid and lame. She wanted to be a great sorcerer, and Djoveeve said she never would be.

Part of her thought Djoveeve was a liar. Just like Fortie Nomstacker had been a liar back at the wizard's school. Making up stuff just to make her mad. Djoveeve liked to make her mad. She did it all the time. Sometimes she was nice, but sometimes she was mean.

And for the last of her magic, the illusion part, well, Pernie didn't see the use. She couldn't even turn invisible like the elves all could. All of them. Her illusion shimmered like a heat wave when she tried. She was weak and her magic was lame and all her dreams were stupid and would never come true. And Seawind would just keep hitting her between the eyes.

She rubbed her head where the butt of his spear had struck her. The thump resounded still in memory, even if the lump was gone. Seawind had, as always, healed the damage that he had done.

"I am not your enemy, little Sava," Seawind said after a time.

"I know," she said. She scooted forward and put her legs over the edge of the cliff, reaching her hands out to feel the cold, damp air blowing up the sheer stone face.

"But you would kill me if you could. You still haven't told me why."

"You won't take me home," she said without the least delay. There was no point in hiding it. She was actually surprised that he didn't already know.

"But who will take you home if I die? Djoveeve hasn't got the magic for it."

"I will find a way," she said. "That's what you told me the

day I first ran with the hunt. That's what you said. So I will."

"If you can get yourself home, then I am not keeping you here. So I ask again, why kill me? Is that not a waste? You learn from me, do you not?"

Pernie let her lips wriggle on that for a time, then nodded. "I do."

"Then there is no value in killing me. There is nothing to be gained."

More wriggling took place beneath her little, slightly upturned nose, as the wind blew the long strands of her dirty blonde hair across her face. She thought he might be right about that. But if she went home, she wouldn't need him anymore.

Except that she also knew she'd never be Master Altin's apprentice either. Never get to spend that kind of time with him now. Not with weakling magic like she had.

"Do you know the difference between dealing death and murder?" he asked. "Has Djoveeve spoken to you of this?"

Pernie shook her head, staring out beyond the waves, ready to tune out another lecture as she defaulted to her favorite pastime these last few months: looking for the right creature to ride right out of here. Right off of the stupid Island of Hunters and all the way gone from the stupid elven lands of String.

"It is the job of the Sava'an'Lansom to know when it is time to kill. When you are ready, you will be able to do it easily. You will become the master of death. And you must deal it out justly."

Pernie yawned on purpose so that he would know that she was bored. She didn't even know what *justly* was. Maybe it meant evenly. Or maybe it meant quick. Gimmel, the groundskeeper at Calico Castle, always told her to be neat about killing things. When he took her out to hunt, he was always very respectful about that. He said, "You can't make them suffer or the Goddess gets mad." Which just went to prove these elves weren't so smart as everybody thought they were. Gimmel already taught her that when she was only a little girl. Now she was almost ten. Kettle told her she'd be a big girl when she finally had two numbers in her age. And now she did, or almost did. Only a few more days. And it was true. Here she was, with an elf telling her things she already knew.

And it was Orli Pewter's fault.

Everything was. If it hadn't been for her, Pernie would never be here. She'd still be at home with Kettle and Gimmel and Nipper and all the rest. She would see Master Altin every day. And so what if she was too weak to be his apprentice? So what about all that? She could protect him with her spear now anyway. And if the orcs came again, she'd carve out all their hearts and give them to Kettle to make into a stew. Master Altin would love her then. Or at least when she was a little older anyway. When her bosom grew. Then he would. Pernie knew.

But first she'd have to put a spear right through Orli Pewter's heart. See what good *her* bosom did her then.

She thought about that for some time, imagining it, imagining jamming it straight through Orli's chest. She knew now how hard the cartilage was, the strength of the breastbone. Djoveeve had shown her. Made her practice thrusting hard enough to pierce a mannequin made of boiled leather and tree bark, merged together with transmutation spells and made as solid as any man. Djoveeve said it was just as hard as a warrior in leather armor, and Pernie practiced killing it with glee over these last eighteen weeks, ever since she'd gotten the spear. Every time, she imagined the look on Orli Pewter's face, just like it had been when she'd nearly shot Orli on her wedding day. The wedding Orli never got. That made Pernie smile. At least she'd prevented that. Or she sort of had. She hoped she had. She had no way to know.

She might not have scored a killing shot, but there was still reason to believe the wedding had not gone off: Kettle had told her that being the flower girl was the most important part of the wedding. She'd said it the day she and that fussy man, Master Needlesprig, had been trying to force Pernie to try on a big fluffy dress. At first Pernie thought Kettle had only said that to trick her into trying on the dress, but now that she thought about it, it was probably true. Master Needlesprig had agreed, and he worked directly for the Queen, so he couldn't lie. So, if it was true, then they had to wait. But how long? Orli Pewter would be in a big fat hurry and want to find another flower girl. Pernie wasn't sure if that was legal or not, but she just knew in her heart that Orli Pewter would try. Which was why Pernie had to get back and finish what she'd started before it was too late.

Master Altin would be mad at her when she did it, though. He'd never marry her after that. So she'd have to make it look like an accident. Which she wasn't quite sure how to do. Which meant she probably should be listening to what Seawind was saying as he squatted there on the ledge. She would listen, but only for a little while.

Chapter 21

Black Sander squeezed into the tiny clean room at the TGS depot in Murdoc Bay, stuffed in with eleven other miners—or at least, with eleven others who were miners. Black Sander was simply dressed as one, magically dressed, of course, draped in the exquisite detail that W-class illusionists are capable of. His lean body and long nose were made squat and broad, his black eyes were brown, his slender fingers, so deft at locks and delicate thievery, made thick as fat sausages. He cast into his illusion the smell of whiskey and rum and set it to emanate outward for nearly a full pace, and he added to that just the right hint of stale sweat and other bodily odors that could be expected from the sort of man who hasn't bathed in a month.

As he stood among the working men in the small teleportation room, he took a careful whiff around him, checking to see if he'd gotten the scent just right. He thought perhaps he was no worse than most and marginally better than a few.

He looked around at his compatriots, all men, all weathered and sturdy-looking folk. A few peered out of bleary, red-rimmed eyes, and the vapors of their liquor-laden breath carried much farther than his illusion did. He smiled inwardly to himself and knew that he would blend in perfectly.

He fingered a topaz in his pocket that was as large as an avocado pit as he watched the TGS teleporter close the door. A small window, a cabinet-like opening cut clear through the wall, held a pair of small shelves upon which sat two blocks of carved wood and a pair of hourglasses. He waited patiently, nodding a bit too late and forcing a smile at some crude joke he hadn't heard, as the attendant outside swapped out the block of wood with the sailing ship signet of Murdoc Bay for a newly emblazoned block, which depicted a great round planet surrounded by seven orbiting moons. It was the signet for Tinpoa Base depot, serving the mines and the spaceport the Earth men were putting up on the moon as it orbited the green gas giant, Naotatica. The attendant then turned over one of the hourglasses, one that corresponded to the new block and had the planet and seven moons etched into its base. Soon after, the little cabinet door outside the teleportation chamber snapped shut, at which point a few of the miners began shifting nervously.

"Hope we don't show up dead," one of them said. His smile lacked the conviction suggested by the cavalier nature of his words. His eyes gave it away.

"That ain't funny, Hoke," said one of the others. "Don't joke around."

"You boys oughta consider sproutin' a pair," said another. "My wee girl don't even get fearful teleportin' nowhere."

"Yer wee girl is only six years old. She don't know what's happenin' ta her in here."

"All of ya shut yer traps," said another, this one with something like authority. "We're likely already there."

Sure enough, the little cabinet door opened immediately after he spoke, and the white glare of the Earth people's artificial light poured in through the opening.

The door opened right after, and soon the lot of them

were shuffling out into a square room made of an all-white material like nothing found on Prosperion. Small, narrow windows looked out into the black night beyond, and through the farthest left of these could be seen the partial green curve of the giant planet Naotatica, believed by many to be the origin of the elves.

Black Sander had heard that Sir Altin Meade had disproved that, but he hadn't enough friends who knew the Galactic Mage personally to verify it, and he was not typically one to spend time with priests. Still, he took a moment to move to the window while the other miners were clogging the entrance to the long hallway. The corridor would take them to the checkpoint where they could be recorded in the Earth people's log. He stared out, looking up into the bright green mass of the giant world, a great swirling ball of varying tones, mainly a bright lime green, but tiered and stratified with darker shades, all swirling around it, whirling in some places into spots, the whole of it like a bucket of green-hued paints that's only been stirred once or twice and hasn't yet mixed properly.

This was his first time up here, though he had seen it in the scrying bowl spell of the marchioness' seer, Kalafrand. He knew the layout of the base well enough, but the sight of the planet in person was enough to give even Black Sander pause.

He glanced back into the bright light of the room, and saw that the TGS teleporter was busy setting the hourglass for the next load, a group of three Earth people who, by the signet the woman had on the table near her, would be going to Crown City. No one was paying any attention to him.

While the Earth people crowded into the teleportation chamber and the Prosperion miners crowded down the hall, Black Sander quietly hid his incantation in their noise. A moment after, he vanished, his invisibility illusion cast. He dropped the illusion of his dirty miner self, and let go the stink he'd cast with it as well. He replaced that with absolute odorlessness.

When there was room to slip past the Earth people, he made his way down the hall, pausing briefly in the silence between them and the miners to add silence to his spell. It was an afterthought, and he could be silent with the careful placement of his practiced feet, but there was no point taking any risks. He muttered the spell under his breath. He had to do it quickly, for he knew, once he was past the range of the teleportation area, he could not add anything new to his spell. They were watching for magic here. On that point the marchioness had been very clear. The Earth people could see magic in the twitter of their electricity, and they would know. That was Lord Vorvington's latest discovery.

He came up behind the last of the miners in the line. They were waiting to be let into the main part of the moon-based mining camp.

"Name?" said the fleet soldier standing before a low desk made of the same white material as the walls. He wore a helmet with a single round bit of glass mounted on it, swung down over his right eye somewhat like a monocle. A second fleet soldier, a woman, sat at the desk and looked into what appeared to Black Sander to be a black picture frame from which radiated a pale blue glow. Black Sander could not see the images in it from where he stood, but he knew from the scrying spell Kalafrand had cast that she was checking to see if the man's name matched his face in her electricity-powered record-keeping device.

"Hoke Rockraker," the man said gruffly. "I been here often enough you people ought to recognize me."

"We know your face," said the woman at the glowing picture frame, "but we still have to make sure it fits your biometric profile."

"I know," he grumbled, but he held out his hand without being asked, and the soldier standing before the desk ran a long, slender object up and down his hand and forearm. When he'd finished the pass, he flipped it around and ordered the miner not to blink. There came a brief movement of green light, and then it was done. The soldier placed the butt end of the device onto a square black pad, and after a moment, the woman nodded and said, "Welcome back, Hoke. Be safe down there."

"Bet I will, missy," he said. "And don't hold up the boys too long in here."

"I'll try," she promised with a smile. The other soldier stepped aside and let the stocky miner pass through the narrow space between the desk and the wall.

Black Sander smiled behind the mask of his invisibility, the nervousness in his guts ramping up his energy. There were few things he loved more than breaking in. And breaking into the first interplanetary spaceport was shaping up to be one of the most entertaining clandestine entries he'd managed so far.

Assuming he managed it, of course.

Slowly the line made its way through, one by one, some of them joking casually with the woman, none of them with the man. But each in turn passed through the line without incident or fuss. Soon there were only three miners left before Black Sander would be able to pass. He was going to need the man with the helmet monocle and the detection wand to step aside, but he hoped that he would as soon as the visible miners passed.

The woman chatted with the next miner in line while the soldier passed his device over the fellow's arm and face. As they scanned the worker, Black Sander moved to the desk and chanced a glance over the top of the picture frame. To his horror, he could see himself peering over it.

The discovery jolted him, but his reflexes were those of a thief. In the time it took the woman to look from the soldier to the miner and back to her screen, Black Sander had, by the grace of Sobrei the Swift, patron deity of crime, managed to dart back into line behind the rest. It was an act of conscious effort to still his breathing, so unexpected had his surprise been. How could they see him?

Suddenly the bright lights in that white hallway seemed blinding. It was as if he stood naked beneath a bloated sun, the whole world watching him. He felt entirely exposed. He could not fathom how it was possible. His cast had been flawless. He'd been casting illusions since he was thirteen. His ability was W ranked. He did not make mistakes, and there were no holes in his illusions. Ever. Not once in all his life.

He looked down at his hands. Of course *he* could see them.

He backed away down the hall some, not so far as to be suspicious, but trying to get back as close as he could to the teleportation room, to the place where twitters in the electricity were expected and ignored by security.

He gently rechecked his spell, pushing his mind into the mana and carefully watching his weave. It was intact, a perfect core of sensory magic and a great radius of groping strings, all those threadlike ends reaching far and near, searching like twitching roots for minds to touch and to deceive. He could see them all, and there were many where the guards at the table were, many, many of those strands, each reaching into the minds of the others and painting the waking dream, coating their own ideas with his contrived reality. They should not see him without having reason to disbelieve. They could not. And yet there he'd been, in that woman's image machine, as plain as if he'd simply walked up to her with no magic at all. Something was terribly wrong. And now there was nothing he could do.

The last miner was being waved through.

The woman looked up at him and beckoned him. "Come on," she said. "You're next."

His mind spun, whirled, as he groped for what next to do.

"Don't be shy. It's just a formality. You're new, aren't you?" She glanced up at her fellow soldier, who nodded, not recognizing Black Sander either.

"Yes, I am," he said, quelling the urge to run back into the teleportation room. It was still an option, though. He could simply tell them he'd changed his mind. By treaty, the space between that checkpoint and the TGS depot behind him was still the territory of the Kingdom of Kurr.

"Well, don't worry. None of this stuff hurts. It's all safe. Our people have been using these for centuries."

Black Sander walked as casually as possible back up to the desk. The situation wasn't entirely alien to him, despite it being, well, entirely alien. This wasn't the first security check he'd had to lie his way through. But still, it was with some effort that he had to put down the shock of discovering his illusion had completely failed.

"What's your name?" she asked. It seemed as if she was making an extra effort to be nice. He let go a long, calming breath as he heard it. He would be fine here.

"I am Stamon Farplain," he said. "Jeweler to Lord Gideon Dovenstake of Dae."

She looked up, her eyes bright and curious. "Jeweler, eh? I didn't think you were dressed for digging down there. Did they find something valuable in that hole besides iron and titanium?"

With practiced stoicism, and equally practiced conviviality, he kept himself from frowning during the moment of his confusion. Then he laughed. "Oh, hah hah, don't we all wish, my dear? No, I'm afraid there's no such luck as that." He glanced up at the man standing there, as if about to share a great secret, then leaned down to the woman. In a low yet jovial voice, he said, "At least not as we know, but who's to say what these fellows are sneaking out in the bottoms of their boots, you see?"

She laughed and leaned back in her chair. "Oh, and we don't even screen for it. They could be making a killing off of us, couldn't they?"

Black Sander's grin was wide beneath his long, long nose, and he set upon her his most charming and innocuous look. "Yes, but the boys work hard, and if your great empire doesn't need all its small diamonds and rubies, and even its little moonstruck pittance of silver or gold, I imagine these lads could stand the extra pints of ale."

She laughed again, and even the stone-faced man beside Black Sander had twitches of humor touching the corners of his mouth. Black Sander felt his feet, and his confidence, settle a bit more firmly on the floor. They were all, in the end, so easy. Toss a bone to the working man, and there they were, appeased. So honest and well-meaning. So easy to deceive.

She was tapping her fingers on a bit of dark glass lying upon the table then, and she frowned for a moment before looking up at him. "How do you spell your name?" she asked. "I'm not finding it in here."

He spelled it out carefully for her.

She shook her head, clearly regretfully, as she tried entering the name again. She chewed briefly on the bottom of her lip before asking, "Did your people send a file to TGS central to be entered in? I'm just not finding you."

Feigning confusion was not difficult for him then. "Why, no. Not that I know of." He recovered quickly enough, and began in earnest to modify his plan. There was still a chance to salvage it. "Lord Dovenstake simply asked that I bring this gift to Captain Hawthorne of the *Lima*."

He pulled the huge topaz out of his pocket and showed it to her. She let go a long, low gasp. "Holy crap," she said. "It's as big as a plasma grenade."

"Well, I should think not quite so big as that," he said with a humble smile, though he had no idea what the object she spoke of was. "But still, My Lord hopes that Captain Hawthorne will accept this small gift in gratitude for all she and her crew have done for the working men of Kurr."

"Well, I can see why you don't care much if anyone's pulling a few little diamonds or rubies out of the mines," she joked as she looked up from the topaz and winked at him.

He muttered the words to an illusion just for her, a low-level charming spell that would paint him in her eyes in a subtly gossamer light, a divine radiance that was just beyond her ability to see. With it he layered in an equally subtle pheromone, the scent of centaur sweat carried on a waft of cocoa and tea. It was all very deft and minor, and all for her. It was all on a bet, and risky, he knew, for it might fail just as the first one had, especially if the lights flickered for having cast it. Which they did, at least those in her monitor did, but she wasn't watching it. She had eyes only for him.

"What's that?" she said, unable to make out the words as he cast his spell.

"It's a little song we sing in Dae, a sailor's prayer begging the Goddess to forgive us our greed."

She was all smiles then, like a little girl pleasing a favorite uncle on whom she's always had a secret crush. "Well, don't worry about that. We won't start checking in their boots. But let's see about getting you logged in. I can requisition paperwork from TGS in Dae and give you a temporary pass for today. Will that work? How long do you need to stay?"

He showed all his teeth as he smiled down at her. "Oh, you are such a sweet thing. Thank you, of course that will be fine. And I think an hour or two will be more than enough."

Chapter 22

Orli leaned over Doctor Singh's shoulder, watching as he worked. She had to bend low enough so as not to hit her head on the thick pipe jutting from the machine. In the absence of an atmosphere, she couldn't hear the roaring hiss of the water jet as it cut through the crystals near Yellow Fire's heart, but the clouds of mist that whirled around them spoke volumes for what she might have heard had he been doing the work elsewhere.

"Suction, damn it," the doctor said for the third time in less than a minute. "Rabin, what are you doing up there?" It wasn't really suction anyway. That was simply the surgeon's reflex. The baby-faced grad student was supposed to be blowing the mist away, angling an air jet at the end of the machine's long arm.

"I'm trying," came Rabin's reply. "There's a big difference between practice and reality."

"Well, get it right. I can't see."

Orli could see the air nozzle move, and more mist came blasting back out of the nearly microscopic incision he had made. It sprayed all over the doctor's facemask blindingly.

"Orli," the doctor said even as she was reaching out with a towel and wiping off his mask. He cut the order short and thanked her instead. They'd worked together long enough on the *Aspect* a few years past, when the first encounter with the Hostile orbs had brought devastating disease to the crew. It was strange how much of that chemistry came right back.

"Move it left, Rabin. Now I'm getting a double shadow from the spotlights."

The large, fine-toothed gears moved across the rack that supported the machine, a long strip of steel with a serrated upper edge running parallel to the wall. The whole rig sat atop a sequence of these tracks, each mounted atop a row of steel columns set ten feet deep in the ground, the ground, of course, being the bottom of the thirty-by-thirty-yard hole that they'd excavated in the bottom of Yellow Fire's cave.

Much of the machine was tank, a twenty-foot-long cylinder, domed at both ends, and wide enough that Orli could have walked the length of it inside without having to duck her head. But the essence of the machine was the enormous sequence of pumps, three of them, each linked to the previous by pipes that looked to Orli more like cable mesh than pipe. From one to the next, the pipe-cable got smaller, and the pumps got squatter, fatter, and thicker of casing. Together, they rammed the water and a few tiny particles of a coolant chemical through the jet that the doctor guided with a pair of specially fitted gloves. Every motion of his hand, every twitch of his fingers, sent signals to the machine. The barest movement of his eyes inside his helmet could move the heavy nozzle in increments too small for Orli to see.

"How's that?" Rabin asked from his place in the water saw's cab, a small, boxy compartment with a seat, three monitors, and the controls that operated the pumps and moved the body of the machine up and back along the tracks.

"A little more; I'm still getting a double edge on this." The steel frame vibrated for a moment after, followed by the doctor's grunt. "That's better. Leave it there." Once again the clouds of mist thrown off by the water jet resumed.

Orli watched breathlessly as the practiced hands of the skilled surgeon eroded away the barest layers of crystal around the velvet-purple pulse of Yellow Fire's heart. Her own heart pounded so loudly she could hear the blood coursing through her ears. She couldn't imagine having to be the one to do it, to actually carve out Yellow Fire's heart. What if she messed up? A cough? A little tremble of a muscle or a nerve?

What if Doctor Singh did?

It wasn't a matter of culpability; it was a matter of death and misery. And guilt. Lifelong guilt. This was all her idea. So much was riding on its success. So much more now, given Altin's promise to kill Blue Fire if it didn't work. Just thinking of that made her temper rise, even though she'd had several months to come to terms with it. She just couldn't. What had he been thinking? So she watched and she fretted. There was so much more at stake. Two lives now. Doctor Singh had nearly refused because of it and, well, because Altin had been with her when she asked.

"So killing comes easily to you now, does it, *Sir* Altin Meade?" That's what the doctor had spat at Altin when he and Orli explained what they wanted, and what was at stake. The way he spoke Altin's title dripped with irony. "Well, I won't do it. I took an oath to do no harm, and your gross willingness to kill anything that inconveniences your road to glory has rendered my help impossible."

Altin had tried to argue, of course. And Orli had as well. "Why impossible?" she'd asked, once the two men had finished their own emotional exchange.

"If I lose a patient trying to save them in earnest, and they have understood the risk, that is one thing. A weighing of risk and reward. That is what you have done, Orli, in asking Blue Fire to approve this procedure you want done. A reasonable conclusion to try the surgery. What harm if he has already been dead, or nearly dead, so long? Only Blue Fire knows how that all plays out long term. So that risk I call acceptable. No harm done. But now this, what you ask, what your ... fiancée asks, is another thing entirely. Now I do harm by simply trying. The attempt is not about risking a patient already all but dead. The attempt is risking another being entirely. The probability for doing harm is now extremely high. Far higher than the chances for success. And all for a death promise from the Galactic Mage. Galactic Assassin, I say." He'd turned such a bitter look upon Altin then, such absolute contempt, and said to his face, "You are in good company with that elf."

Orli had had to stop Altin's response with her fingers placed softly on his mouth, pleading with her eyes that these two men whom she loved so very much would not grow to hate one another any more than the doctor already did the mage. "Please," she whispered, and Altin had relented.

It had been the work of eleven days and countless conversations that had finally gotten Doctor Singh to do the surgery. A lot of begging and a lot of tears. But at last he had relented, perhaps knowing in his heart that it really was the only hope of happiness for Blue Fire. And with Orli's secret promise not to let Altin keep his word.

And so now the doctor worked with a strange tool, not so different than a laser scalpel in its way, but much messier and much more difficult to use. There were no cutting templates for a living planetary heart, and the odd properties of the gray crystals, the gray Liquefying Stone all around, gobbled up attempts to map the surgery properly. They could not get a visual representation with sound, X-ray, neutrino, or Higgs flow. They'd managed a gross sketch between each of those, each having marginal ability to permeate and shape the heart stone, but there were far more blank areas in the organ map than there were details. Which meant the doctor was on his own, though he did have the careful advice of Marks Bryant in his ear, the professor's years of archaeology aiding his great knowledge of geology.

So Orli watched, and the doctor worked, and everyone not operating the machine or the lights, or monitoring the settings of everyone's environmental suits, waited and paced. Which included Altin Meade.

Altin, therefore, paced back and forth on the bridge of the *Glistening Lady*, relegated to that distance at Orli's request. The farther he was from Doctor Singh, the better off everyone would be, especially Yellow Fire, who needed the doctor's hand steady as a steel plate, not quivering with rage. So Altin watched on the monitor of Roberto's ship and waited anxiously.

"You'd think your daughter was late coming home from the prom," Roberto said, trying to break the tension Altin kept painting across the deck. "I know you and the doc ain't really all kissy-kissy anymore, but the man is good. It's going to work out fine."

For a moment Altin was taken aback, the words his friend chose confusing him. Altin was trying very hard to learn the language Orli's people spoke, and he was within the radius of a translation spell now, but some of that made no sense. Besides the enchantment on one of Altin's amulets, and enchantments on the com buttons of the ship's entire crew, Roberto also had enchanted torch sconces mounted all over the ship, a gift from the Lord Chamberlain that Roberto had been too polite and too delighted to send back. Which meant Altin should have been able to understand everything. And yet, with Roberto more than most, he often couldn't. He did know the man well enough, however, to realize much of it was likely some bit of inanity or sarcasm, so he forced himself to let it go. "I know Doctor Singh is competent, the best," Altin said, responding to what he had gotten out of it. "I have absolute faith in his skill. But I'm worried about putting it back."

"What do you mean?" Roberto asked as he laid a card on the table he and his crew had set up on one side of the bridge. He looked to the brawny woman sitting across from him, whom Altin had first seen standing guard at the base of the ship's loading ramp that first day at Murdoc Bay. "Just one, and make it sweet," Roberto said. She seemed to be amused by that, and her muscles flexed beneath tanned skin as she dealt Roberto a card, her arms toned and strong, with veins like blue snakes visible at the inner elbows and down her forearms.

"I mean, when he cuts it out, and we figure out how big it is," Altin replied, "how are we going to get it into the cave on Red Fire? I'm watching the man work, and it occurs to me that we're not going to be able to just stuff this heart into a hole like planting daffodils. It's going to have to be put back perfectly."

Roberto looked like he was going to make some smart remark, but Deeqa Daar, standing beside Altin, saw where the Prosperion's thoughts were going. "You do not think they will be able to cut a new hole for it properly on the red world, despite all of that?" She pointed into the monitor, indicating all the expensive equipment that Tytamon's—that Altin's money had bought. "That is a high-end setup you have there. It is the best that money can buy."

"Yes, I know. And Professor Bryant says they'll cut a hole to match. The machine is monitoring the doctor's every move, and taking notes of some kind. But I'm still worried that it has to be an absolutely perfect match. A hand in a kid-leather glove isn't going to be a good enough fit. It must be more like those flexible gloves Earth doctors wear, and I just can't see how they're going to do that with that water machine. All that money, and I saw no plaster or even mud down there. I had hoped they might at least plan to make some kind of wet mold or something."

"Four ladies, ladies," Roberto announced, slapping four cards onto the table to the groans of both security crewwomen and his navigator. "Good thing I pay you well." He turned a victorious face toward Altin as he raked in a pile of silver Prosperion coins. "Dude, that's your medieval-age thinking going again. You're so backwoods, bro. No offense, of course. But relax. They'll scan that hole when the doctor is done and model it exact. I'm telling you, Singh won't even have to make the cuts on Red Fire. The computer on that rig down there will match the hole way better than he ever could. It's the first template that is the tricky part. That's what Singh will do."

Altin understood most of that very well, and he nodded, pacing right up to the monitor. "I certainly hope so. But I'm still worried about the joint. If it's not close enough, it might not heal. Or grow. Or whatever it needs to work."

"If you want something to worry about, you should be worried about how you're going to get all that equipment teleported to the red world without screwing it up when this is done. Do you guys even have a hole cut out for it yet?"

Altin shook his head. They didn't. He hadn't even gone back since the day Orli blew the life out of the vicious Hostile they all called Red Fire, the day both she and Altin were nearly killed. He hadn't wanted to. There'd been no need. Only a few quick trips with a seeing spell to confirm that the damage was done and that it had stayed that way. He'd looked again after Her Majesty had suggested there was a chance that Red Fire, like Yellow Fire, was merely lying dormant somehow. But he was not. The black, burnt-out remnants of his heart chamber lay open like a caved-in skull. The force of the explosion Orli had ignited with the mining charges had blasted out the bottom of the chamber and broken off a section of the cave wall, which dropped to the cavern floor like an unhinged jaw. There was no pulsing light in it now. Altin had even sent his magical sight scurrying through the debris, crawling with it through the darkness like a tiny insect through the rocks, looking through and beneath each boulder, all around, seeking the slightest pulse of light in the Stygian darkness. There had been none. Red Fire was dead. It was a certainty.

Or at least he hoped it was. He'd cast a divining spell for it, and that seemed to confirm it as well. So did the one the priestess Klovis had cast for him. The young adherent of Anvilwrath, part of the circle of clerics who had helped find Red Fire, had done it as a favor for him when he'd asked.

Now that there seemed to be a real chance that they could get Yellow Fire out, now that the professor's insane-seeming water-knife idea was working as planned, the reality began to settle on him. They were going to have to go back. And if he was there, if Red Fire was lurking in that rubble heap, what might happen to them all?

He decided that perhaps he should put a little more effort into verifying the death than he had. Yes, the priests said it was so. But the priests lied as often as not these days. And when they weren't lying, they simply got things wrong. Snatching up bits of this prophecy and that, trying to tie together the absolute truth.

He decided that, just to be sure, he'd go see Ocelot again. Orli would be busy for a while, and he thought a quick trip to the Z-class diviner would bolster his confidence before going back again. If it were only him, he wouldn't be worried at all, but the whole lot of them would be going there in Roberto's ship. And for the five or six hours it took to restart the ship's systems, it and everyone in it would be vulnerable as it drifted in orbit above the huge red world. He supposed if there were to be bad news, now was the time to get it. And while he was on Prosperion, he would open up some books of transmutation spells. Maybe between him and Ocelot, they could figure out how to meld all that Liquefying Stone. He'd never tried to work with Liquefying Stone and his ring together. And certainly never an entire planet's worth, a very big planet's worth when it came to Red Fire. That world was no moon.

But he'd have to look into it. It was clear from watching this procedure that something most likely would need to be done to facilitate the transplant. The cut that Doctor Singh made now would have to be uncut on Red Fire, the damage undone. So home Altin would go, to Ocelot, and perhaps afterward, a visit to the man with the greatest gift for merging stone that Altin knew: Aderbury.

Chapter 23

Climbing the twisted palm trees in the forbidden cove was easy. Pernie scrambled up the winding slant of one such pair with the ease of a monkey and the silence of a child who'd spent her whole life playing and exploring in nature, one who had learned from hunters and woodsmen on Kurr, and now one with over a half year's being trained by elves.

The cawfrat, a poisonous variety of parrot, flapped away as she climbed. Silent as she was, it did not need to hear her, for it saw her quite easily with its great round eyes. Just as well, Pernie thought as she neared the top of the winding trunks. It was better to be out of its range. She knew from previous experience that cawfrats spat foul acid along with the curses that they spoke. But their range was short, and the parrot only flew to the next tree, not particularly concerned with the little girl in the tree.

That was a fatal mistake. No sooner had it settled in the crook of the palm fronds it had flown to than Pernie's spear ran it through, right beneath the wing and halfway out the other side, pushing that wing out at an acute angle as the spearhead knifed through. It barely had time to squawk before it fell in a flapping spasm into the sand, where it landed with a thump.

Pernie sent the image of it, in particular of its eyes, to Knot, who lay curled up in a ball on the beach where she had left him. He perked up upon receiving the thought, and she guided him to it once he'd unrolled himself and seized onto the idea of food. A moment later, an instant really, given the insect's speed, Knot set upon the still-twitching cawfrat and drove his tongue spike into one of the bird's huge, juicy eyes, happily sucking out the delicious meat.

Pernie watched Knot as she leaned into the tree, her toes jammed into the cleavage formed where the two trunks had come together as the trees had grown. Knot loved eyeballs, it was true, but there were none he loved as much as cawfrat eyes. Each was nearly as big as a papaya, and every time she killed one of the birds for him, he grew a little less obstinate.

She sighed and looked up into the cluster of coconuts that dangled just above her head. She should have gotten one down before she'd thrown her spear. She'd been wanting to try one anyway.

She climbed the remaining distance and drew her knife from her belt. She reached up and had just begun to cut when Djoveeve's shout came up. "Don't you dare, child!" There was such absolute command in it that Pernie's little eyebrows dropped into a concerted line above eyes that focused all the more. She set to the task more earnestly and thrust her little knife into the cluster, sawing for all her worth.

Tremors vibrated through the trunk as she cut, and for a moment it gave her pause. Her sawing slowed as she feared that Djoveeve's stories of the twisted tree spirits, the ghosts that lived in them, might be coming true. What if the tree was shaking because a ghost was coming out?

But then an enormous hand clamped an iron grip upon her leg as Djoveeve, now transformed into a silver-haired gorilla, yanked her free of her perch and dangled her by the ankle high above the sand.

Djoveeve began descending, still holding Pernie at arm's length in one hand and using her remaining three limbs to climb. The motions were violent. The transmuted assassin jumped down with her bottom half, her thick body elongating as she dropped. Her lower legs would catch the trunk and stop the near free fall with a jolt, then she'd let go with her upper arm and let the tree slide through the gray pads of her powerful hand. The sliding made a rapid *tick, tick, tick*ing as the corrugations rasped across her leathery grip, then she'd grab hold and drop another two spans with her bottom half again. She repeated the sequence several times, with Pernie swinging wildly in the air.

The whole descent took only a matter of seconds, and by the end of it, Pernie was shaken rather violently—perhaps on purpose. It was a condition that was not helped much by the fact that, when they were still five feet from the ground, Djoveeve simply dropped her, letting Pernie fall into the sand. She landed with a dull thump not unlike that of the fallen cawfrat, whose eyes Knot was still sucking on, and had to blink some of the beach out of her eyes.

"I told you not to come here again," Djoveeve said, already returned to human form. "And I certainly told you the nature of these trees."

"You tell me lots of things," Pernie said through a pout. "You talk too much, and nobody believes in ghosts." She got up and went to where Knot was, intent on riding him away.

Djoveeve caught her and gently turned her around, looking down into her eyes. Pernie defied her, glaring back as if she were the one with something to teach the old woman instead. Djoveeve stared down into that little gaze of solidity and smiled, first in admiration, and then with fondness and even love.

"What's the matter, little Sava?" she asked at last. "Even

you aren't this angry right away."

"I'm not angry. I want to be alone."

"But why?"

Pernie yanked an arm free and tried to turn away. But Djoveeve still held her firmly by her other arm. When Pernie looked back, she saw that Djoveeve's eyes were closed, and she was quietly muttering a spell. Pernie tried to yank her arm free again, which failed, so she tried to peel Djoveeve's gnarled old fingers away. She might as well have been trying to straighten an iron boomerang.

She thought about stabbing the old woman through the hand, but she knew that would be bad. Too bad. Still, the more she tried to peel those fingers away, the madder she got. Pernie looked up in the old woman's old face as the weathered assassin muttered her dumb old spell, and Pernie decided it didn't matter how mad Djoveeve got. She reached for her knife and saw that she didn't have it anymore. It was still lying in the sand where the gorilla had dropped her.

She bit the old assassin instead. Right across the top of her knuckles, just as hard as she could. The woman did not let go, not even when Pernie tasted blood.

Finally Djoveeve stopped chanting and regarded the child held captive in her strong grip. She smiled sadly, and apologized. "It's your birthday, little Sava, and nobody has done a thing."

Pernie wanted to deny it, to throw it back at Djoveeve as a lie, but it was true. It was her birthday. And nobody even cared. Kettle would have made her a giant cake and hung strips of dyed lace all around the kitchens everywhere. Kettle would have let her eat sugarplums and frostberries for breakfast, all soaked in cream. There would have been no work today either, and Kettle and Nipper and Gimmel would have all sung her the birthday song. Gimmel would have brought her a present too, something from town, a new sharp knife that would make Kettle grouse and worry and smile.

But no, not here. Not on stupid Hunters Isle. She couldn't even get sweet coconut milk from a stupid "sacred" tree. Knot was the only one who got anything special on her birthday.

Djoveeve seemed to see her thoughts as they played out in her eyes, and she apologized again. "I am sorry, little one. I did not realize."

"It doesn't matter," Pernie said. "I'm ten years old today. I'm a big girl now. I don't need sweets and party songs."

"Well, I don't know about party songs, but I think I should like an excuse for sweets."

Pernie thrust out her lips and tried to turn away, once more tugging at the manacle of the old woman's grip.

Djoveeve released her, unexpectedly, and she staggered a step toward Knot, who had just begun slurping out the dead cawfrat's other eye. She meant to go ride him away as soon as he was done.

"Have you ever heard of sugar shrimp?" the old assassin asked to Pernie's retreating back. "They are one of the great joys of String, and the elves say they are the sweetest meat on all of Prosperion. Perhaps the sweetest anything."

Pernie frowned, unseen by Djoveeve, and kept walking toward her bug. She had never heard of sugar shrimp, but she was not going to tell the old woman that.

"I once ate forty-three of them, all in a row," the aged assassin said. "It was a year after I got here, and I discovered them by chance. Oh, you should have seen how old lady Belletelemew fussed. She went on and on about fitness and health, calling them the confection of the sea. She told me that my people, our people, get fat here on String, and that the Assassin of the Vale has to be nimble and swift." She laughed, thinking back on it. "I think I'm plenty nimble and swift," she said. "Even at my ripe old age."

Pernie tried not to care, but it was kind of interesting.

Sort of.

"Well," said the ancient assassin, "since it is your birthday, and now that I've got those sweet delicacies in my head, I think I'm off to have a few to celebrate. It would be more fun if you'd come along, but if you'd rather stay here and pout, so be it. Just do not climb the trees. In this I am in earnest. If you cut them, you could kill them, and with them someone's life-bond will be lost."

Pernie turned back around; she was going to protest that she didn't believe all that sacred soul stuff. Trees holding ghosts and spirits. Kettle told her a long time ago that there were no such things as ghosts. She'd said it many times, and even Master Altin had agreed. He'd been right there in the kitchen that day that Pernie had the bad nightmare, the night after Gimmel told the scary stories around the fire as part of the Festival for the Dead. She'd had terrible dreams about ghosts coming through the walls, just like Gimmel's story said, but even Master Altin had told her that ghost stories were meant for scaring little girls. Both Kettle and Master Altin said they weren't true, and they would never lie. Although, Master Altin had once told her that the stories about the orcs were only meant to scare little girls too.

But Djoveeve was already transformed to her black jaguar form again, running off toward the rocks at the edge of the invisible dissolving barrier, though this time headed for the left side, which was a direction Pernie hadn't explored the last time she was here.

Sugar shrimp did sound promising. And it was her birthday after all.

She turned back and saw that Knot was still at his meal, though the bulging eyeball was nearly half-collapsed. She could wait for him to finish. It wouldn't be fair to deprive him of his birthday dinner just so she could have hers.

She retrieved her knife, then plopped down on the soft pink sand and waited patiently. Watching with her head tilted to the side a little and the sun glinting off the long, shimmering gold of her hair, she let herself enjoy the gross slurping of Knot at his meal. In time, she was in a good enough mood to giggle as Knot got to the bottom of the cawfrat's eye socket. What remained of the eyeball meat mixed with air as he sucked up the last juicy bits, and the noise he made gurgled hilariously in her ears. She was still giggling when it was all done, even as she pulled her spear free of the eyeless corpse and climbed onto her insect's back.

But she fell silent after, as she set her feet and settled in to ride. She took up the rope in one hand and wrapped it several times around her wrist. She gripped the spear tightly in her other hand. She closed her eyes and sent her thoughts into the insect's mind. She listened to its senses, for its thoughts were mainly blank. But it sensed everything. She had discovered that she could hear what it heard, what it knew through its feet, the vibrations of things so tiny no human could hear, so tiny she doubted even elves could hear. But Knot could. Knot's sensitive little feet felt everything, heard everything. And in the span of a few seconds, she could hear the soft pads of Djoveeve's jaguar paws on sand.

With a tap of her spear, and just the barest reminder of pain in places behind the bug, it set off at a run. She caught the black cat in four minutes flat.

Chapter 24

As Altin had feared, the visit to the diviner Ocelot had been useless. Her cryptic answers were more cryptic than usual, and he was reminded, again, of why everyone said she was completely mad. For the most part, it was nothing but a string of the obvious or the insane, as she'd gone on and on about how he could see himself in mirrors—hardly a shocking revelation there—and about the dead rising up again. And of course, the silliest part, or the most mundane, was her emphatic warning of how great danger would come from an Earth wizard one day, which was either total nonsense, since there were no Earth magicians, or simply mundane reality, as it was more than obvious that some sorcerer, many sorcerers, would eventually get to Earth, and while there, who knew what Altin might do one day that could set one of them off. Where the wizard happened to be was, in a way, immaterial given that a magician that wanted to do him harm was going to do him harm, or try to, whether he was on Prosperion or Earth. Or, for that matter, whether he was on Blue Fire, Yellow Fire, Red Fire, Andalia, or anywhere else. So, while it was unfortunate to discover that he had enemies on the horizon, it was hardly a surprise. It seemed the universe never ran out of hateful beings to throw his way.

And it was on that topic, at least in a way, that Altin found himself being confronted upon his return to Calico Castle. He teleported himself back from Ocelot's forest hovel into his old, familiar place behind an old suit of armor, his own sort of unofficial clean room—clean space really—that he'd been using for years. He appeared in the dark shadows behind the ancient plate mail, deep in the recesses of Calico Castle's huge and seldom-used dining hall. There stood, far across from where he'd arrived, a long table, not so long or grand as had been the custom in centuries past, but long enough for a very large family, if one were to attend a meal set there.

Sitting at this table, in a dim little globe of candlelight, sat the keep's kitchen matron, dear old Kettle, staring at the round shape of a bright blue birthday cake. It wasn't a very big cake, and for a woman whose skills were as renowned as Kettle's were, it seemed a rather sad little thing, her usual deft touch with the knife normally giving a playful texture to the frosting, and on other occasions she would have put some time into making little frosting animals or flowers or puffing clouds. But not this one. She'd frosted it with the deft strokes of a woman wanting to have it done, as if she'd planned for no one to see, and there were no puffing anythings fluffing up in folds of fancy frosting at all.

Kettle's puffy red eyes, however, suggested that the birthday cake was not meant for happiness anyway, and it only took him a moment to guess by the ten candles burning there whose birthday it was. He grimaced, hating what he knew was about to come, but there was nothing to be done for it, and he was the master of Calico Castle after all. Not to mention the Queen's Galactic Mage. He sighed. And he was, more than any of those others, Kettle's friend. Part of her family in a way, for what other family had either of them known in these last thirteen years?

He padded across the floor, his bare feet silent as he went. As quietly as he could, he pulled out a chair opposite her.

The chair's old oaken feet scraping across the stones broke her trance, and she looked up at him, wiping reflexively at her cheeks with the back of her hand.

"It's certainly quiet around here without her," Altin said, hoping that his smile would bring happy memories.

"And ya was always fast ta remind her of it too," she said.

Altin exhaled a long, tired breath that fanned the ten little candles, bending the tiny flames toward her like glowing supplicants, bowing in submission to her grief. "She's not dead, you know. She's in very capable hands. She's going to be a great person one day. Perhaps very soon, as I expect those elves have more than they bargained for with her."

She tried to be mad again, to snap at him, but that last bit made her smile. "Oh, and that's like ta be the truth of it too." She almost laughed. "I can see 'em now, her givin' em screamin' fits, like as not bitin' and scratchin' the lot, wantin' ta come home."

Altin nodded. "I imagine she is."

"Ya should be goin' ta check on her regular, ya know. What with her bein' yer ward and all."

"I've already told you I can't, Kettle. You know the laws and the treaty. And this is beyond even that. This is some ancient pact. We've gone over it a hundred times."

"And we'll go over it a hundred and another more. Ya don't even try ta get a message ta her at all. Not even one a them lizards the city folks throw about. Could ya even be bothered to do that much?"

"Kettle, they don't go to String. You were there when I tried. And she can't hear me when I call. I've done that too. She's with the elves. It's done. Please stop throwing it in my face all the time. I've got enough to worry about as it is."

"She worships ya, ya know."

"Yes, I know. And she almost shot Orli too. So, if we're being honest, I think that some training on how to handle weapons properly was way overdue. She is where she needs to be. It is her destiny."

"Destiny." Kettle did laugh this time, though there was no humor in it now. No fond recollections or undercurrents of joy. "Like ya ever gave one lick fer destiny afore."

Altin peered through the bright candlelight to where Kettle glowered as she stared into the fire, her face shadowed some since she'd leaned back in her chair. He thought it was an odd reflection of Pernie sitting there, an older, wizened kind of petulance. He shook his head, and got up. "Well, I wish her a happy birthday," he said. "Wherever she is just now, whatever she is doing. I hope she is happy and with friends."

"As if elves know anythin' 'bout friends."

"Kettle, we have no idea what the elves know. For all we know, she's having a big party right now with a hundred dancing elves playing music and eating cake until she's so full she can barely move."

"I should think that's hardly likely. I may not read all them books as a great magician such as you, but I been round long enough ta know there weren't no elf what ever baked no cake. There ain't no need a libraries to know as much as that."

Altin sighed once more and walked away. He wasn't in the mood to argue with a stubborn old woman hells-bent for a fight.

He went out into the courtyard and saw that there were several of the long, brick-shaped containers that the Earth people used for shipping freight. He noted that they were all closed up and locked tight, and that there were no more scaffolds, cranes, hoists, or sawhorses anywhere.

The setting sun glinted a dull orange off the black-painted metal of his tower, and more so from the black windows that wrapped round it, the image of the horizon at his back reflecting perfectly in them. Were it not for the gap-toothed metal wall that formed the battlements at the top, the whole thing might have looked a bit like a giant version of the projectiles the Earth people used in their guns, the lower half ringed in stone like a bullet casing, and thrusting up from that, the brushed black bullet of the rest. He thought the crown of the battlements made it look regal, though, and he was glad that they had added an extra floor. Four aboveground floors and a basement would give them lots of room. And it would be far better for space travel than being packed into *Citadel* with a fortress full of bureaucrats. Despite how huge and spectacular *Citadel* was, despite how much glory the enormous, diamond-encased space fortress had achieved during the war to save planet Earth from the Hostiles, Altin still felt bad for how that had turned out for Aderbury. Brilliant artist that he was, master of stonework and architecture of the highest kind, yet there he was, stuck with the command of *Citadel*. He only had it because Altin had just never wanted the job. That was the Queen's enthusiasm, not his. And so far, he'd managed to stay out of it, which left it to poor, loyal Aderbury.

Which reminded Altin of one of the reasons he'd come home. He still hadn't been able to get in touch with Aderbury telepathically, and unlike the rest of the continent, Altin hadn't yet taken to carrying homing lizards around with him everywhere he went.

Out of habit, he sent a gentle telepathic nudge to his friend, but as before, he got no reply. Aderbury was blocking or, given the absolute nothingness Altin sensed, being shielded by seers, diviners, and illusionists on *Citadel*. He tried reaching Aderbury's wife, Hether, but she too was blocked. He knew it was inappropriate to do it, but he cast a quick seeing spell and looked around their house, hoping to find her at home—he'd done as much before, and while it would be grotesquely rude for most, he'd known them both long enough, and done as much often enough, that he felt less guilt than he would have otherwise. But she wasn't there, so any guilt at all was pointless then.

As he looked about their house, he noticed a small cage populated by the couple's handful of homing lizards. Feeling more than a little guilty for it, he teleported himself directly into Aderbury's study, where the wind of his arrival blew several parchment designs off his friend's workbench and sent them fluttering to the floor.

He went to the cabinet upon which the cage sat and took a bit of parchment from a tray sitting next to a pot of ink and a quill pen. He wrote a short note to Aderbury, explaining that he needed to talk to him about a very important transmutation spell. Then he tied the note to the back of a black-and-yellow-spotted lizard he'd taken from the cage. He tossed the creature down to the floor as he spoke Aderbury's name, and in that instant the homing lizard disappeared.

Altin busied himself with picking up the drawings his arrival had blown about, and in the time it took him to clean them all up, and gaze at a few—he could hardly help it given that they were right there in his hand—he got his reply.

The note read:

Can't help you. Secret project for the Queen. How'd you get my homing lizard?

It was signed simply "A."

His reply was nearly as brief:

In your house. Sorry. Couldn't be helped. Need special transmute spell to merge living heart stone with surrounding crystals (Liquefying Stone, no less) on new Yellow Fire world.

Altin sat down and studied the drawings on Aderbury's desk again, mostly out of the need for something to do while he waited for a reply. They seemed an odd collection of designs for a gifted stone-melder like Aderbury was. Several of them were designs for what looked like simple frontier-style fortresses, although rather high-walled and, if he was looking at them right, made to set upon some kind of column or cone. One drawing depicted nine of the forts all together, a large central one connected to the eight smaller ones by walled bulwarks that arced up and over the space between like bridges that seemed unnecessarily high.

He flipped through the stack of drawings and found some interior sketches, and as before, most seemed entirely normal but for what seemed a proliferation of murder holes, especially along the bridge routes. He couldn't imagine what possible use there was for such a fortress as this. Although, he and Aderbury had once discussed putting an amusement park up on Prosperion's pink moon, Luria. He supposed the drawings might be meant, somehow, for that. Perhaps they were evidence that Aderbury really did not have his heart into the command of *Citadel*, though he uttered no complaint.

The lizard returned at that moment, appearing with the barest puff of air and setting itself immediately to chewing on Altin's earlobe with its soft, toothless mouth.

Altin pulled the note off and read:

Don't eat all our food, you burglar, or Hether will have at you when we return. Assuming we do, of course. And for your spell, take the book on the shelf to the left of the lizard cage. Get the one with the yellow spine. Look for a spell called "Gorbon Glassblower's Cotton Meld." Don't send the lizard back. We are being watched. You (we) got lucky this time.

Being watched? What in the nine hells did that mean? Who was watching? The war was over. All of the wars were over. Weren't they? By the gods, there'd better not be another one, he thought as he read over the note once more.

He turned, however, to the shelf behind him and found

the book with the yellow spine. It was a squat, fat book with gold leaf painted along the edges of the pages. An expensive spellbook to be sure.

Unlike most, it had a table of contents, making its maker a rare sort of wizard for such things. It did seem appropriate, though, given that most transmuters ended up tinkerers and builders and the like. The very same sorts of people who tended to like things organized.

In a matter of moments he'd found the spell. It was a longish one, sixty-one pages in all, but nothing he couldn't memorize with a little time. It was too long to copy, however, and feeling more guilt about taking the book, he shrugged and took it anyway. What were friends for if not the lending of wondrous books? He only hoped that this one would do what he needed it to do, which was to spare him a much greater guilt than the pilfering of a book: the guilt of killing two living worlds. One he might kill by incompetence, should he fail, and the other would die by his vow.

He grunted and shook his head. All he'd wanted to do just three short years ago was travel to the moon. See the sights. Maybe have a look at some nearby stars. And now look at him.

Chapter 25

Pernie paused and watched, transfixed, as Djoveeve waded out into the surf with her arms out slightly to her sides. The dry, rippled appearance of the woman's skin intrigued the girl, the way the backs of her arms hung loosely from the bone. Just a little, but it was there. The lines of muscle were still visible beneath that leathery flesh, but the muscle was more than lean, seeming almost stringy in the striations visible there. The ancient Sava'an'Lansom was wearing thin. Without her armor, it was obvious. The skin seemed barely attached at the back of her thighs. Oh, those thighs could still leap well enough, and those slender shoulders could still heave a spear hard enough. But bare as she was, Pernie could see age upon her. A little past three centuries she'd had. Not so many as the great Tytamon had, but still a lot of time to be the guardian of the High Seat.

The curiosity that stayed Pernie there on the beach vanished with one backward glance from Djoveeve, who beckoned her to come along. "Don't let me eat them all without you," she teased.

Pernie yanked off the last bit of cloth that covered her, then plucked up her spear and ran out after the old woman, eager to get her first taste of sugar shrimp, the fine feast for her birthday.

"You won't need that, little Sava," Djoveeve said once Pernie had caught up. "Your eyes are your weapons here."

Pernie frowned, but turned and threw her spear back onto the beach, a long, graceful arc that had the black shaft glinting in the sun as it flew true and plunged into the sand near her clothes. She didn't really know how she was supposed to catch shrimp with her eyes, but she supposed anything was possible in the land of elves.

Soon they were deep enough that Pernie could just barely keep her head above the water, and she had to jump to stay above the white froth of the broken waves, which washed over them both in steady, crooked lines.

"Here," said Djoveeve. "Here is where you will find them. They come in with the tide, and they eat the little things that spawned in the sun when the water was gone." She made a show of holding her breath and ducked under the surface. Pernie tracked her as she swam along the sandy bottom. Her splotchy skin was pale beneath the clear blue water, dappled further by the sun.

Djoveeve swam slowly along as Pernie watched, winding between black rocks that stuck up here and there from the sand. The old assassin paused from time to time near this one or that, and she paused here and there beneath clumps of kelp that drifted over her as well, rolling over and looking up at the bottoms of them as they slid through the low, rolling waves. Pernie watched for several minutes until finally she saw the woman's arm dart into one of the clumps. Djoveeve stood up out of the water then, not even a half measure taller than Pernie was, and raised her arm triumphantly. "Got it," she proclaimed.

She made her way over to Pernie, who was still standing nearby, bobbing in the waves as she hopped over the highest ones. Djoveeve picked bits of seaweed off her hand as she approached. She drew near and held out her hand, palm open and up, revealing a lump of dark green seaweed. She pinched out a few more bits of green slime, then briefly made a loose fist and shook it back and forth beneath the water for a moment before lifting it out again. "There, you see?" she said, holding her hand out for Pernie to have a look.

All Pernie saw was the woman's palm again, wet and clean.

"See what?" Pernie asked.

"Well, drat," Djoveeve said. "They change so fast." She ducked down under the water and scooped up a handful of sand from the bottom, then came up again. She sprinkled the wet sand in little clumps onto her hand, and Pernie watched with delight as the shape of a shrimp was formed. For a moment. Then there was only a little heap of sand.

Pernie frowned, then laughed, then frowned again. "Is it gone again?"

"Oh, they're never gone," she said. "But they're clever and they're quick." She made a loose fist again and once more plunged it into the surf and, shaking it again, rinsed out all the sand. "Here, put out your hand."

Pernie reached out, and Djoveeve placed an invisible thing into her palm. Something wriggled there, little feet working as it tried to get free again. "I can't see it," Pernie said. "It's magical!" She was thrilled. She'd been trying to find a magical sea creature for quite a while now, using what time she could steal for herself to find beaches and seek out something that she might ride back to Kurr. She hadn't found a single one yet, and was starting to lose hope that any had magic at all. And now here there was evidence after all.

"Oh, that's not magical," Djoveeve said. "Lots of creatures can do that. Regular old ordinary critters do it all the time. Cuttlefish and octopuses and squid. But so, too, do the great gavenau whales, the shrieker fish, and the blue sea dragons of the Tine. Even in these creatures it's not magic, however impressive it may be. It's a common trick, actually, but very good camouflage."

"Well, I thought you said these things were magical." Pernie began to feel a little bit cheated. Old people always made up magical things. They told stories of tiny badgers living in their beards or danced fake lizards in the air. She used to like it when they did that, but now she knew they only did it to get her to do what they wanted her to do. She began to protest that very thing, but Djoveeve cut her off.

"The magic," said the old woman, "is how they create the wondrous taste."

Pernie looked dubious, but she did want to have fun on her birthday, so she decided to wait and see.

"First, however, my little Sava has to learn how to catch a few. Then I'll show you the trick of the treat. Come, follow me and watch close."

Djoveeve took the shrimp back from Pernie and tucked it into a bag she'd tied to her wrist. Then, without further ado, she ducked under the water and began to swim away. Pernie did likewise and swam beside her, only just a bit behind. Djoveeve swam along through the rocks for a long time, but Pernie, though she had swum a lot since coming here, couldn't hold her breath so long as that. So she came up, took a fresh lungful of air, and plunged back down after the old woman again.

Djoveeve was waiting for her near a rock. The rock was covered with feathery tufts of blue-green algae amongst which nestled several mollusks known as fire limes, named so for their green color and the little bubbles of boiling water that they spat, little round beads of steam that scalded on contact anyone or anything that got too close. Pernie had learned about those the hard way a few months back while trying to connect telepathically to an elephant seal lounging on a rock a few hundred spans offshore. She pulled away from the rock as soon as she saw them, her toes wriggling reflexively as she thought about how that had felt on the bottom of her feet.

"Here," came the gentle thought pushing against her mind. "Share my thoughts, little Sava."

"I am," she replied.

"Look here by this anemone. Just in front of it." She was pointing to the space in the water only a finger's width away from the reach of a deep purple anemone. "Come closer and watch how the tentacles sway with the currents. Look carefully and see how the pattern breaks. There is a delay as our sweet little friend is constantly trying to keep up."

Pernie swam right up next to Djoveeve, whose long gray hair floated wildly around her in the water, making her look rather like an unkempt silver anemone herself.

Pernie peered closely into the anemone, staring down Djoveeve's gnarled finger and looking for a break in the pattern. There was nothing. Just lots and lots of little purple strands.

"It's moving," came Djoveeve's thought. "You have to see carefully. You must be patient and watch. Put away what you think you ought to see. Put away what you expect. Keep those images out of your head. Just shut down your inner voice and *see*."

Pernie stared into the place where Djoveeve pointed, the woman's sticklike finger slowly moving down, apparently tracking the invisible shrimp as it made its slow getaway, working down the rock beneath the anemone and seemingly headed toward the sand.

Pernie tried to stay with her, watching as hard as she could, but her air was running out again, and she had to go back up. She burst above the surface and took a few long breaths, before pulling in as much air as she could and going back down again.

Djoveeve was still pointing, though she was moving

along the bottom now, lying on her side as she pulled herself along, stirring up little clouds of sand each time her elbow or hip grazed the bottom.

Pernie swam up opposite her and turned parallel, facing her, barely the length of Pernie's arm separating them. She stared at the space in the water near the woman's fingertip, a hand and a half above the seabed. There wasn't anything there.

"Stop looking for the shrimp, little Sava," came Djoveeve's thought. "Start looking for what's wrong with me."

That didn't make any sense. Pernie didn't need to send the thought with words; the face she made conveyed it clearly enough.

"Look at my finger. My hand. Look through what you are trying to see at me. Watch what shouldn't be about me. See what is there, not what you believe should be."

Pernie tried again. She watched the woman's finger carefully. She tried to imagine how big the shrimp would be. It was trying to look like a part of Djoveeve, like it had looked like the anemone and then the rock. Like it had looked like the sand.

She stared through the empty space and watched the movement of Djoveeve's arm. The way her stomach wrinkled and movement of her breasts. There were lines in all of that, shapes and forms, shadows and spots of sunlight beaming down. Then she saw it. A double line of fingernail, and the shadow of the old woman's rib. But it was gone right after.

"I think I saw it!" Pernie sent to Djoveeve as she peered even harder through the intervening sea.

The color shifted on Djoveeve's inner arm, the blue veins visible and the little dimples in the soft flesh not quite rippling right. Pernie squinted and moved closer. The line of her shoulder seemed a little too brown, just for an instant, and the sunlight that sparkled on a rippling wave above flashed twice right in a row. Pernie's hand shot out and snatched the little shrimp even as her little lungs began to burn for having held her breath too long. But she caught it. It wriggled in her hand.

She burst up out of the water and let go a *whoop*, holding her arm high. When Djoveeve surfaced right beside her, she whooped a second time. "I got it, I got it!" she yelled.

Djoveeve's smile was just as wide as Pernie's was, and the woman laughed happily as Pernie let her hold the little captive and measure it with her hand. "Why, look there," Djoveeve said with pride, "yours is even bigger than mine."

Pernie would have clapped for joy, but they were in water too deep to make such things easy. And besides, she wanted to get more of them.

"I want to find more," she said. "I think I can see them now."

"You can, indeed. But we must get enough for us both, and I am in quite a mood for sweets. Let's not be lazy. I can eat quite a pile."

"And how will we make them sweet? What is the trick of the treat?"

"You will see, little Sava. But first, let us fill up my bag."

With a smile so wide it seemed as if it might just run right up and clip her ears, Pernie dove back under the waves again. And for the next few hours, she and Djoveeve had a wonderful time, spotting the invisible. By the time they were done, Pernie was nearly as good at catching them as Djoveeve was. It was only the fact that the old woman could hold her breath for what seemed eternity that gave her any advantage at all.

When at last Djoveeve's bag was full, the two of them marched out of the surf together, each with a hunger worked up for all the work they'd done.

"Now for the magic," Djoveeve said as she dumped the bag's contents into the sand. "But you've got to have a good imagination to make it work."

Pernie winced upon hearing the word. Imagination. Hah. She knew there wasn't going to be any magic now. Grown-ups always called lying "imagination," and at ten years old, she was tired of it.

Djoveeve saw the look on her face and shook her head. "You have to have faith sometimes, little Sava, or life is misery. You must learn when to believe."

"Seawind said I shouldn't trust anyone. He says you have to assume everyone is your enemy, and that all words are lies. He says the truth is in the in-between, in the movement of eyes and the beating of their hearts. He said I should listen to their hearts if I want to hear the truth."

"He is right. You should. In that way, listening to your enemy's heart is like seeing the sugar shrimp. A calm face can't hide an excited heart, once you know what you are looking for. It is seeing the difference between what is real and what is meant to deceive."

Pernie made a bored face, one side of her mouth twitching toward her cheek. "I know that." She looked impatiently down at the squirming pile of shrimp. Together they made a shifting pile that looked like water that's turned to gel and filled with sand. They didn't work very well together, Pernie thought.

"These little creatures are liars too," the old woman said, squatting down near the pile. She picked one up, and Pernie watched as it tried to keep pace with the changing backdrop, its appearance changing rapidly as Djoveeve's hand moved, matching in incredible succession whatever it was that lay behind it that would be in Pernie's line of sight as she looked its way. That's when Pernie realized what it actually had to do to hide from her.

"Hey," she said as the idea dawned upon her. "How does it know what I am looking at?"

Djoveeve once again wore that grin of victory. She nodded, clearly pleased. "I had hoped you would see it for yourself. You are a clever girl, and Tidalwrath chose you well."

Pernie didn't care about stupid Tidalwrath. She was moving her head around, moving herself around, changing angles as rapidly as she could, moving her line of sight so that one minute the shrimp was between her and the sand, the next between her and Djoveeve's arm, or her leg, or her hair. No matter where Pernie moved, no matter how fast, the shrimp changed immediately.

"So how does it know that?"

"These little creatures read your mind."

Pernie frowned. "They do?"

"Yes. That is part of their magic. They are the best little diviners in the sea. They know what you see before you do. The only reason we can see them at all is because it takes them that tiniest fraction of a second to adjust their skin. There are no other creatures that can do that."

Pernie nodded, happy to have something interesting to understand. "So what is the trick of the treat?"

"That's where the imagination comes in. You see, they are also little transmuters, though they don't actually know it yet."

"How come they don't know?"

"The same way you didn't know you were a teleporter until you were frightened enough to make your first teleport. I'm sure you remember that."

Pernie nodded that she did. She'd never forget that terrible day when the orcs came and tried to kill everyone. One of them had been about to cut Master Altin right in half. She hadn't even known she was about to do it at all. She just, well, she saw the orc going, and then it happened. She was right there on the orc's back, the distance between them just gone, as if it never was. She simply found herself there on top of it and began to stab the awful thing as fast and furiously as she could. How could she not have?

Djoveeve saw the glaze in her eyes and nodded, watching Pernie watch the memory. "That's right, little Sava. And these tasty creatures work the same way. When they are worked up into a fright, they find their transmutation ability."

"So what do they do, turn into a candy or piece of cake?" Pernie asked hopefully.

Djoveeve tilted her head back and laughed. "No, dear child, not quite. But it is something delicious in much the same way. And this is where your imagination comes in, for they are not shape-shifters like me. Their transmutation ability is not so good as that. At best they might be C class if they could be ranked. But that is quite good enough for this." She laid the shrimp in her left hand and took her knife from where it lay atop her folded clothes. "Before you kill them," she said, with a marginally wicked smile, "you must think of the sweetest thing you can. I always think of maple syrup, the kind that we had when I was a little girl, not much younger than you. My father had a grove of maple trees, and it was the best flavor of my life. Yours will be something different. Perhaps that birthday cake you are wishing for. So conjure that up in your mind, not the image of the cake, but the flavor of it. Remember it so well that you can feel it on your tongue." As she spoke, her words came more and more slowly, her eyelids drooping a little as she allowed herself the memory. "Hold the thought there, and then gently find the place between the shrimp's legs, where they meet at the belly. Feel for it with your thumb." She spent a moment feeling into the invisible shrimp in her hand, probing with her thumb. "Once you have it, slowly push your knife into it, just like this. Not too fast. You have to let it feel the pain. It will flicker, then turn gray, and in that instant, you must plunge your knife in before it can camouflage itself again. You have to be quick, kill it quick, from there."

She stopped speaking for a moment, letting her own memories come back to her as Pernie stared, openmouthed, watching. Then, sure enough, just like the flicker of a candle in a breeze, the shrimp turned gray and Djoveeve stuffed her knife tip right into its guts. She opened her half-shut eyes and smiled.

With a few quick strokes of her knife, she opened up the shrimp, stripped its shell, and cleaned its innards out. She presented it to Pernie, who still stood watching with her mouth still agape.

"What's the matter, little Sava? Is it too cruel for you to do? I admit that there are not many who can make themselves do what needs to be done to the little things for the sugar secret to work. If you haven't the stomach for it, I'll prepare them. Though it will be maple and frostberries in them all. I just can't seem to remember anything else well enough to make it work, and for whatever reason, only sweet memories do the trick."

Pernie shook her head no. She had no qualms about torturing the little shrimp to make them sweet. Pain was a reality. Pain was how she trained her little, low-slung mount. She was rapidly beginning to realize that there was a great deal of good that came from pain. And she kind of liked doing it too.

She ran to where her clothes were and pulled her knife out of the sheath. She ran back and fumbled in the invisible pile of shrimp until she found a nice big one to try it on.

She missed the flicker on the first one, and she stabbed too quickly on the next. But by the third try, she had it, holding it just right, seeing the big pink-frosted cake Kettle had made for her last year and then tasting it in her mind. She tasted it as she twisted her knife into the wriggling shrimp's little guts, pressing the point in just enough until the creature became briefly visible. She plunged the knife in the instant she saw it, so hard she actually stabbed through it into her palm. But it worked that time. She knew it because the creature turned pink just before it died.

"I think I did it," she cried, staring up at Djoveeve hopefully.

"Let us find out," the old assassin said. "Here, push it a bit farther down your knife, and take my shrimp too. Push it on there as well."

Pernie did as instructed.

"Do you remember the fire limes?" she asked, the sunlight flashing in her smiling eyes. Pernie nodded that she did. "Take them to a fire lime and hold the shrimp in the bubbles that come from its shell. Only a half minute on each side or they'll be overdone. Then try one and see."

Pernie could hardly get back into the surf quickly enough to test it out. And sure enough, immediately after the minute it took to cook them, she discovered that Djoveeve had been telling her the truth. One shrimp was maple and the other a sublime shellfish slice of Kettle's birthday cake, three whole bites apiece.

And so went the remainder of the day, Pernie eating shrimp after shrimp after shrimp, and catching more and more until the sun was gone. She kept at it until she couldn't swallow even one more down, no matter how hard she tried, which set Djoveeve to laughing in the sand. They rested, then practiced with the spear, and twice more across the day, they went out and refilled Djoveeve's bag. By twilight, Pernie had broken the old woman's long-held shrimp-eating record by four.

Chapter 26

Black Sander reined his horse in as he approached Galbrun Hall, home of the Marchioness of South Mark and seat of power for the largest of all the duchies on Kurr. He saw descending the long stair the figure of Cypher Meste, guildmaster diviner, accompanied by the captain of the Palace Guard and two younger officers. Cypher Meste did not look pleased, and her long dark hair danced about her shoulders as she shook her head emphatically to something the captain had said. She looked up as Black Sander came to a halt, and she squinted into the noontime sun. He muttered the words of a flashing light spell, to augment the solar effect, and, in the few moments that she blinked at it, shaped his features to match those of the gardener he'd seen working a half measure down the road.

Cypher Meste squinted back at him a second time, still blinking, then apparently lost interest and turned back to the crimson-cloaked captain, who was still speaking to her. Again she shook her head, and the four of them made their way to a small stone house down the lane, in which Black Sander knew was located the marchioness' private teleportation chamber. Black Sander watched them go, his own eyes narrow and calculating until they had disappeared inside the little stonework house. He let the illusion dissolve and rode up to the front, handing his reins off to a stable boy who came running out to take his horse from him.

Once he was inside and admitted to see her—after her chambers and the hall outside them could be cleared—the marchioness glared at Black Sander through pale blue eyes that were little more than slits beneath the drawn curtains of her eyelids, violet eye shadow, and wiry black lashes that quivered at the fringe. Her sneer was a crooked red gash across her gaunt face, and the severity of it was augmented by cheekbones that protruded at such angles it seemed they must cut through the skin at any time. Her whole body was made that way, angular, and so slender her flesh seemed but tissue laid upon a lattice of rapier blades. If it were, all those blades now trembled in ire beneath the opulence of a black-and-gold gown. Black gossamer fabric, webbed with gold, flared like fireworks at her shoulders and hips, a gilded puffery that ballooned as if holding captive clouds of ink.

As he watched anger rattle through the old cage of her bones, Black Sander held his tongue. Slender though she was, thin like split kindling, he understood well enough that she was still the heart of power in South Mark, and the one person on all of Prosperion who could, with a word, actually create a worse fate for him than the War Queen. She and she alone had more connections in the underworld of Kurr than he. Not even her toady, the Earl of Vorvington, could make such a boast.

But this day, they were not comparing notes or arguing cultural realities, though Black Sander could have wished for such levity. No, this argument that they had was one about simple competence.

"It's been five months!" she said in a low, taut tone from her place near the window of her private rooms. "I don't ask much from you. The pay is regular, and I give you your head. And all I asked this time was that you place a simple seeing stone. Just one. And yet, all you have managed to accomplish in that time is to get the royal hounds sicced on me from Crown."

"What did they want?" he asked, immune to the ice in her voice.

She went to an end table by a long divan, which was covered with embroidered lines of writing, each a great quote once spoken by her father, one of the finest orators in all of history. His words had calmed the people after the War Queen had bested his armies in battle two centuries ago. South Mark had been the last to go. She picked up an object roughly the size of a hen's egg that was lying there on the divan and brought it to him, placing it in his palm. "Do you recognize this?"

She pulled away her own skeletal hand and left him staring down into his. At the topaz seeing stone he'd secretly stowed on the fleet spaceship during his brief incursion to Tinpoa Base. He'd hidden it very well. Or so he'd thought, stuffing it in a nest of wiring inside a wall panel he'd found in a vacant corridor. He couldn't imagine why anyone would have been digging around up there, so the only thing he could figure was some sort of mechanical accident. He'd wondered what had happened to it. And why they hadn't heard anything.

She saw the brief flicker of recognition, perhaps even read it in the slight movement of his lashes or some twitch of the cheek. She rolled her eyes and turned back to the window. "She's watching everything," she said, referring to the Queen. "Everything. The fortunes she is spending on defensive spells alone are preposterous, and yet, she's got people sniffing out seeing stones. *Seeing stones*, of all things. How many people on the entire planet even know how to create one?"

There was little he could say, and even less that he was inclined to speak aloud, so he simply watched her as she stared outside.

"Given what they've just asked me, do you have any idea what they must actually suspect?" she went on. "If that child of a guildmaster were not so young or were ranked higher than her V, I'd be on my way to the guillotine. We are being spied on by the capital, and that gold-clad idiot clanking about the throne room is going to bankrupt the kingdom to do it."

Black Sander, long used to enduring hour upon hour in shadowy places waiting for opportunities, watched and waited here. At some point she'd come back to him. Finish her complaints and give him something he could use.

"Have I not given you the names of enough teleporters to get it done?" she asked. "Have I not shown you enough personally?" She swept her arm out toward a large armoire upon which sat a beautiful mirror in a frame made of bone, a great swirling mess of carved white complexity, wrapped around an oval glass, all of which was set into a beautiful black box of enchanted tarwood. Tucked within the lattice of the bony finery were tiny carvings depicting Earth fleet spaceships. And in the mirror itself could be seen the image of Orli Pewter, standing in a vast cavern beside someone else, both of them wearing clumsy-looking suits of white material and helmets fronted by a half bubble of glass. "Is this not enough? I've even given you access to the enchanted seeing spells of Altin Meade himself, made for his little blank hussy. She's regularly to be found on that ship that was sighted outside of Murdoc Bay. Surely it's been to Earth a thousand times and back these last five months. Why can you do nothing with that? Must I go myself and simply beg passage to Earth on the privilege of my rank?"

Black Sander watched the two figures in the mirror for a while, their image the product of some augmentations by the marchioness' personal seer, Kalafrand. Though he was a Z-class master of sight magic, Kalafrand was a well-kept secret, one the marchioness jealously hid from the Queen. Kalafrand was a man with a single gift for seeing, and little else, almost nothing else, but he was a savant. Both genius and imbecile. Somehow, he'd been able to fiddle with Altin Meade's complex spell, and managed to alter it some, making it something the marchioness could use, at least to a degree.

He took a step closer and watched as the Galactic Mage's fiancée went about whatever she was doing. The last time he'd looked into this glass, she had been gardening. Now she was with some other Earth man in what appeared to be some kind of mine. The two of them worked together with the lights of their suits flashing on a patch of faintly glowing purple stone, and whatever they were doing sent out clouds of white mist like fog. There were others around them, people working with a strange Earth machine that he could only partly see in the mirror, a large contraption that had been built at the bottom of a large rectangular pit.

"You see them, thief?" the marchioness went on. "You watch what they do. See where they are. Wherever she goes; I show you everything. The woman has the privilege of Sir Altin Meade and of the Earth royalty. I give you this information freely, anytime you would ask it, and yet in all these months you still can't get a simple seeing stone to Earth for me. Not even on a ship they are on with regularity. I make it easy for you, and yet you cannot get my seer's eyes to Earth?"

"They aren't royalty, Your Grace—"

In the time it took him to breathe, she'd cut him off. "Don't equivocate with me. I pay you to solve problems, not quibble with me about identities."

"But My Lady, it is not to quibble, but to point out that Sir Altin and the Earth woman are well guarded, more so than even the fleet ships. And they are well guarded here on Prosperion, not only in Crown, but at Calico Castle as well.

Sir Altin has shrouded the old keep in nearly as many counter-spells as the Palace has. He's taken on a guard of at least forty men. And while the general and his troops are no longer encamped beyond the walls, he's got more traps and magicks around that place than any other Prosperion but the Queen."

"Of course he does. Vorvington's idiot nephew kidnapped his intended—getting himself banished and killed in the process. You can thank dead Thadius Thoroughgood for the traps. The Galactic Mage watches over her like a beholder hawk now. But it doesn't matter. You don't have to break into Calico Castle. You have to break *on*to Earth. And that requires a simple seeing stone. Just that, so I can get a teleporter there. So you see, I haven't tasked you with all that much, have I?"

He started to explain again the nature of the heavy guard and the way that the Earth people saw through illusions and sensed for magic in the flicker of electricity, but she saw it coming and silenced him with a glare.

Though she did not quite raise her voice when she spoke, she managed somehow to add more ice to it, rising as she did to her full height. At nearly two spans, she looked like a noble razor. "They are blanks!" she said. "And I've hired you because you are supposed to be able to do what no one else can. You're supposed to be the master of traps, the king of illusion, the go-to chap when it comes to circumventing rules, magical or otherwise. That was the on-and-on about you. The 'procurement specialist,' everyone says. That is what I bought you for."

"Speaking of things bought, Your Grace has pointed out herself that the Queen is sparing no expense."

"Your reputation for rising to occasions seems to have been more fiction than I would have liked."

Black Sander would not bother to defend himself. And she, wisely, recognized her own temper on the rise, a circumstance beyond dignity.

"Get me a stone on that infernal planet before it is too late. The sands are running out. If I don't have one of my teleporters on that planet by year's end, all my other preparations will be for naught. All of them, do you understand?"

He didn't. "Perhaps if Your Grace were to give me more information, my divining informants would be of greater use."

Scrutiny shaped her gaze like the blade of an axe. He saw the internal debate that danced upon that edge, and saw that he had won some small victory shortly after.

"I need weapons," she said bluntly. "And I need them before that fool sitting on the golden throne gets us into yet another war. Perhaps several of them all at once. It seems having three enemies this year was not a great enough challenge for our beloved, overreaching monarch."

Few things surprised a man whose entire life had been devoted to ferreting out surprises more than that one did. Another war? It didn't seem possible.

"That's right," she said, seeing it in his eyes. "The ink isn't even dry on the treaties, and she's already making flanking moves for territory in space. She's preparing for war as we speak."

"War, Your Grace. Truly? So soon? There is no sense in it. She's not recovered her treasure or her troops. She's not ready for one."

"Correct. And yet she's at it with all haste, from what *my* divining informants can tell. She's set up a colony on the planet they call Andalia and hasn't mentioned a thing about it to anyone from Earth, at least not as far as Vorvington can verify. His informants tell me that the *Citadel* mages have found another world as well. Again, secretly. And how do you think the Earth people are going to appreciate that little dollop of news?"

He barely shrugged. He had no guess, nor inclination to. Politics was only interesting to him in how the shifting winds might blow something promising his way. But he did think it was too soon for war again. A wasted populace has little of value to barter, steal, or trade beyond picking through the remnants of burned-out domiciles. People are quickly reduced to worries about food, water, and physicians, where real wealth requires an active economy. Another war, several wars, could push Prosperion toward being that kind of place.

"She's hells-bent on infuriating those people, and between her clandestine colonies and the fact that she's pointedly dragging her feet on the TGS platforms, their governance is going to be furious."

Black Sander nodded. "They'll send all those gleaming war machines at us this time. All of us." He thought of the unbridled carnage the fleet ships and the mechanized warriors had done, and how quickly. Magic was too slow to defend against such an onslaught. At least one that came in force or by surprise.

She nodded, though it was barely perceptible. "There's little to keep them from planting a flag right in the center of Crown City and all the other duchies and marks. That was the threat they made when they first landed, just before the great battle began. That was General Pewter's message, straight from the NTA director, albeit the one they've since deposed. But they had the thought once, and they'll have it again if it conveniences them."

"Perhaps that is why Her Majesty seeks to plant colonies on other worlds. Her diviners may have seen something yours have not."

That put a frown upon her face. She regarded him for a time, something dark in her eyes, then paced back to her mirror again. "I've got to stop her before she ruins us all."

Black Sander had a hard time believing that was what

this was all about. "Why not simply tell the new director of the Northern Trade Alliance? Even just get a message to a ship captain at Tinpoa Base? Why the secrecy?"

"It's not enough. It needs to be handled here. Her reign has gone on long enough. She's vain and reckless. It's time to take matters into my own hands. I should have done it forty years ago when I had the chance."

"The Earth people may send their machines to help her if you attempt a coup."

"They won't. They don't want another war either. And this is a domestic feud." She glared at him, her icy eyes narrowing as if she'd just caught him spying on her. "You'll do best to do your job. Get me a stone on that silver ship the next time it comes to Murdoc Bay. Or on another one leaving from here, or from Tinpoa, bound for Earth. Send a damned homing lizard for all I care, but get around the damn blocks and wards, or I'll find someone else who can. It's a planet full of blanks, for Hestra's sake. Get it done."

"Yes, Your Grace." He left with one last glance at the mirror and Altin Meade's precious fiancée. Surely there was something he was missing. Something he'd overlooked. There was always a way around everything. But what?

He climbed down several flights of stairs and made his way back outside, all the while ruminating on what he could have missed. What angle of their defenses had he passed right over for its obviousness? It was always the way. The simple answers were usually best and, with painful frequency, also the most difficult to find. Simplicity was, like clarity, often a matter of hindsight.

He was still thinking about it all as he climbed back onto his horse, his cloak sweeping over the horse's rump as he swung into the saddle, irritating the animal and causing it to flick its tail. He thought back over everything the marchioness had said, everything they'd covered, time and time again. But he'd done all that. The wards were everywhere. The electronics on everything were monitored; the least flicker set off alarms. And even the homing lizard trick was no good. He'd tried that too. There simply weren't enough of the fleet captains set in the network for them to be of any use, and none that were on Earth.

And then it struck him, an idea, the one thing she had mentioned that might still be of some use: Thadius Thoroughgood. Thadius was dead, that much was true. Altin Meade had killed him, that's what the rumors said. But his man wasn't dead, his teleporter, a Northfork Manor magician by the name of Annison.

Chapter 27

Annison bent over the bar near the wall farthest from everyone. A red-and-green light above him kept flashing the unpronounceable name of some beer from some country the blanks called Germany. They called the things that bring disease *germs* too, and why they'd name a country after many of them was hard to say. It sounded like the name of an old-fashioned disease spell from Prosperion history, something Korgon the Beast would have cast with his perversion of growth magic and a subtle transmute. But even as the thought crossed his mind, he let it go. These people had no such history. He was sure it meant something entirely different, but didn't care enough to ask. Nor enough to try the beverage, which he was sure was hideous.

The beers in the place were unspeakably bad, or at least those that Rue's Bar and Grill served. Although they did have one spirit that he counted spectacular. They called it *vodka*, and it was clear delight. The top-shelf varieties, as Rue herself referred to them, were the best, and Annison had taken to pouring this libation down in copious amounts these days. It was the only thing that kept him from losing his mind.

He leaned heavily on his elbows as he stared into his

drink, the light from the blinking sign hypnotically shaping arced lines around the lip of the glass. He watched the two ice cubes in it melting slowly, until they were eventually all but toothpick-sized versions of an ice lance. Frost. He'd never had frost spells. Or fire. Conjurers were the popular ones. The mighty ones. There was little enough use for an illusionist that didn't become a thief or a stagehand. Oh, the Queen had plenty of counter-mages too, but that was boring work. Tedious and time consuming. And teleporting was just as bad. He couldn't imagine sitting in a TGS depot all day, sending scads of nervous travelers all around Kurr. What a ridiculous way to waste your life. He laughed as soon as he thought it. It was hardly worse than being The Incredible Spectacularo. Could that simpleton Slick Danny have conceived a more idiotic name? If Annison had had a better grasp of the Earth language English back then, he would have insisted on something less insipid.

He threw back the whole of his drink and put the glass down loudly enough that the bartender heard. Annison nodded at the middle-aged woman, who nodded back. "One sec," she said in her rustic Earth way. "Same?" she asked as an afterthought.

He rolled his eyes. He'd ordered the same thing twelve times a night every night for something approaching two hundred days. It was hard to imagine that the blanks on Earth might be more vapid than those on Prosperion, but they seemed hells-bent on taking the prize for dullest in all the galaxy.

"Hey, look," called a voice from a table near the center of the small room. "It's The Great Spectacularo!"

A few other patrons turned to see where the young man was pointing.

"It is," confirmed one of the youth's compatriots. Annison recognized the third and only silent member of the group, though he couldn't place him or recall a name.

"You see that, Reggie. That's the 'real-life Prosperion' that freaked you out, bro." They laughed and prodded him, and it was clear from the derisive way they spoke the planet's name that they had no thought in their heads that it might actually be true.

Annison turned away from them and stared in the direction of his empty glass, wishing the barkeep, Rue, would hurry up with his drink.

"Hey, Spectacularo," called one of the noisy youths. "Why don't you show us another magic trick? Reggie here swears you really are one of them magic aliens. He's been taking crap for months. Help him out, would ya? Just one little trick."

"Yeah," agreed the other boisterous one. "Let the Great Spectacularo amaze the crowd. And maybe tell us why he's working in such a shithole like Slick Danny's dump."

"All right, boys," said Rue, coming around from behind the bar. "First off, his stage name is The *Incredible* Spectacularo, not the *great* one. So get it right. And second off, he's my customer, and his money is as good as yours. So leave him alone, and I'll buy you all a round and a game of pool just to keep it nice."

The bigger of the two loudmouths started to protest, but Reggie put a hand on his arm, and shut him down with a look. "Let's just play, all right?"

The aggressive one shot Annison a long, taunting look, but Annison was still ignoring him, or at least trying to. "Fine. Wouldn't want him to get mad and send us super far back in time. We could get, like, eaten by cavemen and their pet dinosaurs."

"*You're* a caveman," Rue said as she gently pushed them all toward the pool tables far across the room. She pulled a wooden cue from a rack on the wall. "Here's your club, stud. Now what do you want to drink?"

Annison glanced over at them, observing mainly out of

the corner of his eye. They'd already forgotten about him. Which was good. He didn't need attention. He just needed to be left alone.

A short time after, a man came and sat down on the barstool to Annison's right. The Prosperion turned from his vodka long enough to look at the newcomer and shake his head. There were five empty barstools between him and the closest patron at the bar.

He drew in a long breath and waited for whatever the man had to say.

"I've been following you for a week," the newcomer said at length. "I've watched your show."

Annison tried to place the man in his memory of any of the recent crowds, but couldn't. He made a point of watching, but there were places in the theater he couldn't see. The stage lights were too bright.

"Yeah, well, I don't sign autographs," Annison said.

"That's a strange accent you have there," the man remarked. "I'm sure I've never heard it before."

Annison had gotten sloppy in recent months. He often forgot to cast the illusion on his voice. It didn't seem to matter much here in the dregs. None of them had ever traveled out of this flea-ridden neighborhood, so they wouldn't know one accent from the next. He could tell them he was from Germany, and they couldn't care less. In fact he had. Nobody gave an Earthly shit down here.

"It's German," he said, making sure to make his tone as conspicuously irritated as possible.

"Really? My mother is from Germany. What part?"

"Piss off," Annison said. "If I wanted company, I'd have gone to a brothel."

"Hmm, interesting," said the man. "I'm not sure I've heard anyone use that word to describe anything around these parts before."

Annison glanced sideways at the man again. Blond hair,

short cropped. Pale eyebrows on a broad brow. A rather large, bulbous nose below wide blue eyes, and narrow, emotionless lips. His expression lacked that dull vacancy that seemed to fog the countenance of most of the people around here. "Piss off," Annison said again.

"I'm not here to turn you in. I have less love for the NTA than you do."

Annison wasn't taking the bait.

"You don't have to live like this, you know. There are other places you can go. Safe places."

"Why don't you go home to your mother in Germany," said Annison. "Like I said: piss off."

"I have friends in Mexico who are interested in meeting you. Who want to protect you from the NTA."

"I have no issues with the NTA," he said. He waved his empty glass impatiently in the direction of Rue behind the bar.

The man shook his head. "The people I work for don't like it when their hospitality is turned down. A couple of days at a nice villa on the bay is all they ask. Hear them out. They just want to buy some DNA. Maybe a little time at the lab. It will be no big deal. Easy money, like when women go donating eggs. Just come listen. Enjoy the scenery. San Francisco has some of the best seafood and highest culture in all of Mexico. You'll have fun. And you will find people there who can, shall we say, sympathize with your plight."

"And what plight is that?"

"Banishment."

Annison couldn't hide the widening of his eyes. He nearly did; it was only barely noticeable. He hoped the man wouldn't see it in the dark. But the man did. He smiled.

"Yes. We know a lot. We don't have to belong to the NTA to find out what happens on its ships. Bureaucracies always have leaks, and our people have been being overlooked for centuries."

Annison took the fresh glass of iced liquor from Rue and whirled it slowly while his mind raced. The ice cubes clinked against the glass. He missed having a decent place to live. He lived in a box that was little more than an old shipping crate, one in a stack of them in a place called the Junction, ironically of course, for it was a junction of nowhere.

But if the NTA found him, they'd want him back. They'd want to put the secret tracker in him again, and they'd want to poke him with needles and suck out more of his blood. They'd want to do the tests they'd threatened him with. They'd offered him money too. For all he knew, these people in this man's *Mexico* would do the same. Or, then again, perhaps they just wanted him to do private magic shows. Or perhaps teleport them into bank vaults or something equally mundane like everyone on the damn planet was afraid Prosperions would do.

He sipped his drink slowly. The man sat patiently at his side.

Finally he shook his head. "I'm sorry," he said. "I can't help you."

"Well, you have a week to change your mind," the man said. He slid him a small piece of paper with a little square of scrambled ink on it: a net signature. "You can find me here. They call me *El Segador*. Just ask for me when you arrive. I hope we can come to an arrangement that benefits us all, as I'd prefer not to come looking for you again." And then he left. Leaving The Incredible Spectacularo to his drink, his vodka, with its melting ice cubes, reminding him of magic he couldn't cast.

Chapter 28

Altin's newly rebuilt tower appeared without a sound upon the surface of the vast red planet they knew as Red Fire, or at least it appeared without a sound that anyone could have heard over the roaring of the planet's incessant winds. Just like their first visit to this world, Altin and Orli both stared out at the atmospheric violence and could not help but feel a sense of awe. Fortunately, this time, they had the thick, tempered glass of the new wraparound, Earth-style windows to protect them, even after dropping the protective magic of the Polar Piton's dome—which he did not do right away.

Satisfied that all upon the surface was as it had been when first they'd come, now nearly a year ago, the two of them ran down the four floors of the new stone-encased steel structure and into its basement, which now sat on the surface of the red planet and likely counted as a fifth floor rather than a basement, given it was not presently subterranean. Made entirely of steel and titanium mined from Tinpoa, with several layers of insulation between inner and outer shells, the basement served the tower as a base, although one that looked rather like a foot. The basement "foot" jutted out on one side like a dull metal shoe beneath the "leg" of the tower. It even had a sock, so to speak, where the stone of the ring-wall was visible around its ankle before giving way to the black-painted steel and glass above. Obviously the battlements at the top ended the foot-and-leg similarities, but the effect was not lost for it, which was why the construction would eventually acquire the marginally inaccurate designation of "the boot."

In keeping with the mix-and-match quality of the boot's dual-planet technological design and asymmetry, inside the basement there could be found an equally assorted variety of equipment and personages, the lot of which came from locations across Prosperion and Earth, making it, therefore, an assemblage from across the galaxy.

At one end of the rectangular chamber was a square stone construct, which looked as if Altin had ordered a small cottage built into the corner of the space, but it was not. It was a clean room, a teleportation chamber five paces square and complete with the standard small wooden door and two-way window for placing signets and hourglasses, should the need arise. It was a thing obviously and entirely of Prosperion.

And as if intending to make things as disparate as possible, in the other corner at that same end of the room was another box, barely a quarter the size of the clean room, which was made of plastic back on Earth. One end of this large crate was open, and inside was a bulky metal contraption that Altin had been told was a "diesel generator," which didn't mean anything to him in either language yet. The Earth men who'd placed it there had attached the big black-and-red-painted monstrosity to the walls via a connection that met with all that gray tubing Master Sambua had called "electrical conduit" and buried in the tower walls. In addition, it had also been attached to a spout in the wall, which the engineer had promised would "pipe out the exhaust." It was all in the service of providing electricity, Master Sambua had promised, again joking about Orli's supposed need to have some way to do her hair.

Altin's protests about the effects of magic on technology had been dismissed in regards to that machine, and Master Sambua had explained that if the effects of ambient magic did not interrupt a communications badge beyond the occasional static surge, they would likely do nothing to that generator at all. "Think of it as the mechanical equivalent of a donkey or a mule," the engineer had said. "Old-school efficiency at its best ... just in case. And besides, you have solar backup and batteries. You're as powered up as you could want to be. It's just clunky."

Altin didn't mind if it was clunky, but he was determined not to rely on it in times of dire need. Still, he could not complain about the possibility that, on those occasions when Orli thought it necessary or useful, she could have electricity.

The center of the room was filled with racks and rows of shelves, all bolted to the ceiling and floor, and all braced together with cross members that were also bolted tightly in a network of stability. Each had a set of iron grates, sturdy as gates, with heavy latches to close them tight. It was as if the designers expected the tower and its contents to endure considerable instability. Altin wasn't sure if that was optimism or an indictment of his power. He thought it might be evidence as to their thoughts about his chances for long-term success. His tower had been a heap of stone when the builders saw it for the first time.

Either way, he had already filled up the largest share of the shelves with a vast supply of spell reagents and devices for various alchemies. The rest were filled with Orli's things. She had ropes and wires and batteries. Canisters, cables, and containers of various sizes. She'd filled up one rack with spacesuits, two apiece for him and her, and several others in sizes to fit her father, Roberto, the Queen, and a spectrum of other visitors. She'd told Altin that "he did not want to know how much they cost," and that had been the end of it. He didn't care anyway. She knew better than he did what sort of thing they needed in that arena.

She'd filled another whole rack with nothing but assorted Earth weaponry, which had actually made Altin nervous. Not that he was opposed to having it, but given how much trouble her own lost laser had caused in Crown City last year, he was concerned about keeping it secure. Had the Queen's assassin not located the man who'd purchased Orli's missing blaster on the black market, who knew what kind of trouble might have come? And yet she'd loaded his tower up with even heavier weapons, the big ones like the soldiers used. Still, in a way, it wasn't technically much different than the rack of swords, bows, and crossbows he'd had set into the wall between the clean room and the generator, so he could hardly tell her not to add them to their supplies.

The remaining portion of the basement, a roughly thirty-by-thirty space at the "toe end" of the boot, was left open. For now it housed only three vehicles, one of which was an electric thing on fat black balloon "tires," over which Altin was corrected for having called "wheels." It had no roof and four seats, and Orli told him it was a "rover" not a "wagon," and assured him it was state of the art. The other two vehicles were really small gravity sleds, more for moving cargo than conveyance, but with a good horse and harness, they'd do quite nicely as lorries any day.

The remainder of the space was open, left that way by design in anticipation of the unanticipated, including such apparatuses as the disassembled parts of the water saw.

And that was why they were here. This was the next part of the mission. They were ready to begin setting up for the final transplant of Yellow Fire's heart into the old heart chamber of the slain Red Fire.

After a few experiments had been done, Altin's initial

test with Aderbury's "Gorbon Glassblower's Cotton Meld" spell had proven that it did work on Liquefying Stone. He'd had to take off his ring in order to control the mana flow through the crystals as they were, but that was the only real limitation. While wearing the ring, he kept popping the crystals, bursting them like glass. Without it, however, he could do it fine, and his fears about drawing too much mana with that much Liquefying Stone around were unwarranted. It seemed that in Yellow Fire's dormant state, the crystals around his heart did nothing to affect the mana flow. Despite casting in contact with a network of millions of them, Altin had had no trouble at all. He'd even practiced on the incision Doctor Singh was making, merging some of the cut closed. The spell Aderbury had given him worked perfectly. So with that evidence, he was confident he could meld the heart stone into place on Red Fire as well.

Doctor Singh was only a few days away from being finished with the cuts. With that done, all that was left to do was to complete the extraction of the dormant heart, and the matter of a day or two to process the cavity. Once they'd done that, they could create the template that would guide the water saw, making the placement of Yellow Fire's heart into Red Fire's vacant heart chamber a perfect fit. And that was why Altin had brought himself and his team to Red Fire.

Professor Bryant was in attendance with the young brothers, Rabin and Prakesh, and the three of them were loading up the gravity sleds as Altin and Orli arrived.

"We're there, then?" the professor asked, making a show of lifting a particularly heavy crate the moment that Orli walked in. He turned sideways and pushed his arm against the corner of the crate so that his barely average-sized bicep would be squeezed to better effect against the plastic lid. "So I guess you need me now." He winked and set the crate down on the sled, slowly, presenting his backside in a way that he clearly thought was appealing. It was such an unnatural movement, so glaringly contrived, that Orli couldn't help but look. Which, of course, the professor caught her at. He smiled and winked. "That's right. Get a look before the enviro-suit covers it up."

Orli pursed her lips, and her eyes bugged a little bit, but she managed not to laugh. Altin was already on his way to the teleportation chamber, opening the door, so he didn't see a thing. He'd seen enough in the weeks prior, however, and his only comment to her on it had been that he could hardly blame the man. "I made quite a fool of myself trying to impress you too, as I recall."

So, beyond the occasional rush of the professor to help her lift items she could have carried one-handed to the sled, they soon had the test and measurement equipment loaded and pushed into the stone box of the clean room.

"Ready to go?" Altin asked, once everyone was inside.

"This isn't going to scramble my parts or anything, is it?" Rabin couldn't help but ask. The whites of his eyes were more than just visible in his face, and they seemed to glow in the dim light of the big stone box once Altin closed the door.

"You've already been through it once, dumbass," Prakesh reminded him. "What do you think we just did? What do you think those TGS guys did to the *Glistening Lady* back at Neptune when we left from the Amphitrite depot?"

To which the other twin nodded gratefully. "Oh, yeah. I forgot about Amphitrite. It's different when you're on a ship that is inside that big black box. Now we don't have a ship, so it's creepier."

"Now you have a spacesuit. Duh," his brother pointed out.

"Don't worry," Orli said in kinder tones. "You do get used to it right away. I mean, there's nothing to really get used to. That's what you get used to. Nothing. It's the best way to travel really."

"Well," said Rabin, still not sounding convinced, "from what I heard, the only reason they built this tower is because the last one came apart during a teleport." He looked nervous then, and turned to Altin apologetically. "No offense, of course, Sir Altin. It's just what I heard."

Altin nodded. "It's true. But it was an accident based on a problem we already knew we had. We were too far from Prosperion, and I was unconscious. Orli had to use a fast-cast amulet to get us out. Just like the ones I've given all of you. But, unlike the ones you wear, the one I had was not made for the distance we had gone. There wasn't enough mana in it, though luckily for us both, only by just a tiny bit."

The older brother, by six minutes, looked to the younger and smiled triumphantly. "See?" he said.

Rabin looked marginally mollified. He couldn't get at his amulet, though, given that it was buried inside his spacesuit helmet like everyone else's was, but he unconsciously raised his gloved hand to the joint where his helmet would clip into place anyway. He smiled. It was better hearing it from the Galactic Mage than his brother, he supposed.

"All right, let's get the lids on you guys," Orli said. "Check your partners." She helped Altin get his locked on and waited until she heard it pressurize before putting on her own. She let Altin check the settings, just as she'd shown him how to do, but the professor came over and double-checked because "what can a Prosperion know?"

Orli grinned at Altin through the rounded glass as the professor made a great fuss about checking her thoroughly front and back. Altin's smile was as amused as hers. The poor fellow. A totally sanctioned opportunity to look her over thoroughly, with Altin approving as he watched, and yet, for it all, the view was muddled completely by the bulky mass of the spacesuit.

When it was confirmed that everyone was buttoned up and airtight, Altin wiggled his gloved fingers toward Orli and asked her for a glow stick. He'd found that the little crackling chemical lights were fabulous devices for seeing into dark places like the one they were headed for.

He teleported it to where he remembered being before, the place on the massive cavern floor where he'd nearly died, and followed the cast with a seeing spell. Even in the dim green light cast by the glow stick, he could see the dark stains where he had lost a considerable amount of blood.

He followed the light to the edges of the jumble where the section of the wall had collapsed after the mining charges Orli planted had gone off. He couldn't quite see up into the huge opening she'd blasted out, but he could trace its outer edges well enough to know he likely couldn't fit the teleportation chamber inside.

So, he moved his sight back to the flattest spot he could find and set the place in his mind. He came out of the spell and turned to Professor Bryant. "All right," he said. "I've got the place set. Are we ready to go down?"

"Go down?" he said, his voice laden with innuendo. He laughed as he glanced back and forth between Orli and Altin. He was waiting for reactions that he never got. The two brothers nodded that they were ready, both now quietly expectant if not entirely on edge. Orli nodded as well.

"Wait," said the professor, all seriousness this time. "One question before we go."

"Yes?" asked Altin.

"How far down are you taking us?"

"I don't know," he answered honestly. "It's very far."

"Oh, shit," Orli said to that. "I can't believe I didn't even think of it."

"That's what you're paying me for," the professor said in a voice that was now low and smooth. He raised an eyebrow and overdid nonchalance.

"Think of what?" Altin asked.

"The pressure." She turned to look at Professor Bryant with widening eyes before she looked back at Altin. "Remember when we were falling down that crevice? The long one, and we just fell and fell for what felt like forever?"

He nodded, flinching at the memory. "How could I forget?"

"Well, do you remember how our spacesuits kept stiffening and eventually that alarm went off?"

Again he nodded.

"Well, the suits had time to adjust to the pressure. This is going to be instant."

Altin's brow only furrowed for a moment. By the time his brow had unfurrowed, however, Rabin's and Prakesh's frown lines were so deep they looked like tire tracks.

"By Hestra, that's likely a bad thing to go hopping right into, isn't it?" Altin said as he noted the twins and their matching chevron-rumpled horror.

"We can set the suits for it if we know where we're going," the professor said. "Orli, do you remember how far down it was?"

"No. I never looked. Or if I did, I was too busy freaking out to remember it."

"Well, I can find out easily enough." He went to a stack of crates at the back of the chamber and opened one. He pulled out a small plastic case and opened that. There was a device Altin didn't recognize inside. The professor pressed a button to activate it, then keyed in a few numbers using a number pad that was large enough to accommodate spacesuit gloves. "Depth measure," he said into it. He waited for a half second, then said, "Record." He tapped the keys on it twice more and said, "Five seconds," to some prompt that went unseen or unheard by the rest in the dim little room. When he was done, he closed the device back up inside the case with all its lights still on.

"Can you send this down there?" he asked Altin as he brought the case to him. "It's in a box, so it should be fine electronically, right?"

"Well, it's a small box, so the relative area around it is rather tight, but it's likely to be all right. I won't destroy it, I shouldn't think."

"Well, we've got another if you do. 'Two is one, and one is none,' as we say in my line of work. You don't get much done in the field if your only one of anything breaks."

"Very reasonable," Altin said, taking the case from him. "Let's see what happens then."

A moment later, Altin had teleported what was essentially a high-tech plumb line down into the depths of Red Fire. A moment right after that, he brought it back. The professor opened it up and read the measurement, which he followed with a long whistle. "Wow," he said. "You guys went that far?"

"H-how far?" asked Rabin in echo of his brother, who actually beat him to it that time.

"Eighteen point six miles."

"Oh, crap," said the twins, still in unison.

Watching them react, and even noting the concern in Orli's pretty blue eyes, Altin suggested, "We could walk, you know. You plan on using your gravity sled to travel up and down the cliff face when we get inside; you said as much yourself. We could just unload it a few extra times along the way and use it ourselves, like one of your 'elevators,' for some of the larger drops. Or we could simply bring the other one. We've got two, you know." He even started moving toward the door to get it, but the professor stepped in front of him with a confident smile. He glanced to Orli and winked, giving the slightest nod, eyes slightly narrowed, lips in a tight, nonchalant smile of supreme confidence. "I've got it," he said as he began setting the controls on Altin's suit. As he worked the settings, he turned a second time to Orli and winked again. "This is what you pay me for."

"We're all going to die," said the twins.

Chapter 29

The Incredible Spectacularo stood upon the creaking stage, playing to a crowd of six. The small table upon which he'd placed his frayed top hat stood between him and his audience. "Behold," he said, squinting into the lights and looking to see if the bulbous-nosed man called El Segador was there. It was too bright to tell.

"Behold," he said again, forgetting he'd just said it. He reached into the hat, muttering as he did the words to a simple illusion spell. When he pulled his hand out, he held by the ears a white rabbit, which wriggled its nose, fanning its whiskers innocuously. As usual, the audience was not impressed, but then The Incredible Spectacularo flung the illusionary rabbit out into the audience, where it spread its ears and began to flap them like the wings of a bird. This made the people duck and gasp at first, but then laughter followed as the rabbit flew about their heads. The wizard sang into the illusion the gentle air currents of the flapping wings, and the sound of them, and soon the audience was laughing and clapping as the little rabbit did loops and twirls in the air above their heads.

After two or three minutes of it, he brought the illusion back and had it settle in his arms, where he held it, infant-like, for a moment before stooping down as if to deposit it somewhere beneath the folds of the tablecloth, which draped to the ground.

The people were still clapping when he stood back up, three of them standing as they applauded. He tried to smile, but it was all so pathetic it nauseated him. Still, it paid the rent, and for the time, the work kept him out of trouble and out of being vaporized by a rampaging Galactic Mage or being dissected by the inquisitive scientists at the NTA. But now he had that damnable El Segador to worry about. The fact that the man had found Annison was troubling. If he could find him, so could the NTA. Assuming they were still looking for him, which he could not confirm. He liked to think he'd made a clean getaway.

When the war was over and all the Hostile orbs went still and turned gray, the fleet people had come to the prison where all the Prosperion crew from the *Aspect* had been held. Annison had stayed among them for the time even though he could have teleported out, mostly because he'd had no place else to go. But when they came and opened the doors and told everyone they were going back onto a ship and heading home, that's when Annison had disappeared. Literally. A quick invisibility spell followed by a teleport to the last place on Earth he could recall, a speck of land viewed through a porthole just before the landing craft flew over the walls at Fort Minot. From there he'd run.

He found his way into the back of a horseless wagon a few days later, which he had since learned were called trucks, and one thing leading to another, he got himself well away from Fort Minot. He drifted generally south for several weeks before he found himself here in this place called "Des Moines," in an outskirt near the dumps where "the dregs" lived. The dregs like him. People nobody wanted anymore.

But he was nervous after that meeting with El Segador.

He knew the people of this world were all blanks, and he could handle himself well enough if he needed to, but they did have a lot of technology. Far more than Annison understood. And the news programs that he watched on what they called the global net suggested that there were already new technologies being made to detect magic as it was being cast. Security companies were selling protection to cowering homeowners who feared losing all their valuables to Prosperion thieves. Global net ads promising security from that threat—and at the same time implanting the idea of it—ran almost constantly. Others warned that magic-using perverts were watching wives and daughters as they bathed. Prosperion pedophiles were only a spell cast away from ruining lives and families. *Buy now*! It was an incredible campaign, and the profits were surely pouring into the companies selling the protective devices and "insurance" policies. Annison could only shake his head as he watched. He knew a great number of criminals, it was true, but by the noise the Earth people's global net made about it, every Prosperion above the age of two would have to be a criminal to justify all that fear. And they'd all have to get here. It was a strange phenomenon, and he found it odd that the people on this world were so easily put to fright.

He also thought it odd that, given the way El Segador made him feel, people on Earth weren't at least as afraid of their own as they were of Prosperions. He certainly was. Yet, even with that fear, Annison hadn't left the dregs. He hadn't even ruled out talking to the man. He just hadn't acted yet. His banishment from Prosperion had left him almost anesthetized, and it seemed every day of his life since had happened in a numbing fog, time passing like molasses through an hourglass.

It was in that state of absentmindedness that he looked up at his audience and smiled. "Oh, you liked that?" he said. "Well, here, perhaps Mr. Wiggles should take a bow." He

knelt down and from a box beneath the table took out the
real rabbit Slick Danny had given him. He stood and
presented the rabbit to them, gazing upon it with affection
he did not feel. He forced himself to coo, "Oh, look, Mr.
Wiggles, they love you." He walked forward to the edge of
the stage and held the rabbit out so that the people in the
front row could come forward and pet it. Two of them did,
and with it, the effect of the magic act was set. The flying
rabbit had been real. They turned back to the others in the
theater and mouthed silent things like "Oh my God" and
"Amazing."

The Incredible Spectacularo bowed, turned with a
flourish of his cape, and then put the rabbit back in the box.
He glanced offstage to where Slick Danny stood in the
wings, nodding with a big smile. This had been his idea,
and he hoped it would bring bigger crowds.

Annison rolled his eyes but smiled back at his employer
feebly. He faced the audience again and prepared to do his
last trick. That's when he felt the gentle pressure in his head.

He'd kept up the telepathic block for the entire year since
he'd been on this world. There was nobody left he really
wanted to talk to. And if Sir Altin Meade found out where
he was, Annison was not vain enough to think he'd stand a
chance against the man in a fight. Not a Seven, and damn
sure not a Seven with a Z. So he'd blocked his mind, and in
all that time, nobody had bothered to come knocking at all.
So the sense of it, so long absent, startled him.

What if it was Altin Meade? Perhaps it would be a
merciful thing. Lord Thadius hadn't lasted a second, from
what Annison had heard while aboard the ship. One massive
burst of energy and the dapper lord was little more than
bloody spray. So, what if it was Altin knocking in his mind?
Could it be any worse than whatever El Segador had
planned?

With a hard swallow, he opened up the mental gate and

let the thoughts come through. But whoever it was didn't say anything. There was only the silent presence of someone there inside his mind. Totally unfamiliar to him, but solidly connected. He knew immediately it was a seer's sense. Seers made the best telepaths, and this one was immensely strong, the contact smooth and even soothing in a way, though, paradoxically, with a frenetic undertone.

"Go on," shouted someone in the audience. "What are you waiting for?"

"Turn around," finally came the voice in his head. "My name is Kalafrand. I need to see."

The two voices, the one external and the one internal, came simultaneously, and for a moment more he stood there as if in a daze.

"Turn around. All the way around," said the telepath he'd let in. "We can send a teleporter if we can get a proper sense of place. So look at everything, and go slowly; indirect sight takes time."

"Who are you?" Annison thought back at him.

"Kalafrand. Seer for the marchioness."

"Are you a Z?" He knew how much power it took to look into a stranger's mind for an indirect sight spell, especially one that reached this far.

"I am. And I've got a few other channelers helping me. And a conduit."

Annison nodded, but wondered why.

"Hey, dumbass, do another trick," someone yelled from the audience. The others shouted in agreement.

From just offstage, Slick Danny hissed at him to cast something as well.

"What do you want?" Annison asked inside his mind. "I'm not supposed to speak to anyone on Kurr. If the Queen's diviners catch me, they'll send the Royal Assassin."

"You'll be able to hire your own assassin," came a different voice into his head, a familiar one this time. It startled him. The conduit, whose role it was to orchestrate large, multi-magician spells, had obviously brought yet another magician in, someone Annison knew.

"Who is this?" Annison asked.

A plastic bottle, half-filled with fizzing soda, struck him in the chest. "Hey, wake up, asshole. I paid good money for this."

"I see you're doing very well for yourself there on Earth," sent Black Sander, his thoughts as snide as his speaking voice ever was. "A fine use of your skills."

Annison nearly gushed with relief when he recognized the voice. Sarcasm was the least of his worries. "Black Sander! For the love of the gods, it's good to hear a friendly mind. I feared you'd been caught or killed."

A second bottle hit him, splashing him with lukewarm beer. "Dude, what the hell?"

Annison's rage, the full fill of nearly a whole year, came upon him in a wave, the second time in five months, and he lost his temper with the audience. With the utterance of a few brief lines, he hurled the great face of a giant dragon forward from himself. It appeared so suddenly and appeared so solid, so real, the six-member crowd all screamed at once, not that anyone could have heard it for the thunderous roar that came from the dragon's mouth. Along with the roar, he sent a blast of illusionary fire much like he'd done last time, filling their liquor-soaked minds with more things to be afraid of.

The people flung themselves over the backs of their seats, stumbling and tripping, falling flat as they tried to straddle and climb over the rows. In moments the theater was empty of patrons again.

Black Sander's voice laughed in Annison's head, and there were rumbles of mirth from the others included in the spell as well, one of which felt tainted with a note of instability.

The Incredible Spectacularo turned to his right in anticipation of the onslaught to come from Slick Danny, surely charging out at him now. But the man was not. He lay facedown on the ground instead, unmoving.

Annison barely had time to turn back and look to the other end of the stage when the dart hit him in the neck. He reached up and grabbed it with the reflex of one who's just been stung by a bee.

He was vaguely aware of Black Sander's querulous thoughts mixing with the seer's tainted ones. Then he slumped forward and fell onto the stage. The last thing Annison saw was a pair of brown leather shoes, polished to a high shine and standing right before his face. For a moment he stared into them, watching in the reflections as the stage lights faded to black.

Chapter 30

Annison woke up slowly, his vision returning bit by bit. As he became aware of that fact, he also became aware of a sharp pain in his throat, like a pin stabbing him. He reached for it, or at least he tried to, and found that he was bound tightly to a chair, straps at the wrist, elbows, ankles, waist, chest, and head. He sat reclined in such a way that he might have been at the barber's for a haircut or at a healer's for the treatment of a tooth. But he was here for neither.

A breeze blew gauzy white curtains into the room at an open window, and on the breeze came the smell of ocean air and the shrill laughter of seagulls not far away. He strained to turn his head to look, hoping vainly to get his bearings on a planet where he'd been almost nowhere, but he could not. There were two padded wedges jammed up against his cheeks, making it so that he could not move his head at all. He might as well have been set in clay and baked in place, he was so securely held.

Something beeped faintly behind him, and from time to time, he could hear the whirring of some small electrical device or another, familiar in a way, but not so much so that he could name it or its function, just some thing of Earth. To his left there was a long counter with jars and boxes along the wall, and above it cabinets, all of it painted a pale yellow. There were pictures on the wall, done in black and white, depicting men in extremely wide-brimmed hats and wearing strangely studded belts that crisscrossed their chests. The men in them looked proud or triumphant, standing before dirty walls or amongst rocky landscapes where tufts of scraggly brush and cactus dominated.

Panic began to rise, and he quickly started a teleportation spell, but the first word wasn't even fully shaped before his throat constricted painfully, instantly, his neck and face and upper chest all contracting with the violence of electricity. It stopped almost as quickly as it began, and he lay there panting, the pinprick in his neck throbbing. His head hurt so badly he could hardly keep from vomiting, and he was dimly aware that if he did, he would likely drown in it.

A door that he could not see opened, and someone came in, a man with brown skin and brown eyes and a very serious look on his face. He wore a wide mustache like the men in the pictures did, though he wore a neatly cut suit of the sort that was in fashion with the well-to-do on Earth, a dark brown jacket in shimmering fabric worn over a shirt that nearly matched the yellow of the walls, and shiny slacks to match the jacket.

The man peered down at Annison lying there and smiled a wide smile that rounded his cheeks to the point where they shone a little in the sunlight coming through the window. He said something in a language Annison had not learned, though Annison did catch the phrase *El Segador.*

The man patted Annison on the cheek, affectionately, as he might a prize racehorse, and then left the room, calling out names that Annison had never heard.

Annison tried to cry out, but just as when he'd started the teleportation spell, his face and neck and chest were once more wracked by electrical agony. He tried to stop speaking, but in the pain of it, he had a hard time stopping the rasping *gahhhh* that came out on its own, perpetuating his suffering. And so it went until somehow, without really any volition of his own, the sound in his throat stopped, the muscles having finally seized too tightly to vibrate any more.

He lay there panting, tears running from the corners of his eyes. He closed them and tried to calm himself. He tried to remember what had happened to him. He remembered the rabbit, and that someone had reached him telepathically. Black Sander had been involved. It hurt his head to think of it. In a few hazy moments he recalled it all, and he immediately sent out a telepathic call to the strange seer again, intent on finding Black Sander and begging for help. Black Sander could come get him. He sent the request across the mana stream, sent on waves of terror and absolute urgency.

He pushed rather brutishly against the mind of the man whose thoughts he'd only ever touched once, the Z-class seer who had found him across all that space. On Prosperion his approach might have gotten him a reprimand from the Seers Guild, whose bailiwick telepathy was. As he concentrated on the thoughts he sent, as he hung there in impatient misery, he noticed the whirring growing more incessant from the back of the room. No sooner had this thought struck him than the door opened again.

In came two women and three men, two of whom he recognized. One was El Segador, and the other was the man in the brown suit with the wide mustache. One of the women went around him and disappeared, but he could hear the now-familiar sound of someone tapping on the glass panel of a computer console. He'd been on this miserable world long enough to recognize that.

"He's trying to use it," she said. "Look at all this activity, only partly in the frontal cortex. It's all down here, like base functions."

"Well, stop it," demanded El Segador. "You're supposed to have set it for that."

The second woman, wearing a white coat that hung to her knees, came forward and touched something just out of sight behind Annison's chair. Again came the painful electrocution in his throat. His face cramped, and he jerked about in his restraints until after a few seconds she released whatever it was she'd touched.

The man in the brown suit was laughing, and he came right up and leaned down into Annison's face. He smelled like cigar smoke, and tattoos ran all the way up his neck and wrapped around his ears. Small x's had been inked at the outer corners of his eyes, three on the right, two on the left. He said something else in the language Annison didn't understand. He patted him on the face again, not quite a slap, once more like a fine thoroughbred. He stood up and spoke to the woman, then said something else to El Segador before he went out. He could not possibly have looked happier.

"Jefe likes you," said El Segador. "He says it's been a long time since he had a gringo he liked."

"Well, damn it," said the woman in the white coat next to him. El Segador looked up with the question in his eyes. She saw it, then directed his gaze downward with her own.

He laughed and shook his head as he looked briefly at Annison's lap. "You pissed yourself already, Prosperion? We're hardly even started yet."

Chapter 31

Altin leaned forward, the spotlight of his spacesuit shining into the hole that the professor had cut out with the machine, cut straight into the cave wall where the old heart chamber had been. Water still ran out of it as he looked, and Professor Bryant was accepting compliments from the team about how perfectly this hole matched the readings, or at least the partial readings, taken from Doctor Singh's carefully excised heart stone back on the moon where Yellow Fire was.

The crystal bed in which Red Fire's heart had lain prior to Orli's blowing it to pieces with mining explosives was laid bare and ragged by the blast. The plain stone, the rocky components that made up the planet prior to its having become host to a Hostile, was visible in places, particularly where they'd had to excavate room for the water saw and its mounts prior to beginning. They knew from the work on Yellow Fire that the barest tip of the heart stone would need to touch this rocky stuff, but all the rest of Yellow Fire had been nestled into the Liquefying stone. This was going to be a problem that had to be resolved.

Before they'd started the cut, Professor Bryant and his team had concluded that the crystal bed here would need to be regrown before the transplantation would work. "It's dead," he'd said. "And I mean *dead* dead, not dormant dead. In fact, I'll bet Orli and the whole *Glistening Lady* crew a massage and a steam bath that the circuit is open right now, in a way it isn't open back on Yellow Fire. Look." He'd made his point by pointing a laser at the crystals all around, and to Altin's and Orli's horror, it acted differently. As in, it shone right through them, altered some by the dull gray of the crystals, sure, but it went right on through. The crystals might as well all have been formations of quartz or salt.

Live Liquefying Stone didn't work like that. Light went in, but it didn't come out. At least not exactly. Not like that. The dead crystals on Yellow Fire hadn't either. They had no glow, but they didn't let light right through. They'd just been sort of dull.

Professor Bryant had then taken a small hammer off of his tool belt and tapped the tip of a long crystal a few times. A portion broke off, and bits of what remained turned to powder like crushed glass. He looked up and grinned. "See. Someone owes me a steam bath and some shoulders time," he'd said.

Altin had grown very nervous at that point. He went to the broken shard of crystal and pressed a finger to the powdered part. It stuck like sand to his glove. He studied it for a moment and then harrumphed. What did it mean? Clearly that something was different. So now what? Was it going to work?

And that was the conversation now that the hole was cut, ready for Yellow Fire's heart. Or nearly ready. Now they had to figure out what to do about the difference. They had to fill that space where the explosives had cleared the crystals away. But should they cut out more crystal from Yellow Fire and transplant that too, or should Professor Bryant actually regrow the crystals that were already here to fill the space? He'd said he could do it. Now they were going to have to decide.

"Well, a perfect cut," the professor concluded. "So now you people just need to tell me which it's going to be, transplanted crystal or regrowth. I can set up a containment field on the open areas, and we can make a bed for it right here. Now that we can actually study the damn things, we've found the valence shell, and it's not really any different than any other crystal from there."

Altin knew better than to ask what that meant, and he relied entirely on Orli to decide. "So we have no way to know if these crystals are any different than those back on Yellow Fire?" Orli asked, standing beside Altin and staring into the opening. "What if there is some subtle difference between male and female? What if there's a huge difference?"

The professor climbed down out of the water saw's cab, splashing into the runoff as he jumped from the last rung of the short ladder bolted to its side. He came over and looked into the hole with them. "What an incredible cut, if I do say so myself. I've done an outstanding job here, I have to tell you all."

"I thought this cut was based on a template created by the cut Doctor Singh made back on Yellow Fire," Altin said. "Wasn't one of the main purposes for this particular machine being employed that it could trace a pattern with absolute accuracy essentially on its own?"

"Listen, Meade, I don't piss in your oatmeal, so you don't piss in mine, okay?"

Altin wrinkled up his face and looked to Orli, who was barely holding in a laugh, as he said, "I have absolutely no idea what that means."

The professor moved on to Orli's question anyway. "Like I said, I can't study that other stuff, the heart stone, anyway, at least not much. So your guess is as good as mine. I suspect when we pull that out all the way, the gray crystals on that moon are going to get just like these, delicate and breakable.

But that doesn't change anything. At some point, somewhere, material from there is going to have to come together with what is here. Which means you need to decide which part and where. Are we crating all this equipment back up and taking it back to Yellow Fire for a skin graft, or are we growing these to fill in the gap? Either way, the semester is going to start in a few weeks. I'm going to have to go back or burn my sabbatical."

Orli looked irritated by that. "Well, I think you need to worry more about Blue Fire and Yellow Fire than whether or not you might have to use up your vacation time."

"Hey, it's not vacation. Sabbatical is serious business. We save that for serious research."

"How is this not serious research?"

"Well, that's true," he said. "I just needed something to bitch about because this is all going so well."

Altin shook his head, having difficulty understanding the man, but Orli was not put off in the least. "Well, let me ask you a question, then," she said.

"By all means," he replied, sending Altin a look that suggested he'd just won some kind of victory.

"Do you love your parents?"

"My parents?" It was the professor's turn to frown. "What do my parents have to do with anything?"

"Do you love them?"

"Of course I do."

"Are they still with us? And healthy?"

"They are. My dad can still shoot his age on the golf course, and Mom is doing cutting-edge research at a lab in Shanghai."

"Good," said Orli. "Then tell me this: if Blue Fire was your mother, and Yellow Fire was your father, and this thing that we are doing was meant for them, which would you do? Transplant crystals from Yellow Fire or grow new ones here?"

"Well, if it was my dad back on earth, we'd just grow him some new skin. Like I said, it's easy once you have the whole genetic code, which we do."

"But what about the fact that the light is going through them, and the shattering part? That's not caused by the same 'code' as what's on Yellow Fire."

The professor's countenance became strictly serious again, like it did when he was focused fully on the work at hand and not trying in his awkward way to flirt. "Well, you have to leave something for life to do. Like I said, I think all this is something like an electrical circuit." He waved his arm around above his head. "When you blew up Red Fire's heart stone, you opened the circuit and killed the power source, including the auxiliary. I realize it's only a guess, but it fits the evidence pretty well. Your magical boyfriend there says the yellow stones on Blue Fire are all fired up all the time, even when they are pulled out and removed from the planet entirely. Yellow Fire's work there on that moon, but in his dormant state, they only barely function. They may be dead in terms of all that magical amplification business, but I think they are still looping his dormant energy; that's what I'm calling auxiliary. Here, they are dead entirely. To me it seems pretty obvious, even if we can't really measure the current, or whatever it is, anywhere. Yellow Fire is going to need the power source and closed loop. That's how I see it, but the only way I can prove it is to try the transplant and see if it all turns on. I have no idea what really binds it all. That whole bit about the stones' working independently throws a big question mark in the middle of everything, but I'll stand by my hypothesis until we come up with a better one."

"My *magical boyfriend* is also your employer, you know. The one who's opened up this opportunity for you to be here on this never-been-tried-before research. Show some respect."

He actually took a step back from her unexpected response. "Hey, no offense. I was just saying. Don't get cranky on me just because this is all frustrating."

She closed her eyes and took a breath. It was all frustrating; everyone present could feel it. She returned to her earlier line of inquiry. "So, to be clear, if this was your father, and his life and your mother's were at stake, you would grow the crystal bed around the heart rather than transplant additional crystal?"

"Well, my mother wouldn't ask to be killed if my dad was dead," he said. "She'd be heartbroken, but she's actually pretty happy with her work. She'd get through it. He'd want her to."

Orli's right eye started twitching, but the geologist saw it and amended his reply. "But yes, I would grow them. I know we can produce identical crystals to those that are here. There is no such guarantee that the crystal bed back on Yellow Fire will match these. In essence, moving them here would be like transplanting two organs instead of one. Twice the opportunity for rejection. Again, that is my guess. But you asked, so that is what I would do."

"I agree," chimed in the professor's assistant, Doctor Walters, over the com. She was in orbit, up on the *Glistening Lady*, using the ship's computers to assist with the work. "Geologically speaking, it's solid. Not sure about how it plays for resurrecting life, but he's right about the rest."

"How long will it take?" Orli asked. "To grow a crystal bed over all of that?" She pointed to the blown-out area all around them where the planetary rock was exposed.

"Probably longer than you want," said Professor Bryant. "Three months, maybe three and a half. We can do some things to try and speed it up, but this is a lot of space to cover. And they are big."

Orli's body moved with the magnitude of a mighty, decisive breath. "Fine," she said. "If you both think that's the way to go, then that's the way to go." She turned toward Altin and put her hands on her hips, staring up at him through the dome of the helmet glass. "So there you have it. Her Majesty asked that we get all our ducks in a row. Well, now we have them. We have a hole; we have the heart stone cut loose and ready to be moved; you have the transmutation spell you need; and the professor and Doctor Walters agree that they can regrow the crystal bed around it all. The only thing left is to convince Her Majesty that it is enough. She's even less inclined to science than you are."

"Hey," he protested. "I'm perfectly inclined to science, and I learn more and more every day."

She smiled. It was true. "I know. I'm just trying to make a point."

"Well, if you want something to be worried about, you should be thinking about how we're going to get past the wedding obstacle with Her Majesty. She fully intends to hold our happiness hostage for whatever it is she really wants."

"You know what?" Orli said, sounding suddenly completely at ease in that regard. "It's been so many months now, and Kettle is still not ready for it, and Pernie is clearly not coming home anytime soon. If all I have to do is wait another year for a ring and an official document, then so be it. If that's what it takes to safeguard Blue Fire's life at this point, I am fine with that. I've already corrupted you, and your honor is surely ruined as far as the purpose of all that delay anyway. I already have what I want." She grinned up at him, and saw that he was blushing beneath his helmet and making a rigid point not to look around. She even spared a glare for the professor while Altin recovered himself.

"Well," Altin said, changing the topic to one more suitable for public discourse, "you are quite right about Kettle and Pernie. But I should think that"—he paused and looked around the chamber filled with what amounted to broken Liquefying Stone—"we ought not mention that you've become suddenly so accommodating to Her Majesty's request." He grinned at her. "I think I've just realized the one thing that will motivate her to give her permission immediately, so long as you don't tip our hand."

Orli wasn't quite sure what he had in mind, but she did like the confidence in his voice.

"Well, then let us get to it," he said. He turned to the professor standing there. "You heard My Lady; get to your project. We'll go see if we can get the last thing we need: the sanction of two worlds."

Altin teleported himself and Orli out of the cavern directly to the lowest level of his tower, "the boot," as it had become known by the science team. They took off their spacesuits, and while Orli ran upstairs to "put on something that won't cause scandal on Prosperion," as she'd said, Altin spent a moment checking the area down below the surface, making sure it was still clear for the clean room. It was, so he sent the little room down to its designated resting place near the heart chamber, where they had been working for weeks. Satisfied it was in order, he checked the jar of fast-cast stones on the shelf near where the teleportation chamber sat when it was in the boot. There were still three of the small garnets inside the jar, none of them worth much for jewelry, but all perfectly suited for storing simple magic spells. If broken, any of the three would send the stone box down into the caverns of Red Fire, precisely as Altin had just done. And inside the chamber he'd just sent was a corresponding bowl in which resided four little blue sapphires, each of which would bring the box back to the boot. He figured that would be plenty for the team should they have need to move back and forth while he and Orli were gone.

With those precautions taken, he ran up after Orli and

found her waiting for him on the battlements, staring out into the blowing sand of the red world as she brushed her hair, still short in the style of Earth, which Altin simply adored.

"You get them all set up?" she confirmed as he came up behind her and wrapped his arms around her waist.

"I did," he replied, though it was muffled in the kisses he placed upon her neck.

"I'm still nervous about leaving them down there like that with us gone. Well, with you gone." She turned in his arms and faced him, looking up into his eyes.

"They're fine. I promise. They have four sapphires in the box to come back with, and they've got three garnets to go back down. You know Her Majesty has a short attention span when it comes to the technical details, so we'll make sure to bore her into agreement and then come right back."

She smiled. "Are you saying I'm boring when I talk about this stuff?"

"Oh, yes. It's dreadful when you start quoting readouts and things. I sometimes think I might have to cast a silence spell on you."

She gasped and shaped indignation on her face. "How dare you, Altin Meade. Don't you ever, or I'll ...."

"You'll what?"

"Well, just try it and see."

He smiled devilishly and kissed her, and for a time he let his hands roam freely. The rise of her breathing matched his own, and he had just begun to push her toward the floor when Orli's com button beeped and Roberto's voice came over it.

"Hey, we can see you guys down there, you know? That magic lid of yours is see-through."

Altin gasped and pushed away, looking up through the transparent barrier of his Polar Piton's Perfect Parabolic Protection shield. All he could see were the whirling clouds of the endlessly red atmosphere.

"You pervert," Orli said as she tapped the com button to transmit. "Don't you have enough hot chicks to look at up there as it is?"

"Who says you are a hot chick?" They could both hear him laughing.

"You know what I mean. Don't make me kill you the next time I'm up there."

"Who says I'll let you back on my ship?"

"You do see who is standing next to me, right, Captain Voyeur? I pretty much go where I want these days, so you better just watch it."

"Oh, I *was* watching it. That was the problem. I thought I might throw up, so I said something."

"Oh my God, you are going to die." She was smiling, however, despite Altin still looking rather uncomfortable about having nearly been caught.

"Hey, you guys are the ones who told me to monitor everything from up here."

That was true enough. "Hey, speaking of that, make sure you do. Keep a close eye on those guys in case they need you for anything. Altin and I have what we need to go talk to the Queen."

"Yeah, Stacy told me. Good luck. But you know she's going to make you guys wait to get married, right? You're going to have to keep doing it in sin. Hopefully not where I have to watch."

Altin turned nearly purple at that, though Orli didn't even bat an eye. "I know. Altin has something planned." She looked up at him with eyebrows raised expectantly. "At least I think he does."

"I do," he said, his neck blotchy as if with some strange blood disease.

Orli laughed, then smiled up at him.

"Hey, who else is that with you anyway?" Roberto asked.

"Who came back up an hour or two ago, before you guys did?"

"What do you mean?" Orli asked. "We don't have anyone else up here."

"Hate to break it to you, lover girl, but, yes, you do. There's someone right there with you, or at least"—he paused, and the feed cut off for a second—"someone seven point three yards southwest of where Altin is standing. I'm looking at the heat signature right now. Not as hot as you two were a minute ago, but there plain as day. I can't get a visual through the storm."

They both looked in the direction Roberto had given them. If there was someone there, whoever it was had to be standing outside the dome of the Polar Piton's shield, out in the fury of the winds and blowing sand.

Orli shook her head. "Are they moving?"

"Nope. Hasn't moved since it popped up. Just standing there."

She went right up to the battlement and leaned against the cool, black-painted steel crenel that had replaced the stone ones that had been there before the tower accident. She peered through the Polar Piton's shield out into the wind, but she still couldn't see a thing. "How much did you pay for that ship again?" she asked finally. "You might want to take the sensor modules back under warranty."

"Seven hundred and thirty-four billion, and the sensors are just fine. Dude, I'm looking right at it. You can't see through that garbage blowing out there, but I can. There's someone there. Or something. Temperature says human. It's plain as day."

"One sec," she said. She frowned at Altin, who glanced up at her long enough to see it before staring out into the wind again. The winds were especially bad just now. He started a seeing spell shortly after as Orli went running off down the stairs.

JOHN DAULTON

She came back with a pair of binoculars and dialed up the infrared. She raised them up and gasped immediately after. "Holy shit!" she said.

"Yeah. See, that's what I tried to tell you," Roberto said over the com.

"But what is it? It's too small to be human."

"It's the right temperature," Roberto said again. "Look at your reading. The static charge in the wind is probably just messing with it some. Thank God, too, because I really wouldn't have wanted to watch you two going at it a minute ago in high definition. Your panting-ass heat signatures were bad enough."

She ignored him and checked the temperature reading. He was right. Definitely human. She turned to query Altin, but his eyes were closed, his vision now beyond the tower in a seeing spell. Though not for long. A moment after, they sprang open as if on a spring.

"By the gods!" he exclaimed.

"What is it?" both Orli and Roberto asked, nearly simultaneously.

"It's Tytamon's decanter. The one that I sent out there to test gravity the day we arrived."

Orli wrinkled up her pretty face. "You mean the little wound-up palm-trees thing with the spinning lid?"

"The very same."

Chapter 32

Pernie's hands trembled as she tried to pour the oleander extract into the small glass vial. Adding to her difficulty, she could hardly see. She'd been dizzy since, well, pretty much ever since the first dose of the stuff three months back. The poison had been Seawind's bitter antidote to sugar-shrimp joy apparently. She knew that wasn't exactly true, but the timing of his announcing it was time for her to build "immunity" sure coincided with that day of sweet discovery. All she knew for certain was that it made her feel sick most of the time. And the world got to tilting and whirling sometimes. But it wasn't as bad as it was yesterday, and that had been better than the day before. And so on.

The oleander oil was the last to go in as she mixed it. They called it *Fayne Gossa*, which translated roughly to "the flavors of nine hells." Djoveeve said it was "all poisons and none," whatever that meant. They'd taught her how to mix it herself a month after they'd started giving it to her. She hated that they made her take it, but it thrilled her to see it at work. They only gave her the barest portions to practice with, at least at first, but recently they'd let her have as much of it as she wanted to take with her when she went out exploring on her own.

She'd taken to trying it out on the way to the beaches she haunted, finding things to kill with it simply to watch it work. So, as she often did, out she went into the jungle intent on having a bit of fun with it again. She started small at first, coating her knife blade and flipping it through the air at a little monkey climbing in a tree. She aimed for its back leg carefully, wanting the poison to do the work, and of course by now her aim was startling—"The truest sort of killer you are," Djoveeve had said to her one day, "forged by the old gods, no doubt." So the monkey fell, and Pernie ran over to watch it. It flopped down on its back and stared up at her, little brown eyes wide, its mouth opening and closing, as if gasping for air, or perhaps wanting to scream in agony. But no sound came out. The poison was wonderful that way. The extract of cottonwood was for that, the essence of muffling, augmented of course by elven magic. Its little gray limbs twitched, tiny black fingers opening and closing like a little beggar after alms, its mouth opening and closing as well. Pernie cocked her little head and studied it, her own mouth moving to mirror what she saw, shaping its unspoken words until finally it was still, looking now into eternity through wide, staring eyes. Death was interesting enough, she supposed, but dying was spellbinding.

She jerked her arms out of the big pack she wore on her back, and threw open the flap. Tipping it over, she dumped Knot out, the insect rolling out in a ball. Pernie sent it a thought to uncurl it, and sent after that thought the idea of food, projecting an image of the little monkey lying there. Knot unwound hastily and in moments had sucked out the monkey's eyes.

Still needing to walk given her dizziness, she sent a telepathic poke into the insect's mind again, the promise of pain, and it rolled right back up again. She almost never had to hurt it anymore. Which was good. She didn't like being mean.

She rolled him back into her pack and put it on again. Djoveeve said carrying him around was good for her and would make her strong. She told the old assassin that she would do so, but the truth was, she was too unstable to ride him very well these days anyway. The poison put her in a perpetual cloud of semi-nausea and random waves of vertigo. She didn't want to admit to being weak. She was too close to the test now. If she could kill the orc, she could go home.

She hated to admit it to herself, but she was losing hope for finding a suitable sea mount. She'd spent months and months chasing creatures around, teleporting across the water at them—teleporting out of their teeth sometimes (oh, how saltwater did sting when something bit into her)—but never finding one with mind enough and magic enough to properly communicate.

She would have asked Djoveeve why that was, for the creatures on land with magic were certainly abundant enough, but she didn't want help for that. She was Sava'an'Lansom, and they kept telling her that she "must find the way" for everything. "That is your great power," Seawind said time and time again.

But she didn't think she was going to find a way to find a sea creature anymore. At least not with her whole heart. And the time was getting close for killing the orc. She would kill it with her new poison. Or at least, she would once she could see straight again.

She pulled her knife out of the monkey's leg and wiped the blood off on its fur. After carefully coating the tip and edges with Fayne Gossa again, she pushed the knife back into its sheath. She headed onward, this time to a beach well north of the little network of caves she'd been living in since coming here, the little network of caves that seemed only to hold herself and Djoveeve, and Seawind when he came. She never saw any other elves, only the hunters when they showed up, but that was only occasionally now. Once a month. And never anyone new.

She still hadn't seen a woman among them, not a girl of any kind. It was as if there were no female elves at all. Only Djoveeve stood for her sex here, and she would tell Pernie nothing about the lady elves. Nothing. As if it were some deep, dark secret to be guarded from everyone, even the Sava'an'Lansom. Some bodyguard Pernie would be if they didn't tell her anything.

She came upon a narrow animal trail that would take her up a long incline. It led to a particular cliff that she intended to climb down and gain access to a hard-to-reach beach. She'd seen a number of large, horned manatee-like creatures down there a few times before, and she thought she might try taming one of them.

She scrambled up the trail and was just about to leap over a few groping lengths of vile ivy, the name earned for its painful acidic burn, when a single pop of a twig sent her diving under it instead. The rotting-meat stench of the *latakasokis*' breath blasted her as its giant teeth snapped shut with a mighty *clack*—right where her head had been a half instant before.

She looked up long enough to see it towering above her, a bipedal dragon, the same as those she'd discovered on that first day, the day she'd first chased the hunt and then the bugs like Knot had chased her. That seemed so long ago now. This latakasokis stood four spans high and was twelve more from nose to tail. It snapped at her again as she muttered the two words for a teleport, which placed her behind it, crouched less than a pace away.

She ducked its tail as it spun on her, drawing her little obsidian knife. Its head shot forward again, the mouth wide enough that she might have stood upright in it upon its tongue and not bumped her head on its jagged teeth. Two more words and she was on its back. She jammed her knife into the soft spot right beneath its stubby little wings, a little pocket like an armpit, the tender hide barely as thick as shoe leather. The elven blade slipped through it easily, and Pernie gripped its little wing in her fist as the great creature went into thrashing fits trying to get at her.

Its eyes widened a moment after, flaring as if in surprise, then the creature went stiff. It tipped over and crashed into the brush, coming to rest against the base of a large tree, which was the only thing that prevented it from rolling down the slope.

Despite her blurred vision and a mild surge of vertigo, Pernie managed to stay atop it. She scrambled around it as it fell and ended up standing upon its ribs when it came to rest. Once it was still, she slid down to stand on its neck. Just like she had with the monkey, she tilted her little head and watched as the latakasokis seemed to try to speak. Its great jaws hinged and unhinged, making shapeless words whose only sound was the rustling of the brush beneath the monster's head. Then it too was dead, staring out at nothing.

Pernie thought Knot would really enjoy eyes as big as that. Nearly as big as cawfrat eyes, which were Knot's favorite treat.

The monster's head was too heavy for Pernie to lift, and it was too large and dense for her F-class teleport to flip, so Knot had to suffice with the one eye for now, though Pernie thought it would be fun to start hunting latakasoki now. If she'd known how easy it would be, she'd have done it earlier. No wonder the elves had made such quick work of those that had surrounded her in that pool.

She debated going back down the slope and looking for more, but decided to stick with why she'd come. She was still a little wobbly on her feet and didn't want to risk a mistake. She wasn't sure she'd be so lucky if she came across two or three, and they did hunt in packs regularly.

She decided climbing down the cliff was a safer bet, and

so she continued toward her original goal, eventually making it to her destination and standing atop the cliff, looking out over the sea. The sun was well above her now, and the sky was perfectly clear. She felt like she could see forever as she stood there in the wind, her long hair shimmering like a golden flag flowing out far behind her as she watched and, in her way, waited patiently. Somewhere out there was Kurr. Somewhere out there was Master Altin—Sir Altin—and, of course, Orli Pewter too. Assuming she wasn't Orli Meade now. Pernie hoped she wasn't. She thought about trying to get ahold of Master Altin and asking, or even trying Fortie Nomstacker, whom she knew from her brief time at the magic school. His was the only other mind she knew, though his mind had always had something about it that made her uncomfortable. But there was no point in trying either of them. She'd already tried a hundred times. Nobody answered her. It was as if no one could hear her from this place.

That thought kicked her out of the reverie, for it was, at least in essence, why she had come to the cliff in the first place. She looked down toward the beach two hundred spans below, but there weren't any of the fat creatures that looked like manatees down there. She hoped that they would come, though, especially the big ones with the great clawed flippers and the forward-facing horns. They shot those horns like spears from their foreheads when they fought. She thought those creatures might have magic in them, if she could just once find one close enough to be in reach of her teleport. They were so skittish, it seemed.

She sighed as she looked down the rock face. The wind blowing up it slicked the black rocks wet with mist from the crashing waves. Before she could even form the thought, she teetered where she stood. It was vertigo caused by the poison in her veins, not by the height she was looking down from. She held no fear of altitude, though she was not keen to fall and be smashed upon the rocks.

She debated letting Knot climb down for her, but she doubted she'd be any better off trying to balance on his narrow sides as he tacked his way back and forth down the side. She definitely didn't want to try it straight down, standing only on his rump. She'd be better off climbing down on her own.

She checked to make sure her spear was firmly strapped to her pack, then belted the pack around her skinny little waist as well. Tightening the shoulder straps so it wouldn't move about, she lay flat on her belly, then turned around feetfirst and scooted her legs over the edge, folding herself at the waist.

Her toes probed for purchase on something, some little edge, some protrusion of any kind. She was, and essentially always had been, an exquisite climber, so she didn't need much. She found one and, with it, gently pushed herself down, holding onto a crag near the top.

Shortly after, she was fully upon the face of it, glad for having gotten over the edge, for that was the difficult part when climbing without a rope. She clung there like a tiny four-legged spider and looked down, searching for the next purchase for her feet. Her hair blew wildly around her face, the golden flag seemingly torn to tatters and whipping all around. She shook her head to throw it all back somewhat uniformly into the wind.

And just like that, she was falling.

She could see the edge of the cliff slipping away as she plummeted, a glimpse of perfect blue sky. Arcing her head back, she looked for the ground instead, deciding in that instant whether to teleport back to the top or wait until she was in range of the beach.

She hadn't tried timing a jump like that before—if the teleport she'd need could be called a jump—but somehow in the calm of that plunge it came to her that the bottom was an option too. So she curled up her knees briefly as she tipped her head way back, looking as far around toward the beach as she could. Her body followed her gaze, and she gently rolled over, at which point she flattened herself out into the fall again, now looking down at the rocks and sand.

They seemed to be hurtling up at her. She twisted and glanced toward the water, looking for a good spot to land. She had to wait the split second until she was in range. She could only teleport fifty spans, and even with the short two-word version of the spell, timing would be everything.

She wished she wasn't so dizzy now.

The craggy black shapes of the rocks were almost upon her when she barked the two words out. And then she was standing on the sand.

Her little chest rose and fell rapidly as she blinked down at her feet. She'd done it.

She looked around a little wildly, staggering as a wave of vertigo hit, poison and the descent combined. Then she looked back up to where she'd just come from and laughed.

With a quick glance around, seeing that there were no great magic manatees around, she trotted back to the cliff, where she began to climb with a huge, ecstatic smile.

She wanted to do that again.

Chapter 33

Orli drew her blaster and pointed it where Altin indicated he'd be teleporting the decanter to. He directed her to move down the stairs a ways, so she could have cover—or a head start—if there was need for a getaway. "Don't shoot it, though," he said. "Only if I tell you to."

"Or if something jumps out and eats his head," Roberto added over the com.

"That's not funny," she said.

"Just trying to lighten it up," Roberto said. "You two are making me nervous with all that readiness. We all know you can't shoot for crap, Orli, and Altin just said you guys had that thing with you when you got here the first time. Altin put it there himself."

"Yes, well, it didn't have life signs then," Orli said. "So something is happening."

"Did you look?" Roberto asked. He had, after all, been the one to point out that it was radiating human body temperature. "I mean before you put it there to begin with?"

Altin glanced up at Orli upon hearing that. It was a good point.

"Well, no," she admitted. "I hadn't thought of that."

"Well, that's all I'm saying. You guys are making me

nervous, and whenever you pull a gun, I get this overwhelming desire to run and hide."

She let herself grin and started to come back up the stairs, but Altin held up his hand. "No, just in case. He's probably right, but a little caution costs us nothing."

She nodded, and he began the teleport spell that would bring the decanter up to the battlements. Casting took him barely beyond a second, and then there it was, sitting right before him on the flagstones, a tall, slender thing made of clear crystal, shaped like a pair of palm trees that have wound round and round one another as they grew. The stopper was made to look like leafy palm fronds, sharp spikes of flat green glass that had spun freely with the force of the wind, and it continued to do so even after it arrived, though it was clearly losing momentum now that they were out of the storm.

Orli shifted her grip on the blaster as Altin watched the decanter, prepared to send it right back out if he had to. He glanced up at her, then right back, both of them anxious to see what might appear. If anything.

Slowly the little palm-frond stopper stopped turning, and at last the thing was completely still. Nothing else happened.

"Wasn't it empty before?" Orli asked. With the movement of her head, she directed his attention to the fact that it was full to the top with a gray-green liquid of some kind.

"It was," Altin agreed.

"So what is it?"

"I have no idea."

"You know," said Roberto, cutting into the tension in the tower's inner atmosphere, "for being the big-shot wizard on Prosperion, I have to say, you say that a lot. I thought you read books all the time."

"I do," he said. "But it seems the more I read, the less I know. It's like every new book simply reveals the existence of whole new stacks of information that I also haven't learned."

"Well, that's not very useful right now."

"No, it's not."

"So what do we do with it?" Orli asked. "Do you take it to Doctor Leopold and have it divined? Or maybe Ocelot?"

"I've had about all of Ocelot I can stand," Altin said. "But I'll get it to the doctor when we get time. For now, let's stick to the mission, and go speak to the Queen. Whatever this is, it has been sitting up here this long, so I'm sure it will be fine waiting a little longer for Doctor Leopold."

"Maybe you should just put it back out there," Roberto suggested. "Just in case, you know, like the wind or something in the atmosphere was working like a refrigerator on that thing. Whatever is in there might just need to warm up before it comes shooting out and opens up a whole new can of whoop ass that nobody really needs right now."

"It was in Tytamon's collection," Altin said. "I doubt it harbors some awful monster or unspeakable plague. He was not the sort of man to leave something like that lying about on a windowsill." To prove his faith in that idea, he went to it and picked it up. It was warm to the touch. "Interesting," he said. He really wanted to open it, but resisted the temptation.

"Well, then let's go," Orli said. "I want to get this discussion with Her Majesty over so we can get Yellow Fire on the road to recovery. Do what you're going to do with it, and let's start moving."

Altin's jaw worked back and forth for a time, and then he closed his eyes. A moment after, the decanter vanished from his hand with a pop of collapsing air.

"Where'd it go?" Orli asked.

"I put it back where it's always been. In Tytamon's window, right where he himself left it last."

"Good. Now let's go. With luck, we can be working on

Yellow Fire before dinnertime."

That, however, would not be the case, for upon their arrival in Crown City some half hour later, they found Her Majesty locked in a private audience with officials from the Transportation Guild Services, including the entire TGS council and the master operators of the three currently functional TGS space depots.

"I'm sorry, Sir Altin," apologized the herald standing between two guards outside Her Majesty's private audience chamber. "But no one is admitted."

"He's the Galactic Mage," Orli reminded him. "There wouldn't be any TGS space depots without him."

"All the same, Miss Pewter, orders are orders."

"It is fine," Altin said, mildly annoyed. The two of them took a walk around the Palace while they waited for a chance to speak with the Queen. When finally word came, the sun had already fallen off the edge of the world, and the Palace glowed like a golden mountain for all across the city to see.

Her Majesty met them in her audience chamber, staying there after the last of the TGS officials had gone. She was finishing off a lamb chop as they came in. Altin bowed and Orli curtsied as was proper in the royal presence.

"Yes, yes," the Queen said, seeing all of that. "So what news have you brought? I'm sure you're going to get on with begging me about Blue Fire's mate again, so let's be on with it so we can be done again."

"Your Majesty," said Altin. "You asked that we gather more information. And we have. It's been several months' work, and at considerable personal expense, but we now have everything we need. Orli has prepared a document that breaks down all the sciences and principles at work, and she details how they have been verified, including the work of several brilliant men and women of science from planet Earth."

Orli lifted the tablet she'd been carrying since they'd come. She pulled up the presentation she had put together, beginning with a brief video in which Professor Bryant explained some of the core geologic principles in language that Her Majesty would surely understand. That was the advantage of having a professor along, as making such explanations palatable to various audiences was part of his job.

But before the professor managed to get even a full sentence out, the Queen waved it away. "Turn it off; turn it off. I already know you'll have the tedious details worked out, assuming it's possible at all. Spare me all that nonsense. I'm too old to try to learn the wearisome workings of another world in that sort of detail. That's what young people are for."

Orli paused the display, but couldn't quite get her mouth closed all the way, so stunned was she by that. "But Your Majesty," she started to protest, but the Queen cut her off again.

"You already know what I want. So say it, and you'll have my permission. I've already talked to Director Bahri about this at length. I was on Earth several times last week, if you didn't know. His opinion on the Blue Fire–Yellow Fire matter remains the same. He wants precautions in case things go wrong, but the rest is up to me. So if I say so, it will be done."

"Fine," Orli said. "We'll wait. I don't care anymore. It's already been a year since Altin proposed, so what's another one? The lives of two living worlds are at stake, and I won't let them be bargaining chips in the debate over a party on our behalf."

"It's on *all* of our behalf, my dear. You have no idea how much people love these sorts of things. The blanks and commoners just adore celebrity, and it will win me a great deal of goodwill. Goodwill that I have lost. You may not be

JOHN DAULTON

aware of it, but there are many who blame me for the losses we incurred in the war. Many. And I have to give them something to prove that things are returning to the happy, untroubled way they were before it all went wrong." She forced a smile at the end of it, but there were stress lines around her eyes.

"Well, you could have married off a duke or something," Orli said. "It didn't have to be my wedding you kept ransoming."

"That insolent tongue sounds an ugly thing in such a pretty mouth as yours, and it would be a shame to lose it."

"Your Majesty," Altin interjected, knowing well how tenuous the relationship between Orli and the War Queen was. There had simply been too much stress put on it since they'd first met. It was going to take time to heal it back to where it should be, if such was even possible. "There is something you should know. It is about the Liquefying Stone."

Her Majesty pushed her plate away and leaned back in her regal chair rather abruptly. The disinterested smile that followed was obviously forced. "Well, go on?"

"Your Liquefying Stones, the eight hundred you have locked up in your vaults, the ones you took from *Citadel* for safekeeping, well, it seems they will no longer function if Blue Fire dies."

That sat her up again. "They what?"

"Yes," Altin went on. "We've seen it firsthand. Orli and I and, of course, the science team that the professor brought with him agree: when they die, the Hostile worlds, or the beings, whatever they may be, when they die, the crystals no longer function for channeling mana. They don't even draw light the way they did. They become little more than hazy gray rocks. If the heart stone is destroyed, they become brittle as glass."

"Well, then you certainly won't be keeping your promise

310

to kill her, should the attempt to revive the other one go bad. In fact, I rescind my permission in that regard." Her tone made it clear that there was no room for argument with that. She even smiled again. "There, you see, Miss Pewter, just like that, you have your argument back."

"I don't want my argument back." Orli looked at Altin and shook her head, exasperated and seeming to say, "Why in the hell did you tell her that?" with her eyes. "Your Majesty, Blue Fire will die anyway. Somehow she'll find a way. Surely at some point simple despair will kill her, whether she believes it or not."

"Perhaps, but for now we have hope that somehow she will revive her spirits, and until such time, we shall just pray to the gods for her quick recovery. Now, if that is all, I have a great deal of things to attend. Your teleporting guildmates at the TGS are a demanding lot and nearly extort gold from me these days. And it appears that Miss Pewter's people remain all aflutter in fear of what will happen if magicians are allowed on their world. I've just come back, and I can tell you, everywhere we went the lights dimmed and the buzzers buzzed and doors opened randomly at times. They actually had the audacity to ask that I take off my armor. I should think more than a few assassins would enjoy such an opportunity."

"Who on Earth would want to kill you? There's no reason for it."

"You are aware of the number of lives that were lost there, are you not?" she said. "Hundreds of thousands. Their previous director paid the price and will rot in jail for life. They're still fighting over his fate, as many are calling for him to be executed publicly, although they've made a big fuss about that not being appropriate. They are a people squeamish about death in that regard. I can hardly believe they considered doing anything but. However, it's not my world, so if they want to feed him until he dies, so be it. But there are those who feel I should be sitting in that cell with him, and it seems I have many enemies on both worlds these days. I have this from Director Bahri's own ... master-at-arms or whatever they call them. It is a threat that, of course, comes with the territory, so to speak, but it was an astonishing moment of clarity when I found them all bewildered by the fact that I would not take off my armor. What was it, did they suppose, that had me wearing it to begin?"

"Your Majesty," said Altin. "I realize that ruling a continent, exploring space, and engaging in interplanetary diplomacy is stressful and time consuming, but we really must bring Yellow Fire back. In the name of decency, you must give us your permission. Orli has already agreed on the wedding ceremony. That is what you said. Please. There are so many people who have worked on this. And, if we are being frank with one another, you are right about my intentions to keep my word. I promised her that if our attempt to bring Yellow Fire back to life failed, I would end her suffering. If you refuse to let us try, then I will have failed to bring him back. You would trap me in my own honor, and so fate will write the rest. So I beg you not to set us on this course."

"I could have my assassin finish you in an instant."

"I can be gone in half of one. Please, Your Majesty. It is the right thing to do. She gave so much to us all. And if somehow it doesn't work, I'll find you another Hostile world. We'll get you more of the stone." He hated saying it even as the words came out. He hated the fact she'd ever found out about the stones at all. Everything that was happening was exactly why Tytamon had gone to such lengths for so many centuries to keep the secret of the Liquefying Stone his own. And now the Queen had eight hundred of them. Hells, the priests of Anvilwrath even had one, the one they'd found, the one he'd lost—assuming they'd dug it out from under the wreckage of the temple somehow. He was fairly sure they would have made a point of it.

The simple truth was that Liquefying Stone was a secret that somehow Tytamon had just known Altin would let out, as if he'd resigned himself to it, even though he'd hoped otherwise. It was a lure to corruption that the great mage knew Altin would release. And now Altin had just vowed to get the War Queen replacements, even more than the eight hundred she already had. He was the pawn of the very corruption he wanted to avoid.

It was a thought so perverse and horrible that he might even have recanted his promise. But he couldn't. And, he hoped, the prospects of finding another Hostile world were unlikely to the point of being impossible.

The Queen glared at Altin for a time, her eyes narrow and her lips taut as bowstrings. Altin was prepared to teleport himself and Orli out, the spell poised in his mind, shaped and ready to go off with a thought. The least flick of her finger, the least movement of her head that might have the assassin moving, he would be gone.

But she did not.

"You are either very brave or very stupid to talk to me that way, Sir Altin. But since the day I first met you, I have never known anyone to be more honorable and worthy of tolerance than you. So, very well. I grant my permission—on the condition of the wedding, just as before, of course."

Orli rolled her eyes and shook her head, but she said that she would agree. Like she already had.

"And with so much at stake, I will provide what assistance I may," the Queen offered, as if she hadn't just run them both through the gristmill. "Do you need anything from me to ensure the success of the work?"

"Yes," he said. "I'd like to have Aderbury do the transmutation that will bind Yellow Fire's heart in place."

The Queen harrumphed at that, the sound resonant

beneath the bright golden breastplate. "That is impossible. He is busy."

"But he is the best transmuter in the land. His hand is the one we need."

"Well, his hands are full on *Citadel*. Find someone else."

Altin shook his head. There was no one else. No one he knew well enough to trust. He was better off doing it himself if they couldn't get Aderbury to do it. His own transmutation abilities were made better than his rank would indicate due to his access to seven of the eight magic schools. What he lacked in the artistry of Aderbury, his raw power could make up for. Or at least they had to hope so, given that there was a life at stake.

"Then there is nothing that we need beg of you," he said. "Except perhaps that you might get word to Director Bahri that you have given your permission for us to be under way, and that it has begun."

"Done," she said. She whisked him away with a backhanded flick of her fingers. "Now be off with you. The two of you have given me a headache, and I wish to close my eyes."

"Yes, Your Majesty." He bowed, Orli curtsied, and together they backed out of the room.

When the doors were shut behind them, Orli allowed herself to grin. "Finally," she said. "Finally Blue Fire has a chance at happiness."

"Yes," agreed Altin. "So long as I don't botch the transmute."

"You won't."

"Let us hope that you are right."

Chapter 34

Annison lay beneath the strange spotted tiles, staring up into them as he had so many times before. So many days had passed that he'd lost count. He'd developed a reflex for looking up there during the first few months of his capture, a revulsion reflex that made him want to look away from the monitor showing the exposed dome of his brain where they had cut away most of his skull. But he was over that now. Mostly these days, he looked up there dimly absent of thought, the horror of what they did to him numbed to passivity. It was almost as if he watched from a distance, as if his mind had gone elsewhere and locked itself in a different room, someplace inside his head where things like having people peeling away parts of your brain didn't matter anymore.

He looked back to the monitor anyway. The big one showed the table behind the reclining chair he still occupied, the same chair he'd been in since he first arrived. The upper part of his brain had been removed, the parts halved, pulled out, and chopped up like some sticky gray cabbage. The parts now floated in shallow trays of fluid, connected by shimmering strands of tiny silver wires to the portions of his brain that remained in his hollowed-out skull. The wires, thin as spider web, were attached to metal pins and long needle probes, each of which was nearly as thin as the silver fibers themselves. All of those things, those alien wires and probes, had been stuck into his butchered brain.

At night the people in white coats filled up his skull cavity with the same fluid that was in the two trays holding the left and right portions of his upper brain, but when they came in during the day to monitor him and investigate, they'd suck it out with a loud, rasping tube.

He found that he couldn't channel mana anymore, not even with the pain-inducing electrode now removed from his throat. Whatever they'd done when they pulled out those brain parts seemed to have snipped his ability to do magic anymore. Though that's not quite what they said.

Doctor Gaspar, the taller and leaner of the two women who worked on him, came in just as he was moving his gaze from his pared brain to the smaller monitor, which showed his emaciated body lying there. He doubted he even made five stone's weight anymore; four might be a stretch. To his eyes, he looked like nothing more than a skeleton lying beneath a drapery of skin.

"Good morning, Annison," the woman in the white coat intoned as she came to his side and looked down at him. "How are you feeling today? Strong enough to do some magic for us this time?"

He knew better than to let hope rise.

"So today we're going to try communicating with your friends again. I want you to try to communicate with those men you told us about, the ones you said were trying to find you. Are you ready to try?"

Oh, he was so ready to try. But he knew it wouldn't work. He'd tried a thousand times since that lost contact on the stage. He could remember it so clearly, more than any other memory. It was the clearest memory he had: him lying there, staring at El Segador's shoes as the theater lights dimmed. And to think how much he had hated being there, doing those magic shows. He would have done anything to be The Incredible Spectacularo now. He could have loved those patrons if he'd wanted to. They were just people after all, perhaps victims of circumstance like he was. But now it was too late.

"Speak up, my friend. Are you ready, or do you need a jolt to get your energy up?"

He didn't need a jolt. They'd attached the electrode that had once been in his throat to a pair of them in his feet. "I can try," he rasped.

"Good," she said. "One second while I pull up the telepathy file. Now be a good boy and don't try anything else. We already know what the patterns look like. Jefe is very pleased with you, but El Segador thinks you are stonewalling us a bit."

If there was anything like humor left in him, any place in his soul where the possibility of mirth, or even irony, remained, he might have laughed. Stonewalling? The energy for any such thing had died in him well over a month ago. Probably longer than that.

"All right, that's got it. Go ahead. Try to call them up. And give me the name of which one you are going for."

"Black Sander," he said, his voice barely audible.

"You said you can't reach that one. Do the one with the Z. You seem to do better with that."

Annison just lay there. The effort of speaking made him tired. He started to drift off to sleep, but the short zap of electricity in his feet snapped him awake again.

"Go on. The Z. Do it."

He let go of the breath that had locked in his lungs when the electricity hit and exchanged it for a fresh one. He closed his eyes and let the air out slowly as he once again reached out for the marchioness' telepath, the man with the frenetic undertones in his mind. He reached for the mana as he had done so many times throughout his life with hardly more effort than it took to see something or notice a sound, the effort of smelling something cooking on a stove, hardly so much effort as even that.

He felt nothing, though. The familiar sense of probing, of finding resistance or acceptance of his thoughts, all of that was gone. He could try to smell the pot on the stove, could even feel the air passing through his nostrils, but there were no odors there. So it was with his attempt to communicate. There simply wasn't anything there.

"Very good," she said. "Now keep it up; don't let it die down like you did last time." She looked up from her monitor, where zigzag lines striped a chart in one quarter of the screen and lines of data scrolled in the bottom half. "Carmen," she called, "reduce the filter another six hertz. Give him a little help."

"Okay, he has it," the other woman said from her place at a workstation across the room.

Both women worked quietly for a time. Annison kept trying to reach out to the Z-class seer somewhere on Prosperion, the habit of hope still working even in this hopeless state.

"Look," said the woman. "They're coming together. Give me another half. We might actually get a match."

The sound of fingers on glass followed, and Annison nearly gave up, but then both women simultaneously cried out, "There!"

"We've got it, oh Blessed Mother, we've got the match," said the woman across the room.

"And look," said the first from her place near Annison's head. "Look there. What is that? See?"

"It's coming from outside. That's not us."

"Oh my God," said the first. "He must have got them. It's working. It's finally working." Her fingers beat a rapid-fire thrum on the console as she worked. "Call them, call them," she said as she worked. "Tell them it's finally happening."

Annison found himself distracted by their noise, but fought to hold on. What had he done? Had he connected with the marchioness' seer somehow? He couldn't feel a thing. But what if he had? He pleaded for help in the same instant he allowed himself to ride the wave of his captors' enthusiasm. He sent cries, weeping cries from the core of his most desperate soul. "Please save me," he sent with thoughts that throbbed with tortured agony. "Please." It felt like shouting into a pillow. Pointless.

His real sobbing broke his ability to concentrate, but, apparently, not the elation of the women in the room. They were both still jubilant when Jefe and El Segador arrived.

Chapter 35

"**D**ude, you owe me," Roberto said as he stared at Altin's image in the monitor before him. "Look at all the stuff I've done for you guys on Red Fire already." He lay on his stomach as he spoke, a buxom woman in the suggestive uniform of the *Glistening Lady*'s crew providing him with a rather rough massage that made his voice surge in volume as she dug into back muscles that lay atop his ribs and lungs.

"It's not for lack of willingness," Altin replied. "I'll gladly accompany you to Murdoc Bay or anywhere else you should like to go, but Orli made me promise specifically that I wouldn't go back there unless it was on the orders of the Queen. She insists it's too dangerous for someone of 'my profile.' I promised."

"You make too many big, binding promises, dude. But I got you covered. Technically, I'm on the Queen's business selling this stuff. And now it's finally been approved by the NTA Department of Health and Agriculture, which means I've only got a few months to build a strong brand in the market before some dickhead company clones it and starts opening up their own chain stores. You know someone is going to try to hose me, man; that's what these big global companies do. You really think the NTA needed all this time to put it through quarantine?"

"I don't think the NTA will go directly against Her Majesty's first trade venture on planet Earth. That's hardly in keeping with good diplomacy."

"The NTA won't. At least not directly. But they will sell it to someone else and have them do it for them. I've actually got my first mate looking for signs of it being shopped around down here already. Deeqa knows people—hell, she's related to people—who would do it in a heartbeat. Trust me; if there's anything these people are good at, it's making money. They ain't the Northern *Trade* Alliance for nothing. They already brought down one world order for cash; don't think they can't get you guys too."

"Well, I think you sell Her Majesty short, but I do understand your concern, and your reason for haste in getting your next load. It's been a long time in coming for you, and you deserve your rewards. Do you really think your people can possibly make an imitation variety of Goblin Tea that will taste as good and have all the same effects? There are creatures of Prosperion involved with growing it, you know. Pollination and that sort of thing."

"Oh, they'll make something close enough. I get all that 'right air, right soil, right bugs' thing, but there's nobody down here that's had it before. If someone beats me to establishing *the* brand, I'll be the knockoff trying to capture some gourmet niche or something. They'll have set the palate, and worse, they can afford to run nonstop net ads convincing everyone that drinking anything else makes you a total loser. People believe that crap. You can't out-info-war the super rich. They'll get all the everyday sales if I don't execute this perfectly. You of all people should understand that I don't want to lose."

Altin nodded. "I do understand."

They exchanged grim nods. "Good. And that is why I

need you with me in Murdoc Bay. Something is up down there, and the last two times we went, we've had people trying to sneak onto the ship, like, right there at the plantation. One of them even tried to do one of those icicle things you guys do, tried to hit one of my girls when she caught him. Deeqa had to shoot his ass."

Altin's lips drew taut and curled in on themselves as he considered that. "Have you told Her Majesty?"

"I have no way to tell her. I sent a message through the TGS depot, just like everyone else trying to communicate with your government does. It's all bureaucratted up now. The TGS might as well be the NTA now, at least when it comes to procedures, forms, and delays."

"Well, I can get word to her for you. She can send a contingent of mages to accompany you."

"She won't. That was my first request four months ago when the two dipshits tried to sneak on board the first time. They thought they could turn invisible and just walk right in, but we can see that crap on sensors. You guys might be able to scramble our brains or whatever with your illusions, but they don't do crap to surveillance feeds."

"Hmm," Altin hummed. "Then you do have a problem, and I can certainly see why having me along would help."

"I'm telling you, man, I don't want to cause an interplanetary incident or anything, but if those assholes keep trying to screw with my people or my ship, I'll burn them down in piles until I get some respect. I know how it goes with blanks down there, especially in Murdoc Bay. And I have Her Majesty's permission to do it, too, although she made me promise to use some restraint, which is why I'm calling you. I guess that bony old hag the marchioness is already pissed off about me being there as it is, so I'm not supposed to become a 'diplomatic problem.'"

"Yes, you're walking more than one fine line in that particular town, to be sure."

"Yeah, so I need you to keep it peaceful. I don't want Her Majesty to think I can't handle it, and I don't have time to wait to hear back from her anyway. The way I see it, if they know you're there, they won't even try anything. Who's going to screw with you?"

"Well, you might be surprised, but again, I see your point. Let me talk to Orli about getting out of that promise."

"I'll talk to her," Roberto offered as his masseuse was working her way down his spine. He seemed to think about what he'd volunteered to do for a second, then said to the woman working on him, "Go back to my neck and shoulders. Orli's attitude is already making me tense, and she's not even on screen yet."

Altin hummed a second time, though this one sounded a different note as he watched the captain of the *Glistening Lady* being rubbed down by a member of his crew. "I should think it might be better if I spoke to her just now," he said.

The look on his face seemed to convey his meaning, and Roberto laughed. "That's true. I think living with you people is turning her into more of a prude than she already was." He winked before going on, though. "Fine, so tell her. But don't mess around. If you guys want me to go back to Earth and pick up the science team for the Yellow Fire meld next week, then I have to pick up my next Goblin Tea shipment tomorrow. If I don't, then I won't have time to get it through customs and security. In a way, it's your schedule I'm trying to work with here more than mine, so I could really use your help in Murdoc Bay. It is technically the Queen's business, and, I mean, not to be a dick or anything, but you kind of owe me. I need you, and I don't think we can keep throwing bodies out the hatch every time we leave, you know? At some point, someone is going to get pissed."

"Well, murder is fairly common down there, but I take your meaning perfectly. Let me talk to Orli, and we'll get right back to you."

"Hey, it wasn't murder. That dude tried to shoot a magic ice arrow through one of my girls. He's lucky he was dead, because it might have gone worse if I got my hands on him."

Altin nodded. "Yes, I understand. That's not what I meant. I'm confident Miss Daar acted in the right."

Roberto nodded. "Damn right, she did," he said. "And my crew depend on me to keep them safe, not just from thugs, but from the authorities. Which I will, but I'm not giving up my Goblin Tea gig just because it's getting a little rough. I'll wait for your call." He reached forward to cut the feed.

Altin shook his head as he stared into the monitor mounted on the tower wall. He still counted it a strange object to be found there, an alien object in his second-floor study, the place where he'd once more begun to assemble his own personal collection of magic books. Although the technology itself was strange, here, amongst those wooden shelves, mounted between a pair of ancient tapestries that Kettle had brought up and hung there to decorate—hide—the brushed steel walls, it seemed especially so. But times changed, and this was an exciting time. His tower, which even he had begun thinking of as "the boot" after having seen it settled upon both Red Fire and Yellow Fire so often in recent weeks, was the nexus of two worlds. He was still getting used to the crosspollination of the two planets even after so much time. It thrilled him, but it also vexed him some. He could see in the aesthetic asymmetry a cultural metaphor, one suggesting that there were some things that would never fit together well, never mix properly. Some things that would want hiding. Roberto's problems were evidence of that as well.

He headed downstairs to find Orli and discuss those problems, figuring she'd be in her garden tending to a very late crop of squash and a pumpkin patch she'd had going since summer began. Sure enough, she was there, crawling about in the dirt with a spade, old Nipper nearby, the two of them working somewhat head to head as they tried to counter an invasion of weeds.

"And a fine thing ta see ya settlin' in, young miss," Nipper was saying as Altin approached. "There weren't enough in one world for some, but most o' us folk find life right fine near enough ta home. As if the mountains ain't high enough ta explore or the forest been all seen as yet." He saw Altin approaching and raised his voice in a way clearly meant for Altin to hear. "Sooner ya both plant roots, the better. With all the dyin' 'round this place these last few years, 'tis about time fer the patter a' little feet again. I actually thought I might like the silence what come from little Pernie bein' gone, off with them elves, but I dunna care fer it no more." He looked up from his work, his tired old eyes rheumy and ringed with lines, lines of age, mainly, but he was tired too. Everyone at Calico Castle was. For those who lived and worked here full time, who had done so for decades and decades, there was little excitement in the discovery of new planets and new people. Only change. Only loss of everything they'd known for all those years, just over two centuries for Nipper, if Altin made his guess, which was pretty astonishing for a blank.

"Well, if that damn woman in Crown ever stops lording over my wedding," Orli replied, unaware that Altin had come up from behind, his movements made silent by his habitually bare feet, "I might be able to get working on that. Hell, I could have had one by now if the stupid elves hadn't shown up when they did."

"Well, missy," Nipper said, "way Kettle tells it, if'n they hadn't come when they did, well, you'd be laid out in the ground feedin' the weeds from underneath. Weren't no baby makin' from there."

Orli nodded, yanking out a clump of wiry vegetation as she did. "Yes, that's true. But you know what I mean."

"She never meant ta do it, ya know."

Orli looked up. "Who? The Queen? Yes she did. She is a stubborn old ... harpy, just like you always say."

"No, not her. I mean wee Pernie. She's a strange one, weren't no lie, an' I'll grant ya that, but she dinna mean that shot. I just know it."

Orli made a face at that, but went back to work. "I don't know. I keep telling myself that too. Kettle insists it's true. But there was sure something scary in her eyes. Like she really meant it. Like she hated me."

"A wee child like her don't know nothin' 'bout hate," he said, glancing up at Altin as he did. Altin could tell the old man didn't approve of him standing there unannounced so long.

"Ahem," Altin said in response. As usual, the old man was right enough on the moral compass side.

Orli turned back, beaming a beautiful smile up at him over her shoulder. "Come to help, Sir Bookworm? Working in the dirt would be good for you, help prepare you for the meld on Red Fire next month. Get you in tune with nature and growing things."

"Well, as much as I'd love to join you two, I've actually just gotten off the com with Roberto."

"Roberto?" She straightened, upright on her knees and rubbing her back absently. "From where?"

"From orbit. He's here to pick up another shipment of Goblin Tea. He wants me to go with him. I guess some of the magicians down there are giving him some trouble."

"Well, he can just get his business partner in Crown City to kick down a wizard to help him out. He can't have mine."

Altin smiled, but pressed the point anyway. "She won't send anyone. She's got problems with the marchioness as it is. Sending a bunch of Crown City magicians is not a good idea—assuming she's got any to spare given all the reconstruction in the city and the TGS depots going up. She's already flatly refused his request."

"Tell him to ask again. Have him try being polite this time."

"He already has. Several times. He can't get through to her, and he's running out of time."

"So he called you."

"Yes. He did."

She made a huffy face and blew out an audible breath through her nose. She looked to Nipper to confirm the exasperation that she felt, and she found by his sardonic countenance and sad, resigning nod that he clearly understood.

"God damn it, Altin," she said. "God damn both of you. You and Roberto. What is wrong with you two? Can't you just ... *live*? Does everything have to be a life-and-death adventure all the time?"

He put his hands up defensively. "Hey, it's hardly life and death." He winced the moment that came out of his mouth. "Well, all right, it has been actually, but that is why he needs my help. To ensure peace."

"And how are you going to do that?"

"My presence will dissuade the locals from attempting to prey on what they obviously think of as a ship full of blanks. The fact that I was there the first time but not subsequently seems to have given them nerve."

She narrowed her eyes at him, glancing once more to Nipper, who shook his head, indicating that he thought Altin's story was as full of holes as was the ancient burlap sack in which the old man had been stuffing the weeds he pulled. "That's all? Just you standing there, and suddenly a whole town full of kidnappers, cutthroats, and slave traders is going to behave itself?"

Altin frowned, a little agitated at her tone, and he too put his hands on his hips. "He's your friend too, Orli. If you prefer I tell him he's on his own down there, so be it. I gave you my promise not to go, and I will keep it if that's what you wish. But I hope you will consider releasing me from it, because I do believe that I will make a difference by simply being there. There is little enough of use that has come with this infernal rank and title the Queen thrust on me, but I should like to think bringing it to bear for a friend who has risked his life for me on numerous occasions would be one of them."

Orli looked from Altin back to Nipper, but this time Nipper suddenly found a weed that needed to be pulled. She glared at the age spots on his bald head, one eye narrow and twitching a little at his sudden abandonment of her cause, but she sighed and shook her head. He was right. They both were.

"Fine," she said. "But I'm not going this time. I'm not going to watch it if it all goes wrong."

"It won't."

"It better not."

"It won't."

"Altin," she said, looking up at him with the frustration already fading from her eyes. "Someday I hope you really will settle down with me. It's all getting, you know, kind of exhausting."

"I will," he said, but he cut himself off before he could say the words "I promise" again. Promises had begun to take new meaning in his life. They were things that bound, given in earnestness and with best intent, but often undermined by unforeseeable reality. He truly did want to settle down, at least in a way that made what he chose to do less risky than running down to Murdoc Bay to play magical bodyguard for Roberto while he did business amongst a den of thieves. But it seemed that's not what fate decreed. So he kept the promise to himself, and kissed her softly on the mouth instead. "I love you," he said; then he ran back upstairs.

Chapter 36

Djoveeve circled warily around the wall, her knives out, one gripped for thrusting and the other held point down, its blade nearly long enough to pass her elbow. Her spear lay on the ground, under Pernie's boot, and Pernie glared at her, crouched like an animal about to spring. She might have were Seawind not approaching her from the left.

Seawind thrust at her with his own spear, and she batted it aside with the haft of hers. She kicked gravel up at him as she did, using the distraction to snatch up the weapon she'd just taken from Djoveeve and throw it at the elf. She cast a teleport spell right after, came up behind Djoveeve, and mashed her in the back of the head with the butt of her weapon. The woman, still fast enough to defeat most anyone, wasn't fast enough for Pernie anymore, and the blow struck with a hollow thud that sent the ancient assassin to her knees.

Seawind's spear struck the wall in the fraction of a second after Pernie ducked, sparks glowing briefly as it did. Pernie pitched herself forward, rolling away but muttering the teleport that put her right behind Seawind again.

He teleported himself out of the space where Pernie's spear tip was, putting himself three paces behind her, where he snatched up his weapon and hurled it again. She sprang backward, a twisting flip over the flight of his spear, and tried to kick him in the head. He vanished again as she came down. She dove for the floor the moment her feet hit the ground, knowing already that she couldn't avoid the strike that was about to come. The sharp point of his knife pierced the leather jerkin she wore. Only a nick, though.

She spun in time to see Djoveeve throwing the spear that Seawind had thrown, and she slapped it aside with her forearm. Seawind vanished from his place in the middle of the room. Pernie flipped her spear in her hand and jammed it behind her, into the place she knew he would have gone.

Her spear shaft *thwack*ed against his as he blocked it, and she muttered the two-word teleport and jumped across the room. But he was there before her, and she only just ducked a two-handed jab with the center of his weapon's haft that would have blunt-force bashed her in the forehead. She punched for his groin, but he was gone again, and she dove forward anyway. Djoveeve was there, anticipating it, and made to kick her in the face. Pernie flipped over on her back, grabbed Djoveeve's ankle, and yanked, pulling the woman off balance and dropping her hard upon her back.

Pernie whipped out her little knife and leapt on the woman, but Seawind kicked her off and set her rolling across the gritty cave floor.

She teleported out of that roll as well, this time into the empty space above his head, and she fell toward him with spear tip down, intent on skewering him cranium to crotch. He vanished before she could.

Djoveeve wasn't moving, so Pernie wheeled back looking for where Seawind went. She muttered her own illusion and became invisible, just as he surely had. She knew her illusion was gauzy in daylight, but it worked well enough in dim caves like this. She moved as silently as settling dew as she worked her way around the room.

Seawind had a knack for finding her, even down here in the caves, and she had to resist the urge to thrust blindly about with her spear.

The blow struck hard, dazing her, and it knocked her right out of her illusion spell and down to her knees. She shook her head, trying to clear it, but it was already too late. Seawind's knife was at her throat.

"I can hear your heartbeat, little Sava. Silence is how quiet you are not to your own ears, but to those of creatures listening for you. Most creatures have better hearing than you do."

Her head drooped, her long hair flowing like silken sunlight into the grit. She sniffled once, then a second time, then filled the cave with the sound of her crying, the echoes of a tantrum, of frustration and rage.

Seawind withdrew his knife and shook his head. "That is disappointing; I'd thought—" he began to say, but her spear butt caught him in the stomach even as she leapt away.

He laughed, actual laughter from the chest, as she crouched halfway across the room, glaring at him with animal ferocity, not the least stain of a tear striping the grit and grime upon her cheeks. "Oh, clever little creature you are," he said. "And with a trick human females have been fooling their men with since the dawn of time."

Djoveeve was just sitting up, rubbing her head and the back of her neck. "It seems that it works perfectly well on elves."

"So it does." He looked very pleased.

Djoveeve turned to Pernie and smiled warmly. "You see, child. You have the advantage of your gender, and are wise to use it when you need. But don't lean on it too heavily. Few of your enemies will have compassionate hearts."

"I won't," Pernie said, also pleased with herself, but not willing to lower her defenses.

"Your magic is still too slow," Seawind said, right back to

business. "You're fast enough for the aging Sava'an'Lansom, but not for one who hasn't lost a step."

Djoveeve couldn't hide the impact of that efficient remark, and her old shoulders drooped a little then. Pernie threw her spear at Seawind for it, and the elf only barely teleported out of the way. "You're a mean old pointy-eared latakasokis," she snarled at him, then went to Djoveeve and helped the woman to her feet.

"You've gotten very fast, little Sava," Djoveeve said, already beyond having been confronted with her age. "But he is right about your magic. You've got to learn to *see*."

Pernie turned and glared at Seawind, but looked back at her human mentor and asked, "What do you mean? I don't have sight magic. I can't just 'learn' it."

"No, Sava. Like the sugar shrimp. Do you remember how patiently you had to see?"

Pernie nodded.

"In much the same way, you have to start watching the mana as you fight. You, as I once had to, must learn to fight with creatures whose magic comes naturally. Which means they need no words at all, not even just two. So you have to see it coming before it's cast."

"How am I supposed to do that?"

"You have to look."

"Look at what? The mana? It's all just waves and choppy pink stuff."

"What were you looking at with the sugar shrimp? There was nothing to look at there either, was there? You had to look at what they weren't. They seem to be seawater and rocks. But they aren't. Their patterns shift, no matter how slightly, and you learned to see it. And now you must do it with the mana too. You must learn to watch the currents as you fight. You must open your mind to them even while you are in combat."

"Well, how can I do that? I can't watch two things at

once. Seawind said as much hisself."

"He said you can only focus on one thing at a time. But you can be aware of many things. Power comes from choosing the *right* thing to focus on at any given time. Shifting from one instant to the next."

"I can only barely focus on two of you. How am I supposed to do that and watch the mana too? Much less look for sugar shrimp in it."

"In time you will see. I did. It will take practice and lots of work, like anything worth knowing does, but you'll get it in the end. But you must start. You must learn to watch for the movement of mana toward a source. The first movements of it, like the twitch of muscle or flick of the eyes that indicates the blow about to come."

Pernie's eyes narrowed, and it sounded like another boring thing to learn. She'd only just begun to think she might actually be able to beat both of them together, and now Djoveeve was telling her to do the impossible, to find the first movement of mana in a tempest of nothing but motion all around.

"I don't want to," she said, thrusting out her chin. "I'm tired of learning now."

"You must," Seawind said. "You're nearly to the test. This is the last thing you will need to try the orc. It is difficult, but I will show you how."

"I don't care about the stupid orc," she said. "Let him go for all I care."

"He's got magic, little Sava, and unlike Djoveeve and me, he will use it on you when you fight."

"Then I will cut his throat and pull his heart out through his neck," she said with such savagery that Seawind actually smiled again, twice in one day.

Pernie's eyes narrowed when she saw it, and the way she cocked her head gave her the aspect of a snake about to strike. "You'll never let me go home," she said. "You're just tricking me again." She turned and stormed out, already calling to Knot to unroll himself and meet her at the mouth of the cave.

Chapter 37

In a time not so long ago, Black Sander would have thought the bright light he watched was a meteor, a daylight shooting star, rare and interesting but nothing more. But not now. In these times, especially here, he knew exactly what that streak of fire was, and he'd been waiting for it for quite a while.

It had been several months since the glimmering silver Earth ship had last settled down outside of Murdoc Bay, and he knew what had kept it away. He'd spent those intervening months rooting out the origins of attempts to board the ship last time it arrived. Someone had tried for it, and he'd heard about a body being found.

Of course he should have known that others would have the same ideas he had, as surely others had tried to get onto Tinpoa Base and aboard ships as well. Already there were thirty-five men in the Crown City jails at last report, eleven in Leekant, and twelve in Hast, plus the three who had been jailed in Murdoc Bay, though of course two of them had escaped and the other bribed his way free. He'd heard it was the same on the west coast as well, though he hadn't gotten any numbers from Dae, Pompost, or Norvingtown, much less any of the smaller port cities or farming towns.

Regardless, it was obvious that the Queen's efforts to stifle attempts by the underground to reach any trade or travel arrangements with like-minded people on Earth were going splendidly for the War Queen. And those efforts had the complete cooperation of the NTA as far as all the information Black Sander could gather confirmed. When it came to locking down access, Crown City was in complete control.

Despite the time and frustration he'd put in, and the badgering from the marchioness, he was more determined than ever now. Chinks in the armor were beginning to suggest themselves, and he thought he might finally have found one that he could exploit.

If there was anything that he had learned in the time he'd spent trying to get aboard Earth spaceships, it was that they could sense magic to an increasingly large degree, and they could absolutely see right through illusions—or at least they could with their technology. In a way, that fact simplified things because it seemed to make boarding a ship a basic matter of brute force. If deception couldn't get it done, then brawn would have to do.

He'd had a group of men waiting on standby for well over a month, and the cost of their silence, not to mention their room, board, and booze, was beginning to infuriate the marchioness. But at last, there it was, a ball of fire entering the atmosphere, and with it, finally, an opportunity for a ship that he knew for certain was headed all the way to Earth. He was going to get on it, and subtlety was no longer the goal.

He rose from his seat, tossing back the last of a warm glass of wine, its contents having sat in the sun untouched for the last hour. He strode across the boards and back into the little tavern that stood at the end of the pier. A greasy little man with a dirty apron worked behind the bar as Black Sander came through. The barkeep reached up with nervous hands and combed back the wet mess of his tar-black hair.

"Seen it coming yet?" he asked. "Or need a splash more wine?"

"Send a homing lizard to Belor. Tell him to bring the rest of them. It's time."

"Yes, sir," the man said, a serpentine smile drawing itself tightly on lips that were stained red by wine.

Black Sander left a silver piece behind him as he passed by the bar and made his way through the sparse crowd, a murmuring bunch of criminals, the lot of them, each too well acquainted with the courtesies of their respective trades to look up at a fellow passing through. This was the End, a place for the best in Murdoc Bay, and only those who knew well the value of silence came in more than twice.

Black Sander made a point of not looking up and over his shoulder at the descent of the bright ship, now no longer a burning streak of light, but instead a blinding, starlike reflection of the sun. His black boots sounded hollowly on the pier as he made his way toward shore, and by the time he'd reached the cobblestones of the waterfront street that ran the length of the seawall, Belor was already arriving with the men.

Belor was by far the most conspicuous of the group, not for his size, his mass, or even the sinister aspect of his countenance, for had he had any of those, he might have fit in quite well. No, Belor was the softest one of the lot, slightly round of belly, round of shoulder in a sloping sort of way, and with a furtive and rather fearful element to the way he moved. The rabble behind him seemed as if Belor might be some wayward innocent from the merchant parts of downtown Crown who'd gotten a gang of thieves on his tail, neighborhood ruffians and brutish deckhands on shore leave for a while.

But Belor walked before them without fear, and they followed immediately behind, quiet but for the sound of their feet on the low boardwalk. Black Sander joined them, falling in beside Belor silently as they passed together along the waterfront and then up a street that took them through the food district and then upwards through neighborhoods heading toward the Decline.

Their passing became conspicuous after a time, and whores peeked out from brothels, and drunkards raised their heads from where they sat against walls or upon street corners. The few riders who passed by on horseback reined in their mounts as the group strode purposefully past, silent while the group was near, but then leaning together to speculate where the little troop might be headed to. Sometimes trouble was obvious, even in that part of Kurr.

Hits and large-scale beatings were not uncommon in Murdoc Bay, and a small army of thugs sent from one crime lord to another was familiar enough, but Black Sander's presence lent the circumstance something extra sinister. Men wealthy enough and connected enough to ride horses into town with an expectation of keeping them would recognize him immediately. They also knew well enough to turn and ride away if he looked back, despite nagging curiosity urging otherwise. But Black Sander did not bother with them. He had work to do.

"How's your Earth tongue coming?" Black Sander asked, looking to Belor as the group began its ascent up the Decline. He said it in the language of that world, the language they called *English*.

"Mine's coming, Master. I've worked on it as you said."

"Me too," said one of the ruffians in the pack, their leader in an undisciplined kind of way. Leader by way of being the biggest and meanest of them, and perhaps a tad smarter too. "That bitch you stole from Crown school taught us good."

"Well, I'm not sure that's quite how you say it," Belor corrected, "but you do have it better than the rest." He glanced sideways at Black Sander to confirm it, though not for long, as his effort was mainly bent on enduring the climb. His round, fat cheeks were already red and huffing, and they'd hardly made it a quarter way up the slope.

"The three of us will be adequate," Black Sander said. "You are called Twane, are you not?" he asked of the man whose Earth English was passing, if not good.

"Yes, sir. Twane, sir," he replied. "'Cuz me mum was twain one husband an' the next." He laughed aloud at that, as if it was the first time he'd said it, and the men with him laughed too, as if it were the first time they'd heard it as well—all but Belor and Black Sander, of course. Black Sander only closed his eyes for a moment, letting a rise of irritation pass. They were who they were, and the mnemonic was how he had recalled the brigand's name.

He turned back and looked skyward, seeing that the ship was now low enough that he could make out its long, graceful lines, the gentle sweep of modest wings lying back along its body like an eagle in a dive, though perhaps a very slender one, for the craft seemed a long sliver of mercury as it swooped down from the sky.

"Listen up, Twane," Black Sander said. "You will be taking three of these men with you in one of the crates. You're going to keep them all quiet. You will keep them that way the entire time. You'll relieve yourselves in the jars we've put in the boxes for that purpose, and you'll keep them corked when you are done. You'll eat quietly and not make one peep no matter how long you sit in there or how dark it gets. You keep them calm if they get antsy or start feeling too confined, and if any of these gentlemen sniffles in such a way that might be overheard, you are to break his neck. And I mean *break* his neck. Not cut his throat, not gut him like a fish or anything else. I don't want blood running out and giving us away."

He nodded that he understood. Belor had explained it to them several times.

"Good," said Black Sander. "Do any of them have

anything enchanted on them? Any weapons, any armor, any lockets, trinkets, or amusement devices? Even a sunscreen enchantment will get us all killed." Black Sander watched as Twane processed the Earth words, watched him grapple with the gaps in diction that he surely was suffering. "Say it back to me, in common," he demanded as he watched.

To his credit, the burly sailor had the essence of it right. Black Sander repeated the last part in the common tongue of Kurr, the part about any last bit of magic spelling doom for them all, or at least, spelling the likely ruin of the plan. If the crew of that spaceship found out there were stowaways packed into three crates of Goblin Tea, they surely wouldn't go straight to Earth. Not without stopping first at a TGS depot and getting the group sent straight to Crown City and the guillotine. Twane nodded that he understood and confirmed that everyone had been checked and double-checked. There was no magic on any of them.

"Good," Black Sander said, once again in English. "And you understand how to work the bellows pump and how to get out when it is time?"

Again the man nodded.

"Good. Then let's be quick, and get this under way. The time for talking is done."

They stopped about halfway up the Decline at a small shop, the front of which was made of faded planks, the rest of which was cut deep into the cliff. The sign above the door read "Gevender's Candle and Lamp."

Black Sander went in, ordering all but Belor to wait in the street and Belor to wait just inside the door. He had to blink into the ironic darkness of the place. It seemed the shopkeeper was stingy about burning down inventory—as well he should be, for his employer was a master of accounts, and the least drop of candle wax unaccounted for would cost the man a finger if not a hand.

"Is the teleporter here?" Black Sander asked the man

working in the back, bent over a box of sand into which he'd shaped a mold for a tabletop candle to be poured.

"He is," said the candle maker. "He's waiting for you."

Black Sander had to duck as he neared the back of the narrowing hollow that housed the business, a crude passage cut into the rock and little more. A sharkskin hung from a wooden frame, creating a room beyond. He pulled it aside and peered into the small space. A thin man in his middle years sat on a stool and looked up at him with fearful eyes.

"You're the T?" Black Sander asked.

"I am," replied the man, brushing nervously at wisps of hair hanging by his ear. "And I got H-class healing should it come to it."

"It won't if you keep your mouth shut and do what you're told."

"I will, sir. Please just don't let them hurt my wife."

"They won't. Just keep quiet and don't lose your head. She'll be fine."

He nodded, quick, anxious movements that were barely perceptible.

"When are you due back to TGS?"

"Not for two more months," he replied, stammering some. "M-Misty, my wife, she's due to give birth any day. Councilman Gangue arranged me leave f-for the delivery and, y-you know, help with the baby for a time."

Black Sander smiled as he watched the man's nervousness mount. "Relax," he said. "I give you my word: do as you're told, and you'll be there for the baby and in time to be back at work. And so long as you never mention the least part of this to anyone, your baby might even make it to university someday. You hear me?"

"I do," rattled the man. "I truly do."

"Good. Then we have an understanding."

The man nodded again, like the last, almost more a facial chatter than a nod.

"You've checked the boxes?"

"I have."

"Mass will be right?"

"As near as I can tell."

Black Sander nodded. That was the biggest risk as he saw it: the weights. That and the smell, if it came to it. But they'd be packed with leaves too. He studied the teleporter for a moment more, watching him and knowing that it was all the man could do to keep from curling up and cowering on the floor. He'd do his job.

"All right, bring them in," Black Sander called out to Belor, who was still waiting near the candle shop door. "It's time to get crated up."

Chapter 38

The *Glistening Lady* flew in low, Murdoc Bay shrinking in the aft video feed and the blue-green line of the southeastern stretch of Gallenwood growing on the horizon ahead. Altin stood behind Roberto's chair as the Spaniard piloted them in. Deeqa Daar, seated beside the *Glistening Lady*'s captain, was already shutting down some of the ship's systems in advance of the teleport that would send them straight back to Earth—a particular convenience of having Altin Meade along. The five hours it would take to restart the ship were nothing compared to the fifteen to forty hours they'd have to wait at the Tinpoa TGS depot—not to mention the indignity of a ship-wide search. It wasn't that they had anything to hide from the authorities, but both Roberto and Deeqa chafed at authoritarian intrusions on principle.

"It's beautiful, man," Roberto said as they approached the sprawling Goblin Tea plantation, which spread before them like a quilt over the rise and fall of gentle hills, miles and miles of them running up a continental slope that disappeared beneath the southern edge of Gallenwood and eventually became the teeth of the Gallspire Mountain Range. "They told me this is the only place on Prosperion

345

where Goblin Tea will grow. Maybe the only place in the universe. I'd sure love to have a spread like this to retire on someday. Not even this big, but enough to, you know, have something to do during the day, then sit out on my veranda and just look over it into the sunset or something."

"It is lovely," Altin agreed. "But it's too fraught with tension and petty—well, and not-so-petty—feuds and turf wars. You'd be ever on guard for thieves and smugglers trying to get in and steal from you; vigilance would be constant and fatiguing. Hardly a relaxing way to settle down in your last decades."

As if to prove Altin's point, they flew over the first of several wide moats that drew shimmering bands across the landscape, dug into the last of the flatlands before the foothills began to rise. Each canal was guarded along its forward bank by a palisade, sharp pales like rows of wooden fangs, and mounted patrols moved back and forth along them at regular intervals, all of them bristling with weaponry.

Roberto, like Altin, peered down at the security and shook his head. "Yeah, well, based on our last two trips, apparently they need more than moats and dudes on horses to keep all the douchebags out."

"Yes, security is difficult in wide-open spaces like this. The cost of maintaining foolproof enchantments would be nearly impossible to sustain, even with the price of Goblin Tea."

"Prepare for touchdown," Deeqa said into her com, alerting the crew. "Chelsea, Betty-Lynn, you set?"

"Set," came the replies.

Roberto brought the ship over a broad, flat expanse of bare dirt, which had been cleared and leveled just for him. The landing site was some fifty yards south of a huge wooden building, the first in a series of ten exactly like it, in which Goblin Tea was dried and processed. Men were running out from a much smaller outbuilding off to one side.

"Look at them," Roberto muttered as he set the ship in place and began shutting the engines down. "They come like that every time. Crossbows and swords everywhere, like we're alien invaders or something. You're right about that tension thing. These guys' assholes are so tight I bet they fart birdsongs."

Deeqa laughed at that, but Altin was too busy watching the men approach. There were six of them, all armed, as Roberto had observed, and a seventh man with them who approached more casually and was therefore well behind.

"Who is that?" Altin asked.

"He's the tea master. He told me his name the first time I met him, but everyone just calls him Tea."

"Sormand Fallowfield," Deeqa supplied.

"That seems contradictory, doesn't it?" Altin observed.

"It does, doesn't it?" said Roberto. "Anyway, he's the plantation big shot. Actually a pretty decent guy. He's one of only three plantation masters down here, apparently, that are entirely loyal to the Queen. I guess some of the other ones are less devoted. Makes for even more tension around here."

"Where there is gold to be had, that's usually how it goes," Altin said. "Especially between the Queen and the marchioness."

"Well, all I know is, I'm going to get me a big fat heap of it back on Earth, so these guys can piss over each other's fences all they want." He shot a wide, gleaming grin across the console to Deeqa, who reflected it right back at him.

A few moments passed, and then Altin felt the ship settle beneath his feet, a thrum that he'd not been aware of since teleporting aboard suddenly gone, making itself conspicuous in its absence.

"That's it," Roberto said, rising from his seat. Deeqa

shifted from her seat to his as he moved out of the way. "Let's go. Deeqa will watch on sensors for any sneaky crap like before, anyone trying to creep aboard invisible or anything else our eyes don't see."

As he spoke, Liu Chun came in, ducking through the hatch. The prominent display of cleavage afforded by her uniform glistened with sweat, and her hair stuck damply to her forehead in places above her dark eyes, suggesting she'd been hard at work somewhere. "Both additional pulse detectors are up around the core," she reported as she slipped past Roberto and took Deeqa previous place at the com. "Our little blind spot is gone."

"Good." Roberto glanced from her to Altin with a satisfied grin. "We may be blanks, but we aren't stupid." Altin smiled back and nodded, and then the two of them went out the way Liu had come in.

Two brawny guards, Chelsea and Betty-Lynn, met them at the top of the ramp, both bearing heavy laser cannons braced on their hips and supported by wide straps around their backs.

"You girls ready?" Roberto asked as he hit the switch that sent down the loading ramp.

"We'll be sure to smile and act nice," said Betty-Lynn, a big, fake smile pushing up her lightly freckled cheeks.

"Not too nice," Roberto replied, then, into his com button, he added, "Going out."

"We got you," came Deeqa's voice.

"Well, for a deal set in motion by the Queen," observed Altin from his place at Roberto's side, "I might have expected a bit less formality between you and your contacts here."

"Yeah, me too," Roberto said. His two guards were already making their way down the ramp, the long, thick barrels of their weapons laid out before them and causing them both to lean back some against the straps. "Let's go."

By the time Altin and Roberto were standing on

Prosperion soil, the tea master, Sormand Fallowfield, was waiting for them. His six men formed a semicircle behind him, a respectful five spans away.

"Well met and welcome, Captain Levi," the tea master began. He noted Altin with a smile and a polite nod of the head. "And Sir Altin Meade. We were unaware that the Galactic Mage would be gracing us with a visit today. Welcome to my humble farm."

"It is magnificent," Altin said. "I had the pleasure of observing it from above as we flew in. An astonishing bit of work to keep it all healthy and growing, I should guess, a testament to your expertise."

"Why, thank you, Sir Altin. We do work very hard to please Her Majesty."

"I can assure you, you do please her. I don't think there is anything the people of Crown City enjoy so much as the product of your labors."

"That is good to hear, Sir Altin. I had feared that the ... incidents of Captain Roberto's last visit might have put Her Majesty off of us a bit."

"I have seen her quite recently, and I assure you she didn't mention it at all."

"Oh, thank the gods," he said. He was visibly relieved too, after which there was, to some degree, a decrease in the rigid formality. "Sir Altin, would you care for a tour of the plantation? I would be happy to take you around personally."

"I would love that," he said, "but I fear that my dear Orli would have my hide were I to do such a thing without her. She rather fancies growing things. I suspect seeing it done on this scale would send her into a fit of giddiness that I am not fain to deny her. I should like to hold you to that offer at another time, however."

"At your least whim, it will be done. I understand that her beauty is famed across the galaxy, and I'm sure such radiance can only be good for the harvest."

Altin laughed, and glanced at Roberto, who shrugged, long used to the ass-kissing the Prosperion big shots passed back and forth before getting to anything. "I shall tell her you said so," Altin said.

The man called Tea gave another brief tilt of his head, a last formality it seemed, and got straight to the purpose of the visit. "Then let us get to work. Captain Roberto, you remember the way to the packing house, I'm sure. Sir Altin, please, this way." He turned and led them toward the huge building nearby, Altin looking it over as they approached.

He gauged it to be perhaps two hundred spans in length, and while he was too close to estimate its width from here, having seen it from the air, and those like it in the row, he speculated it must be something near another hundred spans across. It was easily forty spans high, an expansive place for doing business, and he was eager to see inside.

Soon enough he did. The tea master pulled open a small side door and led them in. Altin was immediately struck by the rich, earthy aroma of Goblin Tea, albeit struck nearly blind with it for the magnitude and overpowering degree to which it filled the air. It was so strong that it seemed to have a solid quality, as if it weighted down the air.

"Good lord," Altin said, his eyes watering. "I hadn't expected that."

The tea master laughed, as did Roberto. "You get used to it," Roberto said, beating the plantation manager to the punch. He'd been told the same thing the first time he arrived.

"Well, I should think there's no need to drink it in this place. Do you simply come in here and take it right in through your skin? I will be shocked if you tell me your people ever sleep at all, Master Tea."

"It's not quite that strong," the tea master said, "but I admit it takes some adjusting to."

"It smells like money to me," Roberto said. "Speaking of

which, where's my crates?"

"Over here, Captain." The tea master led them down a narrow space, just wide enough to walk through one at a time, the space made by the stacking of wooden crates that were a full span higher than Altin's two-span height, and equally as wide all around. They rose high above them, stacked four high, nearly to the roof, and evenly across. They turned left and right and left again, weaving through the maze of them until they came to the far end of the building. They emerged abruptly and found themselves in a clear space some twenty feet away from a simply massive set of double doors. Without word or visible signal of any kind, the doors swung outward, opened from beyond by two of the men that had accompanied Sormand Fallowfield to the base of the *Glistening Lady*'s ramp. Altin sent a glance Roberto's way, accompanied by a single raised eyebrow, but the stocky Spaniard simply shrugged. It had been like this last time too.

Altin had to resist the urge to cast the magic detection spell he'd memorized last night, one he'd learned expressly for the purpose of this trip. He had a feeling an unseen diviner somewhere had attempted to have a look through both their minds as they went weaving through the stacks of crates, the real purpose of an otherwise unnecessary detour. He was sure the blocks he had in place gave whoever might be watching very little to read from him, if they had tried. And he actually hoped that, were there any untoward intentions, the mind-sifters could fathom in some degree the trepidation on Roberto's part, trepidation that had led to his requesting the presence of the Queen's Galactic Mage. They should know that both he and Her Majesty were watching too.

"Bring the team," Master Fallowfield ordered one of the men, who turned immediately and disappeared around the side of the building. Spinning around, he indicated the stack of crates to the left of where they'd just come. "All those with the blue marks are yours," he said. "Ten in all. Shall I have Fleck open them for you?" He inclined his head to his left, indicating the man still waiting by one of the open doors.

"That's all right," Roberto said. "We'll weigh them out before we put them on the ship and let the particle analyzer do the rest. No sense breaking the seal and letting air get in."

"And you're still sure you don't want my transmuter to meld wood on it? I can make them solid as you please, even dip them in wax like we do for shipments traveling by sea. There's no extra charge for it, as I keep mentioning."

"I appreciate your concern, Master Fallowfield," Roberto said. "But we got it. Save the cost of the labor and materials. Call it a tip."

"It's more out of concern for quality, Captain. My name is on those crates, you know. I should hate it if your people's first taste of our wonderful coffee is a stale one."

"Don't worry about that. They're in cold storage all the way, and we're not going to be long getting there anyway."

The tea master nodded, but Altin could tell he wasn't pleased. Altin counted that a good sign and decided in that scrutiny that the man was genuinely concerned. Nothing untoward in his manner at all.

Soon after, the jingle of large harnesses could be heard, and the dull thud of heavy footsteps became tangible beneath their feet. The tea master led them out of the building and off to one side, making room for the massive flatbed wagon being pulled into place.

Two mammoths, their red hair shaved down to short bristles to give them reprieve from the heat, plodded past the doorway. The driver, ensconced in a covered wicker howdah upon the right-hand beast, turned the team as the titanic creatures moved beyond the doors, directing them away from the opening for fifteen spans. He urged them sideways with practiced skill, then, when the wagon was straight enough, he had the team back it up until a half span of it was through the door. That was all, though, and he stopped them there. The work of loading was to be left to one of the plantation's sorcerers.

A woman, clad in brown workman's trousers and a dusty brown tunic, jumped down from the back of the long wagon, nodding to the tea master and his associates as she went past. "Blue, right?" she said over her shoulder, to which Master Fallowfield said, "Yes."

A young man dressed similarly to the woman pulled a long three-legged ladder off the wagon and followed her in, the two of them setting it up against the stack of blue-marked crates. She climbed up it soon after and put her hands on the topmost crate. "Clear," she called out loudly; then she began a chant that Altin recognized immediately, a production-level teleport, a spell written for magicians with power no greater than an H or I. A moment after, the crate vanished with a hiss, then reappeared a half second later on the wagon with another loud huff of air. The wagons springs creaked under the sudden addition of weight, and the leftmost mammoth protested with a rattling snort and shifting of its feet.

The woman, obviously a teleporter despite not wearing guild colors as she worked, moved down a few rungs on the ladder and began again. Once more she called, "Clear," and once more cast the spell, loading that crate onto the wagon bed.

"This would go faster if they'd just let you do it," Roberto muttered to Altin as they waited for her to make her way to the ground. But Altin shrugged. It was true, but everyone had need of work, and this was a fair use of talent for a woman of her youth and ability. It was good experience, and the wealth of the plantation would likely see to her comfort for many years.

Eventually it was done, and Altin and Roberto were invited to climb up onto the wagon for the ride back to the ship.

It didn't take them long to arrive, and soon the teleporter was moving the crates one by one onto a wide, flat gravity sled, which one of Roberto's crewwomen operated. She powered it down before each teleport, so that the magic would not disrupt it and cause some unfortunate, unforeseeable, and unnecessary accident, and then she'd power it back up once a crate was in place. Before moving it anywhere, she would tap up a set of readings that gave the total weight. "Two thousand five hundred twenty-five pounds, eleven ounces," she called out for the first. The second was nearly as much, shy by only forty pounds, and the one after that was twenty pounds heavier than the first. The fourth and fifth were close enough to the expected twenty-five-hundred range, but the sixth crate was off by two hundred and nine pounds, on the short side, which made Roberto frown. However, he kept his opinion to himself and let the weighing continue, at which point he discovered that the seventh crate was over by one hundred and twelve pounds. When asked, the tea master explained it away as "bean density," which varied between younger and older plants.

"They're strange plants. Cultivating them is more art than science," Tea told them with a shrug.

Roberto hadn't noticed that much bean density variation before, but when Altin shrugged it off—the Prosperion wizard knowing little about the harvesting or processing of Goblin Tea—Roberto let it go. The next two crates were more in line with the weights of the early ones, and Roberto would have forgotten it all had not the last crate been underweight by nearly three hundred pounds.

Roberto looked to the woman working the gravity sled

and raised the question with his eyebrows. She tapped one icon on the screen, and got the total cargo weight. "Twenty-four thousand six hundred and fifty-eight," she said.

Roberto's eyes narrowed for a moment as he did the math. They stayed that way when he was done. "Listen, Master Fallowfield, I'm not trying to be a dick here, but that makes us shy by about three hundred and forty pounds. That's several thousand NTA credits, and I understand you've already been sent the gold."

"I have," confirmed the tea master, looking displeased himself. "That is a bit lighter than I'd call an allowable variance."

Roberto nodded and sent a relieved look to Altin, clearly glad that this wouldn't degenerate into an argument.

"Let's open that one up," said the tea master. "Zoie, get that ladder over here."

The young teleporter and her coworker quickly dragged the ladder off the wagon and set it up against the huge wooden crate. The young man handed the tea master a pry bar, and the plantation master went up himself to pry open the box. It took him some time, and two more trips down and back up again after moving the ladder, but finally he had it open. He lifted the lid with obvious effort and then propped it open with a practiced placement of the pry bar. He leaned over the edge and peered into the crate, and immediately began shaking his head. "Shifted," he said. "There must have been a wet clump in there that broke apart. They've been rushing back there since we started packing for you. You can blame me for that. I should have hired a few extra hands. I'll have a word with the house manager about it, though. There's no excuse. This should have been shaken before it was sealed."

"So what's that mean in English?" Roberto asked.

"I'm sorry?" asked the tea master. "I'm not sure what you mean?"

"He means in common tongue," Altin said.

"It means we've shorted you three and a half sacks of beans because I've put my crew in a position where they are in too much of a hurry to do their work properly. We will get you another crate at once. Give me some time to have one reallocated. I'll have it shaken myself."

The level of his dismay was obvious, and the faint reddening at his cheeks showed that he was genuinely mortified by how the shortage made him and his business appear.

"I truly apologize," he went on, but Roberto cut him off.

"Look, just get me three and a half bags like you said. I just want what I paid for. I don't care about the box. It's all good."

"No, it really should be just as it shows on the manifest. I prefer to keep things neat. I can have another ready in less than an hour. And besides, the bags won't keep as well."

"Throw the bags in the box before you close it up," Roberto said, trying to be agreeable. "Like I said, we are going to seal it back up and keep it all refrigerated the entire time. The bags will be fine, and if they are inside the box, well, then it's still only ten crates, right?"

The man frowned, still clearly flustered by the apparent lack of integrity, but he agreed. "Very well." He turned to the two young workers standing nearby. "Go on, then," he said. "Get them fresh off the line. Four of them. They better still be warm by the time you bring them back."

They both nodded and ran off at full speed.

"Shall we see to the paperwork while they fetch them?" Master Fallowfield asked.

"Sure," said Roberto. "Altin, you want to come watch me sign papers, or do you want to stay here and log those bags in for me?" He said it with a barely discernible twitch of his eye, which Altin easily recognized.

"No, I think I should be bored by paperwork. I'll verify

the last of your shipment while you do that. Orli will be wanting me back soon anyway; we've got a few things to do to prepare for that transmute I have coming up. Efficiency is in order here."

"Roger that," Roberto said. "Let's go sign me out, Tea." He clapped the man on the back, a warm gesture meant to prove there were no hard feelings about the discrepancy. But the tea master turned back to Altin before he left.

"Don't take it if it isn't warm," he said. "It should be almost too hot to touch. That's as fresh as it can be. It will clump a little, but that's fine so long as they make weight."

Altin promised that he would check, and the Spaniard moved off with the Prosperion farmer, chatting away merrily about the chain of stores he was opening back on planet Earth, finally, after nearly a year of being "jammed up by bureaucracy."

In the absence of the tea master and his two assistants, Altin immediately cast the magic detection spell he'd recently memorized, placing himself as he cast it into a quasi-mana-channeling state, pushing a wide and tall wedge of the misty pink stuff out before him like an open hinge. He could imagine how unwieldy the spell might have been channeling mana normally, but with his ring, the gift from mournful Blue Fire, he was able to shape a very neat device. He pushed the angled opening of the construct over the open crate before him, moving slowly into the same space occupied by the object, and watching for the misty mana to react to other magic in the area. He enveloped the whole thing and watched for a time, but nothing shimmered or shifted on the surface of the wedge. There was no magic at work in or on that one.

He climbed up the slope of the loading ramp that had been lowered to accommodate the large crates, and entered into the bottom of the ship. Purple-corseted crewwomen were already at work strapping the big boxes down with wide yellow straps, and each crate was being fitted with a round metal device that monitored its structural integrity as well as its location at all times. "Excuse me, ladies, but would you be too put out if I asked you to turn those devices off for a moment?"

They readily obliged, and soon after, Altin had swept through the whole area with the magic detection spell. There was no magic on or in the crates, and the cargo hold was clear.

By the time he was done with his pass and had returned to the singular crate, waiting still upon the dormant gravity sled, the two plantation workers were returning with heavy bags of Goblin Tea beans draped over their shoulders. They approached Altin, and as promised, he felt all four bags, confirming they were still quite warm from the roasting house. In a matter of minutes, all four were added to the open crate. It required a little mashing and packing, but they got them all in; then the box was shut up tightly again. He thanked them both, then nodded to the busty crewwoman operating the gravity sled, who turned it on, logged the weight, and then pushed the sled up into the ship.

In less than a half hour, they were done with the transaction. Soon after, thanks to Altin's teleportation spell, the *Glistening Lady* was drifting darkly in space midway between Mars and Earth.

"Hah, man, I'm so glad to be out of there," Roberto said shortly after the ship's backup lights came on. "Thanks for coming with me for that. It got so weird last time."

"It was my pleasure," Altin said. "And if you'd like, I'll make one more sweep of the ship with the magic detection spell before you power it all back up."

"If you don't mind," Roberto said. "Might as well, since your damn teleport shut everything down anyway. You really do need to figure out a way to cast that without turning off my ship."

"I agree. And I have. Or at least, the TGS has, and I'll be borrowing the idea. Orli and I would like to have our own transport platform at Calico Castle as well. It's not as if I don't have the time. We're still waiting on Yellow Fire's crystal bed, and, strangely, I am certain Her Majesty is avoiding me. So my time is my own. I've already begun gathering what I need to prepare the engasta syrup for the tiles. I will have one for you soon."

"Yeah, you and Orli both keep saying that," Roberto said, but he grinned. He knew perfectly well having something of a personal teleporter was an extraordinary piece of luck, with or without a big black box. A few hours for restarts meant nothing in the greater scheme of things, especially now that there was no need to worry about some angry Hostile swooping in ready to bash in the ship like a tin can. Although, he had hopes that the *Glistening Lady* could take it, if it came to that.

Altin went off to do as he'd said and check the ship for any signs of magic, augmenting in his way what the heat and surge detectors would be doing constantly once main power came back on. In the end, however, all of Roberto's worries were unrealized. There wasn't a jot of mana being channeled, stored, or radiated anywhere aboard. And certainly not after Altin teleported himself back home.

Roberto stood amongst his ten crates after Altin was gone, the robust and shapely figure of Betty-Lynn at his side, her hip-mounted laser cannon now stored away and both of them completely at ease. He laughed, and the dim auxiliary lights sparkled in his eyes as he surveyed his cargo. "God damn, I'm going to be rich," he said. "So rich. And it's about freaking time."

Chapter 39

Pernie stood atop the cliff, gazing out over the sea. The wind blew beneath a dark and overcast sky, bending the knee-high grass and whipping her hair out behind her like pale golden flames. It was three weeks past the end of winter, and still the winds blew, though the air was warm enough. It always had been. She wondered if the island ever got cold beyond the mild chill of night. She peered down to the narrow line of sand that separated the tumble of black rocks at the base of the cliff from those that jutted up from the waves, the latter appearing here and there in the frothy blue tumult and looking like volcano seeds.

As usual, there were no *sargosaganti*, the elven word for the horned, manatee-like creatures of String, and she began to despair, for they were her only hope of getting home on her own. Other options had been eliminated. She had no way to get to the southernmost tip of String, where Djoveeve said the swimming blue dragons were, and there was simply nothing else that would do. The whales were all stupid; she'd found that out already. Or at least, too stupid for telepathy. The sea turtles were twice as dumb as the whales; the ichthyosaurs were both stupid and mean like the sharks. She had held out great hope for the dolphins, but they were too small to be of any use even if they had had telepathy. Even if they had, she could hardly make a journey across that open ocean on the back of a dolphin, though she had given some thought to rigging up some sort of chariot. Kettle used to read her stories of the great kings of Kurr and the chariots they'd driven into war, and old Nipper had even carved her one to play with when she was only three.

But, she had no chariot, and no skill for making watercraft. She knew it perfectly well. So she'd given up on all of it, all but the manatees. But the trouble with the manatees was that the timid creatures were hardly ever here. She'd only seen them four times since first coming to this place, and in those four times only twice had she been able to get to the beach before they were gone, and on only one of those occasions had she made it far enough to even get her feet wet.

She was just about to turn back, however, when fortune seemed to throw a favor her way. A movement upon a rock some hundred spans beyond the beach caught her eye, and she froze and stared with hawkish intensity. She could just see it, a tiny lump that seemed a bit too round along the top ridge of the rock. She watched it, placed the curve of it, and set it in comparison to the cuts and sharp protrusions of the dark rock face on either side. She watched for movement in the gaps between every crag and outcrop, anything dark shifting like the least shadow between fork tines.

Sure enough, it moved.

She muttered the words that would turn her invisible. With the wind stirring the dark clouds above her and the grass all around, her invisibility would work just fine. She cast the silent parts now too, put them into the magic naturally every time—Seawind's spear butt thudding into her skull had set that lesson permanently. If he could hear her heartbeat, so perhaps could the sargosaganti.

She remained motionless, even though she'd vanished

magically, a long habit now with her time on String, and she watched. For the longest stretch of time nothing happened beyond the barest motion of that round shape, but eventually, the creature seemed satisfied that all was safe. It rose out of the sea, letting the rise of an incoming wave push it right up to the highest part of the rock, the surface of which it covered like a great fat sausage, if sausages grew to near the size of mammoths or the woolly rhinos that lived on the western steppes of the Daggerspines.

It lay atop the rocks and spread out wide, grunting and shimmering with wetness as it seemed to ooze over the rock, eagerly extracting what remnant heat it could from the surface. It was a female, Pernie recognized, for it had small horns, barely a span in length. After some thrashing and worming about, it finally settled and lay still.

Dark spots appeared in the water around it then, movements shadowy and graceful beneath the foamy lace of broken waves. And then, one by one, more of the great horned manatees swam up out of the water and flopped themselves upon the rocks, each taking its own rock in turn. In the beginning it was only the females, and soon all the rocks were covered with blotchy black-and-green sausages, lying this way and that like someone had carelessly knocked over a tray of fat links at some seaside buffet. Pernie might have giggled at this idea, or even longed for real food, which she so often did, but she was too focused on the task.

Finally, as they had before, the males came in last. There were only three of them. Two young ones, and the patriarch, a great vast thing with a pair of horns nearly three spans long, each as thick as apple barrels where they came out of its head. It oozed and flopped itself up onto the beach looking as if it were the mutant offspring of a great green pig and a long black whale. It stretched and wriggled like a fat worm until it was halfway up the beach, where it blew out a blast of air from its fuzzy muzzle, sending clouds of sand and gravel flying up the beach to land in a patter upon the rocks and even the base of the cliff.

That was the one Pernie wanted. The big one. She could pitch a tent on its fat back if she wanted to, and camp all the way across the ocean until she was home. She'd even have room to dance about and play. She could practice the death dances she'd learned over the course of eleven months, the flips and spins and vaults that the elves had taught her, maneuvers that had at one time seemed impossible, but that she could now do with some degree of competence. She could stay deadly and strong during her voyage, which would be important when she did finally get home. That big sargosagantis was her way home. She had no need of fighting the orc to prove anything. She'd fought orcs before—though she still shuddered when she thought about it, about their long teeth and wicked roars, their muscles moving beneath their thick green flesh, hands powerful enough to crush her small head. They were abominations in the shape of men. She knew they could be killed, but the thought of facing one again made the pit of her stomach fill with ash. She spoke bravely enough of it when Seawind was around, but as the days drew nearer to that combat, anxiety began to take its toll. Which was why she had to finish what she'd started long ago. She had to tame something to ride away from here. And that sargosagantis was going to be it.

She gave it time to settle, watching its eyelids droop farther and farther down the round black domes of its eyes. Soon the shimmering round bubbles were draped in spotty black-and-green flesh, with pale eyelashes curving upward along the lowest edge like the warped teeth of a comb.

Her plan was simple: she would jump down to the beach as she so often did here for fun, teleport as close to it as she could before she hit the ground—she gauged she could get within twenty steps or so—and then run right up its back.

She would keep the words of her next teleport ready on her lips as she ran, and try to watch the mana as best as she could like Djoveeve and Seawind were trying to teach her to do—though it hardly worked at all like they said, at least not so easily. The creature would, just as she would, just as the elves would, try to blink away with its own animal teleport, but Pernie knew how far it could go. Not far. Barely enough to jump out of danger from predators, just enough to get free of their gnashing teeth. It was a defense she could appreciate, but also one she could do herself if she needed to, though she hoped it wouldn't come to that. Her plan relied on her belief that it wouldn't jump until all the others were away. She'd seen that on her last two attempts to approach one. So she had a plan for after that. The real danger would be the horns.

Once she got on its back, she'd jam her spear into its thick, blubbery hide and hold on for the ride, trying to find its mind in the same way she'd tried with all the other creatures so far, the way she had found Knot's. She'd do it while watching in the mana, trying to beat it to its next teleporting cast. She'd stick it hard enough with her embedded spear to stop it before it could blink away. Timing would be everything, but pain was a very effective tool for training animals. It had worked well enough on Knott, if not for anything else. But she thought there was a chance she wouldn't need it. The sargosagantis might be smart enough to communicate with directly, just like Master Altin's dragon, Taot, was. It was hard to predict, though. She'd had such hope for the dolphins, and they had no magic at all. She'd tried other creatures, several just to see if she could carry it off. Her attempt to communicate with the creatures she'd come to call spider-apes had nearly got her killed, and trying to communicate with a stump-winged latakasokis was pointless. She supposed toadstools had larger brains than those dumb dragon cousins had. There had been many others throughout the months with equally unremarkable results, making Knot legitimately the only success she'd had. Nothing else had mind and magic in the right combination to be of any use, and those that had either hadn't the sense to respond or didn't notice that she was there. Or else she simply didn't know how to get them to. Either way, this was her last hope. The sargosaganti were friendly with one another, protective, and seemed to communicate. And they definitely had magic. So this was her lone remaining option. And she was ready for it.

With a breath to steady her nerves and a quick glance at those horns jutting from the big one's head, she scooted along the cliff face until she was as directly in line with it as she could be. Flipping her spear in her hands so that its point was down, she jumped from the cliff and out into the wind, plummeting toward the rocks. She started her spell.

In the half instant before she hit the largest of the rocks, she finished the last word of her magic and teleported herself to the sand beyond them. She reappeared, already running toward the hulking sargosagantis lying just twenty paces away.

It twisted so quickly toward her that she'd only barely begun to reach out for its mind, watching the mana draw in case it tried to blink, when it shot the first of its horns at her. In that split second of her reaching for mana, the nine-pace-long shaft was on her, through her, and carrying her flying down the beach. She landed with a splash in the surf well over thirty spans away, her invisibility spell gone and her blood being carried into the sea with the receding of the most recent crashing wave.

She could see the great horn rising from her body like the trunk of a beheaded tree, widening as it rose up into the air. Her guts felt like they were aflame. She lifted her head feebly and saw that all the manatees were gone. She was dimly aware of how disappointed she was, but the pain made it hard to think.

She had enough time to call out to Djoveeve telepathically before the sky faded away.

Though she had no sense of passing time, or even much value for measuring it anyway, four days had passed before she woke up again. Even with the spectacular healing power that Seawind brought to bear, she'd still been in great danger for the whole first day after the manatee incident, for it had been that long that the elf had been at work on her. But awake she did, and alive she was.

Not surprisingly, the first words out of her benefactor's elven mouth when Pernie awoke were "Foolish girl. Not even elves trifle with sargosaganti."

Djoveeve, however, was kinder, and the thin slit of her pursed and ancient mouth shaped a smile of genuine relief when Pernie's bright blue eyes blinked bewildered up at her for the first time in days.

"Crazy, brave little thing," the old woman said, pushing strands of Pernie's hair off her pale brow unnecessarily. "You cannot ride a sargosagantis back to Kurr."

Pernie rolled her head, looking away from the woman to the elf. The folded silk blanket serving as her pillow made wispy sounds against her ear as she did, soft against her cheek. "I almost did," she said, glaring up at Seawind. "You'll see."

He looked from her to Djoveeve seated on the ground next to where Pernie lay upon a bed of grass. The convalescing child was covered in a sheet of silk, her slender little body barely a length of lumps beneath. "She is brave. But if she's stupid, she'll die before she is of any use. *You* make her stay away from the sargosaganti. They cannot be tamed. If she won't hear it from me, you'd better find a way to make her hear it from you, or there will be more of that water spilling from your old eyes."

"You brought her here," Djoveeve said. "*You* did. You picked her. She is your responsibility. I only teach her what I know. Neither of us asked to be here in our time. You'll do well to remember that. Your people, your prophecies, choose us. You choose humans because we are not elves. That is why. So don't stand there now and bemoan the difference. *You* make her understand. And hitting her with something won't help. She's past that now. Some lessons can't be taught with the blunt end of a spear."

He frowned across the intervening space at the ancient Sava'an'Lansom and considered what she'd said. It had been a long time since he'd trained Djoveeve, and it was possible that some of what she had said he'd not been considering. He nodded, and left the low-ceilinged room.

Djoveeve turned back to look at Pernie, who was smiling up at her. "You told him good that time," Pernie said. "He's been needing a talking-to."

Djoveeve leaned back and laughed. "Yes, child, I did tell him good, didn't I?" They shared a moment in that happy thought, until finally, once more she spoke. "And you must do it too when time comes, little Sava. You tell them what they need to hear. They will need your candor just as they have often needed mine. It is not for the spear and knife alone that they bring us here. It is for what only we can see."

"You mean like sugar shrimp and mana tide?"

"In a way. You see, the elves have no intuition. Not like we do, at least not the males. They simply can't trust a guess like humans do; they can't go with their gut. They will be the first to tell you they are creatures of reflex, but their reflexes are based on certainty. That's why they fight so well. They don't guess; they know."

"But I thought certainty was why they always win. They're very smart, or at least Seawind is, though he's mostly the only one I know. Sandew and the others were smart too. I saw them fight the latakasoki, lots of them, and with no Fayne Gossa like I had. They never make mistakes. Guessing is silly because they already know everything."

"But they don't. They don't know everything."

"Then how come they never lose a fight?"

"The dead ones lose."

Pernie had to think about that, but she supposed it made perfect sense. She'd never seen a dead elf, but then, she'd never seen a young one or a female either. There were all kinds of elves she'd never seen, so she'd just never really thought about that before.

"How come they never let me see anyone else?" she asked after a while. "Are they ashamed of me?"

"I cannot tell you that just yet, little Sava. But if it is meant to happen, then you will. They are an amazing race, beautiful beyond reckoning. The first time I saw an elven woman, I fell in love."

"What?" said Pernie, sitting bolt upright. "With another woman?"

Djoveeve took her by the shoulders and pushed her back down into the bed, smiling but insistent. "You must lie still for another day or two, child. There is a bit more healing that must happen on the inside still."

Pernie grumbled about that. Nothing hurt when she sat up.

She made a face at Djoveeve but didn't try to sit up again.

"And yes, little one, I did fall in love with a woman, though there was nothing I could do about it. I simply was. But elves don't love the way we do; they don't hold each other or kiss each other in the dark."

"I know about what happens in the dark," Pernie said a bit indignantly. "You can say it. Besides, I've seen the critters at Calico Castle doing it all the time. They climb on top of one another, and Gimmel says they will keep on until a baby comes out."

Djoveeve had occasion to laugh again, but Pernie mistook

it for disbelief, which she wasn't having any of. "It's true," she protested. "All the time I seen Nipper's old bull get up on that bald-faced cow Gimmel brought back from Leekant, and it followed her around and went after her constantly. And that cow had a calf by the end of the year. It just came right out all gooey and covered with snot. And people aren't any different, and even Kettle said it was true because I asked, and she never lies to me."

Djoveeve patted her on the cheek and nodded that it all was true, or at least close enough. "Of course you are right about all of that. People do, just like many animals as well, though not all by any stretch. And elves are like those creatures who don't make love. At least, not until a very specific time." She sat up straighter then, and cleared her throat, though there was nothing in it to be cleared. "The rest of that, you'll just have to wait to learn. I've said more than my vow allows as it is."

Pernie didn't care about vows, though. She was still trying to imagine how any woman could be so beautiful as to make her fall in love. At one time she'd thought Orli Pewter was beautiful, but not enough to be in love. Or at least she didn't think so anyway. She had liked following her around because she was nice to her. But then she tried to take Master Altin away, so now Pernie thought Orli was uglier than Gimmel's bald-faced cow.

Thinking about life at home made Pernie a little melancholy, and for a while she lay back trying to remember things she used to like to do. Much of it was the same as the things she liked to do here, as she thought about it. Climbing trees and jumping streams. Swimming and chasing animals about. Hunting and practicing with whatever weapons someone would let her at or that she could make herself. She had to admit the elves and old Djoveeve were actually much more generous about that last part. Plus she got to use poisons when she wanted to. Granted, they made her drink the poisons she practiced with, dosing her for months and months first to build up her resistance, but eventually they did let her, and she did suppose being immune to them was probably a good idea. She didn't like barfing very much, though. Although sometimes the strangest-looking things came up, which made it not so bad.

She'd also found Knot here, and she really did love him. Thinking of him made her worry, and she sent a thought out in search of him. He'd unrolled himself from her pack and gone back to the fern meadow where she'd gotten him.

That was fine. She could get him to come back now. It was funny to think about it, but in the light of the recent conversation about mates and mating, she thought the little monster sort of saw her as its mate, or something like it anyway. She thought about how Djoveeve must have felt being in love with a woman who could never love her back. It made her sad inside. She imagined Knot loving her like that, hopelessly, and thought about not calling him back to her. But then she knew he was just a bug. She'd been in his head before. There simply wasn't that kind of emotion there. Still, it was a sad thought, unsettling, and she looked up at Djoveeve wondering what it must be like, to love someone and not have that love ever returned. So she asked. "What happened to the elf woman that you loved?"

Djoveeve shook her head and gave a wan, breathy sort of smile. "Nothing," she said. "She's living her life perfectly happily beneath—" She stopped abruptly, saying instead, "We're even friends in our way. In the end, I might as well have loved the sky."

"Was it magic that did it to you?" Pernie asked. "Were you under a love spell like Lord Thoroughgood used on Miss Pewter all that time?"

"No. Not magic. At least not directly, not intentionally. They're all like that. The females, I mean. That's why the elves always take human women to be Sava'an'Lansom. It is said that if a human male sees an elven woman, he will simply give up and die. Apparently they just lose the will to live. It's what happened to the very first Assassin of the Vale."

"Because of how pretty they are?"

"Yes. Because of that. As I said, you will see. And if you are weak like I was, you will carry the heart wound with you always, as I do, like a scar in your heart's memory. But the heart heals over, and you will be stronger for it in the end. It doesn't happen a second time." She looked off into the distant space of memory for a moment, and when she spoke again, her tone was tutorial again. "But only if you pass your test."

"The test of seeing an elf woman or of killing the orc?"

Djoveeve's brow wrinkled a little, only for an instant, before she nodded. "Yes. Most of that, anyway."

Pernie couldn't decide if she wanted to see a woman so beautiful she'd have a wounded heart, but she supposed Seawind could cure anything. And what could be worse than a giant manatee horn through the guts anyway? She did, however, dread that rotten orc.

Chapter 40

Black Sander sat upon the wide lip of a clay jar as if it were a stool. He stared across the pale yellow gloom at his three companions, two men he'd hired for muscle and the teleporter, who still trembled as much as he had at the candle shop before making the teleports. His companions sat, as he did, atop their own clay jars, and at their feet were four more small jars, one filled with almonds and the other three with water, each corked tight. The only light came from the cap of a yellow mushroom, which one of the thugs held in his lap as dearly as a child might a favorite bedtime toy. The man's fingers twitched as he held it, the tips of them caressing its glowing flesh in a searching sort of way, as if he were certain that at any moment it might disappear.

"You're going to break it apart if you keep fiddling with it," Black Sander said in a voice so low it was barely a hiss. The man started at the sound, his eyes wide and the whites jaundiced by the mushroom's light. He followed the direction of Black Sander's gaze to the cap in his lap, and jerked his hands away as if it might bite him.

"Don't like it in here," he muttered back. "It's too dark and too tight. I can't hardly breathe."

"You'll breathe just fine if you stop thinking about it,"

Black Sander hissed back. "Just relax. We'll be there soon enough." He turned to the man to his left, and watched the sand in the hourglass run out. He waited for the man to turn it over, which he did immediately.

The brawny fellow saw Black Sander looking at him, and gave a grim nod. "Twenty-six," he mouthed silently.

Black Sander lifted his wide-brimmed hat and pushed his long, agile fingers through the dark hair beneath, nodding back at the man. He would have liked to have stood and stretched, but there was no room for it. The small space, a square cube made of taut canvas stretched over a wooden frame, would not accommodate such a thing. It was even worse now than it should have been; the unexpected near collapse of one corner of their little hiding place had reduced their headroom substantially on one side. Someone on the outside had thrown in additional weight, and a knot in one of the four main poles had proven a nearly fatal flaw for the plan. Were it not for the quick reflexes of the man now holding the hourglass, they might all be sitting in a Crown City jail.

But he'd caught the drooping canvas and held up that side of their tiny room, all upon his back, his legs trembling and his arms braced against his knees as he held up the weight of well over thirty stone in Goblin Tea beans. They'd had to scramble to aid him, Black Sander and the claustrophobic lad, but they'd strapped a pair of daggers in place with two belts and somewhat splinted up the pole. It still drooped, and they all knew it might give at any moment, but at this point in the plan, they had no other choice but to trust to chance.

The man with the mushroom got up and went to a length of bamboo sticking through a hole in the side of the canvas wall. It had a small bellows-like device affixed to it near its end. He wrapped his lips around the opening and pumped the bellows hungrily, sucking in the air it brought from outside the crate they were hiding in.

"Sit down, you fool. They'll hear you panting like a damn dog. There's plenty of air in here."

He did as instructed, but he mumbled, "I can't breathe."

"Calm yourself. We'll be off the ship at any moment now."

The man slumped back on his clay pot, too late to prevent the aroma of urine from mixing and even overwhelming even the mask of the Goblin Tea for a time.

Another two turns of the hourglass passed after that, but at length, and such a length that even Black Sander began to grow anxious, there were sounds from outside their confinement again. Faint sounds, dull and muffled, but clearly something was finally happening. He glanced to the teleporter sitting there, the man having not uttered one word since they'd left, and gave him a look that promised death to him, his wife, and his unborn baby if he uttered so much as one magical word. The man nodded that he understood.

The crate jolted a moment after, and Black Sander quickly yanked off the bellows from the tube and slid a long wooden dowel through it, stopping where a mark on the dowel lined up with the tube opening. The hole was now plugged up tight.

The crate rocked several more times, then settled. He could make out the faintest hum of voices, but there was far too much wood crate and Goblin Tea in between for him to make out what was being said.

They all tipped at a shallow angle then as someone outside moved the crate. The man with the mushroom looked as if he might cry out. The fellow with the hourglass set it down and slapped a hand over the mushroom bearer's mouth.

Black Sander smiled as their tiny apartment leveled out again, and for some time there was no movement again, or at least none they could detect. The crate jolted once again, then all was silent. No one said a word. After a time, there came another jolt, as if something had been slammed up against the side of the crate. Then silence followed yet again. This sequence repeated eight more times, and after the last, a new type of rumble commenced. They were all jolted once more, this time in a distinctly directional sort of way, as if a wagoner had just whipped a team of draft horses into motion.

They bounced along long enough for half the sand in the hourglass to fall, and once more came to rest. A few more jolts and jostles, more mumbling from outside, and finally all was silent again. Silent for long enough that Black Sander decided it must be time.

"You ready?" he said to the man whose composure had been so admirable all along.

"I am."

"All of you get up and come over here," he said. "Get in close."

When they had, when they were all stuffed into the corner of the little canvas box, Black Sander drew a dagger from his boot, leaned across the small space, and cut through the canvas where it began to droop near the broken part of the frame. The pitch-black beans of the Goblin Tea began to pour in like mud.

The man with the mushroom actually made a whimpering sound, and Black Sander had to suppress the urge to cut his belly open just like the canvas so they could all watch his frightened guts pour out.

With his foot, Black Sander pushed the heaping beans into the far corner as best he could. Confident with the process, he cut the gash a bit longer still. He made another long cut along the bottom of one canvas wall, near where they all stood, cutting the long, angular gash nearly to the height of their knees."Give it a push up," he told the timekeeper.

The man did as told, pressing into the tarp between the crossed wooden braces and causing the beans to pour in more forcefully.

"Can you feel the top?" Black Sander asked.

"Not yet," the man replied.

It was the matter of some long and admittedly nervous minutes, letting more beans in, letting them pile up beneath their feet, until at last the man found the top of the crate. They let out a collective breath of relief, the man with the glowing mushroom most of all.

Black Sander cut away the remaining tarp above them, and with some cringe-inducing volume, they were able to pound the crate open from within. They were immediately met with a rush of chill alien air, air cooled by the electricity-powered machines of planet Earth. In minutes, they had the rest of his crew out from the other crates; all twelve men had made it without a hitch. After so many months of trying, he had finally arrived.

Chapter 41

Altin placed his hands on the new crystals that the professor and his team had grown. It was the first time he'd felt them without the mediating layer of a spacesuit glove. His breath blew in foggy plumes, giving him the aspect of a sea dragon blowing steam. The clouds of each breath played amongst the gray formations of the crystals like clouds around miniature mountaintops. He looked to his left, through the clear plastic sheet of the atmospheric tent that separated him from the rest of the team. Orli stood centermost amongst them, her spacesuit helmet's spotlight glaring in at him along with all the rest, the combination of them making it so that he couldn't see her face. He knew she'd be chewing on her bottom lip, though, like she often did when she was nervous. He made a point of smiling and gave the thumbs-up gesture that the Earth people often used.

The new crystals were just as Professor Bryant had said they would be, exactly like the rest of them had been when they first arrived. They were a little smaller on average, but otherwise they seemed no different, and the professor had assured him they would grow a bit more in time. Altin hoped it wouldn't make a difference for what he had to do.

He scooted to his left a little and got down on his knees, peering as he did into the prickly-seeming expanse of dull crystal where it butted up against the pulsing purple mass that was Yellow Fire's crystalline heart. The science team had done their part, and now it was time for Altin to finish off the work.

He leaned forward and had to stare very closely to find the hair-thin line that traced the edge of the new-growth crystals, the tiny line of separation between the transplanted heart and the "regrown skin," as the professor had been calling it. He placed his hand over the crack, his right hand, upon which he wore his ring. The silver touched the tip of a crystal with a *clink*. He let go another long, foggy breath and opened his mind to the mana, the calm endlessness of its pink eternity. He swept at it with his thoughts, as if waving away a breath of smoke, and in this way he wafted it into the crack between the heart stone and the newly formed heart chamber "skin." He spoke the words of the spell he'd learned from Aderbury's book, forcing himself to cast the magic slowly, meticulously. There was so much at stake. He let himself lean on the rhythms of the spell, since it was so new to him, and soon enough by his measure of it—though a matter of nearly an hour to those observing from outside—he'd traced the gap all around the heart stone. He filled it all with the gentle mist of mana, shaping the surface of the heart stone as he saw it in his mind.

When the mana was all wrapped around and the gap was full, he spoke the words that anchored the transmutation spell in place, the first portion of it anyway, and then opened his eyes, staring down at what he had done. So far there was nothing to see. Just a hairline crack that was nearly impossible to locate with the naked eye.

"Well," Professor Bryant asked, "did it work?"

"He still has to do the other half," Orli snapped. "Be silent. Don't you listen?"

Altin couldn't help the smile that came upon his face. *Be silent.* She sounded like the Queen. But she was right, and he needed to stay focused on the spell.

He turned to his right to reach for reagents, a simple task made still difficult by the heavy spacesuit he wore, despite having the helmet and gloves pulled off. The environmental bubble they'd made for him around the heart stone was perfectly functional, but nobody on the team would let him take any more chances than that, just the helmet and the gloves.

Beside him were two jars. One was filled with soft clay taken from the bed of a hot spring north of Hast, and the other held three cocoons containing the pupae of the rare Endoru moth, found in the northwestern parts of Great Forest, where the gulf breezes cooled the trees and prevented frost come wintertime.

First he applied the clay, smearing it into the crack with his fingertips as best he could, then evening it out with a small brush made of artificial fibers, something manufactured on Earth that was much softer than horsehair.

He worked carefully, brushing the clay evenly so that no gaps or holes were in it. The spell instructions had been clear on that. There must be no part uncovered. He pulled a magnifying glass out of his belt and carefully examined the work all around. There was one tiny gap, barely a pinhole, that had opened up where the clay had been brushed too thin. He was glad he'd had the discipline to check. He only got one chance at this, and if he failed, both the heart stone and the crystal for several spans around would crumble and turn to dust. This was an all-or-nothing spell. Quite terrifying.

He brushed more clay into the crack, carefully blending it with the rest so that it was all even and smooth again. To be sure—that pinhole having made him nervous—he went around the whole thing again, adding just a little more. It was good. The work was patient and thorough.

He put the brush down and wiped off his hands with a chemical-coated towel that Doctor Singh had handed him before he'd been zipped into the atmosphere bubble. The doctor had not looked him in the eyes. He wouldn't anymore, not after, as he saw it, Altin's cold-blooded murder of Thadius Thoroughgood. Altin wondered if the doctor would ever understand. If he would ever forgive him. He wondered if maybe this time, this spell would be enough, the two of them working together with the rest to bring another life back from death. Surely that would be redemption, wouldn't it?

He finished cleaning his hands and tossed the towel down, giving his hands a moment to dry. The cold air within the plastic bubble felt even colder as he waved his hands to expedite the drying process, though he hadn't really needed to.

Altin realized he was stalling a little, and stared down into the jar with the three pupae inside. They wriggled like swaddled things. He didn't have a lot of time to wait. He had to cast the spell before they started to come out, yet just as they were ready to emerge: such were the dictates of the spell and, thereby, the dictate that he do it *now*.

He reached into the jar and took one thumb-sized cocoon out. It might as easily have been a very large grub or a maggot of extraordinary size. He could feel the life inside of it. It made him wonder if he was really redeeming the life he'd taken after all. He would still be down by one. Perhaps Doctor Singh never would have reason to release Altin from his moral pillory.

"Oh my God, go already," he heard Roberto say. "What's he waiting for?" It wasn't a direct link into Altin's suit speaker, though. Roberto's impatience was transmitted indirectly through Orli's helmet feed. She'd been about to ask Altin if everything was okay just when Roberto spoke, giving Altin a glimpse of the tension outside the plastic room. Orli cut off her transmission immediately, leaving Altin in silence again.

He held the cocoon in his fist, firmly but not enough to harm it. "Slowly trickle mana in, shaping it like a heart," the spell had read, so he turned his hand and pressed his closed fingers against his chest. He closed his eyes once more and reached out for the little plume of mana that drifted like a bit of string caught in an updraft, emerging from the mana cocoon he'd constructed around the heart stone. He took the strand up again and once more attached it to the rest of the mana all around, pulling it through the endlessness that seemed all the mana in the universe. He pulled it back out again, as if threading an eternal needle. He pushed it through his hand and wound it around the wriggling object that he held.

He poked the strand into the very center of the creature, the life that was seeking to be reborn, and he prodded with it until he found the creature's little spark of light, the singular pink dot of the mana that animated it. Altin attached his thin filament to that.

The chrysalis popped in his hand. He could feel it, the damp of its innards there.

He had the presence of mind to catch the wisp of mana before it unraveled back and slipped beneath the surface of the crystal stones, if barely before. He locked it into place again, leaving it to dangle its length into nothingness like a lone wisp of hair. He opened his eyes and unfurled his fist. He saw the broken chrysalis lying there, gooey and unfortunate.

"What happened?" Orli asked.

"I'm not sure," he replied. "I think I put in too much mana." He picked up the towel and wiped off his hand, pulling off his ring to clean inside and out. The green marble of the Father's Gift that Blue Fire had given him was buried within the thick silver block. The ring was a crude piece of jewelry made by Altin's own hand, but the stone pulsed steadily, visible only on that underside. It was beautiful. And powerful. He wondered if the phrase "slowly trickle mana in" written into the spell meant more slowly than what he'd done with it. He'd gone very slowly. As slowly as he could. But he thought that perhaps the ring made it too fast. The stone did change the nature of mana significantly, and surely the wizards who had designed the spell hadn't been channeling mana with Hostile heart stone. Perhaps the timing had simply been off. Spells cast over long durations had that kind of temperament, so to speak, and if there was a downside to the stone, that might be it. Usually it was healers, not transmuters, who complained of such things the most, of overchanneling and impatience with patient spells. Still, he supposed he was healing in his way, even with this transmute, so he decided to give it another try. This time he would do it without the ring. Perhaps all he needed was to get the timing right.

He placed his ring atop the towel on the ground and took the second of the three wriggling cocoons out of the jar. With it gripped in his fist as he had the last, he once more reached out into the mana stream. It had been some time since he'd seen the mana this way, the thick, smashing swells of it churning in whorls of pinks and purples, sometimes so dark they were nearly black. It moved in eddies and curling licks like splashing waves and tongues of flame, yet even in doing so it moved like syrup on a cold plate. Compared to the unchanging pink mist, it seemed something else entirely when he looked into it this way.

Nonetheless, this was how the spell authors had seen it when they'd first cast the spell, and Altin was confident that he could channel the mana in its thick and slow-moving ways precisely as it was written in the spell. So he did so, and once again reached out for the tiny wisp of mana that he'd left attached to the surface of the joint he was trying to make.

But now it was no longer a tiny wisp. It was a massive thing, huge, as big around as a Palace tower. It was colossal, and it waggled about in a massive space within the mana stream like the decapitated body of a serpent grown to titan size. It nearly startled him to see how much perspective had changed. He might have laughed were the situation not so delicate. Surely that "strand" was not quite what the spell designers had in mind either. Still, he felt it might work best for the merging of the heart stone to have it that way, usable in its magnificent size, but he understood now why the chrysalis had been destroyed. It wasn't even that he'd delivered too much mana, so much as that he'd delivered the correct amount too fast. Apparently, "slowly" meant *really* slow.

He began the words that the spell had put down for those who channeled mana naturally, slow casters like Altin had used to be, like he forced himself to be now. He took the end of that mighty mana stump and carefully whittled it down to size. Without the ring, it was the work of some time to shape it down to a point, shaving away mana as if he were sharpening some giant wooden stake.

At last he had it reduced to a thin thread, a thread so small that he wondered if he could even see it while he wore the ring. Nonetheless, he gathered it up and once more fed it into the new chrysalis that he held. Again he reached into the wriggling thing, probing and seeking the point of its tiny mana core. The little speck of mana he'd seen in the previous pupa blazed in this one like a great bonfire in the magic eyes of Altin in his ringless state. He nearly lost his concentration for seeing it, and he regarded the conflagration of pink and purple roiling in the tiny creature's mind—its soul perhaps—with awe. He marveled at it for a time, marveled at the brilliance of the spell itself, but he caught himself and stuck to the task at hand.

He said the words and thought the thoughts of joining and becoming something new, of being one thing and then another in a sequence insistent and orderly. The transformative thoughts came clearly as each phrase of the spell argued for the certainty of a change, each word guiding the images in his mind, the concepts and very visceral understandings of what it was he sought to make the gap become: one. In time, much time, he finally had it; the nature of the clay became the nature of the crystal, which became the nature of the heart stone. One thing must become another, which becomes another yet again. He could see it, even feel it in his chest, sensing what it was to be that thing, to be that physicality, each phase of it he understood perfectly. And so, with no hesitation, with certainty born of the recognition that it must be now, he thrust his hand forward, a punching motion with his hand, opening it as he thrust, palm out. He mashed the chrysalis against the center of the heart stone. "Ca'ana Feen stora moore," he shouted in the ancient tongue, and then his eyes flew open, and he stared at what he'd done.

For a moment he couldn't see anything; the spotlights and even the glow from Yellow Fire's pulsing heart seemed blinding to him. But he squinted and leaned forward, peering into the shadowy cracks around the violet light. The red-brown clay he'd brushed on was turning black, black like engasta syrup tiles, absolute black. It seemed to fall away, like the center of a square of wax being melted from underneath. It melted into the crack all the way around, and little wisps of smoke came out in places, emitting a noxious smell. There was a faint hissing for a time, and then nothing for several minutes more.

Then, simply, nothing.

He waited. Those standing outside the swollen arc of the pressurized plastic bubble waited. If they were speaking amongst one another, Altin hardly knew. He craned his neck forward, tilted his head, pressed his ear against the rock. He listened. Nothing.

He sniffed around the edge for a time. The noxious odor was gone. Sucked up into the evacuation vent that was filtering everything in this frigid little room.

It occurred to him that maybe the cold temperature wasn't good for the process at this point.

"I need to get out of here," he said. "We need to take this chamber down. It is usually hot down here. Some of the gases in the air are different. I think it should be that now."

After reclaiming his ring, he pulled his gloves on and reset the seal. He snapped his helmet back in place as well. All the lights were green on the panel on his left arm. "Okay, take it down," he said.

"Come here first," Orli said over the com. "Let me check your suit."

He would have argued, but knew it would be faster to comply. He'd put this suit on enough times over the last year to be quite capable of doing it properly by now.

"Turn around," she ordered, and he went through the ritual she always put him through. When he was done, and she was, she said, "Okay, drop it, Rabin."

The grad student drew down the pressure in the bubble, enough that it could be unsealed from the rock face, and soon after, Altin was standing beside the rest, waiting anxiously as Rabin and his twin brother detached the rest of the bubble and rolled it up and out of the way.

Orli and Professor Bryant were the first to be peering point-blank down at Altin's work.

"Don't touch it," the professor and Altin said simultaneously as Orli began to reach toward the heart stone.

The professor straightened after a few moments of looking at it, and pulled out the blocky device he'd used to take readings from it on his first day at Yellow Fire's original home, the device Altin knew emitted the green light beams.

"Stop," Altin said. "I think it best if you not bombard it with anything at all. Not now." He couldn't help but glance around at all the small crates of explosives lying around the edges of the regrown area; the fleet had already insisted on enough potential bombardment as it was. Poor Yellow Fire's life, if he got one, was going to be lived under the specter of death for a while. Altin hated that it was so, but understood why the explosives and detonation apparatus had to be there. At least for a while.

"This won't do anything to it," the professor said. "We've been taking readings off these things since we got here."

"They weren't infused with tissue-thin mana before," Altin said. "I have no idea how your device works, but I should think if my channeling mana makes your equipment do strange things, then it is likely your equipment might make my channeled mana do strange things too, especially in a procedure as delicate as this. Given what's at stake here, I think patience is called for."

"He's right," Orli said. "Put it away, Professor. Please. You've done amazing work here. The team has. But it's time to let the stuff we don't understand run its course."

The professor looked like he wanted to protest, but then the lines that were forming upon his brow suddenly reversed themselves. "You've probably got a point," he said. "But we're sure going to lose a lot of data about what's happening, especially if it works."

"As a man of science, you of all people know how observation can alter things," Orli said.

"I do," he said. "Which means there's nothing left to do but have a drink and celebrate what I'm sure will be our incredible scientific victory."

"I don't know," said Rabin as he came to stand next to Professor Bryant and Doctor Singh. He stared like the rest of them down at the work that Altin had just done. It didn't look any different than it had before. "What we did is cool and all, but it seems like maybe we should pray."

"Pray?" Altin asked. He could see the deep and gentle way that the young man was gazing down at Yellow Fire's heart.

"Yes," the grad student replied. "We should ask God to help Yellow Fire find his way back. Maybe even ask Him to forgive Red Fire for what he had done, for his sins, you know? We could ask for Yellow Fire's sins too. I mean, we don't really know who he was before. Not that it matters. We should ask for all of us really, for what we might be doing now, meddling." He paused, and looked around, watching them all stare at him as he somewhat lost track of what he was trying to say. He resigned himself to concluding, simply, "It can't hurt. A little humility is all. And what can it hurt to ask?"

"Nothing," said Doctor Singh.

When they began, even Altin bowed his head.

Chapter 42

Social stratification is a constant in the nature of human societies, and it is in the seams between those divisions that the criminally inclined find leverage. Location and patience are all that is required, and a carefully placed strategy can break apart any structure with a very small amount of effort. When water freezes in the tiny cracks of a castle, it can, with time, crumble the mighty thing. Black Sander knew it would be the case as much on Earth as it was on Prosperion.

For the first three days on Earth, Black Sander and his men had struggled to stay out of sight, doing so the old-fashioned way, as it were, by ducking behind shadowy things and creeping along at night. He could not admit to his men that he was lost, but he was, and it took them some time to find their way out of the freight yard into which they'd been deposited as part of the *Glistening Lady*'s cargo. And that might have been acceptable to Black Sander alone, but it had then taken a considerable amount of additional time to locate the less well-manicured parts of town, the parts of town where people could go missing and nobody would care—or at least, where anyone who did care had enough issues with the authorities to keep their mouths shut anyway.

Black Sander and his associates had had to snatch a few people off the streets for a time, and had to knock a few heads together for a while, but eventually they were able to sift through enough wanderers, transients, and prostitutes to find a few with enough wits remaining to be of use. It didn't take them long after to learn that they needed what the Earth people called a "grid pass" or a "net ID." In addition, to make any of it matter, they also needed an account in which to put and store NTA credits.

Black Sander's man Twane continued to grapple with the idea of how, on Earth, nothing actually served as money. "But how can we buy stuff if'n we ain't got no coppers, silvers, or gold?" he'd asked.

"They don't use that here. There are no coins. It's all done by the machines."

"What is?" Twane had asked, scratching his head. Black Sander would have ignored him, but the others were watching too. They had to be confident Black Sander was up to the task of being on an alien world.

"The currency. It's all in the machine. The net. The damned grid. It's not that difficult to see."

"But that's just it," Twane argued. "There's nothing to see. You give them a card and they give it right back when you buy something. Sometimes they just shine a light in your eye. I seen people buying things like that, just a light. Or even a fingertip. Where's the money, then?"

"There is no money. It's all made up," he said. "It's all one big tally kept track of in the machine."

"So there ain't no gold nowhere in the whole world?"

"Good gods, man, of course there's gold. They just don't pass it around. You're in an alien culture. You need to relax and accept things how they are. You'll start to make sense of it in time." Twane never could quite get that down. But Belor had, and Black Sander, of course. None of the others cared. As long as Black Sander had it down, they were content to follow along. Their ignorance did make them loyal, though. They knew they were in it very tight.

With the help of a trembling young man who they found on the third night, they found a proprietor who sold generic citizen numbers and access to net accounts, which they paid for with lumps of gold that they'd made by melting down gold crowns from Kurr. Soon they had clothes, credits, and a small Earth device known as a "tablet" with which they could access the grid, though Black Sander was still frequently frustrated in his efforts to master it.

And it was around this tablet that he, Belor, Twane, and the teleporter sat, their faces lit up and blue in its light as if it were the Earth equivalent of a campfire. He was flipping through slide after slide of satellite images, each depicting various coastal cities of nations within the NTA. They'd been at it for several hours now.

Black Sander, frustrated, sent another telepathic thought to Prosperion, to the addled mind of the marchioness' seer, Kalafrand. "I need to see it again," he conveyed. "Think it back one more time."

"I've sent it a hundred times," Kalafrand sent back. "Can't you hold it in your head?"

"I'm not a Z-class seer, idiot. Just do what you're told."

"I'll tell My Lady if you keep being mean to me."

Black Sander had no worries about incurring any wrath from the marchioness on Kalafrand's behalf, not now, not on Earth. That was what she'd been desperately waiting for. But he let the man think the threat had won him some small victory. "I apologize. Please just think it back to me."

With a sense of smug satisfaction unfiltered from the thoughts, Kalafrand once more conveyed the images of the city from which the missing Annison had been trying to contact them for some time. According to Kalafrand, Annison tried to reach him every day. He did reach him, apparently, but every time the seer opened his mind to the telepathic nudge, Annison said nothing. In fact, rather than saying anything, he simply kept trying to open contact and nothing more. It was as if he had no idea he'd gotten through. It was an odd situation, one that was so odd and unaccountable that Black Sander suspected it might have more to do with Kalafrand's oddness than any quirk of telepathy across all that space.

On the positive side, however, the Z-class seer was able to track Annison's telepathic footprints back, so to speak, and as before, he found where the magician lay, strapped to a barber's chair with his head half hacked away. Apparently someone had opened up his head and pulled apart his brain. Kalafrand had conveyed images of it to Black Sander shortly after the discovery, images of Annison lying there with his skull but a bowl of bone and parts of his brain floating in liquid-filled trays. He'd also sent Black Sander other images, memories gotten when he pushed his magical sight around the complex in which Annison was held. He saw that, and eventually, he'd pulled his vision up as high as a gryphon flies, up through the rooftops and high enough that he could see the city all around. That was the city Black Sander was looking for.

Though some of the buildings were tall and angular and looked to be made from mirrors and nothing more, most of the city was a collection of lightly colored structures that climbed up the hillside and looked down upon a bay. Black Sander found it oddly comforting to see another bay city like that, different from the crime hub of Kurr, but in a way, sister cities across the stars, connected by him. Or at least they would be once he found the damned thing.

The trouble was, there were many bays on this planet, and too many cities, and they needed to find one that matched the images in Kalafrand's mind. They needed to get the name. They were looking for one that had a series of strange towers jutting up from the water near the mouth of the bay, ragged and rusting. They'd been looking for it for three days already when he'd started up again today. Now nearly four days in, he was growing frustrated and losing patience.

But still he looked, and it was nearing midnight on that same fourth day on Earth that Black Sander pushed one image aside in exchange for another in his tablet, and there it was: the city, its rusting red towers reaching skyward from the water and its hillside covered with plain, squat homes. "There!" he announced, pointing at the screen. "Finally!"

He saved the image and immediately tapped up the corresponding data. "It's called 'San Francisco,'" he read aloud. "In an area known as California in the northern part of a country called 'Mexico.' It says here that its trade status is 'friendly,' but it's not a 'subordinate state' of the NTA."

"Whatever that means," Belor commented as Black Sander fell silent for a time, scanning through information about primary local resources, trade, population numbers, and the like. Eventually he found the feature their captive junkie had shown them that would allow the table to make a comparative map for them. When he called it up, he could see that they were on the wrong side of the continent—though he did count himself lucky that they were at least *on* the continent. Some luck was better than none.

He stood and walked the tablet to where the junkie lay on a sagging mattress on the other side of their dark and filthy motel room. "Hey," he said, prodding the junkie with his foot. "Wake up."

The youth, whose name he hadn't bothered to ask, looked up through eyes so red they could have been hot coals. He slurred something in response, and the movement of his tongue pushed a rivulet of saliva out of his mouth and down the side of his face.

"By the gods, how long does that confounded stuff addle them so?" Black Sander asked. "He's useless to us like this. I told you we shouldn't have given him what he asked for."

"It seemed like a good strategy at the time," Belor replied, it having been his idea that they keep the man, since he'd seemed so willing to do anything if they'd just supply him with the money to procure the liquid he injected into his veins. He'd promised to do anything for them for that. It had seemed a very reasonable price to pay for a willingly complicit slave, but, as it turned out, not a particularly lively one.

"I'll go ask the innkeeper," Black Sander said, and with it exited the room.

The motel manager looked up over the stub of a foul-smelling cigar when Black Sander came in, but he did not turn down the volume on the net show he was watching on the big monitor hanging on the wall nearby.

Black Sander laid the tablet on the counter before the man, turning it around so the man could see the map of the continent deemed "North America." He pointed to the mark on the map where San Francisco was. "There," he said. "How do I get there from here? Where can I book passage or post to carry me?"

The man frowned at him, glancing right back to the television show, which was now depicting a fiery crash between two vehicles, around which men were running and shooting at one another while noise that Earth people called music played loudly over it all.

"Hey," snapped Black Sander. "Answer me."

The fellow reached up and scratched at his shoulder, a big, round, hair-covered thing, with a hand that was just as hairy as the itch-afflicted joint. He moved his cigar into the corner of his mouth as he spoke. "Take the eighty tube," he said without peeling his eyes away from the battle waging around the burning wreck depicted on the screen.

"What is 'the eighty tube'?" Black Sander was forced to ask, holding his rising frustration in check.

That had the man looking away from his television show. "What do you mean, what is it?"

Black Sander wanted to grab a fistful of the curling black chest hair that crawled out of the low neckline of the man's grimy, sleeveless shirt. He wanted to hurt him and cut the answer out of that greasy neck with a knife, but he did not. "I mean, as I told you when you asked about my accent a few nights ago, I am not from around here."

"Well, how far ya gotta come from to not know the eighty?"

"Just tell me where it is, for the love of the gods, man. Where is it?" The feral nature of the Prosperion manifested itself fully in his eyes, and Black Sander didn't even have to cast an illusionary red glint of fire in his eyes to augment the effect. A man operating a motel the likes of this one knew that look well enough, and danger was as obvious on Earth as it ever had been on Prosperion.

"Hey, I just never seen anybody didn't know is all. Maybe you got amnesia or something. Fried something with too much hooch. Not my problem. Eighty is upriver, on the other side of downtown. You wanna avoid people, go up the river through town till you see the tube. You can't miss it. Follow it east until you find the station at Northwest Sixth."

Black Sander didn't bother to thank the man.

Chapter 43

Watching them work on his brain was something of an out-of-body experience for Annison these days. He lay there in the loose wrap of his skin, which clung like wet muslin to the skeletal apparition he had become, and observed the proceedings with no emotion left. He had already tried to die several times, but it wouldn't work, and the unfortunate efficiency of Earth medicine continued to find ways to deny him the relief of simply shutting down. So he lay there watching, numb, the molecules of fear and hope in him only rarely flickering to light these days. His captors no longer tortured him. They did still ask him each day as part of the routine to try contacting someone. And he did. He tried to contact someone, anyone—anyone he'd ever known on Prosperion—but it never worked. He did what he was told, but he'd long ago given up on getting a reply.

The doctor they called Gaspar came to him as he watched her in the monitor, and she asked him to try making an illusion spell. They'd been very interested in that particular school of magic recently. "Go on," she said, not gently but not with animosity either. She might have been talking to a potted plant. "Let's see if we can't get one of your mind tricks to work this time."

He didn't resist. The electrocutions left him feeling exhausted now, yet they wouldn't let him sleep, so it was best just to try.

He closed his eyes and reached out for the mana. Even that familiar pink void was gone. He couldn't see it anymore.

"That's it," she said. "Keep going."

She always said that, and yet he never saw a thing. But, he knew how to channel it by long habit, so he did what he'd always done, moving through the spell like a blind man walking through a once visually familiar room.

He thought it would be nice to see the Sansun River flowing by the pastures south of Northfork Manor, a place where he'd spent much happier times. He focused on the memory and set the illusion with a few muttered words, the air that passed through his lips barely shaping them, the sounds of them perhaps sapped by the desert dryness upon his tongue.

With his eyes closed and his expectations buried in the darkness beside the corpses of hope and fear, he was mildly surprised to hear the women shouting happily. He heard them less by the rise in volume than by the presence of their glee. Nothing was gleeful here, and so it was that acidic emotion rather than the escalating pitch that had him open his eyes and see.

Sure enough, he'd cast it. He found himself lying upon the riverbank. He could hear the water running past, even if, from where he lay, he couldn't see that it was there. He looked up into a sunlit sky, and for a moment knew one small morsel of happiness. He pulled in a long breath, wanting to smell it all, the rich scent of the land, the wet, muddy riverbank, the faint hint of salt from the not-so-distant sea. But there was none of it. And he knew in that moment why.

He'd never fallen for his own illusion before. He thought that was almost an interesting oddity, but he didn't have the energy to be curious. He did, however, have enough knowledge of his own magic to recognize it for what it was, and just like that it was gone.

"Awww," both women moaned. "Did you get it all?" the one called Gaspar asked.

"I did," said the other. "Finally."

"Finally what?" came a voice from the window. Annison recognized it immediately.

There followed a scraping sound, and something heavy hit the floor, followed by the breaking of glass when a rack of test tubes followed suit. And then Black Sander was before him looking down and shaking his head.

"Don't say no words," said another voice Annison did not recognize, though it was thick with the accent of someone from the south of Kurr speaking in Earth English. He glanced up at the monitor and saw a large man with a handheld crossbow trained on the doctors.

"They've got cameras," Annison rasped.

"They've got what?" Black Sander asked, then turned to the window as another man was crawling through. "Cover the door," he ordered, then leaned down nearer to Annison's mouth. "Speak up."

Annison repeated what he'd said, his voice like crushing old, dry leaves.

"Well, I can't understand a thing you are saying," Black Sander said. "And you look like all nine hells. I take it they haven't bothered to feed you since you arrived." He glanced around the room before his eyes came to rest on Annison's brain, all neatly quartered and most of it in dishes placed on the tray. "And what have they done to your head? I don't think I've ever seen anything quite like this." He had seen it in the images from Kalafrand, but the reality of it was significant.

He walked to where the women were, and glanced past them into the row of monitors along the back wall. Several of them depicted three-dimensional models of the parts of Annison's brain. The most frequently graphed and illustrated among them was the mythothalamus, which Black Sander had seen on occasion in drawings in books or doctors' offices back on Prosperion. He turned to the two doctors, who were surprisingly calm despite their situation. "What's all this?" he asked. "What are you doing to him?"

"Studying him," the woman said in English, though she had something of an accent in the way she pronounced the words. It sounded different in her mouth than it did in those of the Earth people Black Sander had dealt with in the city called Des Moines.

Annison struggled to wet his lips and called out again. "They have cameras," he said again, more clearly now. "They're going to come."

To suggest his claim might be true, there were two loud reports from outside, short pops of noise that echoed off the walls. There followed a few shouts, some in English, some in the common tongue of Kurr.

Black Sander went to the window and looked down the rope up which he had climbed. Two of his men lay dead, and there was a dead Earth man on the lawn with an arrow in his face. Two of the men from Murdoc Bay were already dragging that fellow into the bushes, though.

"Well, that's done it," Black Sander said. He went to the flat, boxlike object on the counter between a pair of monitors and pulled out the thin wires in the back. He tossed it to the man with the crossbow, who caught it one-handed and stuffed it into the back of his pants.

That's when the door into the room burst open and three men came charging in. A bright streak of red light cut through the space between the first of the men and Black Sander, even as the attacker was running for the left corner of the room.

Black Sander muttered four short words for an illusion,

casting a block of blackness around the man and locking him in absolute darkness. The second through the door had a longer weapon, one made of wood and black metal, like a crossbow without the bow. From it spouted flashes of white fire and loud, concussive reports. It was a weapon the Earth men called a gun. All the gunfire was directed at Twane, standing near the window.

This was hardly the first time the burly Prosperion had been in a room being raided by a group of armed men, and he was already diving for cover when the first shots rang out. He fired his crossbow as he rolled, and his first shot, aimed through the legs and rods of the tables and monitoring equipment around Annison's chair, shot the gun-wielding man right through his ankle, which sent him sprawling to the ground.

The third Prosperion, who had been in wait beside the door, stepped out from behind it and silently slit the throat of the third Earth man through the door. Then he leapt upon the man with the long gun and plunged his knife into the man's heart. He took the gun, and, finding a smaller handheld gun in the man's belt, he took that too. He immediately tossed the smaller one to Twane, who had just regained his feet.

Blasts of red light sprayed out from the black block of the illusion spell Black Sander had cast. The random fire caused everyone to dive for the floor, even the two doctors, who huddled together in a corner where rows of low cabinets met, looking scared but not remotely hysterical.

Annison let out a cry as one blast of laser fire blew off his left kneecap, and another burnt away part of his shoulder, sending him into absolute agony.

"Stay at the door," Black Sander barked, and he crawled across the floor to where the man in the darkness spell was. When he was near enough, he snatched the man's ankles out from under him with a hooking swipe of his arm. The man fell like a rock, his head hitting the wall first, then the corner of a counter before he landed with a thump. Black Sander dismissed the spell as he drew his dagger, and the man had just enough time to stare up wide-eyed at his killer before Black Sander's knife was in his throat.

Black Sander took the man's weapon and stood up, studying it for a time. It was much smaller than those the fleet soldiers he'd seen on Prosperion had carried. This was a remarkably concealable device. He smiled as he tucked it into his belt.

He turned back in time to see three more men arriving, though these came slowly, and looked warily through the doorframe. One of them turned back and said something to someone out of sight, and perhaps just coming up the hall. Black Sander could not tell what they were saying, but he quickly cast a spell of invisibility on himself and his two men.

When the man looked back, he saw that they were gone. He took the time to look quickly around the room to confirm it, then ducked back behind the doorframe again.

There followed more talking. It was a language Black Sander did not know. Then came a loud voice speaking in one he did: English, clear and audible. "Gentlemen, gentlemen," the man outside the room called in. "I had no idea you were from Prosperion. Why didn't you just come in through the front gate?"

Black Sander didn't answer.

Annison moaned. Black Sander figured he was in agony. Blood ran freely from his leg and shoulder both. The emaciated magician was twitching his finger up toward the roof. Or toward the monitor near where he lay. He was pointing. Black Sander followed the direction of the skeletal finger, looked into the monitor there. It was the monitor that showed the room and the table behind Annison. The one showing Black Sander as plain as day.

"They can still see you," Annison rasped. "In the cameras." His hand trembled as he tried to point again.

Black Sander saw it and realized his mistake. From that angle, the men in the hallway couldn't see the monitor. He didn't believe there were any monitors like it outside the room either. He'd been through this whole complex in his mind; he'd had Kalafrand run him through in the memories from his seeing spell.

"Gentlemen," continued the voice. "You cannot escape. Put down your weapons. No one else needs to die."

Several loud gunshots followed, and the Prosperion guarding the door fell forward, his blood leaking out onto the floor, tracing the shape of his body despite the invisibility spell. There were three smoking holes in the wall behind where he had stood.

Clearly the men outside the room had some kind of monitors after all.

"There's no reason for everyone in there to die," said the voice in the hallway. "And I'd rather not have to throw grenades into the lab. We've got a lot of nice equipment in there that would be a shame to waste. Jefe will be upset."

Black Sander muttered the words to a seeing spell; for this situation his D-class sight was more than adequate. In moments he'd assessed the threat.

Gunfire sounded from outside, below the window, along with the hiss of laser fire cutting through moisture in the air. He hoped he'd brought enough men. They weren't magicians, but they were streetwise and experienced. As if in answer, he heard Belor shouting at one of them to get the weapons off the dead Earth men. He sent his magic vision out through the wall, and confirmed what he had hoped: the men arranged around the side of the house had worked efficiently. Four more of the locals now lay dead.

He let the seeing spell go, and looked back at the monitor where he was clearly visible. Invisibility would be pointless within most Earth buildings; that much was becoming obvious. He glanced to Annison, lying there with his brain all carved out, and shook his head. It was also obvious that the Earth people wanted magic for themselves. His hunch had turned out absolutely true.

He wondered how much they'd learned, how much was in that little box he'd tossed to Twane.

"Break it, Twane," he called across the room. "The box I gave you. Stomp it into a thousand bits. Shoot it with that gun."

Twane did as he was told. Black Sander's black brows knit together, his mind ticking through possibilities.

"Do you seek the secret of magic?" he called out to the man behind the wall.

"I do," said the man.

"You're going to need more than one mage to figure it out, you know. Different schools. Different powers. Combinations change what they can do."

"Yes," said the man. "We've learned that much from your friend there."

Annison began to squirm. It was as if he recognized something familiar, something terrible in the lilt in Black Sander's tone, a silky smoothness that the procurement specialist used when negotiating things—things like the price for Orli's capture, for example, and things like more than a few of the ingredients he'd needed for the siren's blood elixir Lord Thoroughgood had ordered Annison to make. "Black Sander, don't," he said.

Black Sander dropped the illusion and came toward the chair where Annison lay. The illusion would have failed them anyway. The men had tablets. They would see him and his men, and they would disbelieve. But he didn't need to hide from them anyway.

He grinned. He drew his knife out again, placing it at Annison's throat. "They're not encouraging travel between the two worlds yet. You understand that, yes?" He spoke it loudly so the man in the hall could hear.

"Yes," the man called back. "We are aware of that. It's very ... inconvenient."

"It is," Black Sander agreed.

"May I come in?" asked the man in the hallway, this time sounding entirely polite. "I'd prefer not to be shot if we are going to negotiate."

"Just you," said Black Sander. "And call off your men downstairs."

There was a brief jumble of voices from beyond, muttering and words in a melodic language Black Sander did not recognize, all of which ended in the negotiator yelling at someone to be still and get it done. That last he understood clearly enough.

"All right," said the man. "I'm coming in. I have no weapons."

Black Sander cast his seeing spell once more, and studied the speaker carefully. He was a heavyset man, with blond hair and a bulbous nose. He wore expensive clothing in the style of the affluent class on Earth. "Yes, I see you," Black Sander said. "What's that lump near your ankle? Lift your pant leg and let me see."

The blond man actually grinned at that. "Yes, I forgot about that," he said, then reached down and pulled a very small version of the laser pistol Black Sander had acquired from the man he'd stabbed in the throat.

"Now you can come in," Black Sander said.

The man moved between the group of his fellows, which had now swelled to five, and came inside, his hands held up near the level of his head, palms out and fingers splayed wide. "They call me El Segador," he said. "If you are not familiar with the local tongue, that means 'the harvester.'"

Black Sander nodded. "And is it your job to harvest magicians from Prosperion?"

407

The man nodded. "Nothing personal, of course, and certainly not for any ill will toward your people or your government. Think of it more in the cause of curiosity. And understanding, of course."

Black Sander smiled. "Of course."

"And who are you, my friend? What brings you to our humble estate with all your ... medieval Prosperion weaponry? It seems a long way to come, and a risky trip, given the measures the NTA is going to. Is our guest here so important to you that you would risk angering the power structure of two planets? Or are you here on the orders of someone else?"

Black Sander smiled and shook his head. "He is a traitor and nothing more. My reasons, and those of an employer, were I to have one, are none of your business. Yet. But I had hoped to arrange some, shall we say, mutual harvesting. I'd planned to start with this one, since he has managed to fall through the NTA cracks from the start." He looked down at Annison again and shook his head. "But it seems you people have beaten me to it. Honestly, you've rather ruined him for my purposes anyway."

"Yes, I am sorry about that. Curiosity makes people do crazy things, you know? Especially when specimens are in such short supply. But we've gone to great lengths to keep him alive, as you can see?"

Black Sander laughed. "Indeed." He pulled the handheld laser from his belt, which caused El Segador to take a step back.

"I thought we were being civil here," El Segador said, lifting his hands higher still.

Black Sander smiled again, though his eyes held a predatory gleam. "I believe we may well be. For you see, from where I stand, where my employer stands, objects like this are in far shorter supply than chaps like him." He lifted the weapon slightly, then tipped his head in the direction of

Annison lying there, a sequence of movements like tipping scales.

El Segador's eyes glinted too. "It's interesting that you say that," he said. "Because we have the exact opposite problem here."

Both men were laughing as Black Sander put his knife and his new laser away.

Chapter 44

Pernie streaked across the ridgeline, balanced easily atop Knot's smooth, slightly rounded back. She rode with her knees slightly bent to absorb the undulations that ran through his body in waves whenever his sinuous length scrambled over some stone or stump or mound. She did it reflexively now, and she did it at full speed. Her hair blew behind her, and her loose silk tunic snapped in the wind of his motion as they scuttled along faster than any horse could run. She ran because today was the day she needed to get away. Tomorrow would be a whole year on String. Tomorrow they were going to make her fight the orc. So today, she had to leave.

She didn't dare turn her head back, for she knew Djoveeve was following her; she'd seen the shift in the mana when the old woman had turned from her jaguar form to that of a flying squirrel. Pernie was much better at noting the shifts now, and she could see them with the least dip into the mana stream. Doing so was not quite so easy as spotting sugar shrimp, but she'd learned to trust her instincts when it came to deciding what was a pattern shift and what was merely a natural eddy, drift, or roil. And so, knowing full well that Djoveeve was chasing her through the underbrush,

Pernie had directed Knot up a ridgeline. In places, it was as sharp as a razor's edge, so narrow that Knot had to scramble along the sides. Pernie shifted easily and hooked her heels over the edges of his shell, her back parallel to the stone rushing by. The shift came to her as naturally as if she'd been born with the insect beneath her instead of her own feet.

But the veteran assassin wasn't thrown off her tail just yet, not so easily as by a run along a narrow ridge. No, the downside of Pernie's plan was that she was highly visible up there. It was true Djoveeve's cat form wouldn't work on the cliff, but the squirrel form would get her high enough to jump to the trees once Pernie was down to the canopy.

She nudged Knot down the cliff face then, straight down, requiring that she slide all the way to his rounded rump and stand upon that, leaning into the rock face, which whistled past her so closely that she could not have put her hand between her shoulder and the rock. There was only room for one of her feet to stand upon him when he went perpendicular in that way, so she stood on one and held the other out for balance. She tapped the cliff from time to time with the butt of her spear as well, leaning on it like a rudder, using it to compensate for the shifts Knot made as he went down, S-curving around cracks or brambles or sometimes predators, any of which could come upon them suddenly when traveling at such meteoric speed.

They plunged toward the canopy so fast it felt like free fall. Every second counted. Pernie knew that Djoveeve would struggle to find her once she got beneath the leaves, if she could just get far enough ahead. She was gaining time now. And the squirrel form would take time to glide down too, even be subject to air currents along the way.

Soon they were down far enough that they came level with the canopy, something of a shoreline where the uppermost foliage pressed against the cliff. The moment they were in the shadows of it, Pernie teleported both herself and Knot some fifteen paces away, across an open space between the cliff face and a long kapok bough that thrust even deeper into the sea of leaves. They shot along its length until it narrowed and began to bend beneath their weight. She spied the dangling length of a vine some twenty spans away, the long, sturdy variety preferred by the spider-apes.

She stabbed the end of her spear out in front of Knot, who recoiled from the unexpected sight, curling back on himself as he tried to stop. Pernie dropped to her bottom and slid along his back with the momentum she still had, right up the curve of his recoil. She wrapped her legs around his middle as she hit the upturned part, and she gripped him tightly just before she teleported them both to the vine.

Knot, in terror, curled up into a ball, wrapping himself around her feet and shins. She could feel all his legs twitching like so many spiny bristles of a brush.

She grabbed the vine as they reappeared, and they fell together toward the jungle floor, plunging in free fall for five full seconds before the vine began to draw tight. Pernie knew she likely would lose her grip when she and Knot hit the length of it, so she began the teleport spell again, right as the jolt of the fall tore her hands loose from the vine. She spoke the last word with the precision she learned from jumping off cliffs, and in that barest blink of time, she put them back on the vine again.

They swung so low she had to curl up her knees, pulling the rounded mass of Knot up against her belly as tightly as she could. He was heavy, and her toes clipped the fronds of several squat and bulbous palms.

In a long and graceful arc, so long and graceful that it would have appeared to an observer that it was quite slow despite the wind-whistling velocity, they swung across seventy spans of jungle floor and then back up again. At the top of the swing, Pernie let go of the vine, just as upward momentum waned. They hung there for a moment, for the barest time feeling as if released by gravity, then Pernie nudged Knot with a gentle telepathic threat, which had him opening by the time they began to descend, falling toward the next limb, this one a long, sturdy bridge provided by another of the massive kapok trees.

Knot landed softly, the strength of his little feet always amazing to her, and she came down without the least shock or jolt. In that same motion, they were shooting toward the tree trunk, and then down they went, around and around, spiraling their way down its fluted altitude in a winding trek that took them barely a minute to complete. Once again they were darting through the brush, silently but for the rare slap of leaf clusters that Pernie could neither duck nor leap.

Pernie blinked, looking into the mana again, careful not to touch it or stir it herself, merely looking, flitting in and out of that place as Djoveeve had taught her to do. It was the only way to win a fight with an elf, the old assassin had said, and Pernie had finally begun to believe. Watching the mana in this way was difficult, though, for it was like seeing in both positive and negative space, like watching lightning and trying to recognize both the shape of the lightning's forks and the shapes formed by the darkness those blinding flashes outlined. Lose one, and you lose the other. Then you see nothing. Djoveeve had told her most humans couldn't do it even if they tried. None could focus on two things at once—by now she'd heard that time and time again—but some, a few, could effectively alternate between, and Pernie was coming along just fine.

And so it was that she saw the shift in the mana again, barely, Djoveeve somewhere far at her back. She cast a scent illusion, the smell of herself and Knot, and she sent it spinning up a tree like an olfactory fireball. She set another upon a cluster of seedpods that were floating down a stream.

For a time she wove back and forth doing the same sort of thing everywhere, perhaps a full five minutes, and with the speed of her insect mount, she covered a great deal of space.

When she was satisfied with her misdirection, she masked herself and her roly-poly ride in total silence. She covered their smells and then shrouded them in invisibility, then set out to the north, bent on getting herself that horned manatee.

Three weeks had passed since her injury, and Djoveeve had been tailing her ever since. The woman made no secret about why, and must have repeated fifty times that Pernie not mess with the sargosaganti. Djoveeve said it was because they were dangerous. Seawind, who had been something of a nag on that topic too, said the same. He explained over and over that they could not be tamed. But when Pernie asked if he had ever tried, he'd had to admit that he never had.

"Why not?" she'd asked.

"Because they are not to be trifled with."

"But why?" she'd pressed.

"Because they are dangerous. And because they do not wish to be tamed."

"How do you know? Have you ever asked one before?"

"No."

"Then how do you know they don't want to be?"

"Because it is known. They are wild things. They are peaceful and timid and, as you have seen, able to pin you to the beach easily and instantly."

"But that still doesn't mean they don't want to be tamed. Not if you never talked to one before. And Kettle says that everyone is different, so even if one says they don't like people, other ones might feel differently."

At which point Seawind had turned his head slightly to the side, something of a bow in deference to Djoveeve, and said, "This is where you must deal with your own species." Then he left the cave.

But Pernie didn't care what they said. She knew she could do it, and now she needed to. She'd tamed Knot, and she was fairly sure she'd just completely escaped the current Sava'an'Lansom for the first time since she'd started trying. She looked into the mana and saw nothing at all that didn't appear as it should. There were a pair of garrote spiders making webs across a spider-ape corridor high above, but that was all. Djoveeve was nowhere to be found.

Soon enough, Pernie found herself once more atop the cliff that looked down upon the favored beach of the sargosaganti. She stepped off of Knot and crawled to the edge, peering down through the grasses toward the beach.

There they were again, all of them, a whole herd of fat black-and-green sausages reclining in the late afternoon sun, only partially filtered through a thin haze that was common in the autumn months here.

The titanic mass of the alpha male stretched out on the beach like a fifty-span seawall of fat and flesh, the blotches of his rough hide appearing as if some painter had thrown a fit. Leaving her invisibility and other illusions in place, she stood and gripped her spear, once again point down, ready to strike. The big one was closer this time, and she thought she might be able to make it all the way onto its back if she got a running start. So she did.

She took several steps back, then ran full speed and threw herself off the cliff. She was going to be close with this teleport.

The rocks grew and grew in her vision as she fell. She watched patiently as she plunged downward, the wind whistling in her ears.

She spoke the words, the largest of the jagged black rocks only a half-hand's width from her face, and then there she was in the middle of its back, the king of the manatees, her spear already plunging into its skin.

She blinked her eyes, looking into the mana, and saw it

whirl only a half instant before the creature teleported itself away. She had just begun to drop toward the beach in its absence when she spoke her own spell, nearly as quickly as the sargosagantis had done, and once again she stood upon it, gripping her spear where it dug into its flesh. She fluttered her vision back and forth between sunlight and mana sight, watching the titanic beast gathering mana again. As it did, she drove down with all her weight upon her spear, pushing it even deeper into the blubbery hide. The great sargosagantis jumped across an incoming wave, ten paces out to sea.

Pernie was nearly underwater before she could speak the words again, and once more she was on its back.

It blinked away again.

She chased it, and again she drove down on her spear. She twisted the shaft with her hands, trying to drill down through its thick, fatty flesh. Her spear was already a third of its length in.

She watched back and forth in and out of the mana as she worked, her breathing coming quickly now. She saw the mana move and jammed down on the spear, wanting to hurt it, and still it got away.

Saltwater splashed into her mouth as she uttered the last word of her teleport, and again she set to work on the spear.

It jumped.

She followed. The spear was into the giant sargosagantis more than half the shaft's length now.

The creature jumped again. She echoed the cast, this time pounding on the butt of her spear, hammering at it with her palm until what protruded from the sea beast's fat bulk barely reached her knee. She saw it draw mana again, and she knew she would be too late. She leapt into the air anticipating its teleport.

It blinked away, and once again she started to fall, but she was halfway through the spell when it vanished from beneath her, so she caught it before she'd fallen far enough to even get her toes wet. She appeared on its back again, and this time she stomped on the butt of her spear as it was gathering mana again. It let go a loud huff that sprayed water in great clouds of mist, white sheets that blew back and soaked her from head to toe. It tried to escape again, twice more, and both times Pernie stomped on the spear and stole its focus away.

Then it dove.

It was only then that Pernie realized that she was now well over a hundred spans from the beach, and the seabed now dropped precipitously away.

With a few powerful strokes of its wide, flat-finned tail, the sargosagantis was streaking like an arrow shot for the depths.

The force of the water rushing up at her swept Pernie right off its back, but she muttered the words even with a mouthful of water and teleported back to her spear, gripping it for all her worth as the monster sped into the darkening water at unfathomable speed. It was all she could do to hang on, flapping in the wake of its dive like a little human flag.

But she wasn't going to let go.

She pushed her mind into the mana and strove to find the manatee's will, its conscious thoughts and its mind. She just knew it had one. It had to be at least as smart as Knot.

She found it. She found fear and something that, in a greater intellect, might have evolved into hate. But it simply ran, and as with Knot, the only sense she got of its thoughts could be translated to an essential negative. It simply told her *no.*

Her ears were in agony as she was struck by the absolute intractability of that mind, the massiveness of its negativity, its conviction to run to the bottom of the sea. Then it blinked away from her in the moments that she'd forgotten to watch.

The air in her lungs began to burn, and she had to think twice about whether she should blink after it again with another teleport, but it was already nearly vanishing into the dark water below. It blinked a second time and was but a tiny bluish spot.

She felt herself making a gulping sound in her throat and chest. It felt as if someone had buried coals in there. She thought her ears might burst, they hurt so bad.

She looked up toward the surface and saw that it was very far away, the sun wearing a hazy blue veil. That was something of a surprise. She began to swim for the surface, stroking upwards with her hands.

Again came the spasm in her chest and throat. It occurred to her that she might not have enough air to make it up that far.

She mouthed the words of a teleport, expelling the last of the oxygen in her lungs. The sun still looked very blue up there when she reappeared. She kicked with her feet, wishing she could be rid of the boots she wore, now heavy and water soaked. She pulled with wide sweeps of her hands.

She tried another teleport, though she could only mouth the words.

Again her lungs convulsed. And a second time. She had to take a breath. She tried to pull upwards with her arms, but they wouldn't move anymore, had become things of inert lead.

She really, really wanted to breathe.

Another convulsion. She had to breathe. She had to.

She looked up, saw that she had started to sink again. Everything in her mind told her not to breathe. Something in her heart told her that it would be okay. And besides, her body was starting to feel as if it burned.

She looked up, thought about ... nothing. There was nothing she could do. So, with one last convulsion, she resigned herself to it. It hurt too bad not to. So she took a breath. The water burned like acid in her lungs. They hurt worse than the rest of her. But only for a while.

She watched with an odd curiosity as the sun began to blue again, the white wriggling of the surface growing darker and dimmer as she sank. She even, absently, wondered if she'd see the manatee again. But she never did.

Chapter 45

Altin looked up into the bright sun, now high above him. It was a hot day for this early in the year, and he wiped the sweat from his brow with a sleeve as he contemplated how tired he was. He could hardly believe how complicated the spell was for making engasta syrup, and even with the added benefit of his ring, it was still the labor of several hours to move all the components into place and transform them, merely to make one single tile of the stuff, just one, not even a half-span's length on a side and less than a half a hand thick. While intellectually he'd understood the process to be laborious and expensive, it wasn't until his third day working to build his own private platform that he began to fully understand why this particular activity had gotten the Transmuters Guild guildmaster elevated to the rank of second on the TGS council in recent months. If Altin found toting around heaps and heaps of stone, barrels of pitch, and wheelbarrows full of wisteria and blackroot, along with thirteen types of clay—one of which happened to be the very same as that which he had used to merge the crystals around Yellow Fire's heart back on Red Fire—then he could hardly fathom what building enormous platforms in space must be like. And that was just the labor. The cost was frightening. A primary constituent was tar wood, which was absurdly expensive, and he'd had to bribe three people to get it, despite being the Galactic Mage and ostensibly–if not actually–working on the Queen's behalf when requesting it. Yes, the desire to have a platform at Calico Castle was turning out to be a much larger project than he'd anticipated. It did, however, keep him near home while working on it, which made Orli and Kettle happy.

Kettle was just coming around the corner of the castle with a tray of mint tea as Orli dumped another load of roots at the base of the stone heap, which Altin had just meticulously stacked, as dictated by the spell. She too was covered with a film of sweat and dust, and the two of them plopped down atop the newly made stack of stone and watched Kettle's approach eagerly.

"I thought the both of ya could stand fer a draught," the woman said as she strode through the knee-high grass, a trail of flour dust blowing out behind her like smoke in the light breeze.

"Well, your timing couldn't be better," Orli said. "It's warming up fast today."

"Aye, it is. And a fine day it would ha' been were it not what it is, what it's about ta be."

Altin looked around and thought it a fine day altogether, if warm for heavy work. "Well, what's wrong with it?" he asked as he took a tall wooden mug filled to the brim with tea and chips of ice.

Kettle looked to Orli, who nodded, her cheerful expression dimming momentarily.

Altin saw the exchange between the two women and, glancing from one to the next, asked his question again. "What's wrong with today? And what does 'what it's about to be' mean? What am I missing?" He gestured back and forth between them with his hand.

"They're all the same, aren't they, dear," Kettle said, her

words directed at Orli in a way that made it seem as if Altin weren't standing right there. "'Tis all the work and the duty, and ne'er a thought fer the livin' bein' done all 'round theirselves."

Again Orli nodded and seemed perfectly aligned with whatever the mystery was.

"Oh for the pearls of String, what is it?" Altin asked. "Out with it, already!"

Kettle looked shocked that he'd said it, and Orli just shook her head. It was as if he'd said the most offensive thing.

"Pearls a' String is the right of it," Kettle said. "My little pearl is there on String. And do ya know what tomorrow is? Tomorrow is the day they stole her from me. The same day the two a' ya were ta wed. And while there's still something fer the wedding, there's naught fer my wee girl. Yet here ya are, buildin' yer fancy spaceship box, and not a thought a' poor Pernie gone a whole year away."

Altin resisted the urge to point out that they had already been over that topic what must have been a thousand times. Instead he looked to Orli, thinking she might understand. Pernie was fine. He was sure of it. If anything had happened to her, they would have gotten word. He'd even cast a divining spell to check on her a few months back, just to calm Kettle down. The indications were certain that Pernie was alive and, at least at the time, feeling fine. Orli's expression didn't exactly gush sympathy.

He gulped down the rest of the tea and put it back on the tray. "Thank you for the tea," he said, then returned to his work. With rather more violence than he had before, he once again began mixing the various types of clay, preparing the blend for the treatment of the stack of stones and roots he and Orli had made. Once it was coated with the mixture, he could convert it into another engasta syrup tile.

Perhaps as a show of mercy, Kettle changed the subject as she looked to Orli and asked, "So how's yer friend Yellow

Fire doin' out there on that red world ya planted him in? Have ya had any luck with the magic takin' hold?"

"Not yet," Orli supplied. "Altin checks in on him every night before we go to bed, but it's always the same. Still nothing."

"Well, things take time," Kettle said. "And no tellin' what kind of time fer a critter such as they are, no doubt. What with the two a' ya talkin' about millions a' years livin' fer them things, it don't seem too surprisin' that they'd be a while gettin' started again."

Orli nodded. "That's very likely true." She turned to watch Altin adding water to the large tub where they'd been mixing clay for the last several days. "Which is why we won't be doing anything rash to Blue Fire for a long time to come." The elevated pitch of her voice made it clear who that comment was really directed to.

Altin glanced up from his work, his eyes shadowed by the angle of his head and his lowered brows, but he did not take the bait. They'd already had this fight several times. He'd given his word; Orli thought it was reprehensible. Both sides understood both sides perfectly. There lay underneath their relationship now the tension of that conflict. Orli had stopped complaining about waiting for their wedding anymore. Instead, on that front she seemed relieved. The timing of the wedding, past attempts and future dates, was not a source of trouble anymore.

However, he also knew that barbs like the one she'd just thrown were going to keep coming as long as they waited for Yellow Fire to wake up. *That* was a source of trouble still. She was still angry about Altin's "threat" to kill Blue Fire, and she just couldn't let it go. He understood. He didn't blame her. It was the collision of two ideals. He also understood that she tried very hard not to say that kind of thing, and that mainly it happened when she was tired, which after several long days of labor under a hot sun and the frustration of having so many things, well, if not quite going wrong, not quite going right either, made such remarks nearly inevitable. The nature of tomorrow's anniversary—combined with the fact that he had forgotten all about it—made it a certainty.

And Kettle was right about Pernie's being gone. The castle had never been the same since she was taken by the elves. Hells, it had never been the same since Tytamon was killed. Kettle had simply lost too much. Even the death of the miner, Ilbei Spadebreaker, in the *Citadel* accident had hit her inexplicably hard. In a very short period of time, Kettle had lost a great deal, and with it, some big part of the spirit that had animated her. Altin had wanted to fill the void of lost Tytamon, and he'd hoped having Orli there at Calico Castle would give Kettle someone new to care about, someone to do things with. And in a way it had, Kettle did enjoy Orli, but there were just too many holes in the kitchen matron's heart these days, a heart that had been, in its way, the very heart of the castle.

He thought it a strange and sad sort of parallel, the grief of Blue Fire and Kettle. Two creatures moved entirely by love. Both living at the center of worlds made of stone, a planet and a castle, and both gentle beings wanting nothing more than to give love, to pour great galactic quantities of it into someone else. And yet both were stymied by a universe, by gods, by something cruel enough to deny them. Both now lived on hope—or perhaps more accurately, survived. Both merely waiting.

Orli was right to fight for Blue Fire's life. The promise Altin had made to Blue Fire was meant to be a merciful one, and it would be merciful if the time was right. But when is any time right in the absence of certainty, and who can be certain of anything that has yet to come? How could Altin know when Yellow Fire would finally wake up, if he ever would? How could he possibly ever know? What day was the right day to end the suffering for Blue Fire out there? Today? Tomorrow? A year from now? The chances that Yellow Fire would wake up in the hour after Altin killed her were as great as the chances that he would wake up right now. That he would never wake up. There was no stretch of time that would make it any different. His ignorance made his promise an agony.

With a sigh, he silently cast a seeing spell back into the dimly lit heart chamber on the world they still called Red Fire. Two small spotlights were directed at the dimly pulsing core that was Yellow Fire. A small camera had been mounted on one of the spotlight stands and attached to a transmitter, beaming images to Doctor Walters on the *Glistening Lady* in orbit high above. As if to remind him of the uncertainty of it all, of the lives at stake, the spotlights also illuminated the plastic crates filled with explosives and stacked around the heart chamber too. Certain death for him if he even twitched wrong. Each with an "entanglement trigger," as Roberto had explained. "They cost more than all the rest of your equipment combined. But there's no chance of interference from the atmosphere, so, you know, the fleet isn't going to screw around."

Altin moved his vision to the edge of the heart chamber and saw the twins loading up crates and stacking them one atop the next. Everything that could be taken apart on the water saw had been, and it now awaited Altin in pieces, ready to be sent back into the *Glistening Lady*'s cargo bays. Professor Bryant had proudly proclaimed it in "great shape" and assured Altin that he would get all of his deposit back on those pieces of equipment that had been rented rather than bought outright. Altin could hardly care. Money didn't matter. For all the expense and effort that had gone into it, they had what now? They had no way of knowing, possibly ever, if there had been or would be any value in any of it for Yellow Fire, or Blue Fire, or for anyone. That's what they had.

He turned his sight away from the brothers at their work and watched the dim, steady pulse of the heart stone again, once more moving close to it. He'd always thought this was a work of optimism, and he'd done it only because Orli had pleaded with him to try. She was so passionately sure it was going to work. Her heart, like Kettle's, beat for the service of others, where his seemed to beat only for his own curiosity. They'd been right about him a moment before.

But how can one be a creature other than one's self? He was a creature of curiosity; his appetite, like Taot's, was dictated by nature beyond his control. And, if truth be told, even as he reflected on it, it was working on him now as he stared at the purple pulse of Yellow Fire's heart.

Why hadn't it worked? Why wasn't it growing or taking hold? He must have done something wrong. But what? It was clear that Yellow Fire's heart still had life left in it. Wasn't it? Or was that pulsing light simply some ambient quality, like the glow of metal that's been heated in a forge? That might be said to have life too, but left alone long enough, that life, that glow, fades away. Perhaps the light in the heart of a dead Hostile simply took a great deal of time to fade away.

Still, if that were the case, then why did the crystals on Yellow Fire's old moon in orbit above R3 have different properties than the crystals in dead Red Fire? If Yellow Fire had been completely absent of life, then those dull gray Liquefying Stones around him on that moon should have been brittle like the ones in dead Red Fire's world were. But they weren't. In fact, they still weren't. Even now, with Yellow Fire cut out and transplanted into the heart chamber of the red world, the stones on the old moon were exactly as they had been. Altin had already checked and rechecked several times. The professor and Stacy Walters had looked in their machines. Nothing had changed beyond the movement of Yellow Fire's heart.

Professor Bryant had originally said the life force must flow from the heart stone through the crystals and back, in some kind of loop. But that loop was broken. Yellow Fire was out and transplanted; he was on another world. And yet, apparently, there was still some kind of connection to the old. He wasn't connecting to the new. But Altin had connected him with the spell. So something was missing. There had to be something else.

Or else it just wouldn't work. Maybe it couldn't. Maybe it was hopeless.

Which Altin refused to believe. Too many people believed. Too many smart people, too many loving hearts, had said that it ought to work. People of faith were praying, for Mercy's sake. Which meant it had to be something Altin had done wrong.

He thought back through the spell he'd cast. It wasn't so long ago that he couldn't remember it clearly now. He was confident he hadn't missed anything. He'd been careful with the clay, spread it evenly. He'd double- and triple-checked all of it. He'd even done it without the ring, channeling the mana exactly as the spell had been written, to the very last phrase, the very last syllable, all precisely as designed with no deviation in any way.

He thought about that, the part of the spell he'd done with the ring, the filling of the seam with mana. He wondered if perhaps he shouldn't have worn the ring for that part either. Perhaps somehow he'd changed the texture of it. It didn't seem likely, but one never knew about such things. Mana had certainly never operated any differently for casting other spells. Ice and fire conjured perfectly with the ring. Teleportation worked exactly as it should. But those weren't spells over time. He wondered if maybe that could be the difference. Some of the mana had been channeled with the ring, some hadn't. Then he'd joined them. He wondered enough to verify.

"We should go back," he said suddenly, looking up at the two women still conversing over tea. Their vacant and surprised expressions prompted him to go on. "I need to go back and check something. I may have made a big mistake."

"What mistake?" Orli asked.

"On Yellow Fire. I might have channeled the mana wrong from the start."

"But you couldn't have," Orli said. "You said yourself that if you cast the spell wrong, the heart stone would have turned to ash. All of it would have."

"Dust," he corrected, biting his lip much like Orli sometimes did. "I did say that, though, didn't I? Still, I think I want to have another look."

Orli set her mug of tea down on the tray that Kettle still held out like a shelf. She couldn't help the look of hope that came into her eyes. "I'll call Roberto and have him tell the team we're on our way." She ran off immediately.

Altin and Kettle watched her go, her shapely legs carrying her swiftly through the meadow grass.

"She's a beautiful creature," Kettle remarked. "'Twas a time I didn't look so different than that."

Altin smiled and looked down into her ruddy face. "You're still beautiful, Kettle. And there's not one person in this castle that doesn't love you through and through, myself most of all."

She smiled up at him, some remark forming on her lips, but she checked it and seemed to relax a little bit, her shoulders rounding a little like some burden had been lifted off, or perhaps at least been set down for a while. "Thank ya," she said. "And I'll be mahself in time."

"I know you will," he said. "But no rush. We'll have you however you are for as long as you'll have us."

She smiled again and reached up and stroked his check with her rough, gentle hands. "You're a good boy," she said.

"Now get off with ya before yer space friends grow weary waitin' on ya out there in the stars. What sorta Galactic Mage is late fer a thing like that, eh?"

He smiled, feeling better than he thought he deserved to, and headed for the gates after Orli, who was already inside.

Chapter 46

Pernie had never seen Djoveeve cry before. She knew that the woman could because Seawind had remarked on it before—after the last time Pernie had nearly been killed by the great sargosagantis. But this time, as she coughed out water into the sand, she saw the tears running freely down the old woman's cheeks. Djoveeve cried, and yet she looked overjoyed, as Pernie coughed and coughed and coughed. The more she coughed, the more water came. It came and came. She could hardly believe so much water was in her, as if she'd choked on the whole ocean. Djoveeve began choking too, on her own saltwater, and as she saw Pernie's blue eyes fluttering and beginning to focus on her, she tried to scold her. She tried, but the words simply couldn't make it past the sobs that came instead. She clutched Pernie to her bony old breast and held her, half yelling, half weeping for joy.

"Infernal child," she finally managed as the sobs subsided some. "Stupid, brave, amazing little child."

Pernie felt a little dim, and she was marginally aware that she'd likely nearly drowned. Her chest hurt very bad, and she suddenly had to throw up.

She twisted in Djoveeve's arms and puked even more seawater for a while, puking so hard she saw spots swimming in her eyes. After a time, that passed, and she sat up and stared at the red-eyed woman, blinking and trying to get her vision right.

She realized someone was standing behind the old woman and looked up to see Sandew there, the lean young hunter shaking his head ever so perceptibly as he leaned upon his spear. Voices blew in upon the wind coming off the sea as well, and Pernie turned to see the lithe figures of three women kneeling in the surf, elven women, wet skin shimmering, a pale green hue that reflected the sunlight as the surf came and went around them. Their slender bodies were unmoved by the passing of the waves, and when the bigger waves came and rose nearly to their necks, crashing past and flowing up the sand, their long opalescent hair flowed in and out with the water like strands of liquid pearl. Their hair was the only motion caused by the movement of the waves, even the big ones, and despite the power of the surf. Their bodies remained unwavering, as if they were part of it, or part of the world. They were beautiful.

Pernie sucked in a breath upon seeing them. She pulled it in so hard it burned nearly as bad as when she'd breathed in all that water not so long ago. The effect of their beauty wasn't much different than a physical blow. It was jarring. She thought in that instant that she might get wounded in her heart like Djoveeve had, like an arrow or the penetration of a knife cutting right through, but she did not. She waited for it, though, remembering what Djoveeve had told her about falling in love with them.

Pernie stared right at them, trying to somehow see them more. A strange tightness gripped her in the chest, an anxiousness she could not explain. Their beauty was inexplicable. Astonishing. Even painful. But she didn't think she loved them.

The most recent wave drew back into the sea, and Pernie realized they were naked. She looked upon their nude figures admiringly. She did not love them, but she hoped someday that she might look like that, strong, toned arms, pert breasts, and a tummy with subtle lines where the muscle lay beneath. She felt certain that if she did, Master Altin would love her instantly. Seeing their graceful strength made her want to climb more trees and run longer in the sand while carrying her pack with Knot rolled up inside.

One of them raised a slender arm and waved at her. She waved back, and the other two did likewise. She smiled at them, and they smiled back, speaking to one another in voices that once more blew inland like songs, melodies swept in from a ship full of music sailing by somewhere out of sight.

She wondered if her voice would ever sound like that, be its own melody.

She looked down at her own body, skinny and straight as a spear. Her blonde hair hung dark and lank against the silk tunic, which in turn lay plastered against her skin. She wriggled her lips contemplatively, then looked up at Djoveeve, who was wiping the last tears from her eyes.

"You've scared the very last years of my life from me," the ancient Sava'an'Lansom said. "I should think you've cost me a decade with that little stunt. How many times must I tell you, must we all tell you, not to approach the sargosaganti?"

"I almost rode it," Pernie argued. "I did. I was very close."

"You were more than close, little Sava," said Sandew, unexpectedly and with more than a touch of awe. "I was there and saw you." He pointed with his spear to the far end of the cliff, where it curved and sloped away out of view. "I heard the caterwauling of the females as they all struck out into the sea, and I watched as you fought with him. You rode him all the way out there, past the shelf where the seabed begins to fall away."

Pernie looked back to the ocean, following the direction of Sandew's spear, but from here, she couldn't tell where the water deepened. She did note that the elven women had all gone away. She glanced up and down the shoreline, but there was no sign of their having walked away.

"Well, she nearly got herself killed for it," Djoveeve said, and Pernie could tell, by the timbre of the woman's voice, the initial shock of fright was fading and real anger would be coming straightaway. It worked the same with Kettle, but Pernie was used to it by now. Djoveeve wouldn't try to paddle her behind like Kettle would, and if she did, Pernie knew perfectly well that she could get away. She could paddle her back if she wanted to. If there was one thing that had changed for the better since coming to the land of the elves, it was that Pernie would never be subject to a spanking again. That made her smile, and just thinking it actually kept the smile upon her lips the whole trek back to the cave, which Djoveeve made them walk because she wasn't going to let Pernie try to run off again, as she put it, "on that obnoxious bug of yours."

When they arrived at the cave, they found Seawind waiting for them with an unexpected guest: the War Queen's Royal Assassin, Shadesbreath, returned from the land of Kurr. It was he who spoke first to her as they came into the dim interior of the cave.

"I hear they are calling you Sava'an'Sargosagantis," he said.

She frowned and wrinkled up her nose. Nobody ever called her that before.

"Word travels quickly, Sava," he said. "And riding sargosaganti has never been done."

"And it shouldn't be done," Djoveeve said. "It is disrespectful and disobedient."

"And very brave," he said. "All three traits of a proper Sava'an'Lansom."

"A dead one eventually," Djoveeve remarked.

"Perhaps," he said. "But we will see. One thing is certain. She is ready for the test."

Cold fear gripped Pernie then, colder than lungs full of salty seawater. She hadn't gotten away in time, and now they were going to make her fight the orc.

"I don't want to fight the orc," she said, her voice rising to near a whine. Her body, cold and tired and exhausted, seemed to have finally given up its last ounce of strength. "I don't want to. Please don't make me fight it. I just want to go home."

The two elves looked to Djoveeve, who took the child into her arms. "She's tired," she told them defiantly. "And today she nearly died. She might well be the great Sava'an'Lansom you all are so cocksure she will be, Tidalwrath's very champion, I am sure, but today, right now, she's simply a tired, frightened little girl."

"Well, tomor—" Seawind began.

"Damn your tests! And damn your prophecies!" Djoveeve's voice was the snap of a whip, a loud crack that struck him to silence. "Get out! Both of you. Before I put a spear in you and ride you both out to sea."

Chapter 47

"**I** won't do it," Pernie said as Seawind brought in the orc captive they'd been threatening her with all year—threats were how she saw it anyway. "I won't fight him. You'll just have to pull his knives out of my guts like the sargosagantis' horn."

"He hasn't got knives," Seawind said. "He'll have only his magic, which you can see if you choose to look. The sargosagantis was proof enough of that."

"Then why must I fight him? You said yourself there is a difference between killing and murder."

Djoveeve laughed from her place next to Pernie. "You see, she does listen."

"You must face this creature and be rid of fear."

"I'm not afraid. I rode the sargosagantis. Djoveeve and Sandew saw." Even she didn't believe it, though. The very sight of the orc, even as thin as it had become for want of proper exercise, filled her with memories of dread. Her whole body shuddered, nearly convulsed, as she thought about it touching her with its green hands, its bruising, powerful fingers biting into her flesh before its wicked fangs got hold. It would eat her if it could. She knew it not just in her guts, but in her memories. She could still feel the coarse flour they'd doused her with as they readied her for the cook pot not even four short years ago. She would have been eaten too, were it not for Master Altin coming to the rescue. He'd even apologized later that she'd been hurt, which is when she knew that he loved her.

Maybe he'd finally come and take her out of here. He had rescued her from orcs before. He might come. Though she knew he wouldn't.

Seawind took the silvery chains off the orc's wrists, neck, and ankles and pushed him into the center of the chamber. A bare room, barely forty paces across, roughly round, with a ceiling a little less than two spans above Pernie's head.

Shadesbreath stood near the entrance where Seawind had come in, holding a spear and a long knife made of steel, a human-made weapon rather than the volcanic glass the elves preferred.

"I can see the fear in your eyes, little Sava," Seawind said. "So can this creature here. You cannot move on in your preparations to become Sava'an'Lansom until you are over this. The time has come. As you said, you have ridden the sargosagantis. This orc should take you mere moments to dispatch."

"I won't," she said, crossing her arms over her chest. "You can't make me."

"We shall see."

Shadesbreath came across the room and tried to hand her the spear and the knife. He studied her out-thrust lips and the petulant defiance in her eyes. She seemed a most curious object to him, judging by the look that moved his features ever so slightly. He made no other expression and simply dropped both weapons at her feet. He resumed his position by the door, though only briefly, and then he vanished without a word.

Seawind vanished as well, and Pernie blinked her eyes and watched the wisps of mana curling around where he'd gone. She couldn't find him in it now, but she saw what he had done.

Djoveeve took her gnarled hand off of Pernie's shoulder. "Just get it over with, child," she said. "You're more than a match for it now. Respect its power, but have it over and done." She sang a few lines of a spell she knew and became a crane fly, which flew up and disappeared into the shadows somewhere near the upper reaches of the room, leaving Pernie in the silence and the near darkness of the cave.

She crouched and grabbed the weapons, then immediately muttered an illusion, her familiar variety of sight, sound, and smell. Then she stood and watched the orc as she fidgeted with the spear and knife. The knife was longer than she was used to, but she could wield it well enough if she needed to. She slid it carefully into her belt.

The orc was just standing there, rubbing its wrists. Her heart was pounding as she waited for it to do something to her.

She also thought that one throw of the spear would end it. It wasn't even moving.

Her eyes fluttered as she watched the movement of mana around the orc. They were rumored to have magic more like animals than men, raw magic shaped by emotions rather than thoughts and words, though she didn't know if that was true. She'd had animal magic at one time too, barely a year ago. It was surprising how quickly that had been lost.

She kept watching the orc for quite a long time, but it simply stared into the place where she stood. She wondered if it saw her. It wasn't channeling any mana that she could see.

She moved carefully around it, silent on her feet despite the silence spells. Illusions failed constantly, especially when cast upon those who knew enough and had reason to disbelieve.

She snuck up right near it, her whole body trembling as

she did. The stink of its unwashed body struck her like a blast of wind, driving her back a step. It smelled like death and misery. She could not help remembering the terror of that day in the courtyard back at Calico Castle. All the screaming and the blood. Fire and smoke everywhere. Tytamon lying on the ground and looking dead. Sir Altin almost cleaved in two. And Kettle. Pernie heard the snap of Kettle's forearm breaking, loud in her memory like the sundering of some great tree branch.

With those images in her head, those sounds, a vision of Kettle standing there, bones jutting through her sleeve, bloodstains spreading dark and terrifying, Pernie thrust her spear straight into the orc, right between its ribs. One rib cracked as the weapon drove for the orc's lung, echoing the sound in Pernie's mind. She yanked the weapon out as the creature fell.

A rattling gasp came from the wound she'd made, and the orc slid down the wall and landed on its back.

It lay there doing that for a time, gasping, gurgling, both from its mouth and from the hole she'd made in its side. Watching it reminded her of the monkey and the latakasokis she'd killed. She watched it staring up at the ceiling, its green brow wrinkled in pain, shaping little Vs in its skin like angular ripples in the wake of its nose.

Pernie watched it, and her fear slipped away, the terror inside her evaporating like steamy condensation from a plate of glass. Clarity followed, and fear was replaced by recognition of a simple fact. The orc wanted to die.

Pernie wondered how that could be.

But if the orc wanted death, then it wasn't going to get it from her.

She dropped to her knee and let go the invisibility. She touched the orc on its clammy green shoulder, and she sang the healing spell she knew, the simple one she'd learned before coming to live with the elves. She sang the song and funneled mana into it, and in the course of a few moments, the hissing gurgle from the orc's lung had disappeared, as had, to a large extent, the wound.

She stood and stepped away from it, prepared to fight it now that it could see her, fully expecting it to leap up and attack. She wasn't going to kill it, though. That's what it wanted her to do. And that's what they wanted her to do.

But the orc just lay there. It didn't get up. It didn't move. It lay prone, motionless, its big dark eyes staring into the black shadows in the ceiling of the cave. Then Pernie noticed the strangest thing. She saw a tear running down its face.

She couldn't believe that such a thing could be real, for it defied everything she'd ever heard and seen. With no thought for her own safety, or perhaps with absolute confidence in its security, she approached the orc again.

It didn't even look at her. It simply stared up at the ceiling still.

She wondered if she hadn't healed it properly. She did know that broken ribs could be very painful things, so she put her arm back on its chest and cast the spell again. She didn't know if it did anything or not. Her training with healing magic was nonexistent beyond her single bit of magic, and that really intended for unwilting daffodils.

The tear had run down and fallen into the grit of the cave floor, and there was not a second to follow. She saw merely the empty sadness of the creature lying there. Which frustrated her to the point of speech.

"What kind of orc is it that cries?" she asked. "I've never heard of anything like that before."

The orc stared at the ceiling.

"Hey," she said, prodding the orc in the hip with her boot. "What's the matter with you?"

Still nothing.

She looked around the room, expecting Seawind or Shadesbreath or Djoveeve to appear, but none of them did.

She called out for them. "I already killed him," she said. "Well, sort of. Then I brought him back. But that means I passed the test. So you can come back now."

She turned full circle, but nobody appeared.

She harrumphed at that and looked back down at the orc.

"Is it because you want to go home?" she asked it after a while. When it didn't answer, she very nearly gave up and left. Orcs were probably too stupid to speak anyway.

"Home," it said as she started toward the exit where Shadesbreath had disappeared. "Death."

She turned back and retook her place, looking down at it. "You want to go home to die?"

"Yes. Home to die."

"You speak pretty good human for an orc," she said, cocking her head sideways and rather caught up with such novelty. "Nobody ever said you could. Is that so you can talk to your food?" The thought came out before the ramifications did, and she took a step back suddenly, her spear pointed at it again.

"Kill Gromf," it said. "Or take home. Kill Gromf or take Gromf home." It sounded more agitated now.

"What is *Gromf*?" she asked.

"I Gromf. You Sava. Sava please kill or take to north clan for die." It was actually a mix of the common tongue of Kurr and the elven tongue, which made Pernie wonder where it had learned any elven words. She wondered if it had been listening somehow while Djoveeve worked with her at night. But the most striking thing to her was not the common words or the elven ones that it spoke. It was the "please." The very thought of an orc saying please was the most confounding thing Pernie had ever considered before.

She had to think about that very hard. Why would an orc say *please* to her if it would eat her when it got the chance? But as soon as she thought it, she realized she often talked to animals that she liked to eat as well. She'd had a pet frog once, yet she could kill them by the basketful when gathering frog legs for Kettle's pot. She'd been quite good friends with the calves that Gimmel's cow gave birth to, and twice they'd had them for dinner and many other things. The more she thought about it, the more she realized that people often talked to their food. And while she wasn't quite happy about the fact that orcs would pick on little girls, she supposed she could understand it in the way of natural things.

She knew for sure she wouldn't let an orc ever try to eat her again.

And as she realized it, she also realized that her fear was truly gone. The orc was no more dangerous than a man, or an elf, or even a sargosagantis swimming in the sea. Likely less so than the last. Likely less so than any of them. She supposed they might always give her the shivers if she thought about them wrong, but in a way, they were no different than poisonous parrots, pythons, or giant mantises. Things to be wary of, but nothing to be feared.

Once again she turned around and looked out into the empty spaces around the room. "I'm not killing it," she said again. "It's sad, and it wants to go home. Keeping it here all this time was mean. You should have killed it or let it go." She turned and looked back at the orc and shook her head, then corrected what she had said. "You should have killed *him* or let him go." Then, as if realizing the possibility of a mistake, she asked the orc, "You are a boy, right?" The orc didn't have any breasts like human women did, or like the glistening bosoms of the splendid lady elves.

It wrinkled its brow at her, less in agony than as if for the first time its own interest had been piqued. "Human whelp?" It seemed like a question. "Whelpling?"

"Well, I don't think that's a polite way of saying it," she said, "but I am a child, if you must know." She looked down at herself, at her skinny little frame, and frowned. She looked back at him. "And I'm a girl, just in case you want to know."

He sat up and stared at her for a time, and for some unknown reason, he began to laugh. It was a great, bass, throaty thing that filled the whole chamber with noise, larger than his emaciated body ought to have been able to produce.

"What's so funny?" she asked him, her hands on her hips.

He said something, five words in a coarse, guttural tongue that she knew was orcish, but that she didn't realize were the words to a spell until it was too late.

A ring of fire appeared, just a half step behind where she stood. Its heat beat upon her back. Her spear was already swinging butt end around in the instant it appeared, and before she realized the wall of fire was washing outward from the orc, she'd already knocked him flat with a solid thwack to the forehead, delivered by the butt of her spear.

The fire spread across the room, and as it passed over Seawind and Shadesbreath, they both emerged from their invisibility spells. Djoveeve dropped down from somewhere near the ceiling just before they appeared, apparently not wanting to risk melting her fragile little wings as the heat filled the room.

Gromf sat back up, rubbing a plum-sized knot that was already growing on his head, and he laughed as he saw the two elves glaring at him with wisps of smoke rising from the leather of their armor.

"Golden Queen's elf not like Gromf's fire still," he said. "Elf need human whelp female for kill Gromf." This apparently was the height of all humor for the orc, and once more, he lay flat upon his back, forced back this time by the power of unchecked hilarity.

The elves and the old Sava'an'Lansom came to stand beside Pernie and watch.

"I think you broke him," Djoveeve said after a time. "His

wits have snapped."

"I confess that I had not anticipated such an outcome," Seawind said. "But it appears you may be right."

Pernie looked first at Djoveeve, then at Seawind, tilting her neck back for each. She looked then to Shadesbreath, who was still simply watching her. He was kind of creepy, she decided, like something in a nightmare. But in a good way. Or maybe not. She wondered if she really could someday be like him. She thought it would be fun to look at people and make them feel that way. She'd love to see Kettle or Nipper try to shuffle her off to bed if she could look at them like that. They'd never even say anything. In fact she was fairly sure she could walk straight into the kitchens and eat all the tarts and berry pies she wanted and nobody would say a thing about it again, ever.

"So what shall we do with him?" Djoveeve asked. "Shall I drag him out and leave him for the jackals and latakasoki?"

Pernie snapped round to face her upon hearing that. "No," she said. "We have to send him home."

"We?" Djoveeve asked with an arched eyebrow. "And how do *we* plan on doing that?"

She spun and pointed at Seawind with a slender little finger. "He said that if I could beat the orc, I could go home. Now he has to send me home. So, he can send the orc back with me."

"We ought to just finish it off," the old woman said. "You know the Queen's army and the warriors from Earth have all but eradicated its people anyway. It has no home."

"It's the difference between killing and murder," Pernie said. She glared at Seawind as she said it.

Djoveeve crooked an eyebrow, but she grinned a moment afterward, glancing up at the two elves standing there regarding the child. "Well," she said, "she's got a point. And she's your weapon, not mine. I'm only helping you sharpen her. You do what you please." She backed away from the orc and took her hand off her knife.

The two elves seemed to be communicating between themselves, though Pernie didn't know for sure. Humans couldn't speak to elves telepathically. For some reason it just didn't work.

Unexpectedly, Seawind agreed. "Very well. We'll send him back when he recovers his wits and health. I'll see to his wounds myself." Pernie smiled. She hadn't won a battle of any kind with the elves since mastering Knot and running with the hunt. "And for you, little Sava, the time has come to complete your test."

Pernie looked stunned. *Complete*? What did he mean by that?

"Where would you like to go?" he asked.

"You already know where," she said. "I want to go home."

"So be it," he said. "Give me your hand." She did. He placed something soft and cool upon her palm and whispered into her ear. Then, just like that, she was home, right back where she'd been standing the moment they took her away.

Chapter 48

To their credit, neither Ramachandran twin complained about being asked to unpack the equipment needed to set up the bubble for Altin again. It was a great deal of work to go through the stacked crates and find the pumps and hoses and filters and sheeting, and then get it all affixed and airtight. They'd taken down the power grid and atmosphere purifiers they'd set up, and getting it all going again, even with everyone pitching in, and Altin's generous use of teleportation spells to move the inert pieces around, was still the work of two full days.

It felt like déjà vu as Altin once again slipped off his helmet and gloves and knelt before the pulsing purple light of Yellow Fire's heart stone. "All right," he said to it, "now we've gone to a lot of trouble for you. Why aren't you cooperating?"

He placed his left hand against the crystals embedded in the cavern wall, half his hand on the luminous edge of Yellow Fire, half on the dead gray crystals all around, his middle finger touching the place where the hairline crevice had been sealed. He felt nothing. No heat. No anything from any part.

Leaning forward, he peered into the gray clumps of the

447

crystals that Professor Bryant had grown, just as he had before. The light from the spotlights behind him, as well as those on the helmets of the others outside the bubble, shone into them, lit them up a little, but mostly shone right through.

Not the least bit of color in them. Definitely not Liquefying Stone.

He drew in a long breath of the cold air being pumped into the chamber and closed his eyes, letting his mind slip into the mana as he had before. The endless pink constant of it was there, just as it had been ever since he'd gotten his own gift of heart stone from Blue Fire—the Father's Gift that Blue Fire had melded with a tiny bit of her own Liquefying Stone. It was with that gift, that ring of heart stone, that he had shaped the first part of the melding spell. It was with that mana, the misty form of it made possible by his ring, that he'd infused the crack. But he hadn't used the ring when he'd shaped and finished the cast. The ring had been off for that. And he wondered now if that was the difference somehow.

He sought the shape of the cast he'd made to finish it, thinking that perhaps it hadn't completed itself somehow, that the joint he'd made between the two halves of the spell was not complete, the texture of the channeled mana different on each side of the joint. He hoped to find some small part of that unconnected or undone, some last loose end in need of being tied off or melded into place.

But there was nothing there. There was no spell for him to connect to, no thread to find, no joints or loose anything. The spell was complete. There was nothing left for him to do.

He let go of the mana for a moment and, on a lark, asked, "Turn off the spotlights, please."

"Why?" someone asked, but someone else hushed the lot of them watching there.

The lights went off, and were it not for the dim luminescence of the panel on his spacesuit's chest pack and sleeve, the darkness would have been absolute.

He had to think for a moment, trying to recall the magic detection spell he'd learned to help Roberto last month, looking for spells or magical devices that might have been planted in or upon the Goblin Tea crates before they were placed in the *Glistening Lady*'s cargo hold. If the transmutation spell was still in effect and in process, or frozen mid-process, if somehow it remained as magic rather than finished physicality, then he thought he might be able to detect it. He had to know. If it truly was complete—if it truly simply wasn't working—he would know that as well.

He spoke the words of the spell, though he hadn't really needed to, and in his mind he saw the wedge of mana, a shimmering pair of planes pressed together in the shape of a V. He pushed the magical fabrication into the wall of the heart chamber and watched it for signs of interactivity.

There were none.

He let go of the spell, and pushed himself away from the rock, his head drooping to his chest as he sat back on his heels. No evidence of anything, either way. Just nothing. Which meant his spell simply hadn't worked.

"So, uh, what's the trouble, dude?" came Roberto's inquiry. "You got everybody's butt puckering up here. Is it going to work or what?"

"No," Altin answered even as Orli was scolding Roberto for his insensitivity. "I don't know what I've done wrong."

"You haven't done anything wrong," Orli said. "It's just going to take time."

Altin let go a long, slow breath, frustrated and resigned. In the darkness, he couldn't see the foggy plume of it, but he knew he blew one just the same. Absently, he reached his hand out to feel it, for what reason he had no idea why, and there in the darkness before him was the gentle pulsing light of Blue Fire's gift to him, a dim green light tracing the inside edge of his ring.

It lay there upon his finger, like a tiny beacon of hope, the very pulse of everything that had brought them all here today. Orli's hope and his. Blue Fire's. The hopes of people long gone for centuries, whose only legacy was the names they gave to stars. Altin filled with it as he looked at that small green light. He knew what he needed to do.

It was all he could do to keep the euphoria of epiphany from his voice when he said, calmly, "I do have one more idea."

"Yeah, like what?" said Roberto. "Because we need to wrap this show up and get out of here. I'm due to pick up another load come the end of the week." He preempted Orli's next remark, adding, "Not that I'm not in here with you guys until the end, of course. It's just, you know, I get tired of restarting my ship all the time."

"Give me a moment," Altin said. He turned toward the bubble where the others stood, each of them shaped by the lights blinking on their suits. "I need a pair of those small shears you people use for clipping wire."

There was a brief pause before Rabin said, "One pair of wire cutters coming up." He jumped on one of the gravity sleds, and then the lights on the back of his suit vanished as he dropped below the edge of the heart chamber for a while.

"So," pressed Roberto in the breathless silence—being up in orbit seemed to have left him unaffected by the sphere of optimism that Altin had inspired—"you going to tell me or not? Because, I'm just saying, once you turned off all the lights, this show got pretty boring up here."

"Roberto," Orli warned for yet the third time, "let the man concentrate. For all we know, he's holding onto half a spell."

"Oh, I hadn't thought about that," Roberto said. "Sorry, bro."

Rabin was already rising back to level with the rest as Altin muttered that it was fine. Rabin held out the clippers and switched on his light to illuminate them in his gloved hand. "These, right?" he said.

"Yes, those are the ones. Give them to Orli."

Rabin did as he was told.

"Orli, I'm bringing you inside."

"All right," she said. "I'm ready."

A moment after, she was at his side, quickly removing her helmet and gloves.

He pulled off his ring and held it out to her, gripping it by the thick silver block into which he'd carved her name. "Cut it," he said, indicating the bottom of the band.

"Really?" she said.

"I'll fix it later. Just cut it, please."

She could hear the urgency in his voice, so she reached down and snipped the ring, the cutters parting the silver easily, directly opposite the setting that held the green stone.

He pulled the two halves of the band apart, opening them as far as he could until both were bent up alongside the setting itself. He held it up and looked at it, verifying that the green stone protruded slightly from the bottom of its mount.

He turned a lopsided smile at Orli. "Wish him luck," he said. "Wish them luck."

Orli realized right away what he meant and muttered, "Good luck, Yellow Fire. There's someone waiting for you."

Altin could hear Rabin and Prakesh muttering it too.

"Here goes," Altin said, and, with that, pressed the pulsing green of his stone to the place where he'd merged the heart stone with the surrounding crystals the professor had grown.

For a moment they all sat watching breathlessly, the long shadow of Orli standing in Rabin's light shadowing Altin's

451

hand. Rabin clicked it off, and for a few moments more they all stared into the darkness, watching as the pulsing green light of Altin's ring lit, then vanished, then lit, then vanished, scattered about by the gray crystals it sat upon.

Altin held his breath as he watched, staring into the space, his heart trying to beat with the rhythm of the ring's pulsing.

He touched the heart stone with the ring, and waited a while more. Still nothing, so he put it back against the joint.

That's when the whole cavern flickered like a lantern in a breeze. It flickered once, then twice, a pale blue color like a springtime sky, then in that instant, the whole chamber flared to brilliant life, as bright as any day on Prosperion or planet Earth had ever been, all around them, so bright they all had to shield their eyes. Not just the heart chamber. The whole enormous cavern, everywhere.

The light flared several times, and everyone began to cheer. Orli burst into tears of joy as she shouted, "It worked, it worked," through sobs of ecstasy.

There came a succession of further flares, and a few dimming right after, all in the span of a few seconds, then the bright, daylight azure turned just slightly green, only just barely so, the palest aquamarine.

Orli gasped and looked frightened, but Altin smiled and nodded his head. "I should think that's him discovering his new sun," he said, and as he said it the color stabilized and did not flicker again.

They all stared into it with open mouths. The professor and both brothers were already on their way down to the stacked crates, bent on getting tools and intent on measuring things.

"Whoa, what the fuck did you guys just do?" Roberto said. He didn't sound happy like all the rest.

"Nothing to worry about," Orli cheered. "We've done it! We've done it! I think he's come back to life. Can't you see the beautiful cavern light?"

"No, dude, I'm serious. What the fuck is that?" He was beyond agitated.

"What?" Orli said, exchanging a glance with Altin. Everyone in the cavern could hear the edge of terror in Roberto's voice. "What is *what*?"

He wasn't answering her, however, and what he said next was obviously intended for his crew. "Tracy, get us the fuck away from that shit. Deeqa, transfer power to the shields. Jesus, man!"

"Roberto, what?" Orli asked. "What's happening?" She was shouting now.

Altin stopped and stared at her, his breaths coming in shorter and shorter waves. Roberto's agitation was frightening. The man never lost his cool.

"You tell me. You guys opened up some kind of shit."

"There's something coming through," said Deeqa Daar, her voice low and tense, but characteristically calm. "Something big."

"What, what?" Orli continued to shout.

"Look at the feed," Roberto snapped. "For fuck's sake, just look at the feed!"

Orli and Altin blinked back and forth at one another, then both stooped and grabbed up their helmets, setting them loosely in place. There in the upper left was the feed from Roberto's ship. Less than four miles to starboard was a huge ... something, a rift, like a great tear in space, an opening that curved like the pupil of a cat, its edges shaped in part by the absence of stars within it, but also by what appeared to be some kind of pink-burning flame.

"Oh my God," Orli breathed.

"Oh my God is right," Roberto said, clearly trying to keep himself in check.

"Here comes another one," reported Deeqa Daar with no evidence of fear.

"Fuck," said Roberto. "Full camo on this bitch. Let's hide, people."

"Camo up," replied Tracy Applegate at the helm. "We're out, sir."

"Let's goddamn hope so."

"There's a third," Deeqa reported as Orli and Altin watched helplessly.

"Third what?" Orli asked. Altin would have asked it too. He was staring as hard as he possibly could into the monitor, but not seeing anything. There was nothing to see beyond that strange opening.

"There's something coming through," Deeqa replied. "Look at the far edge. It smears the pink as it passes by."

Sure enough, there was a blurring of the further edge of the slit in space, the pink rim dimming in one place, the distortion widening for a time, then narrowing, and after a few moments, it was gone.

"You get a reading on that?" Roberto asked.

"Nothing, sir," reported the helmswoman again.

"Well, get a reading on the gap, and do the math."

"Thirty-one point nine miles by thirteen point nine. I'm not picking up a third dimension at all."

"Here comes another one," Deeqa said.

"Do they see us? We getting anything bouncing off us?"

"Nothing, sir."

"Are they Hostiles?" someone asked.

The fourth object passed through the gap, and Altin couldn't help noticing how familiar the edges of the opening appeared.

"That last one was twenty-seven miles long," Deeqa reported. "Nine miles high. They're not orbs."

"Do we need to blow the heart chamber?" Doctor Walters asked.

"No!" Orli shouted. "She just said they aren't Hostiles."

"I said they aren't orbs," Deeqa replied.

"Okay, listen," said Roberto. "So there's some big, invisible shit coming out of the new asshole you guys just opened up in space. We can't dick around with this for long. Altin, you got any theories, or do we need to skip the happy fuck out of here right now and melt this bitch?"

"No," replied Altin as he watched. "I don't have any theories at all."

"We're not melting anything." Orli managed not to shout, but she was close. "Don't you dare even suggest it. He hasn't done anything."

"I suggest you guys bug the hell out of there," said Roberto. "Altin, you should take them straight back to Prosperion. If they aren't Hostiles, they might be headed your way. And if they are, we can watch, and if we have to, I'll push the button myself."

"You'll do no such thing, Roberto," Orli said. "We're coming up, and you're leaving with us. If there are any aggressive actions taken toward Earth, Prosperion, or any bases, my father will push the button just like everyone agreed on. If they aren't, then we should get out of their way until we know what they are."

"Like hell I'm leaving," said Roberto. "At least as long as they can't see me, I won't."

"Can you see them?"

"Yes." He was obviously lying.

"Other than right as they are coming through the opening, can you see them? Like, where they are now? You can see that?"

"No."

As if to prove that point, suddenly Roberto was flying over the top of the camera he'd been talking into, as if he'd been flung into the air by an invisible hand. He was already swearing as he flew over the lens. Altin saw one of Deeqa's boots flash briefly on his screen as well, then he was simply staring at the back of Roberto's chair.

"Roberto?" Orli shrieked.

There was no answer for a while.

"We need to leave," Altin said, snapping his helmet into place and setting the seal. He moved to where Orli was sifting through channels on her suit sleeve, and snapped her helmet down as well. "Leave the equipment. Everyone get to the teleportation chamber, now. We're leaving immediately. That is not a request."

There was no one in the cavern who was not happy to oblige, and soon all were rushing for the gravity sled, except for Orli, whom Altin had to nearly drag out of the atmospheric bubble that Rabin had opened up for them.

They were just stepping onto the sled when Roberto's profanity filled their helmets again.

"Are you okay?" Orli asked though the cussing was still under way. Her voice was anxious and high, catching Roberto's attention again.

"I think they just hit us," Roberto said.

"They're attacking you? Was it an orb, throwing a mineral shaft?"

"No, like, I think they just tried to run us over."

"I thought you said they can't see you," Orli said.

"I don't know," he said. "Maybe they can. Shit, I can't get any readings on these things." To his crew he added, "Are you guys checking all the spectrums?"

"I don't know if our scans helped them find us," Deeqa replied, "but yes, I've run through them twice already. I'm not getting anything. If they are Hostiles, they aren't following any previous patterns."

"Well, if they're not Hostiles, they damn sure ain't ours," he said, "unless somebody back home was doing some really hairy secret research while we were gone."

"They weren't," Deeqa confirmed. "Those are not ours."

"We're sending everyone home," Altin said. "Is the ship safe enough to bring everyone up, or are we all going back to Prosperion?"

"I think we're okay," he said. "Still getting status reports, though. Give me a second. You guys load up and get to the boot."

Prakesh piloted them down the cliff face on the gravity sled, taking a steep angle that was a bit dangerous for a piece of equipment that was meant to lift not fly. He managed it well enough, and in moments everyone was scrambling into the cube of stone that would take them back to the boot sitting on the surface of Red Fire, which was now, technically, Yellow Fire.

Altin waited impatiently as they all shuffled inside, the twins both hauling at the front of the gravity sled while the professor started pushing from behind.

"Leave it," Orli reminded them before Altin could. They were fine scientific minds, but they weren't all thinking clearly at the time.

Altin closed the door and latched it, then took his ring and held it between his thumb and forefinger, making sure his thumb was pressed firmly against the pulsing green crystal inside. He had no doubt that he could teleport them out without it, but he had no interest in wasting time.

Soon, they were once more in the basement of the boot. "Well, Roberto, how is your status?" he asked the moment they appeared.

"Dude, I'm working on it."

Altin looked at Orli, who shrugged, a gesture hard to see given the bulky nature of the suit. Altin made his decision on the spot. "I'm taking everyone to Prosperion. Roberto, I'll be back in a moment. No sense putting everyone at risk." He opened the door of the teleportation chamber. "Everybody out." He went out first to avoid arguments.

When everyone was out of it, he shut the door, then spied out the area of Calico Castle where the tower sat, making sure it was clear. It was, and in moments the tower was back in its place. "Everyone out," he said, again. "Go, go, go. If something happens up there"—he glanced to Orli and then to the rest of them—"Orli and her father will see to it that you all get home."

"No, my father will. I'm going with you."

"No, you are not."

Everyone else was already running for the stairs, Professor Bryant stopping near the top to call back, "Have you let down the tower shield, Sir Altin? So we can get out?"

He did so with barely a thought, fidgeting with the ring as he did.

"Orli, there is no reason for you to go. I'm the only one who can cast the spell, and if there is something going on up there, you will be in danger, and that will distract me from helping the others."

"Altin, I'm going. He's my friend too. If there's trouble, I can bring myself back, remember?" She patted the area of her spacesuit near her throat, where the fast-cast amulet hung beneath, enchanted with the spell that would take her to a safe place behind an old suit of armor in Calico Castle's ancient dining room. They both wore one, each enchanted to take them to safe spots, side by side.

"Gods be damned, woman," he swore. "You are the most stubborn thing."

"It wouldn't bother you so much if you'd just accept it already," she said. "So, are they out of the boot yet or not?"

"It doesn't matter. Let's just take the box."

With that, they both reentered the little stone teleportation room, and Altin once more closed the door. "Helmet sealed?" Orli asked.

"It is," he said, and after ensuring that there was a safe place in the *Glistening Lady*'s cargo hold, Altin set the clean room down inside.

Chapter 49

Immediately upon returning to the *Glistening Lady*, the com feeds inside Altin's and Orli's helmets burst back to life with the sounds of the ship's crew at work. They'd been gone less than a half minute, but already their assistance was in need.

"God damn it, Chelsea, get that ram-jack in here. It's crushing her," Roberto called anxiously. "Where the hell are you?"

"I'm coming," replied the frenetic-sounding bodyguard. "It's stowed. Down below. Three minutes."

"She doesn't have three minutes," Roberto said. "Damn it. A great time to lose our fucking sorcerer."

"Your sorcerer has returned. Where are you, I'm coming now."

"Engine room. Hurry. A refrigerant tank broke loose. You've got to get her out."

Altin looked wide-eyed at Orli, who in a less dire circumstance would have given him a "See, I told you that you'd need me" smirk, but she was too busy yanking her helmet off. By the time Altin was following her lead, she was already running out of the cargo bay.

Altin ran after her as they passed through three sections

of the ship, then turned into what looked like a closet to Altin's untrained eye. No closet, it housed a narrow ladder, leading down into a room in which everything was coated with a white layer of frost, almost too cold to touch.

Roberto was kneeling near a long, silvery cylinder that was at least a full span in diameter, and some five spans long. It matched three others just like it mounted on the starboard hull and two more mounted on the port side, the latter pair with a conspicuous space between them that indicated where the one Roberto knelt beside had come from. His forearms and the side of his face were white and looked as if they'd suffered terrible frostbite.

"It rolled right over her," he said upon seeing Orli and Altin rush into the room. "You've got to get her out of there, or get it off."

Altin and Orli ran up beside him, where they found Liu Chun pinned beneath the huge coolant tank. She wasn't moving and her eyes were closed.

Orli knelt down beside her and checked her pulse, her time serving in the *Aspect*'s sick bay giving her more than enough training in terrible emergencies.

"Pulse is weak," she reported. "If you yank her out of there, a whole lot of other things could go wrong. We need to assess the damage first."

Roberto looked horrified. "How the hell are we going to do that?" He winced with pain as his face contorted with the outburst.

"You don't have a ship's doctor?"

"Nobody answered my ad yet. And Liu Chun is a trained combat medic."

"Oh for fuck's sake, Roberto!" She turned back to Altin, looking just as horrified. "Can you get Leopold?"

Altin was already nudging the doctor telepathically. He found him napping, and it was some work to wake the man up. He quickly relayed the situation, and the doctor allowed himself to be teleported to the scene immediately.

Despite the urgency of the circumstance, Altin couldn't help but note how much weight the doctor had lost. The last time he'd seen the man, he would have guessed him going nearly twenty stone, but there he was, likely just over ten or so. He hardly recognized the man.

The doctor assessed the situation instantly and was soon kneeling beside the woman trapped beneath the tank. He placed his hands on either side of her face and began to sing. He sang for several moments, and, while Altin was not a healer himself—the one school of the eight in which he had no power at all—he could tell that there was something wrong with the doctor's chant.

A moment later the doctor shook his head. "I can't do it," he said. "The mana is wrong."

"What do you mean, the mana is wrong?"

"Look for yourself," he said. "I have no idea how you were able to bring me here."

Altin looked into the mana and found it as it always was, a vast, unchanging constant of pink mist. He realized immediately his mistake. He discreetly stuffed his ring into the band of his spacesuit's utility belt and looked into the mana again.

He gasped aloud at what he saw. It was much like it had been when Altin had approached the planet Blue Fire for the first time. Except that, rather than a wide, flat plane of mana being pulled into the dark absence, the black anti-globe that was her essence in the mana stream, the mana here had gathered into a thick, long column. It ran straight through the center of the red planet that now housed the being they knew as Yellow Fire, as if the planet's axis had been wrapped in the stuff of magic somehow. As if it were wrapping it up as he watched.

Altin knew immediately what was happening. He was looking at mana being channeled by a male Hostile. He'd never thought to look at the mana without his ring, not while he'd been at war with the now-dead Red Fire. Why would he?

He watched the strange phenomenon for quite some time, and dared to move his mind toward that rodlike mana solidity to examine it more closely. It was as if someone had run a great thick version of Master Sambua's conduit pipe right through the center of the pitch-black sphere, and when Altin made the most gentle of taps against it, he found that it had, in the abstract way of mana, the absolute solidity of rock. Steel perhaps. Something harder, harder even than the surface of diamond-shelled *Citadel*. Where the flat mana streaming into Blue Fire had been taffy-like, an impenetrable pliability, this was as hard and round as any enchanted column in the Palace could ever be, although, as he watched, it seemed to flicker in places, cloudy perhaps, where it darkened and looked momentarily soft, as if it were sputtering.

"Harpy spit," Altin swore. He didn't know if there was time to teach the doctor how to draw mana with his ring. The doctor had never even used a Liquefying Stone before. The ring could kill him. It *would* kill him, Altin already knew.

"I'll teleport the whole ship back to Calico Castle," he said. "Unless there is some reason why I should not."

Suddenly the whole ship launched to starboard, throwing all of them to the floor and sliding them toward the port side of the ship. The giant cylinder rolled off of Liu Chun and came toward them like a giant steel rolling pin. "Christ!" shouted Roberto. Altin tried to cast a teleportation spell upon it, intent on sending it down to the surface of the red world, but he could draw no mana at all. His eyes popped wide as he realized it was too late to grab the ring, and he braced himself for being squashed against the hull.

Something heavy and metallic clanked, loudly. The left

side of the tank stopped rolling and the right side slowed, though it kept coming as the tank angled some. Orli reached for Roberto as he scrambled along the hull trying to stay ahead of it. The frostbite was agonizing, and he was moving slowly. Orli caught him by the hair and dragged him to her just as the end of the tank finally slammed into the wall, the four of them heaped together in the wedge of open space, cringing and expecting the end.

Realizing they weren't dead, they all turned to see Roberto's heavyset bodyguard, Chelsea, lying on her stomach, flat on the floor, her arms extended to fullest length and still gripping the ram-jack tool that she had jammed like a wheel block under the tank at the farthest end. From the way she was sprawled out on the deck and the trickle of blood that had just started on her chin, it was clear she'd had to dive headlong to get it there in time.

"Holy crap, that was close," Roberto said. "I think I love you, Chelsea."

"Just doing what you pay me for," she said as she climbed to her feet. She wiped at her chin and shook her head to clear the spots of dizziness the jolt against the deck had set spinning in her eyes.

"Liu Chun," Orli said, and immediately she and the doctor were running out of the angular space, around the tank, and to the ship's weapons officer, who was now out from under it, though she had slid along behind it when it rolled and now lay pressed against it dangerously. Chelsea ran to get another ram-jack.

"Deeqa, what the hell was that?" Roberto demanded into his com link.

"I think another one just tried to fly through us," she replied.

"It's like the damn Hostiles all over again."

"I don't think so," Deeqa said. "That one barely touched us, and we weren't trying to move. It's like they just don't see us. I'm going to drop a probe into orbit and take us out to twenty thousand miles. We can watch from there."

Altin looked to Roberto and shook his head. "How about Prosperion?" he asked, the question imperative in his tone. He extracted the ring from his belt and bent the cut halves of the band around his thumb as tightly as he could.

"Deeqa, scratch that last part. Just kill the engines. Altin's taking us to Prosperion."

"Roger that," she said. There was a stretching quality to her voice, followed by the announcement "Probe away, shutting down now."

Soon after, the *Glistening Lady* sat upon the meadow beyond the walls of Calico Castle, resting easily in the grass, which stirred lazily in the breeze.

Altin teleported everyone present directly to the doctor's office. The doctor went to work, and the rest of them watched breathlessly as the skilled Y-class physician cast his spells.

For nearly twenty minutes no one dared to speak, not even Roberto, who was never without something to say, though he did occasionally let go a faint grunt as the pain in his arms and face began to work on him with the waning of adrenaline.

Orli, upon hearing one of those grunts, and finally realizing what they were, led him out of the room to the front, where Lena Foxglove sat at her desk, oblivious to the fact that the doctor had returned and was treating a patient in one of the examining rooms. A quick look at Roberto's face and arms and Lena was all aflutter, but efficiently so, for in a matter of moments, she had another doctor on the scene, who set to work on Roberto in another room.

Orli sat with Roberto for a half hour, and found that the middle-aged woman casting spells on him was an excellent healing mage. When the woman took her hand away from Roberto's right arm, the wounds were entirely repaired.

"You people sure are incredible healers," Orli observed.

"Doctor Salmbalsam is incredible," Lena replied. "You couldn't have been in more capable hands, Roberto."

Roberto nodded, clearly in agreement, and the woman smiled and thanked them for the compliments. After a few moments' gratitude, the four of them went to check on Liu Chun. Doctor Salmbalsam moved to stand beside Doctor Leopold, where she chanted for a time, apparently looking in on what he was doing. After a few minutes of that, she went to stand opposite him and began to assist, the notes of her healing song weaving in and out of his in a tense yet beautiful harmony.

The rest of them stood quietly, no one even daring to breathe too loudly. Roberto winced and shuddered anytime one of the doctors' rhythms changed too abruptly. From the sounds he made, it was as if he were still suffering the agony of frost burns. But eventually came reprieve, for finally Doctor Leopold looked up from the spell with a satisfied expression on his face.

"She's stabilized," he said. "She'll make it. But we've got a lot of work to do if she's ever going to walk again." He looked up into Altin's relieved green eyes and said, "Not so bad as you were that day Tytamon brought you back from the moon, but bad enough. I'll need her for the next several weeks at least." He turned to the doctor who had come to assist him and thanked her graciously.

Roberto wiped at the corners of his eyes, his own relief so obvious he couldn't wipe fast enough for a time. "God damn, Doc. You're the best. Thank you. Whatever you need. No price is too high, you hear me? Whatever it takes. Give her everything."

He smiled, the loose flesh around his jaws where he'd lost so much weight waggling like empty gloves. "She'll be fine, my friend. I promise. Just need some time."

Roberto let out a long, low breath and shook his head as if shaking off a blow that had dazed him for a time. He looked from the doctor to Orli and Altin standing there. "Thank you guys too," he said. "Man, I don't know what I would have done if—well, if this didn't turn out like it did."

"Well, you need to figure out why that tank came loose," Orli said. "That's inexcusable. I know you said this is only the fifth one of these ships ever made, but that is not acceptable. I thought the whole point of buying that ridiculously expensive ship was because it was so damn tough. 'Bottom of the ocean without a creak,' as I recall. 'Hostile shafts bounce right off,' you said."

"Yeah, I agree with you on that, but if we're being honest, whatever knocked that thing loose hit us so hard the ship spun around seventeen times in eleven seconds after impact. Think about that for a minute. And yet, here we are, not dead. Whatever hit us would have caved the *Aspect* in like a plastic canteen."

Orli's jaw moved side to side, but she nodded. "Still, I'd have a talk with the company."

"Oh, I will," he said. "I'll bet they crap themselves when they see what they have to prepare for with these ships. It's a whole new galaxy these days."

"It is," Orli said.

"So what do you think it was that struck you?" Altin asked.

"Do you people mind taking this outside," the doctor said, not really asking by the way he said the words. "You can come back tomorrow night and check on her. I've put her into a deep slumber that will last at least that long anyway, and you're just distracting me."

Roberto looked uncomfortable with that, but the doctor made a shooing noise. "Altin, get them out of here, please. Every moment counts."

Altin looked to his friends, and they both nodded, Roberto reluctantly, and a few moments later they were back aboard the *Glistening Lady*.

Roberto went immediately to the dislodged coolant tank and checked the braces where they had broken. Chelsea had already welded several temporary braces in place along the deck while they were gone, and she was in the process of strapping the tank in place right where it was on the deck for now.

"Won't hold for another nightmare like that back there," she said, "but it will take more than normal atmospheric turbulence to break it loose. It will work till we get it back to the plant and have them do something different. I'm still deciding if I'm impressed or disappointed in this."

"You alive?" Roberto asked with a sideways kind of smirk.

She looked up from her work and smiled back. "Good point." She patted the deck where she knelt. "Sorry, girl. No disrespect."

"So," said Altin, returning to his question of a moment ago, "what do you think it was that hit you? You mentioned it was similar to a Hostile attack. Do you really think Red Fi–Yellow Fire summoned something and set them upon you already, as fast as that?"

"Well, I don't know what else to think."

"I don't think so," came Deeqa Daar's voice from behind them. She was coming down the ladder as she spoke. "I've run the continuity variances from the plasma shields. Whatever hit us was plasma, just like ours—well, basically like ours, but different. A lot better. If I make my guess correctly, whatever hit us was headed for the planet, and we were just in the way."

"In the way? Twice?" Roberto said. "How bad does our luck have to be to get hit on accident two times in a row? Even if we were totally undetectable."

"The objects are very large," Deeqa said. "And both were on the exact same bearing. If you look at our position after the first impact and compare it to the model we came up with based on light fluctuations as the objects came through the rift, the second impact makes sense. We were hit by the wider part of the second one. So it was only one bit of bad luck with multiple events. And we were in full camouflage, so they couldn't have seen us if they wanted to." She came to stand beside him and handed him the small tablet that she'd been reading from.

Roberto looked into it and let out a low whistle. "So what is it?"

"I think it's a ship," she said. "I think they all were."

"Who the hell builds ships that big?"

"Who the hell sent balls of rock the size of small moons around the galaxy?" she said. "Or hopped around in an old English tower like something out of a fairy tale? This universe is damn sure not what they taught us it was back in elementary school."

"You ain't lying about that."

"So," inserted Altin, "are you saying that the strikes on your ship were merely the mishap of being in the path of enormous spaceships on their way to Yellow Fire's world?"

"That's my guess," Deeqa said, nodding in a way that made the thick golden rings that held up a long column of her hair glimmer in the ship's emergency lights.

"Well, they could only be there for one thing, then," Orli said as she sidled in next to Roberto to look at the tablet. "They're there for Yellow Fire. The timing can't be a coincidence."

"Friend or foe?" Altin wondered aloud. "Though I've never heard Blue Fire mention her species having friends."

"She's got you," Roberto said. "So why don't you ask her if there are others?"

Altin was reluctant to let his enormous planetary friend know that they'd brought Yellow Fire back to life, only to tell her that something else might be going wrong. Orli could read the dilemma in his eyes. "Just ask her," she said.

"She's never been one to run from a fight. If they are enemies of the Hostiles, Blue Fire can help us deal with it. Hope might make her ferocious, and to protect him ... can you imagine? I wouldn't want to get in her way."

Altin nodded and immediately sent his thoughts out across the space that separated him and the living world of Blue Fire. He conveyed through his thoughts the happy news that Yellow Fire had come to life, but added in the potentially disturbing part about the timing and appearance of the rift opening nearby. He showed her his memories of the image he'd seen in the helmet, transmitted from Roberto's ship. He did his best to show her the dulling of the far side of the rift, where the pinkish flames seemed to waver as the objects came through.

Blue Fire, however, already knew, at least the first part. And she could not have cared less, apparently, about the second. The moment he made contact, she blasted him with happiness, and the thoughts that filled him spread his face in a smile so violent the muscles began to cramp. He was dimly aware of the pain of it, but his body was so filled with unbounded happiness that he could only barely hold onto the thought that he might be in some kind of danger.

He staggered back, and for a time those with him gaped at him, wondering if they ought to intervene. Roberto even offered to knock him out, if Orli thought that might break the spell. She shook her head no, but by the way she chewed her lower lip, it was obvious to all in the cargo hold that she was reconsidering as the second minute of Blue Fire's jubilance went by.

Eventually Blue Fire's giddiness abated enough that Altin could breathe and break himself out of the contact, an effort that actually required drawing mana through the ring.

"Well?" Orli and Roberto asked simultaneously.

"Well, she knows that Yellow Fire is alive," he said, panting and leaning on his knees. "Apparently they've been

... doing whatever Hostiles in love do across all that space. She was too happy to use her words, but I saw her joy, and in it the reflection of his. So, I guess they found each other right away. She's going to help him recuperate. Apparently he's still very weak."

Orli jumped up and down and clapped her hands, her eyes glittering. "Thank God," she said, elation still driving her to bounce. "I'm so happy. Finally, after all that time."

"What about the big ships, or whatever the hell they are?" Roberto asked. "Did she tell you what that is?"

"I don't even know if any of what I tried to tell her about them got through," Altin confessed. "I opened up to her with my ideas, but it was like getting hit by Palace-sized fireballs of flaming happiness. I was having trouble finding my own thoughts in all of it."

"Yeah, we saw that, dude. I'll be honest; you looked kind of dumb there for a while. I thought you were going to start drooling or something."

Orli made a ticking sound with her tongue against the roof of her mouth, but Roberto shrugged and put his hands out defensively. "What? You saw it too."

"The point is," Altin pressed on, "I still have no idea what those ships represent, friend or foe, much less what they actually are. I suspect I'm going to have a hard time getting through to her through all of that interstellar mooning for a while. I had thought to be the bearer of good news, but it seems now, she has little enough need of me."

"Well, good," Orli said. "I for one am happy for her. And for you. You hardly needed her in your head all the time. She always put you in a mood."

"Whoa, look who's all sympathy now," Roberto said. "Wasn't even a week ago, and you were on him about that promise that he made."

"Well, that was a hard time for us both. But it all worked out in the end." She glowered at him a little bit, however, for taking Altin's side.

"All except for those big ships," Altin said. "I'm not ready to concede that they are part of an outcome that we can all call 'all worked out.' I believe we ought to go and make sure Yellow Fire is not in some sort of danger now."

"Dude, I'm not trying to be a dick here, but my ship is out of service until I get this tank back up and the rest of the ship checked out," Roberto said. "No way I'm risking it or anyone else on it until we square this away." He patted the tank that Chelsea was strapping down.

"Agreed. But my tower is not."

"Why not just look around with your magical eyeball thing?" Roberto asked. He lifted his hands up, right in front of his face, and waggled his fingers, peering out through the motion. "Just check it out that way. That's way faster and less risky."

"Yes, but you'll recall we can't see those ships with our eyes. In fact, only some of your equipment picked them up at all. But at least some of them did."

"That's true," Roberto said. "But only after they damn near ground us down like cheese. You should look before we leap; you know what I'm saying?"

The events of the last hour had rattled them all. Emotions were high, and it was a few moments before Altin recognized the sagacity of the advice. He took a breath and cast a seeing spell, fully expecting to see nothing. But he was wrong.

There upon the surface of Yellow Fire's new red world appeared four long, wide shapes, each with a huge oblong forward section that flared out and then tapered back liked the end of a shovel or perhaps a pit viper's head. The rest of each ship—long and narrow, seeming as long as a mountain range—stretched out behind the thick forward end with a graceful quality. They were obviously rigid but, in being so, conveyed a certain fluidity. They weren't pretty, per se, all one color, a brownish green that reminded him of the color of seaweed, and the surface of each was knotty and imperfect in a way, like something grown or even eroded rather than something built. If they were ships, they certainly weren't held together with rivets and welded seams, not that Altin could see. At the narrowest end, the enormous length finally split in two, forked like the tongue of a dragon, and in places along the end of each tine, they flared out with flattened extensions that looked like tiny wings. These seemed tiny from Altin's perspective compared to the rest of the ship, but in the context of the real mountains and the large rock formations nearby, which Altin was familiar with, the smallest of these were at least a half measure wide. In short, whatever those things were, they were huge.

Each of them had landed upon the surface with the thick ends, heads, as Altin thought of them, pointed toward one another, as if they were in conversation. They left a space between them that was, by Altin's guess, perhaps ten measures across, and as he watched, a large opening appeared in the top of each ship, roughly midway down its length. Great gusts of smoke or steam poured forth from those openings—the winds on the surface were so violent it was hard to be sure—smearing the emissions to the barest streaks of white, and shortly after, they were gone.

Something long, wide, and flat rolled itself out of each opening, like a tongue lolling out of a mouth upon the ground. These were the same color as the rest of the ship, but they unfurled gradually out over the marginally flat upper surface of the vessels, then down the sides onto the red dirt of the planet. Once they had touched the ground, they straightened and appeared to Altin's eye to become perfectly rigid.

Altin watched breathlessly, though somewhere in the back of his mind, he absently considered dropping the spell and telling the others what he saw, perhaps even setting up a scrying illusion in which they could all watch. But he couldn't make himself let go of the seeing spell just yet. He couldn't stop watching.

Shortly after the four tongues went rigid, four angular contraptions came up from the dark spaces inside the enormous ships, each of them with giant wheels, several on each side of the vehicle—if in fact that's what they were— and around these rows of wheels were wrapped continuous bands of yet more of the blotchy green-brown material, though this time jointed together in small, parallel plates. The rows of wheels rolled upon these bands, the bands themselves moving down and around the front and back wheels in a continuous loop that seemed to him meant to supply traction for the machines.

The machines rolled out from their ships, down the rigid tongue ramps, and onto the storm-churned plain. Each machine sent up a long pole from its top, nearly as thick as the whole machine. When the poles, like enormous, fat masts, reached what Altin thought might be a half measure in the air, they sprouted new growth, which branched horizontally like giant spars.

Altin really wanted to break the spell and tell everyone what he saw. He could hear the muffled anxiousness of them speaking around him. Their curiosity was palpable, and he nearly lost the spell anyway.

But he held on long enough to watch the spars as they in turn sprouted wide ends, like spoons, only flat at the leading edges. When they were fully formed, the mast poles themselves bent downward at the halfway point, suddenly sinuous, and stretched themselves out over the ground as if they were the feelers of some great insect. He almost had time to wonder what they were doing, when the feelers went rigid again and all three machines began to dig.

All four machines plunged their flat-tipped spoons, obviously shovels, into the ground, and what Altin had thought of as stays now began to rotate like the blades on a windmill, driving the spoons into the land and ripping out enormous chunks of red soil and stone. The shovel ends spun round on the pole, an axle now, and flung the dirt into the wind.

Smaller shafts emerged from the sides of the digging machines as the shape of the hole they were making formed. These extended out above the wheels, unfolding like the legs of a giant grasshopper. They angled out to brace against the dirt and thrust themselves deep into the surface, obviously meant to provide greater stability. Then nothing more emerged. The machines set themselves to the work in perfect unison, and soon they were excavating with remarkable efficiency.

It was hard to believe how quickly they dug. Altin watched in growing horror as the movements of the shovel arms became so rapid he could no longer see the shovels turning anymore. All he saw were four plumes of dust blowing out across the vast flatlands, a red stain on the wind like bloody smoke from a fire.

When at last he broke the seeing spell, his friends were staring at him impatiently. He thought about trying to explain it, but instead he anchored a scrying spell to the spot he'd been watching from and linked it to an illusion in the air, allowing them to see it for themselves.

By the time he was done and could clear his head from the casting well enough to gauge their response, Orli was in tears.

Chapter 50

Seawind's teleport spell put Pernie right back where she'd been the day he'd first appeared at Calico Castle: on the seventh floor of the tall central spire, which had been Tytamon's bedchamber for centuries, but which now stood decorated to appease Orli's taste. Orli hadn't been in it since the day Pernie tried to shoot her through the heart with her own laser, and Pernie knew it immediately. There was a film of dust on everything, including the duvet, and the rug still had a burn mark where the laser beam had been redirected toward the floor by the elf. Pernie took it all in, the bed just as it had been when Pernie had been moping there, the boxes of shoes right where they'd been dropped at the base of the stairs leading up to the topmost floor. There could be no doubt. It was clear neither Orli nor Kettle had come back here after that day.

Pernie smiled and was glad. Maybe she really was still in time.

She absently fingered the little pouch of her sling, her old weapon now tied around her waist again like a belt, though the dangling ends no longer dangled quite so far. They'd given her back all her weaponry, her sling, her little knife, and her amulet that was the shrunken version of Ilbei

Spadebreaker's magical pickaxe. But they had taken away her spear and her glass knife, and they wouldn't let her bring Knot with her either. They told her those belonged to the Sava'an'Lansom, a title of which she was not yet fully in possession.

She didn't care about titles, though. She just wanted one thing. To see if Orli Pewter had married Master Altin yet. The untouched room gave her hope.

She went to the great chest, hoping to find Orli's laser in there. It was gone. So the room was not entirely untouched. Pernie glanced over her shoulder and also noticed that Orli's tablet was not leaning next to the hourglass. She'd taken her technology.

Pernie crept down the stairs, listening intently for the sounds of anyone coming her way. No one was.

She came upon the landing that looked into Tytamon's study and saw that the door was locked. The last time she was here, she wouldn't have been able to get in there, but this time she had her power under her control. She leaned forward and peered through the keyhole, careful not to touch it, for she knew that such things were often equipped with magical booby traps.

She spotted a clear space on the other side, and, simply to prove that she could, she teleported herself inside. She turned all about, standing alone in the most forbidden of all places in Calico Castle, and she was exultant for it. She truly was a teleporter of Calico Castle now. Just like Sir Altin. Just like Tytamon had been. She finally was one of them.

She sighed as she thought it, though. She wasn't really. They could teleport very far. All around the world. Altin could teleport all across the stars. She'd never teleport across the stars.

She opened her hand and looked into it, still holding the small mint leaf Seawind had given her. "All you have to do to return to us is tear this leaf in half," he'd told her. "It is your choice. We will not come for you again."

She had been more than happy to let them send her away after that, vowing never to return, still pouting some at having found out she couldn't have Knot with her here. Oh, what fun it would have been to ride him across the open prairies of Kurr. No place on the island was open at all, only a few scarce beaches here and there, and those rarely even so much as a full measure long. She thought that perhaps even Knot did not know how fast he could go. She knew that she had grown stronger and faster with practice and training by the elves. She thought that maybe Knot could grow faster and stronger too, given enough room to run. She was sure he was already faster than any horse she'd ever seen.

But Knot was gone. She thought she most likely would never see him again. Which was fine. Once Master Altin fell in love with her, he would let her fly on Taot's back. She was sure a dragon would be better than some old bug anyway.

Still, she sighed again.

She tucked the leaf behind her ear for safekeeping, and looked around the room. She'd never gotten to come in here before, only glimpsed it through the open door. It was even messier than she recalled, and it looked like a lot of Tytamon's equipment had simply been pushed right off the end of the long table that he'd used all those years for a desk.

She heard voices coming through the window across the room, which startled her. With reflexes she'd long since stopped even thinking about, she whispered the words of her complex invisibility spell. She made her way quickly toward the window, stepping lightly over and around the assorted stacks of ancient artifacts and slipping easily between the carelessly arranged tables that angled here and there across the room. The first thing she saw was a big silvery thing sitting in the meadow beyond the walls. She knew immediately what it had to be. A spaceship! Seeing it made her even more excited to see who was visiting.

She had to stand on tippy toes to lean out far enough through the window to see down into the courtyard below, but see she could, and she started upon seeing who it was, as interest in the spaceship vanished. It was Master Altin and Orli, talking to a group of people Pernie wasn't sure she recognized. One of them looked like the fun and funny Earth man Roberto, but if it was him, he was dressed differently than before. The familiar fleet uniform was gone, and instead he wore a bright purple coat with long tails and very torn and tattered sleeves. But he was the only one she might recognize. She was sure she didn't know the rest.

Orli Pewter was crying, which Pernie thought was good. She would be crying when Pernie was done too.

Pernie reached down and touched her boot, making sure the little vial of Fayne Gossa was where she usually kept it. It was. Master Altin would never know it was Pernie that did it if Orli Pewter died that way, and in time he wouldn't be mad at her and would love her instead.

She stood back upon her tiptoes to look down again. Master Altin was talking emphatically, and the way Orli Pewter was moving made it seem as if they did not agree. Pernie was glad of that too. She would always agree with Master Altin; he was a Seven, and he was the greatest wizard in all the land. Plus he had a dragon, which nobody else had. And he'd discovered outer space. And the moon.

Shortly after, the disagreement ended, and just like that, Master Altin disappeared. Pernie thought that was odd because he didn't say anything or move his hands at all. He cast his spell like the elves of String.

She turned to go, intent on sneaking down to the dining room and waiting until Kettle set the table for them all to eat. Kettle always set the table, every night. And Orli Pewter would sit to the right of where Master Altin sat. Which meant Pernie knew exactly which cup to put the poison in. Then she could simply wait in the shadows until Orli Pewter was dead. She would teleport outside once it was done, and then hide in the forest for a week or two. Then she would "come home" and tell them about her first year on String. They would be glad to see her then, and Orli Pewter would be buried in the ground.

A movement in the window caught her eye.

She turned back and saw that there on the windowsill near where she'd been looking out was a little vase of some kind, or at least that's what she'd thought when she'd first approached—not that she'd given it any real thought at all. But there it was, a fancy thing of glass, the sort of thing only a grown-up would want, boring but for the green spikes of a leafy-looking top, which was the source of the motion that she had seen.

She turned once more to go, but then stopped, and looked back at the vase again. It reminded her of something. She stepped nearer to it and examined it more carefully. Her little brow furrowed as she recognized what it was, or at least what it had been made to resemble with marvelous accuracy: it was a pair of twisted palm trees, just like those in the forbidden cove. The ones that weren't supposed to grow anywhere else at all.

What a strange thing to find at Calico Castle. Djoveeve had told her that nobody could ever know about such things. She said that the sacred trees were an absolute secret that had to be kept from humanity. The old woman had made a big fuss about it when Pernie and Knot had chanced upon the grove. And yet, there one was, a miniature likeness sitting in plain view upon Tytamon's windowsill.

She picked it up and gave the green spikes, obviously little glass palm fronds, a spin. They turned as easily at her touch as they had at the touch of the breeze.

She lifted it and held it up to the fading light coming

through the window. There was some kind of gray-green liquid inside, the same color as the palm trunks in the cove. She thought that was a clever way to make it match the trees, but wondered why whoever made it didn't just stain the glass. She'd seen glassblowers coloring vases several times when Kettle took her to the harvest festival each year, so she knew it was possible.

She wondered if it might be some expensive elven perfume. Djoveeve told her that the lady elves had a natural perfume that came out of their skin as if it were enchanted there, although Pernie hadn't smelled anything when she saw the three of them in the waves. Pernie wondered if maybe this was such a thing, bottled up for humans to use.

She rose up on her toes and looked down into the courtyard where Master Altin had vanished. All the rest of them had moved inside the castle, it seemed.

She looked back to the forbidden-tree decanter and smiled. What if it really was the perfume of the lady elves? Master Altin would love her instantly!

She pulled the stopper out of the decanter and meant to take a whiff. But the moment she did so, the liquid inside vanished with a great sucking of air, much like the sound of someone who has just left by casting a teleporting spell. The decanter jolted her hand with the rapid evaporation, and then it was still and clear, not the least drop of fluid left inside.

She raised it to her nose and smelled it anyway, hoping for at least some lingering scent of the lady elves. There was no smell at all. Now she really wished she'd gotten close enough to the three of them so she could have smelled them too. But she hadn't, so she set the decanter back on the windowsill. She replaced the stopper, shrugged, and headed for the stairs.

She found the people from Earth standing about the kitchen with Nipper, talking excitedly about something that had them all upset. Something about someone digging up some kind of new plant somewhere, or at least something that sounded that way. Pernie knew that Orli Pewter had done things to plants when she was on the Earth ship, and that her favorite thing was flowers and gardening and stuff. Pernie never liked gardening, and she hated it when Nipper and Kettle made her go out to the gardens and pick vegetables and fruit for supper all the time. They made her pull weeds sometimes too. Master Altin and Master Tytamon never had to do those sorts of things. And besides, plants were boring, which was why Pernie had always loved to hunt.

She watched as they talked, thinking her thoughts, when Kettle came into the kitchen from the big pantry where they kept all the most necessary stores. The sight of the flour-doused, red-faced woman made Pernie want to leap for joy, then tears came to her eyes so unexpectedly she had to turn and patter quickly down and out of the hall. She hadn't expected that.

She wanted to run back and hug her, the only mother she'd ever known, the one person in the whole world who loved Pernie more than anything. She wanted to run in there so bad it hurt. But she could hear Orli Pewter's voice coming down the hall, and that harpy's screech put the scowl back on Pernie's face. If Orli Pewter weren't in there, she could have gone to Kettle, but for now she'd have to wait. This was the hunt. This was the one thing Pernie knew better than all else. And patience was everything.

She could imagine hearing Seawind saying those very words in her head, but she shook that away. She wasn't going to listen to him anymore. But she would be patient. If she was patient, she would have Kettle and Master Altin to herself, and that would be the best.

Resisting the urge to go watch them again, to watch Kettle with her smiling eyes and gentle hands—except for spankings, but Pernie already knew that would never happen again—she slunk off into the dining room, where she took up a position in the dark corner beyond the armor that stood there like a statue all the time. It was the same place that Master Altin had appeared all bloody and dying that one terrible day. The day she had saved his life. Again. And the day that Orli Pewter had gone off with him to save some stupid planet, leaving Pernie behind. Also again. She thought it was a good place to wait, though she didn't go behind the suit of armor all the way. She knew enough about teleporting now to know better than that, for he might think to teleport there again today.

She sat upon the floor contemplating how happy Master Altin would be to see her again, a few days from now, when at last she emerged from Great Forest with all the stories she would have to tell. She could tell him about the sacred horned manatee she'd ridden, even if only for a little while, and about the beautiful lady elves. She would tell him all about Knot too. She thought he would be proud of her for that, even if Knot wasn't as good as a flying dragon was.

That's when Kettle appeared.

Sure enough, just as Pernie had planned, Kettle came in with a tray of plates and silverware and began setting places enough to serve all those folks Pernie had seen in the courtyard and several more besides.

A strange young woman Pernie had never seen before came in behind her and helped to set the places too, which put a frown on Pernie's face. That would have been Pernie's job before. True, she'd always hated doing it, but she didn't like having that other person doing it even more.

Still, between the two of them they got all the places set. Pernie counted eighteen in all, which nearly encompassed half the available seats at the table there. Pernie couldn't remember seeing that many places set there more than a time or two, and both of those had come in the wake of the Earth people first arriving at Prosperion. It certainly seemed that the Earth people made everything change a lot. Especially Orli Pewter.

With that thought, Pernie decided to take her chance. She reached down and pulled the little vial of poison from her boot, then padded quietly across the distance between the shadows to the place she well knew Orli would sit, right at Master Altin's right hand. She pulled free the little stopper and let go one single drop, the clear liquid falling out of her illusion spell and glinting diamond-like in the candlelight as it fell.

Pernie leaned over the edge of the table and peered down into the cup, making sure the drop wouldn't be visible. The shadows were dark enough at the bottom of the vessel to hide it well. And no one would look into those shadows closely anyway. Why would they?

Pernie smiled and retreated back into her own shadows in the distant corner of the room and once more lay in wait. She wanted to watch Orli Pewter as she died, wanted to see her eyes blinking with surprise as she gasped out her last silent words, surprised by the unexpectedness of death like a dumb monkey or a dumb latakasokis.

Chapter 51

Pernie waited patiently as Kettle, Nipper, and the nameless serving girl brought out trays of fruits and things to nibble on while the main courses were prepared. The girl, who Pernie guessed might be at least four years her senior, carefully poured the wine around the table. Pernie watched, judging her as she went about the work, satisfied to see her spill twice and several times having to add wine to a pour because she'd pulled away too soon the first time. Pernie wouldn't have done that.

Eventually the diners were brought in. First came Orli Pewter, smiling at something Roberto was saying. Pernie saw that it was in fact Roberto as well, despite the lack of the uniform he'd always worn before. She rather liked his long-tailed purple coat, especially now that he wore a fresh one that wasn't torn apart at the sleeves. Behind them came several women who, all but one, wore the same bright color Roberto did. Their tightly fitted corsets marked them as being of one crew—likely the silvery spaceship in the meadow—while the variety of their flesh tones marked them as being as different from one another as elf from man from orc.

But they were, to the last of them, exquisite to gaze upon.

Pernie marveled at how pretty they all were, though not so beautiful as the lady elves. She noted, however, that the lady elves could not possibly be as strong as some of these women, for there were four of them who were sublimely powerful. They sat together, and Pernie marveled at how the smooth skin of their round shoulders and bulging biceps was drawn tautly enough that the candlelight could shape the definition of the muscles underneath. Pernie had seen far more than a few men who were not near so strong as that. Seeing them made her smile, and she thought they must be great warriors from Earth. The fact that she couldn't talk to them made her squirm where she leaned against the wall. It was as if the most exotic and wonderful women of Earth had come all the way across space just to eat with the people of Calico Castle. Well, with Master Altin and everyone else at Calico Castle except her. Not with Pernie.

Pernie wished she could eat with them. Or even just pour them wine. She wanted to so much that she was tempted to kill her illusion spell and just walk out into the room. But she didn't. One glance at Orli sitting there was enough to keep her on course.

At length, all the seats but Altin's at the head of the table were filled, and Pernie knew that there would be no more to arrive. From the angle she had at the table, twice she saw the long arm of a very dark woman—the only one besides Orli not in the purple uniform to match Roberto's coat—reach for a wine cup in a way that seemed as if she might be going to grab the one that sat before Orli instead of her own. Both times Pernie nearly jumped out to warn her off of taking a drink, but both times, Pernie realized her mistake. Still, it made her shift to the nearer side of the armor, where the shadows weren't quite so dark. She knew her illusion wavered some, but it was still dark enough. No one was looking for her anyway.

After a time, when she was done appreciating the beauty

and the alien nature of Calico Castle's visitors, and as she shifted uneasily waiting for Orli to take a drink of wine—*Why is she not drinking her stupid wine*? Pernie thought repeatedly—Pernie was able to catch the gist of the conversation. It seemed the plant that she had heard them talking about in the courtyard was a "trans-plant," and it was on some planet somewhere. She didn't know what a *trans-plant* was, but aliens were trying to dig it up.

She couldn't imagine there being any more aliens than there already were. How could there be so many? Why would there be? But she supposed aliens might be like the creatures in nature in that way. Just lots and lots of them, and no sooner had she thought she'd learned about them all than she'd find some new one sitting in a tree. Or else someone would bring her a book filled with new descriptions and sketches to go along. Or maybe someone might come along and take her off to a place like String, where there were all sorts of new animals to learn about—and be eaten by. So it seemed to her, upon considering for a moment, that there likely were as many aliens as the night sky could hold. She supposed it could hold a lot if it wanted to, just as a jungle could.

As she continued to eavesdrop, she learned that Master Altin had gone off to see Her Majesty to ask for help with the new problem of the aliens digging up whatever he and Orli Pewter and Roberto and all these strong, pretty Earth women had buried there. Orli Pewter didn't think help was going to be allowed.

"Her Majesty is off doing something sneaky," Orli explained. "Altin hasn't been able to reach her, even by her messengers, for most of this whole last year. He's convinced she's up to something that she doesn't want anyone, including him, to know about."

Roberto nodded as he stuffed a chunk of roasted boar into his mouth and chased it with a draught of wine. "I got that feeling a long time ago myself. When I tried to get help with the wannabe stowaway problem at Murdoc Bay, she pretty much blew me off. When I did get in contact with her two months ago and told her people were trying to sneak onto my spaceship—*our* spaceship—she patted me on the side of my face like I was five and said, 'Just be a good boy and make us both rich back there on Earth.' Then she blew me off again. I haven't gotten through to her since."

"Altin says he's seen some strange designs too, some things he found in Aderbury's office, strange fortress designs. He thinks she might be trying to colonize another planet somewhere. It would certainly explain the complete and total absence of *Citadel* all year."

"But why would the Queen keep such a thing secret from the Galactic Mage? Isn't that what she pays him for?" Pernie tilted her head sideways as the woman who asked the question spoke, marveling at her lithe, long limbs, her skin as dark as the shadows Pernie was hiding in. She looked to Pernie like the statue of the Huntress she'd seen once on a trip to Leekant with Gimmel and Nipper a few years ago, all grace and strength, a beauty that, while still entirely feminine, spoke of solidity and deadliness rather than something soft and simply pleasing to the eye. Pernie decided that if she couldn't be beautiful like the lady elves, then someday she would be beautiful like that.

"Well, she says she's paying him to discover things," Orli said. "But I think, if I'm being honest, our Yellow Fire project irritates her to no end. I think Deeqa is right about Her Majesty in that. It seems like she ought to really want Altin working on whatever she's doing—assuming she's doing anything at all. I'm pretty sure that's part of why she still just doesn't like me very much. I'm always keeping Altin from what everyone else wants him to do."

"You are," came Altin's voice as he himself came through the doors. "And it does vex her to no end." He strode across the intervening distance and took his place at the head of the table. "But, she is not quite so disinterested in the Yellow Fire project as she would have you believe. I know for a fact that she covets Liquefying Stone worse than any drunkard does his wine."

Pernie's eyes shifted from watching him to watching Orli's wine cup, realizing she'd forgotten to watch it for a time. It still sat right where it had been, though. Pernie had grown so used to watching things carefully since her first encounter with the sugar shrimp that she was sure of it, sure that the distance between the base of Orli's cup and the tip of her soupspoon was exactly as it had been.

It occurred to Pernie that Master Altin would be very sad to watch Orli die. He would try to take her to the fat doctor in Leekant, and he would try to save her with his high-ranked healing spells. But it wouldn't work. Fayne Gossa worked too fast. Pernie felt bad about making Master Altin sad. Still, he would get better in time. Kettle had stopped crying about that old man, Ilbei Spadebreaker, soon enough, and though Pernie hadn't seen the woman in a long time now, she thought she might have stopped crying about dead Tytamon too.

Even with Master Altin's mention of wine, and despite the fact that he took a long draught of his own, Orli still didn't reach for her cup. Pernie wanted to run over there and pour some down her throat. Waiting was unbearable.

And wait she did, because all through the dinner, Orli never had a drop. She drank water all evening through. They ate five full courses and then sat about talking long after, the nameless girl coming in repeatedly and pouring more and more wine for everyone, but the unendingly uncooperative Orli Pewter just sat there. In fact, the serving girl came so many times that Roberto and several of his crew had grown louder and louder, and soon they were using words that they would not have had they known

Pernie was listening—not that she cared, of course. Gimmel had taught her all the bad words, and they'd once had fits of giggling over the course of a wagon ride back from town. Roberto had once taught her some good ones from the Earth language as well. Who would have thought there could be so many words for the private parts of men? And there were at least twice that many for the private parts of women, up top and below.

But no matter how loud Roberto and the women got, at least those that had not gotten up and gone back to their berths on the silver ship, Orli simply never touched the wine. Not the whole time, even after Roberto and the last of his crewwomen were gone. Pernie knew they were his crew after listening so long. But they were gone, and soon it was only Master Altin and Orli left. Pernie thought they might have some kissy-kissy romantic toast, but when the serving girl came back to clear away what remained of the dessert plates, she asked if Orli was going to have any of her wine, to which Orli said, "No." Then the girl took it away.

The whole evening ruined.

Pernie would have teleported herself out in disgust, knowing that she wouldn't get another opportunity today, but she also knew that with just the two of them there, Altin would recognize the sound of her teleport when the air sucked into the empty space. He would know someone had been there, and then he would come look. She knew he'd found his divining powers too, which meant for all she knew he could sniff her out magically. So she had to continue to sit and wait. A long hunt she'd been on, and never got to take a shot.

When the serving girl was gone, Altin leaned across the table toward Orli and took her hands in his. What he said next was poison in Pernie's ears.

"You've been right all along about Her Majesty and the wedding. And even trying not to be selfish, I've managed it anyway. I—"

Orli cut him off. "No," she said. "You haven't. And whatever Her Majesty made you come here and say, it's fine. I was serious before, and I am now. I don't care when. We already have each other, and since things keep unfolding as they do, well, I realize how silly it was for me to be in such a rush. I've been the selfish one, Altin. The very fact of that guilt you've felt all this time is proof. I've been married to an old idea—not that marriage is an old idea—just that, I don't know, that I needed some ceremony to signify something, when in truth I really don't."

He smiled, and Pernie saw the love in his eyes as he gazed upon Orli Pewter. It made Pernie's skin burn and her chest ache. Master Altin would never look at her like that. Not while she was just a little girl. It didn't matter how many words Pernie knew for private parts if she couldn't make him look at her like that. Watching made her stomach turn.

"Well, that's not exactly what I was going to talk about," Altin said. "Yet it is precisely, though in another way. Her Majesty didn't say a thing about it, to be frank. She was irritated at my insistence to see her for about three blinks of an eye, and then, upon learning of this strange new set of machines on our new Yellow Fire's world, she's suddenly in a different sort of huff. I pressed her on it, and got her to agree to send *Citadel* ... as soon as she can. But she said she wants me on it when it arrives."

"Like, as in, you have to take command of it finally?"

He nodded.

Orli rolled her eyes at that, and looked as if she were about to protest. Pernie was glad Orli was mad. Orli was always mad when Altin wanted to do something fun and dangerous. Pernie had seen it more than once. But Altin stopped her before she could speak.

"You're coming too. I made sure of it," he said, which

irritated Pernie and seemed to pacify the woman some. "But first there's something I want to do."

"What's that?" Orli asked.

"Well, that gets to the other thing. Let's go have your ceremony right now."

"Now?"

"Yes, now. We can call up Captain Jackson on your old ship, the *Aspect*, and have her marry us right this moment. You've still got your maid of honor in Roberto"—he paused long enough for them both to laugh—"though he is a bit on the tipsy side just now, and I'll have Nipper stand in as my best man. Let's have it done."

"Altin, you don't have to do that. I can wait. Her Majesty will be happier if we wait, and that will only make your life, and our lives, easier down the road."

"Perhaps," he said as Pernie's heart turned to ash inside her chest—she was actually siding with Orli Pewter's arguments as she watched, forced into an unholy alliance with the very source of her private agony. "But I see how fate has written it for us. Look how time passes; look how events continue to conspire. We've opened up the frothy ale keg of the universe, and it is foaming still. We've had this conversation before. So many times. And yet, here we are, unmarried still, once more as the gods see fit to amuse themselves with our lives. I won't go another day without you as my wife. You must agree, as I will not allow you to refuse."

"Oh, really," she said, laughing. Teasing. "And what will you do if I do refuse? Smite me with lightning? Set me on fire with your nastiest fire spells? Turn me into a horny toad?"

Pernie could not believe she was saying what she said. Even though, with her whole body, she wanted Orli Pewter to say no, to put it off, to give Pernie a chance to win him for herself, she was simply flabbergasted that the woman could refuse such an offer, such sincerity. Making jokes no less. Killing her would be the greatest favor Pernie could do for him.

And yet Master Altin laughed as well.

"Oh," he said, and his eyes took on this strange, sinister sort of look that Pernie had never seen before. His brows came down, and then he vanished. Right after, he reappeared standing next to Orli's chair, leaning over her. The gust of air upon his return blew the nearest candle out. She gasped. He lunged for her, like a predator pouncing on prey, stopping just short of her, their faces a finger's width apart. "You'll have your fire," he said in a low voice, "and your horny toad." She giggled, then he kissed her on the mouth, leaning into the kiss and pressing his face onto hers for far longer than Pernie could abide. She actually found herself halfway to them when he pulled away, saying, "So, what say you?"

Pernie froze, her heart pounding in her chest.

"I'll take it. The ring and the burning toad," Orli said, grinning. "When do we leave?"

"Go get your best man and mine," he said. "I shall go find the royal dressmaker and retrieve your dress. Surely he's repaired it by now."

"Oh, that's going to piss him off," she laughed. "This late, plus you're going to have me married in it while he doesn't get to watch everybody gape at his epic work?"

"They can gape at the video the *Aspect*'s cameras take."

She nodded happily. He kissed her again, once more long and awful as viewed from where Pernie stood, now so close she could hear the wet sounds and the breathing that they made. She loved Master Altin an awful lot, but she wasn't sure about all of that. Still, if Orli Pewter would do it, then she would too if it came to it.

Then Master Altin was gone.

Chapter 52

Pernie froze, still as stone, staring across the room as the remaining candle flames wavered with the movement of air that followed Altin's teleportation spell. She watched him vanish, watched Orli stare into the vacancy where he had been. Orli had this wistful little smile upon her face that filled Pernie up with hate.

Orli reached out, as if by reflex, for a wine cup that was no longer there. At first Pernie didn't realize what she was doing, but it became clear when Orli said happily to herself, "Oh, *now* they've taken the wine away."

It took Pernie that long to clear her thoughts, and by the time she was reaching for her knife, Orli leapt up and ran out of the room, giggling as gaily as any child.

Pernie watched her go and couldn't believe what she'd just seen. In the span of time required for a dinner, she'd had a victim, lost a victim, discovered she had a chance for a husband after all, and then lost that, and then had a victim and lost it once more, the last costing her yet another shot at claiming Master Altin for herself. How hard could it be to kill one Orli Pewter after all? She'd killed a latakasokis by herself, while in a poison-induced stupor no less. She'd ridden the king of the horned manatees. She'd even gazed upon elven women and not fallen in love!

But still there was a chance. Altin was gone, and now Orli was alone. Pernie needed to calm herself.

She set off after her, intent on finally finishing what she had begun a year ago.

She crept to the massive oaken doors through which Orli had run, and peered out, left, then right. She knew there were patrols in this part of the keep these days, ever since the orcs invaded, so she kept up her invisibility spell. She slipped through the doors and found the shadows of an alcove, pressing herself to the wall so tightly she might have been moss growing there. She listened for Orli's voice or the sound of her footfalls made distinct by the riding boots she wore. Nothing.

By the time she got to the double doors leading out into the courtyard, Orli was running back her way, having already gone into Altin's strange-looking new tower and retrieved the Earth tablet she always spoke into. "Yes, now," Orli was saying as she walked briskly up the steps. "And no, you cannot wear that ridiculous hat. So comb your hair."

"Look who's talking, helmet head," Pernie heard Roberto say.

Orli tapped the front of the tablet for a moment, then laughed before tapping it again. "Yikes, you're right," she said, but she was smiling as she acknowledged it. "I'll fix mine too."

Pernie slipped back and hid against the wall, melting into scant shadows beneath one great black iron hinge.

Orli came through without so much as a glance in Pernie's direction and turned down the long hall, heading for the kitchens by Pernie's guess. She couldn't kill her in the kitchen, so she waited, knowing Orli would either come back this way or go out the back and circle around to Master Altin's tower once again.

She heard Orli's voice coming before she saw her again.

"I know, Daddy, but he doesn't want to wait. And I agree. Those things I told you about on Yellow Fire are going to open up who knows what kind of trouble. It may be nothing. They might even be friendly. But I doubt it. If it *is* trouble, and the whole universe goes to hell again, well, at least Altin and I will finally be together all the way. It will finally be official, you know? I'll be Lady Meade. Can you imagine?" She giggled again, and Pernie wanted to jump out right then and go stab her in the heart. But she didn't.

The general's reply came from the tablet, echoing ahead of Orli as she rounded the corner and strode down the hall. "All right, Orli girl. I'll be there. I'll get Jackson to agree to it. There are no worries about that. You all come and get me before you go."

"We will."

Orli's teeth flashed brightly in the light of the tablet, then right after, she cut the connection and tucked the tablet into the waistband at her back. She was still smiling as she walked by Pernie's hiding place.

Pernie drew her knife and moved in behind her. She hadn't poisoned the blade, which meant she needed to get in quick and be precise with a fatal blow. There were big veins in the throat and the inner thigh. She could get to those easily enough.

But then Orli began to run. She ran to the end of the hall, down the short flight of stairs, and out into an open hall that led to the base of Tytamon's tower, the mounting of which, by the time Pernie caught up, Orli had well under way.

Pernie thought about teleporting up ahead of her, but she didn't know where Orli was, and unlike Master Altin, she had no magic sight to see her way in advance. So she had to follow on foot instead. She wished she had Knot for this. Orli Pewter was not so swift as an elf, but for a human woman she was terribly fast. Nonetheless, where she was going there was no other way out. So Pernie would go as quickly as her own legs could. That would be quick enough.

When she found Orli Pewter again, the woman was brushing her hair, standing much like she had that day one long year ago, staring blissfully at her own reflection, her eyes alight with the joy of finally stealing Master Altin from Pernie.

This time Pernie wouldn't miss. This time Pernie had mastery of her weaponry.

There came a blast of air then, a great blast of it that nearly staggered her, and with it a great pain in her right hand, terrible pain all along the fleshy side between the wrist and the first joint of her little finger, so much so that she dropped her knife.

She shouted, silently in the sealed illusion of her spell just before it broke, and her knife clattered to the ground for everyone to hear.

Altin shouted as well. "By the gods," he proclaimed. "Pernie, what in nine hells?"

He made to pull away from her, shocked to see her standing there right where he'd just teleported to, or nearly so, but he couldn't quite pull away. The sleeve of his robes was merged with Pernie's hand.

As he jerked a second time, not yet realizing what had just been done, Pernie yelped again as her hand sent throbbing agony up her arm.

She looked down at it, saw the gray silk and golden filigree at the long, loose cuff where it disappeared beneath her skin.

But she'd known pain before. She spoke the two words of her own teleport and leapt across the room.

Blood poured freely from her hand. She glanced to the floor where her knife lay, then up at Altin and now Orli, who were both staring at her opened-mouthed.

"Pernie, by the gods, what are you doing here? You could

have gotten us both killed."

Pernie looked from them back to her knife. They followed her eyes and saw it too.

"Oh no," Orli breathed. "Again?"

Pernie thought to blink herself to the knife and get it done before Altin could do anything, but she glimpsed into the mana and saw that he was already casting a spell. Too fast for her to do anything about it, the big bed against the wall vanished, only to reappear directly over the knife, separating Pernie from it and from the person she intended it for.

"Pernie," Master Altin said. "Stop. Don't do this. *Why* are you doing this?"

Pernie glared at Orli, who stared back at her, the Earth woman watching her like she would a snake that's crawled into the room. Pernie was glad of it. She was a snake, and she would bite Orli too. Except her fang was underneath the bed.

She wished she had her spear now. She could have thrown it right through Orli's face. Right through. She wouldn't miss. And Seawind wouldn't show up to stop her this time.

But she didn't have it. The only weapon she had was her hands.

And Ilbei Spadebreaker's enchanted pickaxe.

She snatched the shrunken pickaxe from her neck with her wounded hand, and the pressure of squeezing it tight enough to yank it off sent a jet of blood a full span into the air.

She slid her fingers down the length of the tiny pickaxe. "*Serend'orr*," she said, remembering the magic word, and in that instant it was its full size again.

It clanked heavily against the stone, heavy enough for a strong man, far too heavy for her.

"Pernie, stop it this instant," Master Altin said. "What's gotten into you?"

Pernie spoke the words again, this time sliding her slick, bloody hand up the haft as she did, shrinking the weapon to the size of a hatchet. Its two steel points gleamed.

She hoisted it and circled around the bed, but Altin kept moving, keeping himself between her and Orli.

"Pernie, whatever Orli has done to you, whatever I have done to you, we can make it right. You need to put that down. You're putting us in a very dangerous place, right now. Please, just put it down."

Pernie knew that she would have to be fast. She'd have to cast back-to-back teleports. He wouldn't be expecting that. And she'd come in from above.

She muttered the two words, vanished, then reappeared, feinting with the pickaxe even as Altin conjured a wall of ice between them, two hands thick. But Pernie was already gone, behind them both in two words, the pickaxe swinging for the back of Orli's neck.

But then Orli and Altin were across the room.

"Pernie, I swear by all nine planes of hell, I don't want to hurt you," Altin said.

Pernie let her vision shift between the realms of mana and light. She saw the mana move toward him, but again he was gone.

She spun round and round, but he was nowhere to be seen.

She ran to where they'd been, reaching out with her hands as much as with her mind for the mana, to see if he was channeling invisibility in the corner of the room. He wasn't.

She turned back, looked for movement in the mana, watched for the subtle shifts that she'd worked so hard to learn to see. For the longest time there was nothing, but then came movement from beneath her feet. Just once, a ripple like a teleport.

He was down below.

She ran down the stairs, unwilling to let off looking into the mana, and unwilling to give herself away by using it—though she thought it might be possible Master Altin did not know how to watch patterns like she did.

The door to Tytamon's study was locked, as it had been before. She blinked in and out of the mana stream, watching. She held Ilbei Spadebreaker's enchanted pickaxe. "It can cut through anything," Master Altin had marveled when he read aloud the runes inscribed along its two long, arcing blades.

She swung it at the door handle, a great iron thing, and it went through it as easily as glass. The lock and handle fell apart, as did a portion of the door. Pernie kicked it in and ran inside, pickaxe raised on high, ready to split Orli Pewter through the head.

So it was with some alarm that she found Master Tytamon standing there instead. The longtime master of Calico Castle appeared just as ancient and weatherworn as he always had, and he looked up at her with gray eyes as piercing as ever from beneath the partial curtain of his bushy white eyebrows.

"I should think, child," he said, regarding the pickaxe and pushing just one of those bushy eyebrows up, "that running about with a thing like that, breaking down doors no less, will get your ears boxed by Mistress Kettle straightaway."

Pernie could only stare at him, pickaxe still on high and her little mouth open wide.

Just then Altin came up from behind her, catching her in that moment of perplexity and snatching the pickaxe out of her slick, bloody hand.

"Sweet Mercy, but I thought she was going to strike us all down with this thing," Altin declared. Then he paused, blinking several times at what might be an apparition, before he, like Pernie, began to realize who it was standing there. He staggered back a step, nearly dropping the pickaxe to the floor. "Tidalwrath's teeth. It can't be!"

"Well, it can, boy, and no thanks to the lot of you leaving me out there in that infernal windstorm. It blew me back to spirits straightaway, but you never came back. I thought the worst had happened after you were gone so long. And when you finally did send me back to my windowsill, you didn't come let me out, so again I was sure you'd met some horrible fate. A long time to worry."

Altin's mouth, like Pernie's, fell open, the two of them a pair of seeming dullards.

Tytamon saw it, watching Altin closely for several long moments. He harrumphed, then twitched his thin lips around. "You did know what you were doing when you left me up there, didn't you?" Tytamon asked. "Bringing me up there into all that wind? That was the point, to speed it up, yes?"

"I ...," Altin began, but had nothing else to add.

"Well, I'll be. An accident, then." He turned and resumed what he'd presumably been doing before Pernie came barging in, which was getting to the window to check the decanter with the spinning palm-frond stopper. "Well, that would explain why you let me sit so long." He turned back. "How long?" he asked. "How long was I gone?"

"Nearly a year you were up there," Altin managed to stammer at last. "But you've been dead—or, well, presumed so—for a year and a half. A little more. But I did not know you were—that we had ... put you up there on Red Fire."

"Hmm. I think the breeze coming off the mountain would have had me back by now anyway."

"But how?"

"A bit of elven gratitude, my boy. Long ago. Right after Duador. The High Seat called me 'the one human worth saving if such a disaster should ever befall the world again.' I admit it was vanity that allowed me to agree. And fear, of course. We all fear death from time to time."

Pernie watched the old man watching Altin, not daring to turn around. She understood what had happened, though. She realized she actually understood it better than Master Altin did. He'd never been to the forbidden cove before. It all made perfect sense now.

And while confusion distracted him, she could slip away.

Two words and she was gone, as far down the stairwell as she could get, and, with four more casts, she was at the bottom again.

She recast her illusion and snuck out of the castle proper, heading straight for the armory. There were other weapons there.

The door was locked. It never had been before.

Easy enough, however. She'd been in there a thousand times. She knew it was dangerous to teleport without looking—her throbbing hand was proof of it—but she had to take a chance.

She appeared just inside the door, in one piece, unmerged with anything else.

As if to remind her just how much of a chance she'd taken, her hand throbbed. She looked down at it. It hurt terribly, but she didn't care. But she did see that it was still bleeding a steady stream. There was already a pool nearly the size of a silver piece on the floor beside her foot.

By the time she realized that Master Altin and Tytamon would see the blood trail leading here to the armory, that they would see the blood dripping right out of her onto the ground, ruining her illusion, Master Altin was standing there. "Pernie, stop at once. I demand it. You are not going to harm Orli, do you understand? I won't allow it. I don't know what's got into you, but I won't stand another moment of this. There are places where bad wizards and magical lunatics go, and there are no ways out of them, elf tricks or not. Do you hear me?"

Pernie muttered the teleport and was back in the courtyard again. Where Master Tytamon grabbed her by the scruff. His sticklike fingers, gnarled and ancient as they were, were strong and powerful, and he lifted her right up off her feet. She made to speak the teleport again, but he clapped his other hand over her mouth, pressing his thumb and middle finger into her cheeks, pushing the soft flesh between her teeth.

"Enough!" he shouted, and there was something terrible and compelling in the sound of it, something thunderous that reached right inside of her. She could not explain it, but she knew she couldn't disagree. It was as if he'd cast a spell on her. She was stunned into compliance by the raw force of that command.

Altin appeared beside him even as the command was rebounding off the high cliffs of Mount Pernolde, in whose shadow Calico Castle dwelled.

"She's lost her mind," Altin said. "She needs to be taken to Goffa House in Hast."

Tytamon studied her then, looking into her face like she might have done were she looking into the face of some bug she'd found, some inexplicable little creature with too many eyes or curious pinching mandibles, some *thing*.

She could see it then, see it in Tytamon's eyes, sure. And worse, far worse, she could see it in Master Altin's too. It was a look very far from love. Nothing like the way he looked at Orli Pewter.

Pernie realized in that moment that she had made a terrible mistake. He was looking at her like she had looked at Knot. Like the lady elf that Djoveeve fell in love with must have looked at her.

Thinking of Djoveeve made her realize another mistake: she'd gotten caught. Djoveeve said the Sava'an'Lansom must never be caught. Seawind had said it many times too. It was practically the definition of the term.

And here she was, caught. Tytamon looking at her like a bug. Altin looking at her like a bug. Some stupid creature to be stepped on or smashed with an old book.

He'd never love her now.

"Pernie," Tytamon said. "If I put you down, are you going to tell us what is driving you to such things? No magic, now. Just the truth."

She wanted to cast another teleport. She was sure she could get outside the castle wall. Run off into the woods and hide. She'd get another chance at Orli Pewter some other day. She really hated her now. She'd ruined everything. Everything.

But she couldn't cast the spell. She tried to. She started the words, but she couldn't speak them. They wouldn't come out.

"I've trumped your magic, girl," said Master Tytamon, looking very grizzled and severe. "You won't cast that spell for ten minutes at least. Perhaps even a week, for all I know, as I've never cast it on a child. And if you try too hard, too soon, you'll get it halfway out and hurt yourself. So be a smart girl and don't try for at least five days."

Pernie growled at him, her brows lowering slowly, deliberately, like that first considered placement of the executioner's axe before the killing swing. She aimed her hatred at him for a time.

"By the gods, look at that," Tytamon said. "Have you ever seen such a thing?"

"I'm not sure what the elves have done to her," Altin said, "but they've certainly begun sharpening her into a nasty little knife. By the gods, it's rather unsettling."

She heard him talking about her as if she wasn't even there, and the tears burned in her eyes. She tried to stop them. She didn't want Master Altin to see her cry. He might not ever love her now, but she didn't want him to think she was weak.

Tytamon saw the first of those tears as they began to run, and he set her gently back on the ground. "Go get Kettle," he said to Altin, then he knelt down next to her and looked her in the eyes. "This is the girl without the elves inside."

Pernie watched Master Altin go; he went so quickly and obediently it made the anger burn even worse. She didn't want his pity, and she didn't want to see Kettle looking at her like they had. Like an insect.

"Come now, Pernie. It's okay." He made to pull her into a hug, thinking to console her, but she pulled away. She looked down at her feet instead. She fidgeted with her hands, fumbled with the cords of the sling she'd tied around her waist. She reached for her hair, curled a strand around her finger, fussing with it. "Well, at least talk to me, child," he said. "What is it?" She pulled the mint leaf from behind her ear as he repeated the question a second time, even more gently than the last.

She looked past him, saw Kettle coming out into the courtyard. She could already hear the mutters and admonitions of the woman's worry shaping up.

She looked back to Tytamon and shook her head, blinking dry her eyes as the last tear fell to the flagstones, splashing unseen into the pool of blood she was standing in. "What is it?" he asked yet again. And then she was gone, the tearing of a leaf quite beyond the scope of even the great Tytamon's compulsion spell.

Chapter 53

Pernie appeared in the cave that had been her home for over a year, the one that was her only home now. There was no one around, the room empty but for the table-topped boulder, the coral seats around it, and her spear, which someone had brought back and leaned against the wall. She snatched it up and went out, calling for Knot telepathically. He arrived in a matter of minutes, flowing like a short, silvery river over rocks and roots as he swept in on his silent feet.

She jumped on him and stooped long enough to snatch the length of rope, winding it around her wrist reflexively. She set him off at full speed, the two of them rushing through the jungle like a demon breeze. They arrived atop the cliff that overlooked the manatees, and Knot hadn't even come to a complete stop when she leapt over the edge, using his momentum to sail out over the rocks. She was already falling before she looked to see if the sargosaganti were there. They were.

She didn't know whether it had been ten minutes since Tytamon had stolen her ability to cast the spell, and she didn't care. She spoke the words anyway.

She landed barely fifteen steps from the head of the great

bull that dominated the group, and she took three sprinting steps toward him before casting her teleport a second time. She hadn't bothered looking into the mana to see if the great beast's horn was about to be cast at her.

It was. The horn flew through the empty space where she had been as she reappeared closer to her prey. She vanished a second time just before the monster's second horn was whistling through the space, the snap of air when she vanished the only thing that the horn encountered as it flew.

The sargosagantis' natural defenses had it teleporting out to sea just as Pernie reappeared, falling toward the water, ten feet above the surface, ten spans beyond the edge of the surf. Her spear was already on its way. Not headed for where the creature was, but for where she knew it would be.

Sure enough, the sargosagantis reappeared right where her spear was. It appeared around her spear, in the same place, like her hand and Altin's robe had. And it was not in the same place she'd stabbed into the creature's back. Not this time. Her spear was in the same place as its brain. Aimed by instinct.

The momentum the sargosagantis had taken with it when it teleported was still with it when it reappeared, and it carried it forward anyway, despite the fact that it was in that instant dead. Its great bulk sliced through the water for another hundred spans, slowing like some fleshy sailing ship that's lost its wind.

Pernie landed upon it with her teleport, near the bubbling scar she'd made in its thick, blubbery hide the day she'd tried to ride it not so long ago. She looked down at it with contempt. That time had been failure, but not this time. She looked back toward the beach, at the surf that was drifting farther and farther away as the sargosagantis drifted away, the momentum of its last teleport already nearly arrested by the incoming waves. She let go a breath that felt as if she'd been holding it for an entire day.

She'd finally ridden the king of the sargosaganti, and this time he did not get away.

When she returned to the cave, it was well after dark, but the long shadows and golden flickers coming from the mouth of the cave proved that she would not be alone inside. Upon entering, she saw that Djoveeve sat with her feet up on the central boulder, and Seawind sat across from her taking a turn at some sort of elven game. Both looked up at her as she came in.

"You've come back," observed Djoveeve needlessly. "And you killed the sargosagantis king."

"He's not a king. He's just a big, stupid animal like all the rest."

"You were told the elves consider them sacred."

"The elves are stupid too."

Seawind smiled. "Then you have passed your test."

"I already passed my test. That's why you sent me home."

"Sending you home was the test."

Pernie frowned at that, looking from the elf to Djoveeve, who had raised one eyebrow and the better part of one cheek. The old woman nodded that it was true. Pernie didn't care anymore.

"I want to learn how to kill Orli Pewter," she said.

"That is what you asked when you first arrived," Seawind replied.

"You said you would teach me how to kill her. But I can't. I tried."

"I said you would be able to kill her," Seawind said. "That is not the same as succeeding in your attempt."

Pernie frowned again. She knew he was playing word games with her, but she had spent enough time on the Island of Hunters to know she didn't want to play it back. She was too tired. Her whole body ached like it used to ache in the early days when she'd first come here, the days when she'd spent all that time running and climbing, trying to keep up with the hunt hopelessly.

She looked at the elf sitting there, so calmly, the absolute image of deadly confidence, and somehow it exhausted her too completely to contain. She simply dropped to her knees and began to cry, tears of fatigue more than anything, but also of frustration, waning anger, and more than a little broken heart.

No one came to comfort her, and so she was allowed to sit and pour it all out, the hot, salty tears running from the pools in her palms and down her wrists, soaking her elbows before running into her pants, where they mixed with the salty water that remained from her having had to swim back to shore.

When she was finished, when her sorrow and rage had finished washing out, she looked up to see that Seawind was gone, leaving only Djoveeve sitting there, just as she had been, with her feet up on the boulder still.

"Welcome back, little Sava," she said, a smile warm upon her face.

Pernie's lips wriggled as she got up and sat herself down across from the woman somewhat glumly. "I suppose the other elves will kill me now," she said. "Since I killed their dumb sargosagantis."

Djoveeve's smile grew a little wider as she shook her head. "Oh, I don't think it is as bad as that. And I expect they'll all know about it very soon. It's not easy to kill one of them without Fayne Gossa, you know."

"They could kill it with a lightning bolt or a fireball. A big bolt of ice."

"Sargosaganti don't suffer the effects of fire and electricity. And elves don't conjure the elements at all."

"They don't?"

"Have you ever seen an elf cast a fireball? Throw an ice

spear or summon lightning?"

"No," she admitted. Her little brow wrinkled beneath her bangs, which were plastered to her forehead by the salty sea. "But I've only ever been with them on the hunt."

"Well, they don't. And without poison, you've done something just short of impossible for many of them, I should think."

"Shadesbreath could kill one with his pinkie nail," Pernie said.

"Perhaps," Djoveeve said. "But I certainly would never try. Not even when I was young and fast like you."

Pernie looked up, her eyes still luminous with remnant tears, glittering in the light of the torches Djoveeve had placed in sconces on the wall. The old woman nodded, confirming it was true. Pernie shrugged and started fidgeting with her hands. The one where Master Altin's sleeve had been throbbed miserably.

"Kettle will hate me forever now," she said. "And Master Tytamon too. He's back alive, you know." She looked up then, her features momentarily alight with the thought of that. "He came back because of the ghost tree. Just like you said he would. Except that you never said he would. But he was a ghost, and now he's real. I saw him. He even grabbed me by the neck."

Djoveeve leaned forward in her chair, her own expression contemplative for a time. "That explains the missing tree the elves were discussing this afternoon." But she spent only another half second on the thought before asking, "And why did the old master grab you by the neck? Caught you on at that Miss Pewter, did he?"

She nodded, looking back into her lap. "He did. And Master Altin took my pickaxe. The one that Master Ilbei gave to me. And he almost appeared right on top of me too." She held up her hand for the old Sava'an'Lansom to see. The edge of it was swollen and puffy, a mottled mixture of purples, blacks, and blues. Most of the crusting blood had washed off, showing only a raw pair of splits where the skin had burst open to accommodate the pressure caused by the fabric of Altin's sleeve, rents like an overdone sausage.

Djoveeve took the child's small, battered hand in her own cracked and leathery ones, turning it slightly so she could see it better in the light. "I'll call Seawind back," she said, starting to rise.

"No, I can fix it for myself," Pernie said. And she did so, though the spell nearly exhausted her to unconsciousness before Djoveeve could stop her from beginning to sing it yet again.

"You need to learn better healing magic than that," the old woman said. "You may never be a great healer, but you can certainly do better than a child's song. That magic, however, is one you'll have to learn at a human school. The elves can't teach you, and I haven't got the gift."

"I'm not going to a human school," she said. "I want to learn how to kill Orli Pewter from the elves. I want to marry Master Altin, and now he's married her. They were going to do it this very night. So now I have to kill her and wait for him to be sad for a long time before he'll ever love me again."

Djoveeve watched the intensity of the look that came upon the child's face. The old woman's expression clouded some as she did.

"He'll not love you after, child. You won't win him that way."

"Yes I will."

"Saying so won't make it true. You can't kill her and expect him to fall in love with you simply because she is gone."

"But there isn't any other way."

Djoveeve considered that for a time, her wrinkled face wrinkling all the more. "I was told that Earth people only live a hundred years or so before they die. Their 'technology' is weak in that way."

Pernie looked up at that, her face a question of hope and possibilities.

"It's true," Djoveeve went on. "Their ancient ones reach a hundred and thirty years; perhaps one or two make a hundred and fifty at best."

"Who told you that?" Pernie asked, her little blonde brows drooping skeptically. "Even blanks live longer than that. Orli Pewter says her people are all blanks. Not even one of them has got any magic at all."

"I have my sources," the leather-clad master assassin said. "And I get more day by day."

Pernie fell to thinking on that for a while, and Djoveeve rose and got Pernie something to eat, salt fish and a bunch of wild grapes.

"My point, dear girl," she said as she sat back down and pushed the food at her, "is that you'll have a better chance if you simply wait. Patience is your ally, young Sava. You've learned that as a hunter, both at home and here. How is this any different?"

Pernie's lips set to wriggling again, which in turn wriggled her nose. That was true, she knew. And it was likely that Master Altin, as a Seven, would live very long. And Pernie was a Three. Threes lived a very long time, especially if they could heal or had close doctor friends.

But still, a hundred years was a long time to wait. She didn't want to wait that long. She was fairly sure that was too much patience for something as important as this. Besides, what would happen if she died before Orli Pewter did? She'd almost died several times since coming to the island, after all. The world was a very dangerous place. What if she died before Master Altin finally had a chance to love her again?

What if he died? There were likely very many monsters

out in space!

But it was possible. She didn't know why, but it seemed like he must have loved her at some time, so it only made sense that he would love her again. She'd rescued him from the tree that had nearly killed him and taken off his arm. She saved him from the Hostiles out in space when he was all but dead. Granted, she had just tried to kill Orli Pewter again, so he might not love her right now. But she would make up for that somehow.

But she didn't want to wait.

Thinking about waiting made the lower of her two wriggling lips push itself into a pout. Djoveeve asked what it meant, to which Pernie simply said, "I want him to love me before a hundred years."

Seawind came back into the room before her words were out, and he answered as if the statement had been meant for him. "Your race hardly bonds in pairs with anything approaching exclusivity."

Pernie looked up at him as he approached her, unfurling a length of cloth that shimmered wetly in the flickering torchlight. He took her hand and wrapped it with the cloth, which burned as if with extreme chill. She made a point of not showing that it hurt, but she jerked her hand away.

He snatched it back. "I'm undoing that butchery of a healing spell you cast. Sit still, or your hand will never work properly."

When he unwound the cloth, her hand looked as it had before she'd sung her healing song, swollen with angry red rents and bruising over the back of the hand and up past the wrist. But it only looked that way for a moment more. As soon as the cloth was removed, Seawind took her little hand between his two larger, stronger, and exquisitely delicate ones, and, in moments, the wounds were gone. "Next time, little Sava, let me do it properly. You need that hand to fight. And to use what you will learn in the human school."

"I'm not going to a human school," she said. "I'm never going back. Not until Orli Pewter is dead." She nearly threw herself back into the chair as she said it, the sneer on her face suggesting she'd just realized what she'd said, what she'd resigned herself to. She couldn't kill Orli Pewter. It was stupid to ever think she could. Of course Master Altin wouldn't love her after that. She should have known.

"You *are* going to a human school," Seawind said. "We believe it is essential for you, in fact. Part of your training as Sava'an'Lansom no less."

She looked up, her whole face pinching, her pouting lips now defiant. She crossed her arms across her chest, shaking her head. "I won't." She jerked her gaze toward Djoveeve. "She never did. So I'm not either."

"Well, I did spend time on Kurr across the years, and there was much I had to learn," Djoveeve said, but Pernie could tell by the way she said it that they both knew that wasn't what Pernie meant.

"I'm not going back there," Pernie said. "I won't." Her eyes brightened suddenly, eyebrows leaping on high with a new idea. "Teach me how to kill her so I don't get caught." How foolish she had been, almost sucked into their plan, whatever it was. The answer had been there all along, the very same answer she'd had when she dropped the poison into the wine cup. "That's the school I want."

"He'll still not love you," Seawind said. "That's not how your species works."

"Yes it is," she spat out reflexively. But she paused, and amended with "Why not?"

"A human male will love a human female if he becomes enamored with her. The practice of ring ceremonies has nothing to do with it at all. If you truly are determined to have this man for yourself, then you must win him in the way of women of your race."

Pernie looked down at where her arms were crossed. She

uncrossed them and, after staring there for a time, looked back up at him. "But I can't," she said. "Not until I grow."

"You can't win him like that," Seawind said. "Even your race isn't quite so simple as that. Not all of them, anyway. Certainly not Sir Altin Meade."

"Then how?"

He walked up to her and poked her with the tip of his finger, a single thrust right on the breastbone. "It's not here that you need to grow, little Sava." He moved his finger up and tapped her firmly between her eyebrows. "It's here. This is what will secure him for you, if anything can," he said. "That other will simply make him look."

Pernie had never thought about that before. She supposed Orli Pewter was pretty smart after all. With all that Earth technology she had. She knew everything about the stars. She even knew about a lot of Prosperion, especially the plants. She'd even known some of them before she ever got there. She was the first one from Earth to learn their language too, like really learn it, so you could talk to her outside of the castle where there weren't any translation spells. Pernie knew it was true because she'd been the one to help her do it.

The idea came upon Pernie then, slowly at first, like the first droplets of a melting icicle, drip, drip, drip. But then it broke loose, the whole thrust of it all at once: what if that was why Master Altin loved Orli? What if he loved her for all that Earth stuff she knew?

She looked back to Seawind and glanced to Djoveeve, then back again, her furtive eyes desperate like a cornered wolverine.

"As I said," Seawind said. "You will be attending a human school." He smiled as if he was looking right into her thoughts before he added, "And it won't be on Kurr. You will go to school on Earth."

Pernie didn't like the idea too much, but she nodded

because she realized she had to agree. Earth was the only way. And anything was better than waiting a whole century.

Chapter 54

"**W**ell, you sure know how to show a girl a good time on her honeymoon," Orli teased. She stood between Altin and Roberto, staring out the thick, narrow window in the boot section of Altin's tower, looking through a rather violent storm at the alien excavation taking place on the surface of Yellow Fire's new world. "Nothing says romance like howling sandstorms and watching alien construction equipment digging holes."

"Yes, well, as always, we can thank Her Majesty for meddling in our marital affairs."

"At least we have *marital* affairs now," Orli pointed out, lifting her slender hand and holding aloft the gleaming diamond ring that she now wore.

"Dude, if you ever cheat on her, I'll come kick your ass myself," Roberto said. "Even if you turn me into a cockroach or something, I'll crawl up your ass and eat your spleen."

Altin laughed. "We're both lucky to have such a friend as you, Roberto."

Roberto grinned. "You are. And I'm serious." He winked at Orli, then looked out at the excavation again. "So, what do you guys think? We've been here for ten minutes. They're not exactly falling all over themselves to send a welcome party out."

"Well, I don't know about welcome parties," Altin said, glancing briefly to Roberto before looking out again. "But I should think you'd be grateful that they haven't sent out any troops. I'd hate to see the soldiers that came out of those things." Altin watched through the whirling gusts, great sheets of red sand flinging about as if giants threw it at them by the fistful. It struck with such force sometimes that the sound made it through the thick layers of steel and glass, a loud and sudden rasp that startled them and set all three of their heads jerking back reflexively.

However, despite the sandy thickness of the bestirred atmosphere, he could see the enormous digging machines reaching out with those monstrous spoon-ended arms, scooping up dirt and tossing it into the wind as well. Mechanical giants steadily at work. From the perspective they had there in the boot, the ships from which the machines had come blocked out the horizon, the four alien vessels rising up out of sight into the churning sky and vanishing into the distance left and right.

"Oh, don't think I'm not glad about that," Roberto said. "You're worried about soldiers, but can you imagine the war machines people like that would make? I mean, look at what their damn diggers look like."

"I think I'd rather not imagine such vehicles," he said. "So I really do hope they are friendly in the end."

"If it was me in those ships, I'd have sent out a security detail by now to find out who in the hell we are," Roberto said. "At least a probe or a robot scout or something."

"As would I," Altin agreed. "So I think it is a good sign."

"Maybe they don't even know we're here," Orli suggested, moving away from the window and sitting at the computer console near the wall. "We are pretty small compared to them." She pulled up the feed from the probe Deeqa had launched shortly after the objects first appeared. Readings began to come through, but the screen flashed, and the computer reset. She waited patiently for the reboot, knowing well that the cause of the fluctuation was the shield Altin had cast around the tower to protect them from the elements. The tower could be pressurized if need be now—all but the battlements anyway—thanks to Master Sambua's clever design, but that was a process, and one they hadn't begun just yet.

"Or maybe they don't care," Roberto said. "We could be like ants or something."

The computer came back to life and called up the information again. It was only a minute before she had the numbers up from before. "There's still nothing else we can get from them," she confirmed after going through several different scans. "And the hole is already two and a half miles deep."

"What the hell are they after? Is there gold down there? Titanium? Uranium? Something I never heard of?" Roberto asked.

"Given the timing of their arrival, I think we've already established it could only be one thing," Altin said.

Orli returned to stand between them again. "They are sitting right above him," she confirmed. "And at the rate of three-quarters of a mile per day, they'll get to the heart chamber in three weeks."

Altin harrumphed, though it was barely audible. "Well, that's why we're here. Her Majesty is as curious to find out why they are here as we are. She's stopped short of claiming the world for Prosperion, what with Yellow Fire coming to life, but let's just say she's very interested in his safety all of a sudden."

"Let's just say she's very interested in any potential source of Liquefying Stone," Orli clarified.

Altin's lips curled in tightly, but he said nothing.

"When is *Citadel* supposed to arrive?" Roberto asked. "If

she is so concerned, why are they taking so long?"

"I confess to wondering that myself," said Altin. "But Her Majesty is most reluctant to distribute the Liquefying Stones already in her possession, so I'm sure she's accounting for each one as she hands them out, creating the delay."

"Really?" Orli's incredulity was entirely rhetorical. "The *Citadel* mages were the ones that handed them over to her to begin." She rolled her eyes and looked at Roberto, hoping he shared her impatience for the royal stinginess, but Roberto only shrugged. He was getting used to it.

"Her Majesty has things afoot that I am not privy to just yet," Altin said, staring back out the window at the alien excavation under way. "And the fact I am not privy to them suggests that they are not the sort of thing your people would approve."

"Why *my* people?" Orli asked.

"Because of you and me, of course. Whatever she is doing she intends to keep to herself. Or at very least from you. I believe it is quite likely she's briefing her people on that very thing as she hands out the Liquefying Stones."

"Well, if that's the case, then why did she tell you she wants you back in command of *Citadel*? Why now? Is it really just because of these aliens?"

"I truly do not know."

"Well, whatever she's doing," Roberto said, "I think we ought to go check that stuff out. If they aren't going to send a welcome party out to us, we should send one to them. You know, grab a couple of bottles of good Prosperion booze and go say hi."

Orli made a gasping sort of sound at the back of her throat. "Roberto, that has to be the lamest idea I've ever heard."

"What? Why?"

"Umm … because it's stupid. Do you really need another reason after that?"

"Why is it stupid? We're sitting here waiting for them to send a welcome party out to us, but now we're too good to do the same?"

Altin's cheek twitched up on one side. There was some truth to that. He glanced to Roberto and nodded that he agreed.

"See?" Roberto said, squaring on Orli. "Let's go check it out. This is boring. And you said yourself they might not have seen us. Look at all this dirt blowing around. And compared to them, we're tiny. We're like some weird little piece of bacteria to them, sitting here hoping they'll discover us in all this blowing dust."

"Yeah, and then when they do discover us," she said, "they'll hit us with an antibacterial blast and get back to business before any of them gets sick."

"Fine, then we can be like an amoeba or something. They don't make people sick."

She groaned, exasperated, and put her hands on her hips. "Yes, they do. God, Roberto. Be serious. You know exactly what I mean."

He looked to Altin and shrugged, hands out to his sides, helpless, his expression the very essence of innocence. Altin knew him well enough to know better by now. But that changed little. Altin was in agreement, and his adventurous nature had already begun to get the better of him. "I say we do it," he said. "And I'll admit, I've been curious to try out that wheeled contraption you've parked in here." He nodded in the direction of the rugged ground rover Orli had brought into the boot. "Every time I see it, I can't help but feel it might be fun to take it out and see what it can do. I should think this is the exact reason we have it here, which was your idea, I'd like to point out."

"I should think it is, most indubitably too," Roberto said, doing his best approximation of Altin's Prosperion accent and making taunting faces at Orli all the while. "I'll drive!

Besides, I want to set up a signal relay to boost the satellite. These storms are a bitch to see through. It will be easier to watch from orbit. Two birds with one stone, you know?" He was already going for his spacesuit.

Orli ran to intercept. "Absolutely not. This is the dumbest idea either of you have ever had since ... since your last dumb idea. What is wrong with you two? I just barely got married, for Christ's sake, and now you want to get us all killed?"

"Sometimes you're such a candy-ass, Orli," Roberto said. "Grow a pair. Life is short. Have some fun." He pulled a spacesuit down off the rack. Altin was beside him doing likewise.

"Oh my God!" Orli said. "Are you serious? Both of you?"

"It will be fun," Roberto insisted.

She looked to Altin, who smiled as he went around the back side of the suit rack to step out of his robes. He took his spacesuit from its place and began pulling it on. "Yes, it will be," he agreed. "Come along, Orli. Not every alien in the universe will be the nasty kind. Just look how nicely you and I got on."

"Yeah," said Roberto. "Just look."

Orli could have brought up the body counts of the last interplanetary war, but she saw that it was useless. The two of them were already devoted to the plan. With a sigh, and less modesty than Altin, she reached for her own spacesuit. In short order she had it on and pressurized.

Soon after, the three of them were bouncing along the rocky terrain, often having to drive around large boulders or deep crags in the ground. The wind blew so hard against the vehicle that, at times, Roberto had to fight to keep it going straight. Orli pointed out with each successive blast that what they were doing was a terrible idea.

They stopped long enough for Roberto to set up a signal repeater for his satellite and to get a camera pointed at the dig site, then continued on their way.

Soon after, they were very close, and still no giant, mechanized soldiers appeared, no multi-headed aliens with prodigious blasting rays arrived to decimate them. Nothing came out to do anything to them at all. In fact, they drove right up to the side of one of the enormous digging machines, and Roberto, despite Orli's protests, parked the vehicle, got out, and climbed up one of the giant tracks that encircled its many massive wheels—each of which measured ninety-five yards high.

He climbed it easily—with a helpful gravity adjustment via the Higgs prism on his belt and the fact that the track's trailing side protected him from the wind—but the moment he conquered the ascent and climbed atop the wide track, a gust of wind blasted him so hard he flew right off over the edge. Were it not for the fact his sealed spacesuit worked just like a "box" for teleporting, he might not have survived, but Altin's quick reaction with a teleport spell snatched the screaming Spaniard from the teeth of the wind before he could be blown entirely away. Unfortunately, however, the use of magic reset Altin's suit controls to default settings, at which point Orli had to immediately put herself to work getting the mixture, temperatures, and timers set properly again.

"Holy shit, holy shit, holy shit," Roberto muttered the whole time Orli was at it. "That was so fucking close."

Orli's gloved fingers played the controls of the wizard's spacesuit with the dexterity of a pianist, but, busy as she was, she managed to unleash a barrage of I-told-you-so remarks, completely unsympathetic to Roberto's fright. Something about that seemed to calm him, though, and before she'd finished fixing Altin's suit, he was grinning again.

"God damn, Altin. I swear, if you hadn't married her already, I'd marry you right now," Roberto said. "That was some piece of timing, bro."

Altin grinned through his helmet at his friend as he nodded. "I'm happy to have helped. But let's not do anything that reckless going forward, shall we? It seems my suit doesn't like that particular spell at all, and my dear wife may not be in the mood to fix it next time."

Roberto grinned, the adrenaline receding enough that he could laugh. "Man, you should have seen the view up there. It's no wonder they haven't sent anyone out to talk to us. Seriously, you guys were invisible down here. I seriously think they don't know we're out here."

"I wonder if perhaps we should consider knocking," Altin said.

Orli paused long enough to look up at him, her expression beyond bewilderment, but when she saw that he was completely serious, she sighed, shook her head, and resumed the muttering of profanities as she continued working on his suit.

"Knocking?" Roberto asked. The exultation of his experience still burned brightly in his eyes, a sort of pleasant madness settling upon him, the euphoria of risk.

"Yes. Perhaps they have some sort of ... I don't know, a knocker or cord," Altin postulated.

"You mean like on that big tongue thing these backhoes came out on? That's kind of a welcome mat, if you ask me."

Altin frowned at the unfamiliar term, but knew by the movement of Roberto's thumb what he was talking about. "Yes. There may be something there we can activate. A button or a lever, perhaps a symbol to push, something of the sort your people use for everything."

Roberto's grin might have been described as maniacal as he agreed. "Let's do it!"

"You guys are making me feel like the old, fuddy-duddy grandma here," Orli said as she finished the reset on Altin's suit, "but how many times do I have to point out that this is a terrible idea? You could have died just now, Roberto, and Altin might have too if something worse had happened to this damn suit."

"But we didn't die," Roberto said. "And I am actually having fun. Aren't you, Altin?"

"I am," Altin replied. "It's been a while since being the Galactic Mage was this exhilarating. It's how it ought to be. Just fun without several billion lives at stake."

"What about our lives?" Orli said. "And aren't we supposed to be waiting for *Citadel* to arrive? Couldn't we have more fun with them? You know, the more the merrier—but with a whole bunch of magicians and several regiments of cavalry in case 'fun' becomes screaming and dying all of a sudden." She winced even as she said the last part, knowing full well what was going to come. Which it did.

"Cavalry will be of no use here," Altin said. "And I'm still not convinced Liquefying Stone will be enough to channel with that great column of mana Yellow Fire has made of everything. I should think even with the Liquefying Stone, they'll be fighting over the barest wisps. By comparison, Yellow Fire's mana draw is a torrent to Blue Fire's gentle stream. And he's still convalescing. I can't imagine what it will be like when he is at full health. I continue to be awed by the capacity of this universe to redefine my understanding of what the word 'power' means."

"Come on, Orli, you're an adventurer," Roberto said. "Ever since I've known you, you've never been a sissy inside girl. Now you sound like somebody's mom. I was serious when I said you need to grow a pair."

"I don't want a pair if having them means I'm going to start climbing giant space tractors and getting blown to my death."

"Hey, I didn't die. Your boy had my back. And if I'm being honest, that was pretty damn fun. We could start a whole sporting industry out of that. Alien track jumping.

We could make a fortune selling trips out here to adrenaline junkies."

"As if these ... whatever they are ... are just going to park their equipment here for your amusement," she said. "Besides, you have a coffee fortune in the making. I'd think you'd want to live long enough to spend what your Goblin Tea empire is going to pile up for you before you get yourself killed trying to make a second heap." She looked to Altin for support on that, but he was already turning the vehicle around, Roberto having let him drive this time.

They lurched forward awkwardly as Altin got used to the controls, and Roberto helped him get it down over the course of the next several miles. By the time they'd gotten to where the tonguelike ramp seemed to loll out of the nearest ship, the Prosperion was nearly a master at it.

They came to a stop at the base of the giant, sinuous-seeming ramp. Roberto jumped out and went to the edge where it touched the ground. He knelt down and took what readings he could with the helmet's sensors as Altin and Orli approached the side of the ship itself some two hundred yards away.

The body of the thing rose so high above them that, by the time they were close enough to the hull to touch it, they were well beneath an endless-seeming, upward-curving overhang.

"By the gods, this thing is enormous," Altin said. "Every time I get a little bit closer to it, it seems to expand exponentially."

"A ship that's almost thirty miles long will do that to you," Orli said.

He reached out and tentatively tapped the hull before she had time to tell him to stop. He tapped it like he might have tapped the handle of a pot that's been off the cook fire for only a little while. Nothing untoward happened.

He touched it again, longer this time. "I wish I could take

off my glove," he said. "This stuff has a really strange look to it. It's not wood, but it kind of looks like it. Or maybe bone."

Orli pulled her tablet out of the pouch on her belt and scanned the hull closely. "It's some kind of protein," she said. "I'd need to get a sample and take it to a fleet ship to tell anything more." She thought back to the last time she'd tried to take a sample from the surface of an alien thing, the plug that the first Hostile orb her people had ever seen stuffed into the hole it had drilled into the *Aspect*'s hull. That event had portended a deadly sequence of events.

"Hey," said Roberto over the com. "Something's coming."

"Something what?" Orli asked. She turned to see Roberto jump down off the edge of the ramp, which he had apparently begun to climb. "What is it?"

"I don't know," he said, backing away from the ramp, looking up over the side as he did. "But whatever it is, it's really big."

A glow began to make itself obvious against the blowing storm, illuminating the dust in a way that promised whatever the source was, it was very bright. The glow increased, bouncing off the violently stirred airborne topsoil like a wide-beamed spotlight on clouds. A rumble became apparent both in the air and beneath their feet.

Altin and Orli began to back away from the hull, craning their necks back in their spacesuits as best they could, trying to see what it was that was coming down the ramp, though doing so was like trying to see what was on a bridge while standing underneath.

The light grew very bright, and then, like a small sun in the grip of a glimmering metallic tentacle, the light swung out over the edge of the massive ramp and dangled high above the two newlyweds.

"What the hell is that?" Roberto asked.

"I can't see it from down here," Orli said. She and Altin

hustled backward all the more. "What's it look like from over there?"

"I don't know. Like two huge hoops rolling side by side around a giant glass egg. There's some puffy balloon thing or something in the middle of it with a bunch of spaghetti arms. I'm getting it on video, though."

"Well, maybe this is the creature coming to greet us finally," Altin said, drawing up his courage. He raised his hand and waved, on the chance that the creature could see them by that bright light high above.

The light began to descend, and it became so bright he had to turn away.

"Green button on your sleeve," Orli said. "Darken the helmet glass."

Altin looked down to his spacesuit sleeve, seeing as he did that the light was so bright he now cast a shadow as black as pitch behind him, a short, stubby version of him like an ink stain.

He found the button, though its green hue was nearly washed out to white in the brilliance of the light.

"Oh, shit!" Roberto said.

Altin almost had time to ask him why.

The End

For more information about the author, his
other novels and his works in progress, please visit
DaultonBooks.com.

If you would like to be notified when
new releases are made available, sign up for the
Daulton Books newsletter.